Dear Reader,

Welcome to the first of three books starring a new trio of Creed men—Steven and his cousins, twins Conner and Brody! These relatives of the Montana Creeds and the McKettricks were raised as brothers in the ranching community of Lonesome Bend, Colorado. Now, after years as a hotshot Denver lawyer, Steven has suddenly become the adoptive father of his best friend's five year-old son and wants a new lifestyle. He buys a ranch in Stone Creek, Arizona, home of some of his McKettrick kin, and sets up a law practice. When he encounters Melissa O'Ballivan, the local prosecutor and a McKettrick in-law, watch the sparks fly!

I also wanted to write today to tell you about a special group of people with whom I've become involved in the past couple years. It is The Humane Society of the United States (HSUS), specifically their Pets for Life program.

The Pets for Life program is one of the best ways to help your local shelter: that is to help keep animals out of shelters in the first place. Something as basic as keeping a collar and tag on your pet all the time, so if he gets out and gets lost, he can be returned home. Being a responsible pet owner. Spaying or neutering your pet. And not giving up when things don't go perfectly. If your dog digs in the yard, or your cat scratches the furniture, know that these are problems that can be addressed. You can find all the information about these— and many other common problems—at www.petsforlife.org. This campaign is focused on keeping pets and their people together for a lifetime.

As many of you know, my own household includes two dogs, two cats and six horses, so this is a cause that is near and dear to my heart. I hope you'll get involved along with me.

With love,

Linda Lael Miller

LINDA LAEL MILLER

A CREED IN STONE CREEK

Recycling programs
for this product may
not exist in your area.

ISBN-13: 978-0-373-77555-2

A CREED IN STONE CREEK

Copyright © 2011 by Linda Lael Miller

Printed in U.S.A.

HARLEQUIN®
www.Harlequin.com

Also available from

LINDA LAEL MILLER

and Harlequin HQN

For Sheri and Kat
You're brave and you're funny and I love you both.

A CREED IN STONE CREEK

CHAPTER ONE

SOME INSTINCT—or maybe just a stir of a breeze—awakened Steven Creed; he sat up in bed, took a fraction of a moment to orient himself to unfamiliar surroundings. One by one, the mental tumblers clicked into place:

Room 6. Happy Wanderer Motel and Campground. Stone Creek, Arizona.

The door stood open to the fresh high-country air, which was crisply cool on this early June night, but not cold, and the little boy—Steven's newly adopted son—sat on the cement step outside. A bundle—probably his favorite toy, a plush skunk named Fred, rolled up in his blanket—rested beside him, and the boy's tiny frame was rimmed in an aura of silvery-gold moonlight.

Something tightened in Steven's throat at the poignancy of the sight.

Poor kid. It wasn't hard to guess who he was waiting for. Matt was small, with his dad's dark hair and his mother's violet eyes, and he was exceptionally intelligent—maybe even gifted—but he was still only five years old.

How could he be expected to comprehend that his folks, Zack and Jillie St. John, were gone for good? That they wouldn't be coming to pick him up, no matter how hard he hoped or how many stars he wished on, that night or any other.

Steven's eyes burned, and he had to swallow the hard ache that rose in his throat.

Jillie had succumbed to a particularly virulent form of breast cancer a year and a half ago, and Zack had only lasted a few months before the grief dragged him under, too—however indirectly.

"Hey, Tex," Steven said, trying to sound casual as he sat up on the thin, lumpy mattress of the foldout sofa—he'd given the bed to the child when they checked in that evening. Steven shoved a hand through his own dark blond hair. "What's the trouble?" His voice was hoarse. "Can't sleep?"

Matt looked back at him, shook his head instead of answering aloud.

He looked even smaller than usual, sitting there in the expanse of that wide-open doorway.

Steven rolled out of bed, shirtless and barefoot, wearing a pair of black sweatpants that had seen better days.

He crossed the scuffed linoleum floor, stepped over the threshold and sat down beside Matt on the step, interlacing his fingers, letting his elbows rest on his knees. There was enough of a chill in the air to raise goose bumps wherever his skin was bare, so he figured Matt had to be cold, too, sitting there in his cotton pajamas. With a sigh, Steven squinted to make out the winding sparkle of the nearby creek, sprinkled in starlight, edged by oak trees, with night-purple mountains for a backdrop.

Matt leaned into him a little, a gesture that further melted Steven's already-bruised heart.

Carefully, Steven put an arm around the boy, to lend not only reassurance, but warmth, too. "Having second thoughts about turning rancher this late in your life?" he teased, thinking he couldn't have loved Matt any more if he'd been his own child, instead of his best friend's.

In the morning, Steven would attend the closing over at the Cattleman's Bank, and sign the papers making him the legal owner of a fifty-acre spread with a sturdy though run-down two-story house and a good well but not much else going for it. The rickety fences had toppled over years ago, defeated by decades of heavy snow in winter and pounding rain come springtime, and the barn was unsalvageable. Yet something about the place had reached out to him and grabbed hold, just the same.

The small ranch had been a home once, and it could be one again, with a lot of elbow grease—and a serious chunk of change. Fortunately, money wasn't a problem for Steven, which wasn't to say there weren't plenty of other things to chap his figurative hide.

Sometimes, he felt just as lost as Matt did.

Matt's mouth quirked up at one side in a flimsy attempt at a smile, all the more touching because of the obvious effort involved. "I'm *only* five years and three months old," he said, in belated reply to Steven's question, in that oddly mature way of his. "It's not late in my life, because my life just got *started*." The little guy had skipped the baby-talk stage entirely; he hadn't even *tried* to talk until he was past two, but he'd spoken in full sentences from then on.

"Five, huh?" Steven teased, raising one eyebrow. "If you weren't so short, I'd say you were lying about your age. Come on, admit it—you're really somebody's grandfather, posing as a kid."

The joke, a well-worn favorite, fell flat. Matt's small

shoulders moved with the force of his sigh, and he leaned a little more heavily into Steven's side.

"Feeling lonesome?" Steven asked, after clearing his throat.

Matt nodded, looking up at Steven. His eyes were huge and luminous in the predawn darkness. "I need a dog," the boy announced solemnly.

Steven chuckled, ruffled Matt's hair, gleaming dark as a raven's wing in the night. Relief swelled inside him, flailed behind his chest wall like a living thing doing its best to escape. A dog was something he could manage.

"Soon as we're settled," he promised, "we'll visit the animal shelter and pick out a mutt."

"Do they have ponies at the shelter, too?" The question cheered Steven; Matt was pushing the envelope, so to speak, and that had to be a good sign.

They'd already had the pony discussion—repeatedly.

"You know the deal, Tex," he reminded the little boy quietly. "The fences need to be replaced before we can keep horses, and the barn, too."

Matt sighed again, deeply. "That might take a long time," he lamented, "since you'll be working in town every day."

Steven fully intended to settle down in Stone Creek, build a normal life for his young charge and for himself. And to him, *normal* meant showing up somewhere on weekday mornings and putting in eight hours—whether he needed the paycheck or not.

He'd had to fight just to get through high school, let alone prelaw in college, and then earn the graduate degree that had qualified him to take the bar exam—a frustrating variety of learning disorders had all but crippled him early in his life. Although they'd been corrected, thanks to several perceptive teachers, he'd had a lot of catching up to do.

Still felt as if he was scrambling, some of the time.

Steven ruffled Matt's hair. "Yep," he agreed. "I'll be working."

"What about me? Where will I be when you're gone?"

They'd already covered that ground, numerous times, but after everything—and everybody—the little guy had lost over the past couple of years, it wasn't surprising that he needed almost constant reassurance. "You'll be in day camp," Steven said. "Until you start first grade in the fall, anyhow."

Matt's chin jutted out a little way, the angle obstinate and so reminiscent of Zack that the backs of Steven's eyes stung again. Zack St. John had been his best friend since middle school, a popular athlete, excellent student and all-around good guy. Losing Jillie had been a terrible blow, knocking Zack for the proverbial loop—he'd gone wild and finally died when, driving too fast down a narrow mountain road, he'd lost control somehow and laid his motorcycle down.

"Couldn't I just go to the office with you?" the boy asked, his voice even smaller than he was. "I might not like day camp. Anyhow, it's summer. Who goes to day camp in *summer?*"

Steven sighed and got to his feet. "Lots of kids do," he said. "And you might just wind up thinking day camp is the greatest thing since 3D TV." He extended a hand. "Come on, Tex. Let's get you back to bed. Tomorrow might be a long day, and you'll need your rest."

Matt reached for the stuffed skunk, and wound up in the now-tattered blanket he always kept close at hand. Jillie had knitted that herself, especially to bring her and Zack's infant son home from the hospital in, but the thing had been through some serious wear-and-tear since then.

Steven supposed that Matt was too old to be so attached to a baby blanket, but he didn't have the heart to take it away.

So he watched as the little boy got to his feet, trundled back inside, took a brief detour to the bathroom and then stood in the middle of the small room, looking forlorn.

"Can I sleep with you?" he asked. "Just for tonight?"

Steven tossed back the covers on the sofa bed and stretched out, resigned to the knowledge that he probably wouldn't close his eyes again before the morning was right on top of him. "Yeah," he said. "Hop in."

Matt scrambled onto the bad mattress and squirmed a little before settling down.

Steven stretched to switch off the lamp on the bedside table.

"Thanks," Matt said, in the darkness.

"You're welcome," Steven replied.

"I dreamed about Mom and Dad," Matt confided, after a silence so long that Steven thought he'd gone to sleep. "They were coming to get me, in a big red truck. That's why I was sitting on the step when you woke up. It took me a little while to figure out that it was just a dream."

"I thought it was something like that," Steven said, when he could trust himself to speak.

"I really miss them," Matt admitted.

"Me, too," Steven agreed, his voice hoarse.

"But we're gonna make it, right? You and me? Because we're pardners till the end?"

Steven swallowed, blinked a couple of times, glad of the darkness. "Pardners till the end," he promised. "And we are definitely gonna make it."

"Okay," Matt yawned, apparently satisfied. For the moment, anyhow. He'd ask again soon. "'Night."

"'Night," Steven replied.

Soon, the child was asleep.

Eventually, though he would have bet it wouldn't happen, Steven slept, too.

MELISSA O'BALLIVAN WHIPPED HER prized convertible roadster, cherry-red with plenty of gleaming chrome, up to the curb in front of the Sunflower Bakery and Café in downtown Stone Creek, shifted into Neutral and shoved open the door to jump out.

It was a nice day, one of those blue-sky wonders, so she had the top down.

Setting the emergency brake and then leaving the engine running, she dashed into the small restaurant, owned and operated by her brother-in-law Tanner Quinn's sister, Tessa, and made her way between jam-packed tables to the counter.

Six days a week, Melissa breakfasted on fruit smoothies with a scoop of protein powder blended in, but most Fridays, she permitted herself to stop by the popular eatery for her favorite takeout—Tessa made a mean turkey-sausage biscuit with cheese and egg whites.

"The usual?" Tessa grinned at her from behind the

counter, but she was already holding up the fragrant brown paper bag.

Melissa returned the cheerful greetings of several other customers and nodded, fishing in her wallet for money as she reached the register. Out of the corner of her eye, she spotted a face she didn't recognize—a good-looking guy with dark blond hair, a little on the shaggy side, perched on one of the stools in front of the counter. He wore black slacks and an expensive sports shirt that accented the periwinkle-blue of his eyes.

For some reason Melissa couldn't have explained, she was suddenly picturing him in old jeans, beat-up boots and the kind of Western-cut shirt most of the men around Stone Creek wore for every day.

She looked away quickly—but not quickly enough, going by the slight grin that tugged at a corner of the stranger's mouth as he studied her. Who *was* this? Melissa wondered, while she waited impatiently for Tessa to hand back change for a ten-dollar bill.

Just somebody passing through, she decided, completing the transaction and noticing, somewhat after the fact, that the mystery man wasn't alone. A small boy sat beside him, busily tucking into a short stack of Tessa's incomparable blueberry-walnut pancakes.

Melissa accepted her change and her breakfast and turned on one high-heeled shoe, consulting her watch in the same motion. Her meeting with Judge J. P. Carpenter was due to start in just fifteen minutes, which meant she'd have to gobble down the sandwich instead of savoring it at her desk while she listened to her voice mail, as she usually did on Fridays.

Even without looking, she knew the stranger was watching her leave the café; she could feel his gaze like a heartbeat between her shoulder blades, feel it right through her lightweight green corduroy blazer and the white cotton blouse and lacy bra beneath.

Outside, Alice McCoy, the oldest meter maid in America, by Melissa's reckoning, had pulled up beside the roadster in her special vehicle, a rig resembling a three-wheeled golf cart. A yellow light whirled slowly on the roof as, ticket book in hand, mouth pursed with disapproval, Alice scribbled away.

"Not another traffic citation, Alice," Melissa protested. "I was only gone for two seconds—just long enough to pick up my breakfast!" She held up her sandwich bag as evidence. *"Two seconds,"* she repeated.

Alice bristled. "This is a no parking zone," she pointed out firmly. "Two seconds or two hours, it makes no never-mind to me. A violation is a violation." She made a little huffing sound and tore off the ticket, leaning to snap it in under one of the windshield wipers, even though Melissa was standing close enough to reach out and take the bit of paper directly from the woman's hand. "You're the county prosecutor," Alice finished, still affronted. "You should know better." She shook her head. "Leaving your car running like that, too. One of these days, it's bound to get stolen and *then* you'll be piping a different tune, young lady."

Melissa sighed, retrieved the ticket from her windshield, and stuffed it unceremoniously into the pocket of her blazer. "This is Stone Creek, Arizona," she said, knowing this was an argument she couldn't possibly win but unable to avoid trying. She was, after all, a lawyer—and a card-carrying O'Ballivan. "Not the inner city."

"Crime is everywhere," Alice remarked, with a sniff. "If you ask me, the whole world's going to hell in a handbasket. I shouldn't have to tell *you* that, of all people."

Melissa gave up, climbed into the sports car and set her bagged breakfast on the other seat, on top of her briefcase. She drove to the single-story courthouse, a brick building that also served as the local DMV, town jail and sheriff's office, parked in her customary spot in the shade of a venerable old oak tree and hurried inside, juggling her purse, the briefcase, and her rapidly cooling sandwich.

Melissa's official headquarters, barely larger than her assistant Andrea's cubicle, opened off the same corridor as the single courtroom and the two small cells reserved for the rare prisoner.

Andrea, at nineteen, wore too much eye makeup and constantly chewed gum, but she could take messages and field phone calls well enough. Because those things comprised her entire job description, Melissa kept her opinions to herself.

Dashing past Andrea's desk, Melissa elbowed open her office door, since both hands were full and her assistant showed no sign of coming to her aid, set the bag from the café-bakery on her desk and dropped her purse and briefcase onto the seat of the short couch under her framed diplomas and a whole slew of family photos. She ducked into her tiny private restroom to wash her hands and quickly returned, stomach grumbling, to consume the sandwich.

Andrea, popping her gum, slouched in the office doorway, a sheaf of pink message forms in one hand. Her fingernails were long and decorated with what looked, from a distance, like tiny skulls and crossbones.

A sparkle indicated that the design might include itty-bitty rhinestones.

The girl wore her abundant reddish-brown hair short, with little spikes sticking straight up from her crown, and her outfit consisted of black jeans and a T-shirt with a motorcycle logo on the front.

Melissa sighed. "We really should talk about the way you dress, Andrea," she said, plunking into her chair and rummaging in the paper bag for her wrapped sandwich and the accompanying wad of paper napkins.

"It's Casual Friday," Andrea reminded her, with a faintly petulant note in her voice, fanning herself with the messages and frowning. Her gaze moved over Melissa's expensive slacks, blouse and blazer, and she shook her head once. "Remember?"

The sandwich, though nearly cold, still tasted like the best thing ever. "Is there coffee?" Melissa chanced to inquire, once she'd chewed and swallowed the first mouthful.

Andrea arched one pierced eyebrow, still fluttering the messages. "How should I know?" she asked. "When you hired me, you said it wasn't my job to make coffee—just to file and answer the phone and make sure you got all your messages."

Melissa rolled her eyes. "Speaking of messages?" she prompted.

Andrea sashayed across the span of floor between the door and the desk and laid the little pink sheets on Melissa's blotter. "Just the usual boring stuff," she said.

Melissa glanced at the messages, chewing.

There was one from her twin sister, Ashley. Ashley and her husband, Jack, were in Chicago, showing off their adorable two-year-old daughter at a family reunion.

Olivia, Ashley and Melissa's older sister, was looking after Ashley's cat, Mrs. Wiggins, but there were long-term guests—a group of elderly pals—staying at the B&B, and Ashley, who owned the establishment, was counting on her twin to stop by once a day to make sure the wild bunch were still kicking. Since one of them was a retired chef, they cooked for themselves.

The second message was from her dentist's receptionist. She was due for a six-month checkup and a cleaning.

The third: the biography she'd ordered last week was waiting at the bookstore over in Indian Rock.

"Sometimes," she joked dryly, losing her appetite halfway through the sandwich and dropping it back into the paper bag, which she promptly crumpled and tossed into the trash, "I wonder how I stand all the pressures of this job."

Andrea looked blank. "Pressures?"

"Never mind," Melissa said, resigned.

Just then, Judge Carpenter appeared behind Andrea, wearing a nifty summer suit some thirty years out of style and a wide grin. His hair was a wild gray nimbus around his face, and his blue eyes danced.

He'd always reminded Melissa of Hal Holbrook, doing his Mark Twain impersonation.

Andrea moseyed on out, and Melissa saw that J.P. was holding a steaming cup of coffee in each hand.

"God bless you," Melissa said.

J.P. chuckled and advanced into the room, pushing the door shut with a jaunty thrust of one heel. He set a cup before Melissa and sipped from his own after pulling up a chair facing her desk.

"He's here," J.P. announced. He wasn't much for preambles.

Melissa frowned, confused. "Who?" she asked, watching the judge over the rim of her cup.

J.P. leaned forward a little way, and dropped his voice to a confidential tone. "Steven Creed," he said.

Melissa's mind flashed on the drop-dead gorgeous man she'd encountered at the Sunflower that morning. He and the little boy were probably the only people in town she didn't know, since she'd grown up on a ranch just outside of Stone Creek.

Except for college and law school, and then a stint in Phoenix, working for the Maricopa County prosecutor, she'd lived in the community all her life. So, by process of elimination...

"Oh," she said. "Right. Steven Creed."

Word had it that Creed was a distant cousin of the McKettrick clan, over at Indian Rock, and he was in the process of buying the old Emerson place, bordered by Stone Creek Ranch, the sprawling cattle operation that had been in Melissa's own family for better than a century. Her brother, Brad, lived there now, with his wife, Meg, herself a McKettrick, and their rapidly growing family.

"He rented that space next door to the dry cleaners," J.P. went on. "He's a lawyer, you know. He'll be hanging out a shingle any day now, I'm told."

"Stone Creek could use a good attorney," Melissa said, largely uninterested. Was this the reason J.P. had asked for a Friday morning meeting—because he wanted to shoot the breeze about Steven Creed? "Since

Lou Spencer retired, folks have had to have their legal work done in Flagstaff or Indian Rock."

J.P. took a loud sip from his coffee cup. "I hear Mr. Creed plans on working pro bono," he added. "Championing the downtrodden, and all that."

That caught Melissa's full attention. Stone Creek wasn't exactly a hotbed of litigation, but it had its share of potential plaintiffs as well as defendants, that was for sure. There were disputes over property lines and water rights, Sheriff Parker hauled in the occasional drunk driver, and some of the kids in town seemed to gravitate toward trouble.

"That's interesting," Melissa said, vaguely unsettled as some pertinent recollection niggled at the back of her brain, just out of reach. As for Mr. Creed, well, she tended to be suspicious of do-gooders—they usually had hidden agendas, in her experience—but she was also intrigued. Even a little pleased to learn that Steven Creed wasn't just passing through town on his way to somewhere more fashionable, like Scottsdale or Sedona.

She remembered the child, his ebony hair a gleaming contrast to Creed's light-caramel locks. "The boy must take after his mother," she mused.

"Boy?" J.P. echoed, sounding puzzled. Then a light seemed to go on inside his head. "Oh, yes, the boy," he said, shifting around on his chair. "His name's Matthew. He's five years old, and he's adopted."

Melissa blinked, a little taken aback by the extent of his knowledge until she recalled that J.P.'s youngest daughter, Elaine, had moved back to Stone Creek after a divorce two years before, and opened a private, year-round preschool called Creekside Academy.

Of course. Creed must have enrolled the child in advance—and Elaine had passed the juicy details on to her father.

J.P. finished up with a flourish. "And there's no *Mrs.* Creed, either," he said.

According to Elaine—she and Melissa had gone through school together—from the day she'd jettisoned the loser husband and returned to the old hometown to make a fresh start, her dad had been after her to "get out more, meet people, kick up your heels a little... As if Stone Creek were *overrun* with single men," Elaine had grumbled, the last time Melissa had run into her, a few days before, over at the drugstore.

Melissa, who hadn't had a date in over a year herself, had sympathized. Between her sisters, Ashley and Olivia, and her big brother, Brad, somebody was always after her to go on out there and find True Love.

Easy for *them* to say. Brad had Meg. Olivia had Tanner. And Ashley had Jack. The unspoken question seemed to be, *So what's your problem, Melissa? When are you going to get with the program and corral yourself a husband?*

Melissa frowned.

J.P. either missed the expression or ignored it. Rising to his feet, he lobbed his empty coffee cup into the circular file with the grace of a much younger man. Back in the day, during high school and college, Judge Carpenter had been a basketball star, but in the end, he'd chosen to pursue a career in the law. "Well," he said cheerfully, "I hereby declare this meeting over."

"That was a meeting?" Melissa asked, arching one eyebrow. The subtext was: *I wolfed down the one turkey-*

*sausage biscuit I allow myself per week just so you could
tell me Steven Creed is single?*

"Yes," J.P. said. "Now, I think I'll go fishing."

Melissa laughed and shook her head.

J.P. had just left when Sheriff Tom Parker peeked
in from the doorway. Tom was a hometown boy, a tall,
lean man with dark hair and, usually, a serious look on
his face.

"Hey," he said.

"Hey." Melissa smiled. She and Tom were old friends.
Nothing more than that, though—he was attractive, in a
rustic sort of way, if shy, and he'd been divorced from his
high school sweetheart, Shirleen, for years. Everybody
in Stone Creek knew he'd fallen head over heels for
Tessa Quinn the day she opened the Sunflower Bakery
and Café—everybody, that is, except Tessa.

"Just wanted to remind you that Byron Cahill gets out
of jail today," Tom said, looking spiffy in his summer
uniform of brown khaki.

Melissa felt a mild shiver trip down her spine. Two
years ago, when Cahill was still a teenager, he'd gotten
high one Saturday afternoon, compounded the problem
with copious amounts of alcohol, swiped his mother's
car keys and gone on a joyride. The joy was short-lived,
as it turned out, and so was fifteen-year-old Chavonne
Rowan, who was riding shotgun.

When the "borrowed" car blew a tire on a sharp curve
outside of town, it shot through a guardrail, plunged
down a steep cliff into Stone Creek, teetered on its nose,
according to witnesses, and went under. Two fishermen
had rescued Byron; he came out of the wreck with a few
cuts and bruises and a really bad attitude. Chavonne, it
turned out, had died on impact.

Byron was arrested as he left the hospital in Flagstaff, where he'd been taken by ambulance, as a precaution. Although uninjured, he'd been admitted for a week of detox.

Melissa had successfully petitioned the Court to have young Cahill tried as an adult, over his mother's frantic protests that he was a good boy, just a little high-spirited, that was all, and then Melissa had thrown the proverbial book at him.

It was a slam dunk. Byron was convicted of second-degree manslaughter and dispatched to a correctional facility near Phoenix to serve his sentence—just over eighteen months, as it turned out.

Velda Cahill, his mother, who cleaned motel rooms and served cocktails to make ends meet, rarely missed a chance to corner Melissa and tell her about all the things poor Byron was missing out on, all because she, Melissa, "a high-and-mighty O'Ballivan," had wanted to show off. Let everybody know that the new county prosecutor was nobody to mess with.

Melissa felt sorry for Velda. Never reminded her that Chavonne Rowan was missing out on plenty—*the rest of her life*—and so were her devastated parents.

Tom Parker knotted one hand into a loose fist and tapped his knuckles against the framework of the door to get Melissa's attention, bring her back to the present moment.

"You be careful now," he said. "If Cahill so much as looks cross-eyed at you, call me. Right away."

Melissa blinked a couple of times, dredged up a smile. "You don't think he'd come back to Stone Creek, do you?" she asked. "It's not as if the town would throw a parade to welcome him home, you know."

Tom tried to smile back, but the light didn't spark in his eyes. "I think Cahill's the type to move back in with his mother and mooch for as long as she'll let him. And you know Velda—she won't turn her baby boy out into the cold, cruel world." He paused, rapped at the door-frame again, for emphasis. "Be careful," he repeated.

"I will," Melissa said. She wasn't afraid of Byron Cahill or anybody else.

Tom hesitated. "And speaking of parades—"

Melissa, who had turned her attention to a file by then, looked up. She was getting a headache.

"That was a figure of speech, Tom," she said patiently.

"We've got Stone Creek Rodeo Days coming up next month," Tom persisted. "And Aunt Ona had to resign from the Parade Committee because of gallbladder problems. She's been heading it up for thirty years, you know. Since you and I were just babies."

Melissa saw it coming then. Yes, sir, the light at the end of the tunnel was actually a train. And it was bearing down on her, fast.

"Listen, Tom," she said earnestly, leaning forward and folding her hands on her desktop. "I'm a good citizen, an elected official. I vote in every election. I pay my taxes. On top of all that, I fulfill my civic duty by keeping the town—and the county—safe for democracy. Believe me when I tell you, I feel as much sympathy for Ona and her gallbladder as anyone else does." She paused, sucked in a deep breath. "But that doesn't mean I'm going to join the Parade Committee."

Tom blushed a little. "Actually," he said, after clearing his throat, "we were hoping you'd take over, sort of spearhead the thing."

Again, Melissa thought of her siblings.

Olivia, a veterinarian and a regular Dr. Doolittle to boot, apparently able to converse with critters of all species, through some weird form of telepathy, oversaw the operation of the local state-of-the-art animal shelter, and directed the corresponding foundation.

Ashley, too, was almost continually involved in one fundraising event or another—and their brother, Brad? He was a country-music superstar, even though he'd technically retired around the time he and Meg McKettrick got married. *His* specialty was writing whopping checks for pretty much any worthy cause—and doing the occasional benefit performance.

"You have the wrong O'Ballivan," she told Tom, feeling like a slacker. They were overachievers, her sibs, with a tendency to make her look bad. "Talk to Olivia—or Ashley. Better yet, have Brad *buy* you a parade."

Tom grinned faintly and then gave his head a sad little shake. "Olivia's too busy," he said. "Ashley is out of town. And Brad has his hands full running Stone Creek Ranch—"

"No," Melissa broke in, to stop the flow. "Really. I wouldn't be any good at organizing a parade. I've watched a lot of them, on TV and right here in Stone Creek. I've seen *Miracle on 34th Street* four million times. But that's the whole scope of my experience—I wouldn't know the first thing about putting something like that together."

The sheriff colored up a little, under the jaw and around his ears. "You think Aunt Ona was an expert on parades, back when she took over? No, ma'am. She just pushed up her sleeves and plunged right in. Learned on the job."

"There must be someone else who could do this," Melissa said weakly.

But Tom shook his head again, harder this time. "We got the Food Concession Committee, and the Arts and Crafts Show Committee, and the committee to deal with the carnival folks. Everybody's either already volunteering, doing something else or out of town."

Melissa set her jaw. By then, she was starting to feel downright guilty, but that didn't mean she was going to give in.

Out front, Andrea chirped a sunny greeting to someone. Melissa felt an odd little zip in the air, like the charge before a summer thunderstorm.

"Then I guess you'll have to cancel the parade this year," Melissa said.

And that was when the little boy she'd seen at the café that morning, eating pancakes at the counter, popped into her office.

He looked up at Tom, then over at Melissa, his dark violet eyes troubled. His lower lip began to wobble.

"There isn't going to be a parade?" he asked.

CHAPTER TWO

QUICKLY—BUT NOT QUITE quickly enough, as it turned out—Steven pursued Matt through the open doorway, scooped him up from behind and immediately locked eyeballs with the certifiably hot woman he'd checked out while he and the boy were having breakfast earlier that morning, over at the café.

When their glances connected, his-meets-hers, there was an actual *impact*, it seemed to Steven. He half expected things to explode all over the place, walls to tumble, ceilings to collapse, founts of fire to shoot up out of the floor, as in some apocalyptic action movie.

Damn, he thought, dazed by the strength of his reaction. He'd known plenty of beautiful women in his time, none of whom had ever affected him in just this way. Was it the amazing body, the face, the crazy mane of thick brown hair, falling past her shoulders in spiral curls, the jarringly blue eyes that seemed to see past all his defenses?

Who knew? He glanced down at the nameplate on her desk.

Melissa O'Ballivan. Prosecutor.

Uh-oh, he thought. *Been there, done that.*

After what Cindy Ryan had done to him, he'd sworn off dating other lawyers—especially DAs and their assistants.

"Sorry," Steven said, finally finding his voice and dredging up the patented, lopsided grin that had been serving Creed men well for generations. "We stopped by to pay a parking ticket, and Matt here got away from me."

It was only then that he noticed the uniformed lawman standing just inside the small room, arms folded, assessing him with a certain noncommittal detachment, as if he might be running through a mental database of wanted criminals, in case he could match up Steven's face to one of them. Here was a man who took his job seriously.

Maybe he'd been the one to write that ticket and place it neatly under the windshield wiper of Steven's old truck.

Either way, Steven liked him right off, and figured that liking would stick. His first impressions of people were usually, though not always, accurate ones.

"County Clerk's office is just down the hall," the cop said, relaxing visibly. "You can settle up on the ticket there." That said, he put out his hand in that quintessentially small-town way Steven knew so well. "Tom Parker," he said.

"Steven Creed," Steven replied, setting a squirmy Matt on his own two feet.

"How come there isn't going to be a parade?" Matt piped up. He wheeled to look up at Steven. *You said there would be a parade.* And a rodeo, too. That's the main reason I didn't run away from home when you told me we were moving here!"

By that time, the spectacularly sexy Ms. O'Ballivan had pushed back her chair and stood, soon rounding the desk to face the boy. There was no telling what she thought of Steven, if he'd even registered on her radar, but the lady had obviously fallen for Matt, hook, line and sinker.

"Hi," she said, with a smile that tugged at Steven's gut like a fishhook, even though she was looking down at the child, not at him. "My name is Melissa O'Ballivan. What's yours?"

"Matt Creed," the boy responded, somewhat warily because he'd been taught to be careful of strangers, and Steven felt another tug, this time at his emotions. He'd given Matt the choice, when the adoption became final, of keeping his folks' last name—St. John—or taking on his new father's. And it still touched him that Matt, who remembered Zack and Jillie with a clarity Steven did everything he could to maintain, had decided to go by *Creed*.

"Matt," Steven managed, clearing his throat. He still had that weird feeling going on inside and he wanted to get away, so he could mull it over, come to terms, make some sort of sense of it.

Whatever "it" was.

"Let's go take care of that parking ticket," he prompted, after an entirely rhetorical glance at his watch, failing completely to note the time. "We're due to sign the papers for the ranch in a few minutes."

"You said there would be a parade," Matt repeated, turning away from the dazzle of Melissa O'Ballivan to frown up at Steven. The kid could be bone-stubborn when he'd made up his mind about something, which meant the Creed name would suit him just fine.

The lawman, Parker, cleared his throat. Slanted a glance at Ms. O'Ballivan. "Aunt Ona already did most of the work," he told her. "Laid the groundwork, signed off on the different floats and even arranged for all the permits. Only thing you'd have to do is oversee a couple of meetings, check stuff off on a clipboard. Make sure folks live up to their commitments."

Melissa laid a hand on top of Matt's head and ruffled his dark hair slightly. Her shoulders rose and fell as she drew in a big breath and sighed it out, looking cheerfully doomed. "Welcome to Stone Creek, Matt Creed," she said. "And here's hoping you'll enjoy the parade."

Mollified, Matt punched the air with one small fist and turned to Steven. *"Yes!"* he said, with a grin.

By then, Steven had pieced the scenario together in his mind, or part of it, at least. Ms. O'Ballivan hadn't wanted to oversee the upcoming event, but she'd been roped in anyhow—by the sheriff, from the sound of it.

Steven allowed himself a long look at Melissa—an indulgence, considering the way she shook him up. The Realtor who'd sold him the Emerson ranch had touted both the parade and the rodeo as "longstanding community traditions," in addition to other selling points, and Steven had made a big deal about the festivities so Matt would have something to look forward to, besides the relatively immediate dog and the eventual pony.

"Thanks," Steven told Melissa, and the word came out sounding gruff.

She made a comical face. "Don't mention it," she replied, rueful.

"Maybe I could help out somehow," Steven heard himself say, as he took Matt's hand and started to turn away. "Not that I know much about parades."

"Join the club," Melissa said, with another of those lethal smiles of hers.

Steven grinned, nodded and managed to peel himself away.

He forgot all about paying the parking ticket, though, because his mind was full of Melissa O'Ballivan, and it was bound to stay that way.

All through the closing, held in a meeting room over at the Cattleman's Bank, Matt fidgeted. Steven signed papers, handed over a cashier's check covering the cost of the property in full, probably came across as a man who knew what he was doing.

Adopting a little boy. Quitting the prestigious Denver firm where he'd worked since he'd left the family business. Winding up so far from the Creed ranch outside Lonesome Bend, Colorado, which had been in the family for well over a hundred years, only to buy a run-down spread in another state.

Was he a man who knew what he was doing? Before he'd encountered Ms. O'Ballivan, Steven would have answered with an unqualified "yes." Now, he wasn't so sure.

"WHAT JUST HAPPENED HERE?" Melissa asked, widening her eyes at Tom Parker and laying the splayed fingers of one hand to her chest. Steven Creed and his little boy, Matt, had probably been gone for all of thirty seconds, but it seemed as if they'd taken all the oxygen in the room away with them, leaving a vacuum.

Tom chuckled. "Stone Creek has itself a new chairman for the Parade Committee," he said, looking pleased and maybe a little smug on top of that. Then, about to leave, he paused in the doorway to wink at her. "And unless I miss my guess, the earth just moved." With that, he was gone.

Melissa stood in the middle of the office floor for a few moments, flustered. Then, because she was nothing if not professional, she walked over, gave her door a firm shove with one palm to shut it and marched back to her desk.

She didn't have many cases to prosecute; things had been pretty quiet around Stone Creek since Byron Cahill got himself sent up, but there were a few, and she always had reports to make, files to review, emails to read and respond to. If she'd been smart, she thought to herself, she'd have gone fishing with J.P.

At midmorning, Andrea rapped on the office door and stuck her head in to say that she needed to go home because she had cramps and there was nothing to do around that place anyway.

Peering at the girl over the tops of her reading glasses, Melissa mouthed the word *go* and logged on to her computer. Andrea might or might not have been suffering from cramps, but there was no arguing with the fact that both of them were, for today at least, underworked.

Melissa, grateful to be putting in eight-hour days, like normal people, didn't miss the high stress levels and double workweeks of her previous jobs. She liked having the time to paint the rooms of her little house evenings and weekends, read stacks of books, enjoy her growing gaggle of nieces and nephews and even garden a little.

Okay, so she'd been through a romantic —not to mention sexual—dry spell since her breakup with Dan Guthrie, several long and eventful years before. Nobody had everything, did they?

Something sagged inside Melissa when she asked herself that question. Her *sisters* had everything a person could reasonably want, it seemed to her—babies, hunky husbands who adored them, work they loved—and it went without saying that Brad had caught the brass ring. During his amazing career, he'd collected more than a dozen awards from the Country Music Association, along with a few Grammys for good measure, his marriage to Meg McKettrick was beyond happy, and they were building a beautiful family together.

Melissa sighed. Time to put away the tiny violin, stop comparing herself to her brother and sisters. Sure, she was a little lonely from time to time, but so what? She was healthy. She had kin, people who loved her. Stone Creek Ranch, with its long and colorful history, was still home. She had a fine education, no mortgage, a jazzy car custom-built to look just like a 1954 MG Roadster, and enough money socked away to retire at forty if she wanted to.

Which she probably wouldn't, but that wasn't the point, was it?

For Melissa, success meant having options. It meant freedom.

If she had a notion to pull up stakes and throw herself body and soul into a job in a more exciting place—say, L.A. or New York—she could do that. There was nothing to tie her down: she could simply resign from her present position, rent out her house or even sell it, say another goodbye to Stone Creek and boogie.

She loved her sisters and her brother. She had lots of friends, people she'd known all her life. But it was the idea of leaving her nieces and nephews, not being there, in person, to see them grow up but instead settling for digital photos, phone calls, rare visits and emails that made a hard knot form in her throat.

And why was she even thinking these thoughts, anyway? Because Tom had been right, that was why.

Steven Creed and his little boy had appeared in her office and, at some point, the earth *had* moved. Shifted right off its axis. Gravity was suspended. Up was down and down was up, and the proof of that could be stated in one short, simple sentence: She'd agreed to head the Parade Committee.

Melissa drew in a breath, huffed it out hard enough to make her bangs flutter, and scanned the list of new messages on her computer screen.

Tom Parker, sitting three doors down at his own keyboard, IMed her to say that time was wasting and she really ought to schedule a meeting so she could get on the same page with everybody on the Parade Committee.

The response she sent was not something one would normally say to a police officer, face-to-face *or* via email. But this was Tom, the guy she'd grown up with, the man who'd named his dog Elvis, for Pete's sake.

Tom replied with a smiley-face icon wearing big sunglasses and displaying a raised middle finger.

Melissa laughed at that—she couldn't help it—and went back to the official stuff.

Eustace Blake, who was ninety if he was a day and nonetheless managed to navigate the public computer over at the library just fine, thank you very much, had hunted-and-pecked his way through a complaint he'd made many times before, with subtle variations. Visitors from some faraway planet had landed in his cornfield—*again*—and scared his chickens so badly that the hens wouldn't lay eggs anymore, and for all he knew, they'd contaminated his stretch of the creek, too, and *by God* he wanted something done about it.

Smiling to herself, wishing mightily for a fresh cup of coffee, Melissa wrote back, politely inquiring as to whether or not Eustace had reported the most recent incident to Sheriff Parker. Because, she assured the old man, he was absolutely right. Something had to be done. She even included Tom's cell number.

The next half-dozen messages were advertisements— find love, get rich quick, clear up her skin, enlarge her penis. She deleted those.

Then there was the one from Velda Cahill—Melissa would have known that email address anywhere, since she'd practically been barraged with communiqués since Byron's arrest. This time, the subject line was in caps. FROM A TAX PAYING CITIZEN, it read.

Melissa sighed. For a moment, her finger hovered over the delete key, but in the end, she couldn't make herself do that. Velda might be a crank—make that a royal pain in the posterior—but she *was* a citizen and a taxpayer. As such, she had the inalienable right to harangue public officials, up to a point. She'd written:

My boy will be coming home today, on the afternoon bus. Not that I'd expect you to be happy about it, like I am. Byron and me, we're just ordinary people—we don't have anybody famous in our family, like you do, or rich, neither. What little we've got, we've had to *work* for. Nobody ever gave us nothing and we never asked. But I'm asking now. Don't be sending Sheriff Parker or one of his deputies by our place every five minutes to see if Byron's behaving himself. And don't come knocking at our door whenever somebody runs a red light or smashes a row of mailboxes with a baseball bat. It won't be Byron that done it, I can promise you that. Just please leave us alone and let my son and me get on with things. Sincerely, Velda.

Sincerely, Velda. Melissa sighed again, then clicked on Reply. She wrote:

Hello, Velda. Thank you for getting in touch. I can assure you that as long as Byron doesn't break the law, neither Sheriff Parker nor I will bother him. Best wishes, Melissa O'Ballivan.

After that, she plunked her elbows on the edge of her desk and rubbed her temples with the fingertips of both hands.

She really should have gone fishing with J.P.

"IT'S ALL OURS," Steven told Matt, as they made the turn off the road and onto their dirt driveway. "Downed fences, rusty nails, weeds and all."

Matt, firmly fastened into his safety seat, looked over at him and grinned. "Can we go to the shelter and get a dog now?" he asked.

Steven laughed and downshifted. The tires of the old truck thumped across the cattle guard. *Now to buy* cattle, he thought, trying to remember when he'd last felt so hopeful about the future. Since Zack and Jillie's death—hell, long before that, if he was honest with himself—he'd concentrated on putting one foot in front of the other. Doing the next logical thing, large or small.

What was different about today?

It wasn't just the ranch; he could admit that in the privacy of his own mind, if not out loud. Today, he'd met Melissa O'Ballivan. And he knew that making her acquaintance would turn out to be either one of the best—or one of the worst—things that had ever happened to him. Thanks to Cindy, he figured, the odds favored the latter.

"I liked her a lot," Matt said, as they jostled up the driveway, flinging out a cloud of red Arizona dust behind them.

"Who?" Steven asked, though he knew.

"The parade lady," Matt told him, using a tone of exaggerated forbearance. "Miss O—Miss O—"

"O'Ballivan," Steven said. It wasn't that she was anything special to him, or anything like that. He'd always had a knack for remembering names, that was all.

"Is she anybody's mommy?" Matt wanted to know.

Steven swallowed. Just when he thought he had a handle on the single-dad thing, the kid would throw him a curve. "I don't know, Tex," he answered. "Why do you ask?"

"I like her," Matt said. Simple as that. *I like her.* "I like the way she smiles, and the way she smells."

Me, too, Steven thought. "She seems nice enough."

But, then, so had his live-in girlfriend/fiancée. With the face and body of an angel, Cindy had been sweetness itself—until Zack died and Steven told her that Matt would be moving in for good so he thought they ought to go ahead and get married. They'd planned to anyhow—someday.

He'd never forgotten the scornful look she'd given him, or the way her lip had curled, let alone what she'd actually said.

"The kid is a deal breaker," she'd told Steven coolly. "It's him or me."

Stunned—it wasn't as if they'd never talked about the provision in his best friends' wills, after all—and coldly furious, Steven had made his choice without hesitation.

"Then I guess it has to be Matt," he'd replied.

Cindy had left right away, storming out of the condo, slamming the door behind her, the tires of her expensive car laying rubber as she screeched out of the driveway. She'd removed her stuff in stages, however, and even said she'd thought things over and she regretted flying off the handle the way she had. Was there a chance they could try again?

Steven wished there had been, but it was too late. Some kind of line had been crossed, and it wasn't that he *wouldn't* go back. It was that he *couldn't*.

"So if she's not already somebody's mommy, she might want to be mine," Matt speculated.

Steven's eyes burned. How was he supposed to answer that one?

"*And* she's going to make a parade," Matt enthused.

As they reached the ruin of a barn, Steven put the truck in park and shut off the motor. Off to the left, the house loomed like a benevolent ghost hoping for simple grace.

They had camping gear, and the electricity had been turned on. The plumber Steven had sent ahead said the well pump was working fine, and there was water. *Cold* water, but, hey, the stuff was *wet*. They could drink it.

Steven could make coffee. And if the stove worked, they could take baths the old-fashioned way, in a metal wash-tub in the kitchen, using water heated in big kettles.

Shades of the old days.

"Yeah," Steven said in belated answer, getting out and rounding the truck to open the door and help Matt out of his safety gear. The pickup was too old to have a backseat, but Steven had a new rig on order, one with an extended cab and all the extras. "Ms. O'Ballivan is going to make a parade."

"And you offered to help her," Matt said. That kind of confidence was hard to shoot down. In fact, it was impossible.

The reminder made Steven sigh. "Right," he said. Then he lifted Matt down out of the truck, and they started for the house.

"This place is *awesome*," Matt exclaimed, taking in the sagging screened porch, the peeling paint, the fall-ing gutter spouts and the loose shingles sliding off the edges of the roof. "Maybe it's even haunted!"

Steven laughed and put out a hand, gratified when Matt took it. "Maybe," he said. The boy would be too big for hand-holding pretty soon. "But I doubt it."

"Ghosts like old houses," Matt said, as they mounted the back steps. Steven had paused to test them with his own weight before he allowed the child to follow. "Especially when there's renovation going on. That stirs them up."

"Have you been watching those spooky reality shows on TV again?" Steven asked, pushing open the back door. There was no need for a key; the lock had rusted away years ago.

"I wouldn't do that," Matt said sweetly. "It's against the rules and everything."

Steven chuckled. "Far be it from you to break any rules," he said, remembering Zack. Matt's father had *lived* to break rules. In the end, it seemed to have been that trait that got him killed.

The kitchen was worse than Steven remembered. Cupboards sagged. The linoleum was scuffed in the best places, where it wasn't peeling to the layer of black sub-flooring underneath. The faucets and spigot in the sink were bent. The refrigerator door was not only dented but peeling at the corners, and the handle dangled by a single loose screw.

"Are we going to live here?" Matt asked, sounding a little worried now. So much for his interest in ghost hunting.

"Not right away," Steven said, suppressing a sigh. This place wasn't even fit to *camp* in, let alone call home. The thought of returning to the Happy Wanderer Motel depressed him thoroughly, but there weren't a lot of choices in Stone Creek, and the next town, Indian Rock, where there was a fairly good hotel, was forty miles away.

"Good," Matt said, sounding—and looking—re-lieved. "The people at the shelter probably wouldn't *let* us adopt a dog if they knew we were going to bring it *here* to live."

Steven laughed. It seemed better than crying. He crouched, so he could look straight into Matt's face, and took him gently by the shoulders. "We'll make this work," he said. "I promise."

"I believe you," Matt said, breaking Steven's heart,

as he often did with a few trusting words. "Can we look at my room before we go back to town?"

"Sure," Steven said, standing up straight.

Matt, always resilient, was already having second thoughts about leaving. "Maybe we ought to stay here," he said. "It's better than the motel."

Steven grinned. "I won't argue with you on that one," he said, "but the Happy Wanderer has hot water, which is a plus."

"We could skip taking showers for a couple of days," Matt suggested. Unless he was going swimming, the kid hated to get wet. "Where's my room?"

Steven led the way through the dining room. Although there was a second floor, there was no way anybody would be sleeping up there before the renovations were finished and the fire alarm system had been wired and tested.

"Here you go," he said, opening a door and stepping back so Matt could go inside. It was, as Steven remembered from his visit with the Realtor a few months before, a spacious room, with lots of light pouring in through the tall, narrow windows.

"Where's your room from here?" Matt wanted to know. He stood in the middle of that dusty chamber, his head tilted back, staring up in wonder like they were visiting a European cathedral instead of an old ranch house in Arizona.

Steven smiled. Cocked a thumb to his right. "Just next door," he said.

"Can I see?" Matt asked.

Steven ruffled the boy's hair. "Sure," he said.

His room was smaller. There was a slight slant to

the floor, and the wallpaper hung down in big, untidy loops.

Steven thought of his expensive condominium in Denver and wanted to laugh. There, he'd had a fine view of the city, skylights and a retractable TV screen that disappeared into the ceiling at the push of a button.

What a contrast.

"It's not so bad," Matt decided, taking in the results of years of dedicated neglect.

Steven rubbed his chin, considering options. "I guess we could go back to town and buy ourselves a tent," he said. "The weather's good, so we could take baths in the creek. Carry our own water, cook over a campfire, sleep under the stars. Back to the land and all that."

Matt grinned. "Awesome," he said. "Let's go buy a tent."

"Better unload the camping gear and the grub first," Steven answered. "If we don't, there won't be room in the truck for a tent."

"They don't come all set up, silly," Matt informed him as the two of them headed back through the house, toward the kitchen door. "They're sold in *boxes*."

"Thanks for bringing me up to speed on that one," Steven said, mussing Matt's hair once again.

Matt supervised while Steven carried in suitcases, supplies of dried and canned food, sleeping bags and the camp stove, piling everything in the kitchen.

He returned to find Matt standing in the bed of the truck, one hand shading his eyes from the sun, following a trail of dust down on the road.

"Look," the boy cried, sounding delighted. "Some-body's coming!"

Steven was relieved when the rig, a big, fancy red

truck, turned in at their driveway. Matt would have been pretty disappointed if they'd gone on by, whoever they were.

He recognized his cousin Meg right away. She leaned out the window on the passenger side and waved, beaming, her bright blond hair catching the dusty light. Her husband, Brad, was at the wheel.

As soon as the truck came to a stop, Meg was out, sprinting across the yard to throw her arms around Steven's neck. "You're here!" she cried.

Steven laughed. It had been a while since he'd felt this welcome anyplace.

Matt scrambled down out of the truck bed, eager for company.

Brad unfolded his long, lanky frame from the interior of the pickup and approached, and the two men shook hands while Meg bent to look into Matt's eyes and smile.

"You must be Matt," she said.

Matt nodded. "And you must be Steven's cousin," he replied. "I forget your name, though."

"Meg," she said gently.

Brad, looking like a rancher in his old jeans, long-sleeved chambray work shirt and ancient boots, jabbed a thumb in the direction of the house and said, "Looks like this place is in even worse shape than I thought."

Meg surveyed it with her hands resting on her trim, blue-jeaned hips. Her white cotton top was fitted and sleeveless, and it didn't seem possible that she was old enough to be married, let alone the mother of a couple of kids.

She could have passed for seventeen.

"Brad O'Ballivan," she scolded, sounding wholly

good-natured, "I've told you a thousand times that it's a train wreck over here."

Brad grinned. "It's better than the barn, though," he drawled.

Matt had recognized him by then. "Are you that famous guy who's on TV sometimes?" he asked. Before Brad could answer, he went on. "We know somebody *else* with the same last name as yours. Melissa."

"Melissa is my sister," Brad said, obviously enjoying the exchange.

"You have a sister?" Matt made it sound like the eighth wonder. He was an only child, of course, and so was Steven. Did the child long for a sister, the way Steven himself had, growing up?

Brad crouched, so he could look directly into Matt's face. "Actually," he said, "I have *three* sisters. There's Olivia—she's a veterinarian and she can talk to animals. And Ashley—she and Melissa are twins."

Steven felt a pang at the mention of twins, the way he always did when the subject came up. It made him think of his cousins Conner and Brody and their complex family history. They were a matched set, those two.

"Do they look alike?" Matt asked. "Ashley and Melissa?"

"Nope," Brad answered. "They're not those kind of twins."

"Oh," Matt said, absorbing the information. Then he brightened, looking from Brad, who straightened to his full height and must have looked pretty tall to the child against that sunlit Arizona sky, to Meg, then back again. "You're famous, though, huh?"

"Yeah," Brad admitted, sounding almost shy. "Sort of."

Matt nodded and moved on, over the celebrity aspect

of the encounter, evidently. "We're going to get a tent and camp out!" he announced. "And we're adopting a *dog*, too!"

Meg beamed. "That's great," she said.

Matt absorbed her approval like it was sunlight.

"You could use Brad's old tour bus," she told Steven, a few moments later. The two of them had only known each other for about six months; turned out Meg was something of an amateur genealogist, and she'd tracked him down on the internet and sent him an email. Steven didn't have a lot of kin, and he wasn't taking any chances on alienating his cousin by imposing on her generosity.

Brad nodded, though, and rested a light hand against the small of Meg's back. "That's a good idea," he said, before Steven could get a word out. "It's pretty well-equipped, and nobody's used it in a while."

Steven opened his mouth to say something along the lines of "It's okay, I appreciate the offer, but the tent will be fine for now," but Meg already had her cell phone out. She dialed, stuck a finger in her free ear, smiling fit to blow every transformer within a fifty-mile radius and asked whoever was on the other end to please bring the bus next door.

Brad, meanwhile, had wandered over to look at the barn. Or what was left of it, anyway. "Good for firewood and not much else," he said, scanning the ruins.

Steven nodded in agreement, shoved a hand through his hair. "Listen, about the bus, I wouldn't want you and Meg going to a lot trouble. We'll be okay with a tent...."

Brad listened, grinning. But he was shaking his head the whole time.

Steven's protest fell away when he heard Matt give a peal of happy laughter. He glanced in the boy's direction and saw that Meg was leaning down again, her hands braced on her thighs, so she could look into Matt's eyes. Her own were dancing with delight.

Matt must have told her one of his infamous knock-knock jokes, Steven thought. The kid did tend to laugh at his own jokes.

"Never look a gift bus in the grillwork," Brad said.

Steven looked back at him, blinked. "Huh?"

Brad laughed. "Never mind," he said, and started off toward Meg again.

It was almost as though the two of them were magnetized to each other, Steven observed, feeling just a little envious.

Ten minutes later, the gleaming bus was rolling up the driveway, and it was a thing of beauty.

CHAPTER THREE

It was 5:30 p.m., by Melissa's watch. The bus from Tucson and Phoenix would have disgorged any passengers it might be carrying—Byron Cahill, for instance—at 5:00 sharp, before heading on to Indian Rock and then making a swing back to stop in Flagstaff and heading south again. She was familiar with the bus route because she'd ridden it so often, as a college student, when she couldn't afford a car.

Although she usually looked forward to going home after work, today was different. Home sounded like a lonely place, since there wouldn't be anybody there waiting for her.

Maybe, she thought, she should give in to Olivia's constant nagging—well, okay, Olivia didn't exactly *nag;* she just *suggested* things in a big-sister kind of way—and adopt a cat or a dog. Or both.

Just the thought of all that fur and pet dander made her sneeze, loudly and with vigor. Since she'd been tested for allergies more than once, and the results were consistently negative, Melissa secretly thought Olivia and Ashley might be right—her sensitivities were psychosomatic. Deep down, her sisters agreed, Melissa was afraid to open her heart, lest it be broken. It was a wonder, they further maintained, that she didn't sneeze whenever she encountered a man, given her wariness in the arena of love and romance.

There might be some truth to that theory, too, she thought now. She adored the children in the family, and that felt risky enough, considering the shape the world was in.

How could she afford to love a man? Or compound her fretful concerns by letting herself care for an animal? Especially considering that critters had very short life spans, compared to humans.

Feeling a little demoralized, Melissa logged off her computer, pulled her purse from the large bottom drawer of her desk, and sighed with relief because the workday was over. Not that she'd really done much work.

It troubled her conscience, accepting a paycheck mostly for warming a desk chair all day; in the O'Ballivan family, going clear back to old Sam, the founding father of today's ever-expanding clan, character was measured by the kind of *contribution* a person made. Slackers were not admired.

Telling herself she didn't need to be admired anyway, dammit, Melissa left her office, locking up behind her. She paused, passing Andrea's deserted desk, frowned at the ivy plant slowly drying up in one corner.

It wasn't her plant, she reminded herself.

It is a living thing, and it is thirsty, that self retorted silently.

With a sigh, Melissa put down her purse, searched until she found the empty coffee tin Andrea used as a watering can—when she remembered to water the indoor foliage, which was a crapshoot—filled the humble vessel at the sink in the women's restroom, returned to the cubicle and carefully doused the ivy.

It seemed to rally, right before her eyes, that bedraggled snippet of greenery, standing up a little straighter, stretching its fragile limbs a bit wider instead of shriveling. Melissa made a mental note to speak to Andrea about the subtleties of responsibility—she wasn't a bad kid. Just sort of—*distracted* all the time. And little wonder, given all she'd been through.

Andrea had arrived in Stone Creek as a runaway, when she was just fourteen, riding the same bus that had probably brought Byron Cahill back to town that very afternoon. Out of money and out of options, she'd spent her first night sleeping behind the potted rosebushes in the garden center at the local discount store.

Upon discovering her there, first thing the next morning, the clerk had called Tom Parker, a natural thing to do. Especially since Andrea sat cross-legged against the wall, stubbornly refusing to come out.

Tom had soon arrived, accompanied by his portly mixed-breed retriever, Elvis, who pushed his way right through those spiky-spined rosebushes to lick Andrea's face in friendly consolation. After a while, Tom—or had it been Elvis?—managed to persuade Andrea to take a chance on the kindness of strangers and leave her erstwhile hiding place.

Over breakfast at the Lucky Horseshoe Café, since closed, the girl had confided in Tom, told him about her less-than-wholesome home life, down in Phoenix. Her mother was on drugs, she claimed, and her stepfather, who had done time for a variety of crimes, was about to get out of jail. Rather than be at his mercy, Andrea said, she'd decided to take off, try to make it on her own.

Of course, Tom checked the story out, and it held up to scrutiny, so agencies were consulted and legal steps were taken, and Andrea moved in with the elderly Crockett sisters, Mamie and Marge, who lived directly across the street from Tom's aunt Ona, she of Parade-Committee fame, as a foster child. Andrea still lived in the small apartment above the Crocketts' detached garage, proudly paying rent and looking after the old ladies *and* their many cats.

Melissa was thinking all these thoughts as she left the courthouse, head bent, rummaging through her purse for her car keys as she crossed the gravel lot.

"Did you get my email?"

The question jolted Melissa and she came to an abrupt halt, her heart scrabbling in her throat.

"Velda," Melissa said, when she had regained enough breath to speak. "You scared me."

Byron's mother, probably in her early fifties and emaciated almost to the point of anorexia, stood near the roadster, dappled in the leaf shadows of the oak tree. Velda wore an old cotton blouse without sleeves, plastic flip-flops and jeans so well-worn that the fabric couldn't have been described as blue, but only as a hint of that color.

"Sorry," Velda said, her voice scratchy from several decades of smoking unfiltered cigarettes and half again that much regret, probably, her expression insincere. Lines spiked out around her mouth, giving her lips a pursed look. "I wouldn't want to do that. Scare anybody, I mean."

"Good," Melissa said, steady enough by then to be annoyed instead of frightened.

Velda stood between Melissa and the driver's-side door of the car, her skinny arms folded. Her hair was iron-gray, with faint streaks of yellow, and fell well past her shoulders. Pink plastic barrettes, shaped like little hearts, held the locks back at the sides of her head, creating an unfortunate effect of attempted girlishness.

"Did you get my email?" Velda asked again.

"Yes," Melissa replied, holding her keys in her right hand. "And I answered it. The situation is really pretty simple, Velda. As long as Byron stays out of trouble, he won't have to worry about my office or the police."

Velda smiled wanly, shrugged her bony shoulders. She sidled out of Melissa's way, rather than stepping, as if it would be too much trouble to lift her feet. Clearly, there was more she wanted to say.

Melissa got behind the wheel of her car and turned the key in the ignition, but she didn't drive away. She waited.

"It's hard enough for him," Velda went on, at last, as if Melissa hadn't said anything at all, "knowing that poor young girl died because of what he did. Byron's got to live with that for the rest of his life. But he's not some hardened criminal, that's all I'm saying. He's not some monster everybody ought to be afraid of."

As she'd spoken, Velda had curled her fingers along the edge of the car window, so the knuckles whitened.

Melissa sighed, something softening inside her, and patted Velda's hand. "Byron is your son," she said quietly, looking straight up into the faded-denim blue of the other woman's eyes, "and you love him. I understand that. But, Velda, the best thing you can probably do to help Byron right now is to lighten up a little. Give him some time—and some space—to adjust to being back on the outside."

Tears welled up in Velda's eyes; she sniffled once and stared off into some invisible distance for a long moment before looking back at Melissa. Her voice was very small when she spoke.

"Byron wasn't on the bus," she said slowly. "He was supposed to be on that bus, and he wasn't."

Melissa felt a mild charge of something that might have been alarm. "Maybe there was some kind of delay on the other end—didn't he call you?"

Velda's expression was rueful. The bitterness was back. "Call me? Not everybody can afford a cell phone, you know."

Melissa looked around. Except for Tom's cruiser, the roadster was the only vehicle in the lot. "Where's your car?"

"It's broken down," Velda said, still with that tinge of resentful irony. "That's why I was late getting over to the station to meet the bus. It was gone when I got there, and there was no sign of Byron. I asked inside the station, and Al told me he didn't see my boy get off."

"Get in," Melissa said, nodding to indicate the passenger seat, leaning to move her purse to the floorboards so Velda would have room to sit down.

Velda hesitated, then rounded the hood of the car and opened the door. Once she'd settled in and snapped on her seat belt, she met Melissa's gaze.

"What are we going to do now?" she asked.

Melissa leaned to dig her cell out of her purse and handed it to Velda. "Call Byron's parole officer," she said, by way of an answer, certain that Velda would know the number, even if she couldn't afford a mobile phone of her own. "He—or she—will know if there was some sort of hitch with his release."

Velda hesitated, then took the phone from Melissa. She studied the keypad for a few moments, while

Melissa shifted into First and gave the roadster some gas, but soon, Byron's mom was punching in a sequence of numbers, biting her lower lip as she waited to ring through.

BRAD O'BALLIVAN'S TOUR BUS, it turned out, was equipped with solar panels, satellite TV, and high-speed internet service. It boasted two large bedrooms, a full bath and a kitchen with full-size appliances.

"Must have been tough," Steven joked as Brad showed him and Matt through the place, "having to rough it like this while you were on the road."

Outside, a couple of workers from Brad and Meg's ranch were already hooking up the water supply and installing the secondary generator. That would serve as backup to the solar gear.

Brad grinned modestly, shrugged, slid his hands into the front pockets of his jeans in a way that was characteristic of him. "The band used it, mostly," he admitted. "I traveled by plane."

"Right," Steven said, amused. "More like a private jet, I think."

Brad shrugged again and looked away for a moment, the grin still tugging at the corner of his mouth.

Steven had never met a famous person before—not one from the entertainment world, anyway—and he was pleasantly surprised by this one. O'Ballivan was not only a down-to-earth guy, he was generous. He clearly loved his wife and kids more than he'd ever loved bright lights and ticket sales.

"I appreciate this," Steven said.

"Just being neighborly," Brad answered, his tone easy. *No big deal,* was the unspoken part of the message. He turned, paused beside the door to scrawl a couple of numbers onto the small blackboard above the desk. "Let us know if you need anything," he said.

Steven nodded. "Thanks," he replied.

He stood in the doorway and watched as Meg and Brad drove away in their truck. Matt was so excited, he was practically bouncing off the walls.

"This is *amazing*," he marveled. "Can I have the room with the bunk beds?"

With a chuckle, Steven turned to look down at Matt. The kid's face was joy-polished; his eyes glowed with excitement.

"Sure," Steven replied.

"Can we go back to town and get a dog now that we don't have to live in a tent while our house gets fixed up?" The question itself was luminous, like the boy.

Steven felt like a heartless bastard, but he had to refuse. "Probably not a good idea, Tex," he said gently. "This bus is borrowed, remember? And it's pretty darn fancy, too. A dog might do some damage, and that would not be cool."

Matt's face worked as he processed Steven's response. "Even if we were really, *really* careful to pick a really, *really* good dog?"

"*Good* has nothing to do with it, Bud," Steven said, sitting down on the leather-upholstered bench that doubled as a couch so he'd be at eye level with the child. "Dogs are dogs. They do what they do, at least until they've been trained."

Matt blinked. Behind that little forehead, with its faint sprinkling of freckles, the cogs were turning, big-time. He finally turned slightly and inclined his head toward the blackboard over the desk. "Maybe you could call Brad and Meg," he ventured reasonably. "You could ask them if they'd mind. If we had a dog, I mean."

"Tex—"

"I'd clean up any messes," Matt hastened to promise. He seemed to be holding his breath.

Steven sighed. Got out his cell phone. "You're the one who wants to get the dog now instead of later," he said. "So you can do the asking."

Matt beamed, nodded. "Okay," he said, practically crowing the word.

Steven keyed in one of the numbers Brad had written on the board, the one with a *C* beside it in parenthesis. When it started to ring, he handed the device to Matt.

"Hello?" he said, after a couple of moments. "It's Matt Creed calling. Is this Mr. O'Ballivan?"

The timbre of the responding voice was male, though Steven couldn't make out the words.

"My new dad says we can go to the animal shelter in town and adopt a dog if it's all right with you," Matt chimed in next. Inwardly, Steven groaned. *My new dad says...*

The boy listened for a few more seconds, nodding rapidly. "If my dog makes any messes," he finished manfully, throwing his small shoulders back and raising his chin as he spoke, "I promise to clean them up."

Brad said something in response, after which Matt said thank you and then goodbye and finally snapped the phone shut, held it out to Steven with an air of *there-you-go*.

Steven accepted the phone, dropped it into his shirt pocket, and ran a hand through his hair. "Well?" he asked, though it was pretty obvious what Brad's answer must have been.

"It's okay to get a dog," Matt announced, all but jumping up and down with excitement by then. "Let's go." He grabbed for Steven's hand, tried to pull him to his feet. "Right now!"

Laughing, Steven stood up. Mussed up Matt's hair again.

Someone rapped at the door just then, and Steven answered. The ranch hands Brad had sent over were standing outside, thumbs hooked into the waistbands of their jeans, sun-browned faces upturned beneath the brims of their hats.

"Electricity ought to be working," one of them said, without preamble. "Water, too."

"Mind flipping a switch and turning on a faucet to make sure?" the other one asked.

"No problem," Steven said. "Come on in."

He'd spent a lot of time on a ranch, so he wasn't surprised to glance back and see they hadn't moved.

Matt was already switching the light on and off.

The faucet in the kitchen sink snorted a blast of air, chortled out some brown water, then ran clear.

"All set," Steven said. "Thanks."

The ranch hands grinned and nodded, and then they got into their beat-up work truck and drove away, dust pluming behind them.

Steven locked up the bus. Matt scrambled into their old pickup and expertly fastened himself into his safety seat, but Steven still checked to make sure every snap was engaged, just the same.

A minute or so later, they were on the road, making a dust plume of their own.

Stone Creek's animal shelter was a sight to behold, a two-story brick structure with Dr. Olivia O'Ballivan

Quinn's veterinary clinic occupying part of the first floor. The entrance to the shelter itself was at the other end of the building, so Steven and Matt headed that way.

The walls of the reception area were decorated with original paintings of dogs, cats and birds, of the whimsical, brightly colored variety, and there were plenty of comfortable chairs. A display of pet supplies occupied a corner, fronted with a handwritten sign saying all proceeds went toward the care of the four-legged residents.

There was no one behind the long, counter-type desk, but a young man in jeans and a lightweight sweatshirt crouched on the floor, a scruffy duffel bag beside him, ruffling the lopsided ears of a black-and-white sheepdog.

The girl Steven had seen at Melissa's office that morning stood by, watching, and for some reason she blushed when her gaze connected with his.

"You could adopt him," the girl said, addressing her companion.

But the young man shook his head, straightened with a sigh. "Not without a job, Andrea," he said quietly. His hair was brown, a little long, his eyes a pale shade of amber, and full of sadness. "How would I pay for his food? And what if he gets sick and needs to go to the vet?"

"*I've* got a job," Andrea said. "I can help out with expenses for a while."

"You work for Melissa," Matt piped up happily, smiling at Andrea.

Her smile faltered slightly, but it was friendly. She

nodded, then turned back to her friend. "Byron—" she began.

But Byron silenced her with a shake of his head.

Just then, a chubby woman with frizzy brown hair came out of the back, greeting Steven and Matt with a cheerful hello and an I'll-be-right-with-you before turning her attention to Byron and Andrea and the sheepdog.

"Well?" she asked hopefully. "Have we made a decision?"

Steven thought he detected a note of compassion in her tone.

Once again, Byron shook his head. "It just won't work," he said. "Not right now."

The woman sighed. Her nametag read *Becky,* and she wore print scrubs in bright shades of pink and green and blue. "Your mom must be happy to have you back home," she said gently.

By then, Matt was down on one knee, petting the sheepdog, and Byron watched with a sad smile.

"She doesn't know I'm here yet," Byron answered, his gaze bouncing off Andrea once before landing on Becky. "I got off the bus to hitchhike the rest of the way, but then Andrea came along and picked me up just this side of Flagstaff. I needed to be around a dog to get myself centered, so we came here first."

Andrea winced slightly, as though Byron had inadvertently revealed some vital secret.

Byron looked at Steven briefly, then at Matt. "He's a nice dog, isn't he?" he asked, indicating the hopeful critter.

Matt nodded. "We're here to get ourselves a dog," he told Byron. "We have a ranch. Right now, we live in a bus, but we're going to have a house and a yard pretty soon."

Byron smiled, but there was still something forlorn about him. "Sounds like you'd be a good match for this fella, then."

"Don't you want him?" Matt asked. He might have been only five years old, but he was perceptive. He'd picked up on the reluctance in Byron's decision not to adopt this particular dog.

"He needs a home," Byron said. "Just now, I can't give him one—not the right kind, anyway. So if you think he's the dog for you, and your dad says it's okay, you probably ought to take him home with you."

Andrea started to cry, silently. She turned away when she realized Steven was looking at her.

Becky, on the other hand, was still on the other subject. "You'd better let your mom know you're home, Byron," she said in motherly tones. "Velda's been looking forward to having you back in Stone Creek. She probably met the bus. And when there was no sign of you—"

Byron's shoulders drooped slightly, and he sighed. Nodded. Turned to Andrea, who had stopped crying, though her eyes were red-rimmed and her lashes were spiky with moisture. "Give me a ride home?" he asked her.

"Sure," she said.

"We can always use volunteers around here, Byron," Becky added. "Folks to feed the animals, and play with them, and clean out kennels."

Byron smiled at her. "That would be good," he said. Then after pausing to pat the sheepdog on the head once, in regretful farewell, he followed Andrea out of the building without looking back.

"That poor kid," Becky said, and her eyes welled up as she stared after Byron and Andrea. Then she seemed to give herself an inward shake. Turning her smile on Steven and Matt, she said, "May I help you?"

"We're here to adopt a dog," Steven answered, still vaguely unsettled by the sense of sorrow Byron and Andrea had left in their wake.

"Well," Becky said, with enthusiasm, gesturing toward the sheepdog, "as you can see, we have a prime candidate right here."

The dog's name was Zeke, Steven and Matt soon learned, and he was about two years old, housebroken and, for the most part, well-behaved. His former owner, an older gentleman, had gone into a nursing home a few weeks ago, suffering from an advanced case of Alzheimer's, and his daughter had brought Zeke to the shelter in hopes that he'd find a new home.

"Can we have him?" Matt asked, looking up at Steven. "Please?"

Steven was pretty taken with Zeke himself, but then, he'd never met a dog he didn't like. He'd have adopted every critter in the shelter, if he had his way. "Wouldn't you like to check out a few others before you decide?" he asked.

Matt wrapped both arms around Zeke's neck and held on, shaking his head. "He's the one," he said, with certainty. "Zeke's the one."

Zeke obligingly licked the boy's cheek.

Steven glanced at Becky, who was beaming with approval. Clearly, she agreed.

"Okay," Steven said, smiling.

He filled out the forms, paid the fees and bought a big sack of the recommended brand of kibble. Zeke came with a leash and a collar, left over from his former life.

He rode back to the ranch in the bed of the truck, since there was no room inside, but he seemed at home there, in the way of country dogs.

Matt sat half-turned in his car seat the whole way, keeping an eye on Zeke, who'd stuck his head through the sliding window at the back of the cab.

"I bet Zeke misses his person," the boy said.

Steven felt a pang at that, figuring there might be some transference going on. It was no trick to connect the dots: Matt missed *his* people, too.

"Might be," Steven agreed carefully.

Matt had referred to him as "my new dad" that day, as he sometimes did. It was probably the only way he could think of to differentiate Steven from Zack. And the boy wanted desperately to remember his birth father.

He had slightly more difficulty recalling Jillie, since he'd been younger when his mother died.

"Do you miss anybody?" Matt asked. His voice was slight, like his frame, and a little breathless.

"Yeah," Steven said. "I miss your mom and dad. I miss my own mom, and my granddad, too."

"Do you miss Davis and Kim? And your cousins?"

Davis was Steven's father, Kim his stepmother. They were alive and well, living on the Creed ranch in Colorado, though they'd turned the main house and much of the day-to-day responsibility over to Conner.

Brody, not being the responsible type, had left home years ago, and stayed gone.

"Yes," Steven answered. They went through this

litany of the missing whenever the boy needed to do it. "I miss them a lot."

"But we can go visit Davis and Kim and Conner. And they can visit us," Matt said, as the sheepdog panted happily and drooled all over the gearshift. "My mommy and daddy are *dead*."

Steven reached across to squeeze Matt's shoulder lightly. As much as he might have wanted to—the kid wasn't even old enough to go to school yet, after all, let alone understand death—he never dodged the subject just because it was difficult. If Matt brought up the topic, they talked it over. It was an unwritten rule: tell the truth and things will work out. Steven believed that.

Matt lapsed into his own thoughts, idly patting Zeke's head as they traveled along that curvy country road, toward the ranch. Toward the borrowed tour bus they'd be calling home for a while.

Steven wondered, certainly not for the first time, what Jillie and Zack would think about the way he was raising their son, their only child. Also not for the first time, he reflected that they must have trusted him. Within a month of Matt's birth, they'd drafted a will declaring Steven to be their son's legal guardian, should both of them die or become incapacitated.

It hadn't seemed likely, to say the least, that the two of them wouldn't live well into old age, but neither Jillie nor Zack had any other living relatives, besides their infant son, and Jillie had insisted it was better to be safe than sorry.

He'd do his damnedest to keep Matt safe, Steven thought, but he'd always be sorry, too. Much as he loved this little boy, Steven never forgot that the child rightly belonged to his lost parents first.

He slowed for the turn, signaled.

"Will you show me my daddy and mommy's picture again?" Matt asked, when they reached the top of the driveway and Steven stopped the truck and shut off the engine.

"Sure," he said. The word came out sounding hoarse.

"I don't want to forget what they look like," Matt said. Then, sadly, "I do, sometimes. Forget, I mean. Almost."

"That's okay, Tex. It happens to the best of us." Steven got out of the truck, walked around behind it, dropped the tailgate and hoisted an eager Zeke to the ground before going on to open Matt's door and unbuckle him from all his gear. "Now that we're going to stay put, we'll unpack that picture you like so much, and you can keep it in your room."

Matt nodded, mercifully distracted by the dog, and the two of them—kid and critter—ran wildly around in the tall grass for a while, letting off steam.

Steven carried the kibble into the tour bus and stowed it in the little room where the stacking washer and dryer kept a hot-water tank company. He spent the next twenty minutes carrying suitcases and dry goods and a few boxes containing pots and pans from the house to the bus, keeping an eye on Matt and Zeke as they explored.

"Stay away from the barn," Steven ordered. "There are bound to be some rusty nails, and if you step on one, it means a tetanus shot."

Matt made a face. "No shots!" he decreed, setting his hands on his hips.

Zeke barked happily, as if to back up the assertion.

Without answering, Steven went inside, filled a bowl with water and brought it outside.

Zeke rushed over, drank noisily until he'd had his fill.

That done, he proceeded to lift his leg against one of the bus tires.

"That's good, isn't it?" Matt asked, observing. "He's going *outside*."

Steven chuckled. "It's good," he confirmed. "How about some supper?"

Matt liked the idea, and he and Zeke followed Steven back into the bus. Steven opened the kibble sack, and Matt filled a saucepan and set it down on the floor for the dog.

While Zeke crunched and munched, Steven scrubbed his hands and forearms at the sink, plucked a tin of beef ravioli from the stash of groceries he and Matt had brought along on the road trip, used a can opener and scooped two portions out onto plates, shoved the first one into the microwave oven.

"Time to wash up," he told Matt.

"What about the picture of Mommy and Daddy?"

"We'll find it after supper, Tex. A man's got to eat, if he's going to run a ranch."

Matt rushed off to the bathroom; Steven heard water running. Grinned.

By the time Matt returned and took his place at the booth-type table next to the partition that separated the cab of the bus from the living quarters, Steven was taking the second plate of ravioli out of the oven.

"Ravioli again? Yum!" Matt said, picking up his plastic fork and digging in with obvious relish.

"Yeah," Steven admitted, joining the boy at the table. "It's good."

I might have to expand my culinary repertoire, though, he thought. Couldn't expect the kid to grow up on processed food, even if it was quick and tasty.

Maybe they'd plant a garden.

Chewing, Steven recalled all the weeding, watering, hoeing and shoveling he'd done every summer when he came home to the ranch in Colorado. Kim, his dad's wife, always grew a lot of vegetables—tomatoes and corn, lettuce and green beans, onions and spuds and a whole slew of other things—freezing and canning the excess.

The work had been never-ending.

Maybe they *wouldn't* plant a garden, he decided.

Zeke, meanwhile, having finished his kibble, curled up on the rug in front of the door with a big canine sigh, rested his muzzle on his forelegs and closed his eyes for a snooze.

Matt eyed the animal fondly. "Thanks," he said, when he was facing Steven again. "I really wanted a dog."

"I think I knew that," Steven teased. "And you're welcome."

Matt finished his ravioli and pushed his plate away.

Steven added *milk* to a mental grocery list.

"Can Zeke go to day camp with me?" Matt asked, a few minutes later, when Steven was washing off their plates at the sink.

"No," Steven answered. "Probably not."

Matt looked worried. "What will he *do* all day?"

"He can come to the office with me," Steven heard himself say.

Fatherhood. Maybe, in spite of the ravioli supper, he was getting the hang of it.

CHAPTER FOUR

VELDA RELAYED THE parole officer's remarks to Melissa, after saying goodbye and shutting the phone.

"Byron got out this morning," she said, the cell resting on her lap now, her gaze fixed on something well beyond the windshield of Melissa's quirky little car. "Just like he was supposed to. He had a ticket back to Stone Creek, and somebody dropped him off at the bus station, right on schedule."

Parked at a stop sign, Melissa didn't move until the driver behind her honked impatiently. Then she made a right, pulled up to the curb and stopped the car. "Maybe he decided to get off in Flagstaff or somewhere," she said. With permission from the authorities, Byron could settle anyplace in the state, after all—except that he would have needed his parole officer's permission to do that.

Color flared in Velda's otherwise pale cheeks. "You'd like that, wouldn't you?" she snapped, glaring over at Melissa. "If Byron didn't come back to Stone Creek, I mean? That way, you wouldn't have to think about him, now would you? You or anybody else in this crappy town!"

Melissa sighed. "Velda, calm down. I'm only trying to help you figure out what's going on here and find Byron."

But Velda shoved her door open and practically leaped out of the car. "If you *really* wanted to help," she accused, "you wouldn't have pushed so hard for my boy to do time!"

"A girl died," Melissa said quietly.

The reminder fell on deaf ears, apparently. Maybe it was just too much for Velda to face, the reality that her only child had caused someone's death.

"Do you know what he did while he was in jail, Melissa?" Velda ranted on, standing on the shady sidewalk and trembling even though it was warm out. "Do you know what Byron Cahill, the horrible criminal, *did* every day, while he was locked up?"

Melissa swallowed, shook her head, braced for some dreadful prison story.

"He helped train dogs from the shelters to be service animals. Search-and-rescue, seeing-eye dogs, dogs to help deaf people, too. He's a *good boy,* dammit!"

"Velda," Melissa said, after nodding to acknowledge that Byron Cahill might actually have an admirable side, like just about everybody else on the planet, "let me take you home. Maybe Byron's there. Maybe he caught a ride with somebody instead of getting on the bus, or something like that."

But Velda shook her head. A tear slipped down her right cheek. Then she pivoted on the worn heel of one flip-flop and marched off down the sidewalk, probably headed toward the trailer park where she rented a single-wide, but maybe not.

Melissa, feeling as though she'd aged a decade in the last half hour, watched as Velda's thin frame disappeared into a copse of trees. She hoped Byron would be at home when his mother arrived but, at that point, nothing would have surprised her.

After checking to make sure the way was clear, Melissa pulled back out onto the road, executed a U-turn, and headed for Ashley's B&B.

Mentally, she reviewed her original impressions of young Mr. Cahill. He'd been sixteen when he was convicted and sentenced. Against the advice of his duly appointed public defender, but apparently with his mother's encouragement, Byron had waived a jury trial.

Melissa, in her capacity as prosecutor, and the public defender, a newly minted attorney imported from Flagstaff, had tried to negotiate some kind of deal, but in the end, they couldn't come to an agreement.

The defense wanted probation, with no jail time, and comprehensive substance-abuse treatment in return for a guilty plea. After all, the argument ran, Byron was very young, and he'd never been in any real trouble before.

Melissa had been in favor of the treatment program, but probation wasn't enough. Chavonne Rowan had been young, too. And thanks to Byron Cahill's reckless actions, she wasn't going to get any older. She would never go to college, have a career, fall in love, get married, have children. Naturally, the girl's family was devastated.

Not that Byron's going to jail would bring Chavonne back.

Secretly, Melissa had agonized over the case, but she'd presented a strong, confident face to the public, and even to her own family and close friends. She'd examined her conscience repeatedly, taken her responsibilities to heart, and she had the reputation as a ruthless legal commando to prove it.

Except for those few who knew her through and through—Brad, Olivia, Ashley and one or two close girlfriends—most people probably thought she was a real hard-ass. Even a ballbuster.

And when Melissa allowed herself to think about that, it grieved her.

Sure, she'd wanted an education and a career. She loved the law, complicated as it was, and she loved justice even more. Justice, of course, was an elusive thing, very subjective in some ways, too often more of a concept than a reality, but without the *pursuit* of that ideal, where would humanity be?

She thrust out a sigh. Shifted the car *and* her mood. She'd done the best she could with the Cahill case. And that had to be good enough.

With no reason to hurry home, Melissa decided she might as well stop by the B&B—the octogenarian guests were due in the night before—thereby fulfilling her promise to Ashley. She'd look in on the old folks, make sure they were having a good time. And still breathing, of course.

Five minutes later, she bumped up the driveway next to the spacious two-story Victorian house Ashley had turned into the Mountain View Bed and Breakfast several years before.

Ashley.

Melissa felt a stab, missing her twin sister sorely. Although they were different in many ways, Ashley domestic, Melissa anything but; Ashley blond, with a love of cotton print dresses and gossamer skirts, Melissa dark-haired, fond of tailored suits and slacks—they had always been close.

Hurry home, Ash, Melissa thought, as she parked and got out of the car.

A shrill wolf whistle from the front yard of the B&B stopped her in her tracks.

She shaded her eyes with one hand, since the sun was still bright, and spotted an elderly gentleman standing just inside the fence, in the shadow of Ashley's prized lilac bush, wearing white Bermuda shorts, a white polo shirt, white shoes and white knee socks.

"Now that," the old man said, gazing past Melissa to the roadster, "is *some* car." He shook his leonine head of snowy hair. "Beautiful. Simply beautiful."

Melissa smiled. At least he wasn't a masher. "Thank you," she said, pausing to look back at the car with undiminished admiration. "I like it, too."

"You must be Mrs. McKenzie's sister," the man said, shifting his focus from the car to Melissa.

Mrs. McKenzie, of course, was Ashley.

Melissa was still getting used to that—Ashley married, and a mother. Sometimes, it seemed incredible.

"You must be one of the current guests," she replied, smiling, extending a hand across the picket fence. "Melissa O'Ballivan," she said.

"I'm John P. Winthrop IV," the man replied, with a nod and a very wide—and very white—smile. "But you can call me John."

"How's it going, John?" Melissa asked, thinking she might be able to wrap up this interview quickly and dash off an honest email to Ashley when she got home, assuring her that the B&B was still standing. "Is there anything you or any of the other guests need?"

He beamed. "Well, we can always use another croquet player," he said, making a grand gesture toward the nearby side gate, which led into Ashley's beautifully kept garden of specially cultivated wildflowers.

A teenage boy from the neighborhood did the watering and mowed the lawn, so the flowers, a profusion of reds and blues and pinks and oranges, looked good, if a little weedy here and there.

"I wouldn't be an asset to any self-respecting croquet team," Melissa smiled. She ran two miles every morning, but that was the extent of her athletic efforts. "But I would like to meet your friends."

John P. Winthrop IV rushed to work the latch and swing the gate open. "You look like you could use an ice-cold glass of lemonade," he said.

Try a shot of whiskey, Melissa thought wryly, recalling the Velda debacle. She hoped Byron Cahill *had* been waiting when his mother got home. If he'd taken off for parts unknown, he was in all sorts of trouble.

"Thanks," she said aloud, bringing herself back to the moment. "Lemonade sounds good."

Mr. Winthrop closed the gate and sprinted to catch up to Melissa on the flagstone walk. He seemed pretty agile for a man of advancing years.

Maybe it was the croquet playing.

"There is one thing," he said hastily.

Something in his tone, a sort of mild urgency, made Melissa stop and look up into his kindly and somewhat abashed face.

"We're a little—different, my friends and I," Mr. Winthrop said.

"Different?" Melissa asked, while inside her head, a voice warned, *Here we go*.

Mr. Winthrop cleared his throat. "Mabel should have told your sister in advance, when we booked the rooms," he said. "But we were all counting so on this little get-away and when it turned out we were going to have the whole place to ourselves, well, it all just seemed meant to be—"

Melissa squinted, still several beats behind. "Mabel?"

"Mabel Elliott," Mr. Winthrop said helpfully. "We're all retired, living in the same community, and relatively comfortable financially, and we take a lot of these little jaunts. Mabel knows how to use the internet, so she's in charge of arranging accommodations."

"I see," Melissa said, still mystified, and beginning to wish she hadn't agreed to that glass of lemonade. She could be home in a couple of minutes, taking a cool shower, donning shorts and a tank top and sandals, puttering around in her struggling vegetable garden and generally minding her own business.

Mr. Winthrop took her elbow, in a courtly way. "And with all the foliage surrounding the backyard," he added, dropping his voice, "there's really no harm done anyway, now is there?"

He still sounded nervous, though. And Melissa could relate, because she was feeling downright jittery by now. What could possibly be going on?

They rounded the back corner of the house, and Melissa froze, her mouth open.

Five people, three women and two men, all having a grand old time, were playing croquet in the green, well-shaded grass.

And every last one of them was stark naked.

THE PICTURE OF JILLIE AND ZACK, taken on their honeymoon, showed them parachuting in tandem, somewhere

in Mexico, their faces alight with celebration as they
mugged for the skydiving photographer jumping with
them.

There were lots of photos of the St. Johns, but this
one was Matt's favorite.

"Tell me again about when this picture was taken,"
Matt said, snuggling down into his sleeping bag, while
Steven perched on the edge of the lower bunk and Zeke
made himself comfortable on an improvised dog bed
nearby.

Holding the framed photograph in his hands, Steven
smiled, taking in those familiar faces. Even now, it
seemed impossible that two people with so much life
in them could be gone.

"Well," Steven began, as he had a hundred times
before, since he'd become Matt's legal guardian and
then his adoptive father, "we all went to school together,
your mom, your dad and me, and right from the first,
they were a real pair—"

"Tell me about the wedding," Matt prompted, with
a yawn. It was all part of the pattern—he would fight
sleep for a while, then lose the battle. "You were the
best man, right?"

"I was the best man," Steven confirmed huskily.

"And you and my daddy had to wear *penguin
suits.*"

Steven chuckled, wondering if the kid was picturing
him and Zack dressed up like short, squat birds from
the Frozen North.

But, no—he knew what a tuxedo looked like. Matt
had seen the wedding pictures a million times—usually,
he asked why he wasn't in them.

The answer—*you weren't born yet*—never seemed to sink in.

"Yeah," Steven said belatedly. "We had to wear penguin suits."

"Mommy had on a pretty white dress, though," Matt chimed in.

"Yep."

"And out of all three of you, she was the best-looking."

"A rose between two thorns," Steven said, playing the game.

"A petunia in an onion patch," Matt responded, on cue.

They laughed, the man and the boy. There was a ragged quality to the sound.

"Tell me more about my mommy and daddy," Matt said.

Steven talked, his heart in his throat much of the time, until the boy finally nodded off. When he was sure Matt was asleep, he left the room, stepping carefully around the dog.

Out in the living room/kitchen area, Steven opened his laptop, booted it up and logged on. He hadn't checked his email in a few days.

Once he'd weeded out the junk, and the stuff he didn't feel like dealing with at the moment, he opened a recent message from his stepmother, Kim. It was dated that afternoon.

"Are you there yet?" she'd written. "Let us know when you get settled in Stone Creek, and your dad and I will come for a visit."

Smiling, Steven tapped out a brief reply. Kim had always treated him with warmth and good humor during those growing-up summers, never trying to take his mother's place. "We're here," he wrote, "and living the high life in a country-music star's tour bus. There are bunk beds in Matt's room, so you and Dad could sleep there."

The thought of that made his grin widen.

He added a description of Zeke, the sheepdog, recounting the pet-adoption saga, assured Kim that he and Matt were both fine, and signed off with love.

A second message came from Conner. "I'll be in Stone Creek for the rodeo next month," it read. "Save me a bed."

And that was the whole thing.

Steven chuckled. His cousin was definitely a man of few words.

He hit Reply and told Conner he was always welcome and there would be a bed waiting when the time came. Compared to his cousin's email, Steven's was downright verbose.

A low whimper distracted him from the computer; he looked up and saw Zeke standing with his nose to the door crack, wanting to go outside.

Steven left the laptop on the table and accompanied Zeke out into the yard.

It wasn't quite dark, but a few stars had begun to pop out here and there, and the ghost of a three-quarter moon peeked over the horizon, like a performer waiting in the wings.

Zeke sniffed around for a while, did his business and went back to the door, ready to go in.

Steven opened the door and the dog mounted the steps, then went directly back to Matt's room.

Wide-awake, already bored with the internet and in

no mood to watch TV, Steven sat on the fold-down metal steps in front of the threshold and looked out over what he could see of his ranch.

Some ranch, he thought. *Most of the fences are down, the barn probably collapsed ten years ago and the house is a disaster.*

He sighed and combed the fingers of his right hand through his hair, something he always did when he was questioning his own decisions.

His dad and Conner had both tried to persuade him to stay in Colorado and raise Matt on the family's spread. Set up a law practice in Lonesome Bend.

He wasn't sure they understood, his father and his cousin, why he'd needed to strike out on his own, create something new for himself and Matt and any generations that might follow.

He wasn't sure *he* understood, either.

The Creed ranch was rightfully Conner's, Steven figured, Conner's and Brody's. Their dad, dead since the brothers were hardly more than babies, had been Davis's older brother and, therefore, the heir to the kingdom.

Not that anybody knew exactly where Conner's identical twin brother was keeping himself these days. He'd had some kind of knock-down-drag-out with Conner, Brody had, and except for a Christmas card every few years, with a terse message scrawled somewhere inside, the family hadn't heard from him in a decade.

Conner, like the good elder brother in the parable of the Prodigal Son, had worked shoulder to shoulder with Davis to make the ranch prosper, and it had. Even with the ups and downs of the economy and the ever-changing beef prices, it was a profitable operation.

When he was younger, shuttling back and forth

between his mother's place back East, where he lived fall, winter and spring, and the ranch, which he'd thought of as home, Steven had been more than a little jealous of his cousins. Two years younger than he was, the twins got to live on the land year-round, and Davis was a substitute father to them, the kind he couldn't be to Steven, for the better part of every year, because of the distance between Lonesome Bend and Boston.

So, Steven had essentially lived a double life. Summers, he'd been a ranch kid, a cowboy. He'd herded cattle on horseback, mended fences, skinny-dipped in the lake, brawled with his cousins like a wolf cub in a litter, competed in rodeos.

All too soon, though, fall would roll around, and he'd find himself on an airplane, wearing preppy clothes instead of jeans and a T-shirt and old boots, with his hair cut short and brushed shiny.

In Boston, Steven played tennis and held a spot on the rowing team. He dated girls with trust funds. Even as a relatively little kid, he had his own suite of rooms in his grandfather's sprawling mansion, and it was generally agreed—make that, *assumed*—that he would one day join the prestigious law firm, founded well before the Civil War broke out, where his mother, two uncles and, of course, Granddad, carried on the family business.

School was difficult for Steven, at least in the beginning, a fact that troubled his mother to no end, but he'd worked hard, gotten the grades, made it through college and law school, and joined the company as a junior clerk, just like any other newbie.

Within a year, both Steven's mother and his grandfather were gone, his mother having died of pneumonia, which had started out as an ordinary case of the flu, Granddad of a heart attack.

Steven had soon realized he couldn't work for his uncles.

They resented the fact that he'd inherited his mother's share of the family fortune, as well as a chunk that had been set aside for him at birth and gathering interest ever since. His uncles had never understood what had possessed their sister to hook up with a cowboy in some shithole town out West during a summer road trip with her college roommates, get herself pregnant and compound the everlasting disgrace by keeping the baby.

But there were other reasons for the break, too; Michael and Edward Fletcher had never shared their father's commitment to excellence, not to mention integrity, and his death hadn't changed that. Nor could they match their sister's keen intelligence.

A few months after the second funeral, his grandfather's, Steven had called his best friend from school, Zack St. John, and Zack had recommended him for a position at the Denver firm where he worked.

The rest, as they say, was history.

In Boston, in the operation his mother had referred to as the "store," Steven had practiced corporate law. As soon as he'd made the move to Denver, however, he'd switched to criminal defense.

And he'd loved it.

He and Zack had worked together a lot, and they made a crack team. Steven was proud of their record, not just the wins, but the losses, too.

In every case, they'd done their absolute best.

Just then, Steven's cell phone rang in his pocket, and the sound jolted him. For the briefest fraction of a moment, he'd forgotten that Zack was dead and gone, expected to hear his voice.

"Hello?" he said, still sitting in the doorway of the tour bus, realizing that the night was turning chilly.

"Why didn't you call?" Kim asked, with a smile in her voice.

Steven went inside, shut the door, kept his reply low because he didn't want Matt waking up. The boy needed his rest, especially since he'd be starting day camp on Monday morning.

"Because I sent an email instead," he answered. His dad and stepmother had never had any children of their own, which was a pity, because they both had a real way with kids. They were good people, decent and responsible, and he loved them.

"So tell me all about Stone Creek," Kim said.

MELISSA PLUCKED her formerly frozen diet dinner out of the microwave and plunked it on the kitchen counter to cool, getting a mild steam-burn in the process. With her other hand, she held the cordless phone to her ear.

"I tell you that there are eighty-plus-year-old *nudists* cavorting on *your property,* Ashley O'Ballivan, and all you can do is laugh?"

"The name is McKenzie," Ashley replied cheerfully. "What did you *expect* me to do, Melissa? Call out the National Guard to restore order?"

"I didn't think you'd *laugh,* that's all," Melissa said, miffed and not entirely sure why.

"Why wouldn't I laugh?" Ashley asked reasonably. "It's *funny.*"

"Not to mention illegal." A belated giggle escaped Melissa. "I guess you're right," she admitted, eyeing her food warily. The microwaved dish looked more like a plastic replica of lasagna than the real thing, the kind that might be sold in a joke shop—assuming there was even a market for stuff like that. "But trust me, it was also a shock. You haven't lived, my dear, until you've seen a pack of bare-ass naked senior citizens engaged in a lively game of croquet."

"And you without a fire hose," Ashley quipped.

"Ha-ha," Melissa said, carefully peeling the cellophane cover from her lasagna. Ashley was the one with the cooking talent; Julia Child was her patron saint. Melissa had never really caught the culinary bug; in fact, she'd all but had herself vaccinated against it. "When are you coming home? I miss the pity suppers."

Ashley laughed again, but the underlying tone was gentle, and betrayed a slight degree of worry. "'Pity' suppers, is it?" she countered. "You *know* when we're coming home. I've told you nineteen times, it'll be early next week." She paused, drew in a breath. "Melissa, what's going on? Besides the nudist uprising, I mean?"

"Interesting choice of words," Melissa commented dryly, giving up on the lasagna and shoving it toward the back of the counter. "And it's already Friday, so 'early next week' might be—"

"Okay, Tuesday," Ashley said with a chuckle, then waited stubbornly for an answer to *Melissa, what's going on?*

"Byron Cahill got out of jail this morning," Melissa told her.

"Yes," Ashley prompted, sounding only mildly concerned.

"He didn't show up on schedule," Melissa said. "Velda was upset."

"What else is happening?" Ashley pressed. "Velda's *been* upset for years, and you knew Byron's release date all along."

I met a man, Melissa imagined herself saying. *His name is Steven Creed. He's all wrong for me, and I think he's beyond hot.*

While she might well have confided in Ashley in person, she wasn't ready to talk about Steven over the telephone. And, anyway, what was there to say? It wasn't as if anything had happened.

Still, Ashley was an O'Ballivan and, among other things, that meant she wouldn't give up until she got a story she could buy.

So Melissa threw something out there. "I was roped into heading up the Parade Committee," she said.

"Oh, my," Ashley replied, sounding taken aback. "How did *that* happen?"

"I'm not sure, beyond the fact that Ona Frame can't serve on the committee this year because her gallbladder exploded."

"It—*exploded?*"

"Not literally, Ash. And thank heaven for that, because you can just imagine the fallout—"

"Melissa," Ashley groaned.

"Sorry," Melissa lied brightly. She had always loved grossing Ashley out.

Another chuckle came from Ashley's end. "Not that you deserve this," she began, "but as soon as Jack and Katie and I get back from Chicago, I'll see what I can do to help you get the parade—well—rolling."

It was Melissa's turn to groan. "Bad pun," she complained, but she was grateful—wildly and instantly so—and she wanted Ashley to know it. "You're merely saving my life," she said next.

"How hard can it be?" Ashley asked. "One small-town parade with—what?—fifteen floats, a high-school marching band, Veterans of Foreign Wars and the sheriff's posse riding their horses?"

How hard can it be?

"Don't tempt fate," Melissa said. "Just because poor Ona has made it *look* easy all these years, that doesn't mean it is."

Ashley sighed. "Try to stay calm," she said, but she still sounded buoyantly optimistic, and why wouldn't she? Ashley was happy. Completely in love with her husband, Jack, and thoroughly loved in return. The mother of beautiful Katie and expecting a second child in six months or so. "And since when are you superstitious enough to worry about tempting fate?"

Maybe since always, Melissa thought.

In many ways, their childhoods hadn't been easy—their mother had left home for good when she and Ashley were small, and their father had been killed in a freak accident while herding cattle on Stone Creek Ranch, struck by lightning.

After that, the four young O'Ballivans had been raised by their grandfather, Big John. While Big John had really stepped up, loving them with all his strong, kindly heart, of course there were issues. Weren't there always issues?

Did *anybody* make it to adulthood unscathed? Melissa didn't think so.

"Melissa?" Ashley said, when she'd been quiet too long.

"I'm perfectly fine," Melissa insisted. She bit her lower lip, peering into her fridge now, finding nothing that appealed to her. "But what do you want me to do if the vice squad raids your house on grounds of lewd conduct?"

Ashley laughed.

It was a sound Melissa knew well, and loved.

As much a part of her as it was of her sister since, at some level, it sometimes seemed they were one and the same person.

"What do I want you to do?" Ashley teased. "Well, you could maybe loosen up a little. Sign up for the cro-quet team or something."

"You are just too hilarious."

"Melissa?"

"What?"

"Thanks for calling. I love you, I'll see you in a few days and goodbye."

Melissa made a face at the receiver and hung up.

Hunger finally drove her to get back to her car, drive to the supermarket, and invest in a salad from the deli department, a carton of low-fat yogurt for breakfast and the new issue of *Vanity Fair*.

She was on her way back to her car, shopping bag in hand, when she saw Andrea drive up. Spotting Melissa at the last moment, it seemed, the girl didn't have time to hide her guilty expression.

Melissa smiled cordially and waited until her assis-tant got out of her old car, slung her purse strap over one shoulder, and nodded a shy "Hello."

"Feeling better?" Melissa asked, keeping her voice sunny. "Cramps can be pretty terrible."

Andrea's taste in clothing was questionable, and so was her memory for watering plants and things like that, but she was basically honest, and Melissa knew she was intelligent, too. If Andrea ever learned to believe in herself, there would be no stopping her.

"I was faking," the girl said miserably, her confession coming in a breathy little rush. "I didn't really have cramps."

"No kidding?" Melissa chimed.

Andrea didn't catch the faint sarcasm in her boss's tone. "I went to pick Byron up," she said, looking down at the asphalt of the parking lot instead of directly at Melissa. "Byron Cahill, I mean."

"I see," Melissa said, though she was genuinely surprised. She'd had no clue that Andrea and Byron were friends.

With obvious effort, Andrea made herself meet Melissa's eyes. Now, there was an obstinate set to the girl's jaw as she waited for—what? Recriminations? A lecture? The verbal equivalent of a pink slip?

"Byron's mother was pretty worried when he didn't get off the bus this afternoon," Melissa said, feeling weary again. "She thought something bad must have happened."

Andrea nodded, and her shoulders dropped a little. "I know," she said, small-voiced. "But everything's all right now. I took Byron home, and his mom was there, and she's making pizza. I just came up here to get some sodas and rent a couple of movies." She had the good grace to blush. "Since it's Friday night and everything."

"And everything," Melissa said lightly.

Andrea straightened her spine. "Are you going to fire me?"

"Probably not," Melissa answered, thinking how ironic it was that Andrea, Velda and Byron would spend a chummy evening eating pizza and watching DVDs together, while she dined alone on a deli salad. "For future reference, though, if you have personal plans that will take you away from work, just say so. Unless there's something pressing I need you to do, Andrea, I'll be happy to give you time off."

Andrea took that in, looking ashamed again. "It's just that I thought you'd disapprove. Of Byron and me going together, I mean."

Melissa looked around to make sure none of the local gossips were hovering nearby, with an ear cocked in their direction. "'Going together'?" she repeated. "How could you and Byron be—'going together'—when he's been in jail for the better part of two years?"

"We were pen pals," Andrea said. "I'd see Velda around town sometimes, and she'd tell me how lonesome Byron was, locked away like some kind of criminal—"

Melissa put up a hand. In a courtroom, she would have snapped out, "Objection!" In the supermarket parking lot, facing a young woman who'd had a drug-addicted mother and the very elderly Crockett sisters for her main female role models, she took a different tack.

"Hold it," she said, very quietly. "Byron *did* get high, consume alcohol, then climb behind the wheel of a car and get into a terrible accident. And someone died in that accident, Andrea."

Andrea's eyes widened. She swallowed visibly and then nodded. "I was just telling you what Velda told me," she said reasonably, softly. "I started writing to Byron, because I know what it's like to feel all alone, and he wrote back. We got to be friends." She paused, drew in a breath. "Byron understands how wrong it was, what he did, and so do I."

Melissa closed her eyes for a moment, surprised to find that they were scalding with tears. "Yes," she said. She was remembering Chavonne's funeral, and the graveside service, and how the dead girl's mother had let out a cry of such raw grief when the coffin was lowered into the ground that Melissa could still hear it, sometimes, in her nightmares.

Andrea stooped a little, peered at Melissa. Moved to touch her arm and then drew back. "Are—are you all right? You look sort of—I don't know—pale or something."

Melissa shook her head, not in answer but to indicate that she didn't want to talk any more that night, and stepped around Andrea to get into the roadster.

It wasn't until she'd set the grocery bag on the passenger seat, fumbled for her keys, started the engine and driven to the edge of the lot that she looked into her rearview mirror and saw that Andrea hadn't moved.

She was still standing in exactly the same spot, staring down at the ground.

CHAPTER FIVE

MATT, STEVEN AND ZEKE the Wonder Dog were up early the next morning, even though it was a Saturday, normally a sleep-in day.

Steven showered, then Matt, and both of them dressed "cowboy," in jeans and boots. Matt wore a T-shirt, while Steven pulled on an old cotton chambray shirt, a favorite from years ago when he was still riding and roping on the ranch.

"Here's the plan," Steven said, sipping from a mug of instant coffee while Matt fed Zeke his morning ration of kibble and put fresh water in his bowl. "We'll go into town, have some breakfast at the Sunflower Café, or whatever it is, then take a spin by the day camp so you can get a look."

"Can Zeke come, too?" Matt asked, stroking the animal's back as he spoke.

Zeke didn't slow down on the kibble.

"Sure," Steven replied. "Today, anyway."

Matt nodded, but it was obvious that he had reservations.

"What?" Steven asked, setting his coffee mug in the sink.

Matt looked up at him, eyes wide with concerns that probably wouldn't even have occurred to most five-year-olds. "Zeke can go to work with you when I'm in day camp, right? And this fall, after school starts?"

"Right," Steven said, reaching for the truck keys and his cell phone. "But there will be days when that won't be possible, Tex."

"Like if you have to be in court or something?"

Steven smiled, gave the boy's shoulder a light squeeze. "Like if I have to be in court or something."

"But sometimes he'll be out here all alone? Shut up in the bus?"

Steven dropped to his haunches. Some conversations had to be held eye to eye, and this was one of them. "I plan on having the contractors put in a yard and fence it off as soon as the renovations are under way," he said. "We'll outfit Zeke with a nice, big doghouse and he'll be fine while I'm working and you're at school."

By then, Zeke had wiped out the kibble and moved on to lap loudly from his water bowl.

"What if the coyotes get him?" Matt asked.

Back home in Colorado, it hadn't been uncommon for people to lose the occasional pet to coyotes, even in the middle of town; as their habitats shrank, the animals were getting ever bolder. Because they traveled in packs, even large dogs were often at a disadvantage in a confrontation.

"We'll make sure the fence is real high, so they can't get over it," Steven said, straightening up because his knees were beginning to ache a little in the crouch.

"How high?" Matt persisted.

"Really, *really* high," Steven promised.

Matt brightened. "Okay," he said, making for the door, with Zeke right behind him. "Let's roll."

Steven laughed and, fifteen minutes later, they were

nosing the truck into a parking spot in the lot beside the Sunflower Bakery and Café. Recalling yesterday's parking ticket, he made sure there were no fire hydrants within fifty feet.

They brought Zeke as far as the front of the restaurant and secured one end of his leash to a pole with a sign on it that read, "Park pets here." An oversize pie pan full of fresh water waited within reach.

Steven was just straightening his back, about to follow Matt inside the café, when Melissa O'Balliv an came jogging around a corner and up the sidewalk, straight toward him.

She wore pink shorts, a skimpy white T-shirt, and one of those visor caps with no crown. Her abundance of spirally chestnut-brown hair bobbed on top of her head in a ponytail.

Her smile nearly knocked Steven over—even if it *was* focused on Matt and the dog with such intensity that he might as well have been invisible.

Holy crap, Steven thought, because the ground shook under his feet and the sky tilted at such a strange angle that his equilibrium was skewed. He gave his head a shake, in an effort to clear away some cobwebs.

"Morning," Melissa said, jogging in place.

All the right things bounced, Steven noticed, grinning down at her like a damn fool. "Morning," he responded, after clearing his throat.

She looked up at him with a surprised expression in her blue eyes, as though she'd momentarily forgotten that he was standing there. Or never noticed him at all.

She apparently wanted to give that impression, anyway, and he was intrigued.

"Would you mind opening the door?" she asked, unplugging the white earbuds attached to an armband MP3 player from her head.

It took Steven a moment to register what that simple phrase actually meant.

She wanted to go inside the café.

Feeling his neck warm, Steven pushed the door open and held it, so she could jog over the threshold and across to the take-out counter.

Morning greetings and the scents of fresh coffee, baked goods and frying bacon washed over Steven, but starved though he was, he barely noticed. He couldn't seem to take his eyes off Melissa O'Ballivan's springy, perfect little backside.

"Over here!" Matt whooped, mercifully distracting Steven. If he was lucky, maybe nobody had seen him staring like a pervert while the county prosecutor ran in place in front of the counter, placing a breathy order for a bottle of *very cold* water to go.

The boy had found a table by one of the front windows.

Zeke, just on the other side, put his big paws up on the sill and pressed his nose to the glass.

Steven laughed, and that broke the tension—until Melissa jogged past again, water bottle in hand. A truck driver got up from his booth and opened the door for her, and Steven felt a stab of irritation—or was it plain old ordinary jealousy?

Outside, Melissa trotted by the window, favoring Zeke with a smile Steven wanted for himself.

"What'll it be this morning, fellas?" a pleasant female voice asked, and Steven turned to see Tessa Quinn, the lovely owner of the establishment, wearing a floral print cobbler's apron over jeans and a tank top and looking gorgeous.

He'd recognized her on sight the day before—she'd had a major role in a long-running TV series when she was younger—but evidently she'd exchanged her SAG card for a small-town café and an apron.

Matt asked politely for a short stack of blueberry pancakes and a big glass of milk, and Steven went for coffee and the ham-and-egg special.

Tessa smiled and said, "Coming right up," and the smile lingered on in her eyes when she glanced up briefly at the window Melissa had just passed.

MELISSA'S NORMAL JOGGING ROUTE took her by the B&B most mornings, but not that one.

What was she afraid of, she asked herself, giving a wry chortle as she picked up her pace, going two streets out of her way just to avoid passing Ashley and Jack's place. That the nude croquet game might have been moved to the front yard?

You're getting to be a real party pooper, Melissa O'Ballivan, she told herself.

At home, she went through her front gate and did a few cool-down moves and some stretches on the lawn. She finished off her water, started for the porch and nearly choked, she was so startled.

There, in the shadows of the grand old lady peony bushes on either side of the walk, their huge white blossoms already fading as June wore on toward July, sat Byron Cahill.

Andrea was beside him, and seeing Melissa's expression, the two kids touched shoulders, maybe trying to give each other courage.

"Well," Melissa said, not sure what to think. "Good morning."

Byron got to his feet. He was probably just being polite, and there was nothing threatening in his stance, but he was a big kid, and Melissa automatically took a step back.

"Andrea tells me you might need somebody to mow the lawn and trim the shrubbery and stuff," Byron said gravely. He'd filled out in jail, and he was neatly dressed in inexpensive jeans, high-top sneakers and a clean T-shirt. While he was away, his acne had cleared up, too.

He was actually quite good-looking, though still a kid.

Melissa *had* made a few noises around the office about hiring somebody to whip her yard into shape, but it had never occurred to her that Andrea was listening, let alone planning to bring her recently released boyfriend by to apply for the job.

"Well—" she said, looking at the overgrown peony bushes.

The grass was so deep that small animals could get lost in it, and the branches of the venerable old maple tree were practically scraping the sidewalk in front of her picket fence. Which could use sanding down and painting.

"I can borrow a mower," Byron said, and there was a catch in his voice. One that gave Melissa a twinge of sympathy.

Times were tough. There weren't a lot of jobs in Stone Creek, especially for kids with a police record.

Andrea watched Melissa hopefully, chewing on her lower lip before blurting, "Miss Mamie and Miss Marge hired Byron to reline the koi pond in the backyard over at their place. You know, empty it out and put down new plastic and then fill it and put all the fish back in—"

Evidently, this was Andrea's idea of a sales pitch, but it fell away in midstream when Byron gave the girl's hand a squeeze.

"I thought I'd ask," he said to Melissa. There was resignation in his tone, but his gaze was direct. If she'd stepped aside, he would have walked past her, toward the gate.

But Melissa didn't step aside.

"It's a big job," she said, sizing him up again. "And probably temporary." Mike Smith, the teenager who took care of Ashley and Jack's grass and flowerbeds, usually did yardwork for Melissa, too. This year, though, Mike was attending summer school, and he was running short on spare time.

Byron's eyes widened slightly, and a smile tugged at a corner of his mouth. "I'm not afraid of big jobs," he said. "As for the temporary part, I can deal with that."

Melissa wondered if Andrea had nagged him into asking her for work, or if he'd thought of it on his own. Either way, it took guts to come over here and make the request, considering past history.

"When could you start?" Melissa asked. She named an hourly wage that seemed to please him.

He shoved a hand through his sandy-brown hair. Considered his answer. "Well," he said, "Miss Mamie and Miss Marge need to come first, since all their fish are swimming around in buckets waiting for me to clean out the pond."

Melissa smiled at the colorful image that popped into her mind. "Tomorrow, then?" she asked.

"Sure," Byron answered.

Melissa finally moved, so he could descend the steps. He paused, facing her, Andrea still clinging to his left hand.

He put his right out to Melissa. "Thanks," he said.

She hesitated only a moment before taking the offered hand. "If you screw up," she told him, frankly but in a friendly tone, "you are so out of here."

He laughed. "Yes, ma'am," he said.

He started toward the gate, and Andrea double-stepped behind him, looking back at Melissa and mouthing, "Thank you!" as she went.

Hoping she'd done the right thing, Melissa went on into the house and walked straight through to the kitchen. There she popped her empty water bottle into the recycling bin and hesitated in front of her old-fashioned wall phone.

It was Saturday morning—*early* Saturday morning.

Surely no emergencies had taken place while she was out for her run—she hadn't been gone more than an hour.

Even prosecutors had weekends off, didn't they?

Melissa's mind flashed on Steven Creed, standing in front of the Sunflower Café a little while before, when she stopped by for water, not that she expected *him* to call or anything.

But *hot damn,* the way he looked in those rancher's clothes she'd fantasized about seeing him in the day before. It ought to require some kind of legal permit, being that handsome.

Melissa sighed—not being able to ignore voice mail was the curse of the competent, she reminded herself—and reached out for the receiver. If she didn't check for messages, she wouldn't relax and enjoy her time off.

There had been one caller.

Ona Frame's recorded voice rang over the wire. "Melissa? I hope it isn't too early to be calling you, dear, but I was just so excited when Tommy stopped by this morning and told me you were willing to fill in for me on the Parade Committee this year—" Here, the older woman paused, turned tearful. "You see, I'm going to have to have this darn ol' gallbladder of mine removed, and there's nothing for it, but we've kicked off the annual rodeo with a parade every single year for nigh on half a century now and I don't mind telling you, it almost broke my heart to think of canceling—"

While she was out for her run, Melissa had come up with seven or eight really good excuses for turning down parade duty, but they all flew away as she listened to Ona rant on. And on. The message lasted so long, in fact, that Ona had to call back because she'd timed out on the first run.

The essence of it was that the committee meeting had been scheduled for three o'clock that very afternoon, all along. It was to be held in the community room over at the Creekside Academy, and since the whole crew had been planning on attending anyway, she thought it was the perfect opportunity to present Melissa as their new leader.

"Call me and let me know if you can make it!" Ona finished off merrily. "And I do hope you weren't sleeping in or something, and I spoiled it by calling—"

Melissa hung up, let her sweaty forehead rest against a cupboard door while she drew slow, deep breaths.

There was no getting out of it. She was stuck. Might as well accept the fact and move on, she thought.

She did allow herself one indulgence before returning Ona's call and committing herself to the job, though. Melissa took her shower first.

DURING BREAKFAST, Steven got a call on his cell phone from the Flagstaff auto dealership he'd contacted several weeks before; the extended cab truck he'd custom-ordered was in, and they could deliver it that day if he wanted.

Steven agreed, relieved that he'd have a backseat for Matt and Zeke to ride in now. Plus, his old rig looked like it had been driven West in the '30s by some family fleeing the Dust Bowl, though, of course, it wasn't quite old enough for that scenario.

He smiled, remembering his dad's apt description of the vehicle.

Steven's got himself one of those two-toned rigs, Davis Creed had told a friend, tongue firmly planted in his cheek. *And one of those tones is rust.*

"Do I have to clean up my plate?" Matt asked, anxious to get outside and keep Zeke company.

Steven was still thinking about rigs. In Denver, he'd driven a candy-apple-red Corvette—also unsuitable for carting around a little boy and a dog.

But Melissa O'Ballivan would look mighty fine riding shotgun in the sports car, he thought. He pictured her wearing a blue-and-white polka-dot sundress, strapless, with her hair tumbling down around her bare shoulders and her lips all glossy.

"Steven?" Matt said, waving one hand in his face.

"Go see to Zeke," Steven replied, with a chuckle,

as he pushed away his plate. "While I take care of the bill."

Matt scooted away from the table and zipped to the door, and Steven waited until he saw the boy with Zeke before he turned from the window.

A few minutes later, he joined them outside.

"We might as well go over and see if the office is fit for human habitation," he told Matt, shoving his wallet into his hip pocket as he spoke.

"Okay," Matt said, conscientiously, "but Zeke drank all the dog water." He held up the empty pan as proof. "See?"

Steven mussed the boy's hair and nodded. "Good call," he said. "You figure you're tall enough to reach the faucet on the men's room sink and fill it up again, then get all the way back out here without spilling?"

Matt nodded and headed for the door, pausing only to say, "Keep an eye on Zeke while I'm gone."

Steven grinned and executed an affirmative half salute.

Matt proved to be a competent water bearer, and they headed for the office on foot, since it was just down the street.

As it turned out, the place was in fairly good shape. The property management people had had the walls painted a subtle off-white, as requested, and the utilitarian gray carpet looked clean.

Two desks, some file cabinets and a half-dozen book-shelves had been delivered, and when Steven picked up the handset on the three-line phone his assistant would use—once he'd hired an assistant, anyway—there was a dial tone.

"Looks like we're in business, Tex," he told Matt, who was busy exploring the small place with Zeke.

There wasn't much *to* explore, actually—just an inner office, a storage closet and a unisex restroom that was hardly big enough to turn around in.

And all that was fine with Steven.

He probably wouldn't have all that many cases anyway, even though his services would be free. Stone Creek wasn't what you'd call crime-ridden, after all, and that, too, was fine with him.

It was one of the main reasons he'd chosen to come here. He'd wanted to raise Matt in a small town—a small town that *wasn't* Lonesome Bend, Colorado.

"Are we going to look at the day-camp place now?" Matt asked, once he'd peeked into every corner of the office. He didn't sound overly enthusiastic about the prospect.

Steven checked his watch. "The dealer said we'd have our new truck within an hour and a half," he replied. "Why don't we go back out to the ranch and wait for it to be delivered, then swing into town again and visit Creekside Academy?"

Matt liked that idea, and it was settled.

They headed back home, and when they got there and piled out of the ancient pickup, Zeke ran around and around in happy circles in the grass, glorying in his freedom or maybe just glad to be alive, and obviously a country kind of dog.

Two and a half hours later, the new vehicle was delivered, sky-blue and shiny, with the chrome gleaming fit to dazzle the eye. A second man followed in a small car, to give the driver a ride back.

Steven signed for his purchase, accepted the keys and waved the deliverymen off in the second car.

Matt, meanwhile, had climbed onto the running board, probably hoping to stick his face against the driver's-side window and peer inside. Too bad he was so short.

Chuckling, Steven walked over, hooked the boy around the waist with one arm, and opened the truck door with the other. He hoisted Matt inside, and watched, grinning, as he plunked himself on the seat, gripped the wheel and made that time-honored, spit-flinging *varoom-varoom* sound kids use to mimic the roar of an engine.

"It won't be long," Matt crowed, steering speedily, "until I'm old enough to drive!"

The words saddened Steven a little, because he knew they were true. Like all kids, Matt would grow up way too soon.

"Yeah," Steven agreed, with a laugh, "but as of today, you're still too vertically challenged to see over the dashboard."

"Varoom!" Matt yelled, undaunted.

Steven went to the other truck for Matt's car seat, brought it over and installed it carefully in back of the new rig while the boy continued to "drive" up front. Zeke, evidently feeling left out of the action, put his front paws up on the running board and whined to get inside.

With a shake of his head, Steven finished rigging up the car seat, shut the door and went around to the other side, whistling for Zeke to follow.

He opened the door behind the driver's seat and Zeke leaped right up, nimble as a pup, and sat panting happily on the heretofore spotless leather upholstery, waiting for the next adventure to begin.

"Come on, buddy," Steven said to Matt, when the kid didn't move from behind the wheel. "Time to switch seats."

"Can't I ride in front, like I did in the old truck?" Matt asked. He sounded a touch on the whiny side—probably needed a nap—but since Steven knew the boy wouldn't take one, he couldn't see any sense in allowing himself to dream of an hour or two of peace and quiet when there was no hope of it happening.

"No," Steven said firmly, "you can't. Anyhow, Zeke will get lonely if he has to sit back here all by himself."

Matt couldn't argue with that logic. The dog's well-being was at stake, after all.

So the boy scrambled between the front seats to the back and only sighed a couple of times while Steven was buckling him in.

"Let's see how this thing runs," Steven said, when Matt was secure.

Zeke had moved over next to Matt, probably lending moral support, and when Steven got into the truck and started it up, the dog's big hairy head was blocking the rearview mirror. So Steven had to reach back and maneuver Zeke out of his way, a tricky proposition at best.

By the time they finally hit the road, Steven was starting to think they ought to save the visit to the day camp for another day, but he decided against the idea because their wheels were already turning and, besides, Matt was supposed to start on Monday morning.

The place would probably be locked up tomorrow,

since it was Sunday, and that would mean no advance reconnaissance mission for Matt. He was five, a new kid in a new community. Steven wanted to give him every chance to get his bearings.

On the way back into Stone Creek, Matt nodded off. Zeke, ever the sport, sank down on the seat and went to sleep, too. The peace and quiet was a wash, though, because that dog snored like a buzz saw gnawing into hardwood.

As soon as they pulled up in front of Creekside Academy, a long, low redbrick structure with green shutters on the windows, a large fenced playground and a tall flagpole, with Old Glory up there flapping in the breeze, Matt and Zeke woke up.

Zeke barked jubilantly. Maybe he was patriotic.

Considering that it was Saturday afternoon, it seemed to Steven that there were a lot of cars in the paved parking lot, which looked out over the creek mentioned in the school's name. He knew Creekside was open six days a week, though, and figured the camp must be doing a brisk business.

He parked the truck beside a spiffy replica of a 1954 MG Roadster, looking over one shoulder to admire it while he stood beside the rear passenger door of his new truck, helping Matt with all his fastenings.

They walked Zeke, cleaned up after him and put him back in the truck, where he promptly curled up on the seat, with a big dog sigh, and resumed the nap he'd started earlier.

Elaine Carpenter, owner and founder of Creekside Academy, greeted Steven and Matt at the front desk. She was an interesting character, Elaine was, her buzz cut at

considerable variance with her ruffled cotton sundress
and ankle-strap sandals.

Steven introduced himself and Matt, since he'd never
met Elaine in person, and she made serious business of
leaning down, looking straight into the little boy's eyes,
and solemnly shaking his hand.

"Welcome to Creekside Academy, Matt," she said.
"I know you'll like it here."

Matt returned the handshake—and the solemn gaze.
"I don't suppose you allow dogs to come to school," he
ventured.

Elaine smiled at Steven as she straightened, but her
expression was regretful when she looked at Matt again.
"Only on show-and-tell days, I'm afraid," she said. She
held out her hand to Matt, and he took it. "Let's have a
look around."

"Where is everybody?" Matt asked, not pulling away.
"There are lots of cars in the lot, but I don't see any kids
around."

Elaine tilted her head toward a closed door, opposite
her desk. Through the glass window, Steven saw several
heads moving around, most of them female, but it was
the sign taped beneath that caught his attention:

PARADE COMMITTEE MEETING
3:00 P.M.
HELP US WELCOME MELISSA O'BALLIVAN
TO OUR GROUP!

Steven smiled.

Guided by Elaine, he and Matt toured the day camp,
checked out the mini-gym, the art room, the music room
and the colorfully decorated classrooms.

The place was kid-heaven, and Steven was impressed, though part of his mind didn't make the journey but stayed right there in front of that door with the sign on it, coming up with all kinds of ways to welcome Melissa O'Ballivan—to all kinds of places.

Like his bed, for instance.

It was an inappropriate train of thought, for sure, but there you go.

He was an adoptive father, settling his young son into a new community, introducing him to a new school.

He was also a man, one who'd been alone too long.

And Melissa was definitely a woman.

By the time they'd gone full circle, Elaine wanted to meet Zeke in person, so to speak, since he must be a pretty magnificent dog, given the way Matt sang his praises.

Elaine raised an eyebrow at Steven, who was lingering outside the community-room door. "Would that be all right?"

Steven nodded, handed her the keys to his truck, so she could open the door and meet Zeke face-to-face.

Matt, holding Elaine's hand as he led the way outside, didn't even look back at Steven. He was busy chattering on about life as he knew it. As they disappeared through the front doors, Matt was explaining how their barn had fallen down and there were rusty nails in it, and that it would mean a "titanic" shot if he stepped on one. As soon as the barn was fixed, he was saying, when the doors started to close behind him and Elaine, he was going to have his very own pony to ride.

Steven waited until the woman and the boy had vanished. Then he drew a deep breath, pushed open the door with the sign taped to it and walked into the community room.

Melissa was up front, clad in linen slacks and a matching top, her hair twisted and then clamped into a knot on top of her head with one of those plastic squeeze combs. She wore almost no makeup, but her toenails, peeking out of her simple sandals, were painted hot pink.

It was harder to think of her as the county prosecutor when she looked like that, so he silently reminded himself that there was surely another side to the lady. She might *appear* soft and sexy, but in court, pushing for a guilty verdict, she'd be ruthless and barracuda-tough.

Like Cindy.

Noticing Steven, Melissa widened her eyes for a moment, then turned her attention back to the people filling the rows of folding chairs, studiously ignoring him.

Steven took a seat in the back, watching her, struggling against a strange and not entirely unpleasant sensation that he was being reeled in, like a fish at the end of a line.

Mentally, he dug in his heels. But the truth was that even from that distance, he could see the pulse pounding at the hollow of her throat. He wanted—hell, *needed*— to kiss her there.

And a few other places.

This is crazy, he told himself, and shifted in the chair, but that didn't help much.

He folded his hands loosely in his lap, as a camouflage maneuver, and listened to Ms. O'Ballivan as earnestly as if she'd been conducting a White House press conference.

"I'm counting on all of you to follow through with your original plans," Melissa said, in the process of bringing the gathering to a close, it would seem. "We have less than a month until Rodeo Days start, but after reviewing all your presentations, I think we have a handle on the situation. Questions?"

A plump woman near the front raised a hand.

"Yes, Bea?" Melissa responded pleasantly.

"I'd just like to remind everyone about the rule we instituted last year, concerning the use of toilet tissue in place of crepe-paper streamers on some of the more— creative floats." Bea stood and made a slow half turn, sweeping the spectators up in one ominous glance. "Toilet tissue is in very bad taste and it has been banned in favor of good old-fashioned crepe paper."

No one argued the point, but when Bea faced front and sat down, there were a few subtle raspberries from the crowd.

Seeing the expression on Melissa's face, Steven wanted to laugh out loud.

Talk about somebody who didn't want to be where she was.

He raised his hand.

"Mr. Creed?" Melissa acknowledged, blushing slightly.

"Steven," he corrected. "Are you still looking for volunteers?"

CHAPTER SIX

ARE YOU STILL LOOKING for volunteers?

Melissa narrowed her eyes at Steven Creed for a moment, wondering what the heck he was up to. Wondering what he was even *doing* at the Parade Committee meeting in the first place.

Okay, sure, he was new in town, and he'd said something in her office the day before about helping out. Joining groups was a good way of getting acquainted with the locals, and all that, but, *still*. Could he really be all that concerned about whether or not toilet paper could be used to bedeck floats in the Fourth of July parade?

"I guess," she said, well aware that her tone was lackluster.

A low, speculative murmur moved through the crowd.

Stone Creek liked to think of itself as a friendly place, extending a ready welcome to newcomers, and it was.

Mostly.

Steven Creed merely grinned, probably enjoying Melissa's discomfort, though only in the kindest possible way, of course.

And he waited for the proverbial ball to bounce back into his court.

Melissa worked up a smile. "Sure," she said. "We can always use another volunteer—can't we, people?"

Everybody clapped.

"Okay," Melissa went on, wobbly-smiled, ready to bring this thing in for a landing so she could go home, weed her tomato plants, dine on canned soup or something equally easy to prepare and curl up in the corner of her couch to read. "Remember—we're doing a walk-through next Saturday afternoon, in the parking lot behind the high school. Nobody bring an actual float, though. We'll be tweaking the marching order, that's all."

There were nods and comments, but the meeting was finally over.

Melissa collected her purse and her clipboard, hanging back while the dozen or so parade participants and general committee members meandered out.

Steven Creed didn't leave with them.

He stood near the door now, watching her, his arms folded, a twinkle in those summer-blue eyes.

Hoping he'd just go because, frankly, she didn't have the first idea how to deal with him, Melissa nodded, coolly cordial, and got busy folding up the chairs and stacking them against the far wall.

Steven remained. In fact, he helped her put away the chairs.

"I didn't expect to run into you here," she said, when the work was done and there was no avoiding looking at him.

"Matt starts day camp here on Monday, so I brought him out for a tour," he explained, just as the boy appeared behind him, half dragged by the sheepdog she'd seen them with that morning, at the Sunflower.

Elaine Carpenter, J.P.'s daughter and a friend of Melissa's, brought up the rear, smiling.

"Ms. Carpenter said I could show Zeke the inside of the school building," Matt told his father. "So far, he likes it."

He was such a cute kid, and so bright. Just looking at the little guy made Melissa's biological clock tick audibly. And here she'd thought the battery was dead.

Seeing Melissa, Matt beamed at her and said hello.

Melissa relaxed a little, though she was still conscious of the man standing so nearby that she could actually *feel* the hard warmth of his body.

Okay, maybe she'd just assumed the "hard" part. It wasn't difficult to make the leap, since he looked so lean and yet so muscular...

What was it about him that set off all her internal alarm bells?

"Hello, again," she told the child.

"We're staying in your brother's tour bus," Matt told her exuberantly. "He says you've got a twin sister, but the two of you don't look anything alike."

Melissa smiled, nodded. "Ashley and I are fraternal twins," she said.

The boy frowned, holding Zeke's leash in both hands to restrain the animal. "What's *fraternal?*" he asked.

Steven Creed's eyes twinkled at that, and his mouth had a "you're-on-your-own" kind of hitch at one corner.

Not about to explain the fertilization process to a child, Melissa brightened her smile and replied, "I think you should ask your dad about that."

"My real dad died," Matt said, wiping that smile right off her face. "But I could ask Steven."

Melissa saw pain mute the twinkle in Steven's eyes, and she felt a twinge of regret. J.P. had mentioned that the child was adopted, but she'd forgotten. "Oh," she said.

"We haven't exactly worked out what I should be called," Steven told her.

Elaine had already left the room by that time, so it was just the three of them and, of course, the dog.

Melissa felt a strange, hollow ache in her throat. This time, she couldn't even manage an "Oh."

For the next few moments, the room seemed to pulse, like a quiet heartbeat.

Then Steven smiled at her and said, "I've never helped out with a parade before, but I'm pretty good with a hammer and nails."

"It's kind of you to offer," Melissa said, finding her voice at last.

"Do you want to come out to our place and have supper?" Matt asked her, out of the blue.

Steven looked a little taken aback, though he had the good grace not to come right out and say it wasn't a good idea.

Melissa was oddly reluctant to see Steven Creed go, even though she hadn't wanted him there in the first place.

He was just too—*much*. Too good-looking. Too sexy. Too lots of things.

All of which worked together to make her say the crazy thing she said next.

"What if you and your—you and Mr. Creed—came to *my* house for supper, instead?" *I'm not the greatest cook in the world,* Melissa thought to herself, *but my sister is, and I'm willing to raid her freezer for an entrée even though it means risking another encounter with a naked croquet team.*

Matt giggled, probably at the reference to "Mr. Creed," and then swung around to look up at the man standing behind him.

"Can we?" he asked eagerly. "Please?"

Steven's smile seemed a touch wistful to Melissa; he probably thought she'd suggested supper at her place to be polite, as a way of letting him off the hook for the impulsive invitation Matt had issued.

He'd be right, if he thought that, Melissa concluded, but she still hoped he'd say yes. And it surprised her how *much* she hoped that.

"Six o'clock?" Melissa added, when Steven still hesitated.

He sighed, looked down at Matt, shook his head. "We didn't leave the lady with much choice now, did we?" he said to the boy.

"It would be nice to have company," Melissa heard herself say. Her voice was softer than usual, and a little tentative. It came to her that she was going to be very disappointed if Steven refused, which was just one more indication that she was losing her ever-loving mind, since she should have been relieved. "And it's no trouble. Really."

That last part was certainly no lie. She'd snitch one of the culinary triumphs Ashley always kept on hand, in case of God knew what kind of food emergency, slip some foil-covered casserole dish into the oven at her place, and gladly accept all the accolades.

Without actually claiming the cooking credit, of course. If anybody asked, she wouldn't lie. If they *didn't* ask, on the other hand, why say anything at all?

Steven still looked troubled, but Melissa could tell that he wanted to take her up on the offer, too, and that knowledge did funny things to her heart.

"How else are you going to get to know people in Stone Creek," Melissa urged, starting toward the door as though supper were a done deal, "if you don't let them feed you? It's the way we country folks do things, you know. Your best bull dies? We feed you. Your house burns down? We feed you. Not that being new in town falls into that kind of category—"

Why was she rattling on like this, making an idiot of herself?

At last, Steven made a decision. "Okay, six o'clock," he said. "Can we bring anything?"

Matt let out a whoop of delight, and the dog joined the celebration with a happy bark.

"Just bring yourselves," Melissa said.

Steven, Matt and the dog followed her out into the brightness of afternoon. Splotches of silver and gold sunlight danced and flickered on the waters of the creek as they burbled by.

A smile flashed in Steven's eyes when Melissa tossed her purse and clipboard into the passenger seat of her roadster.

"That's some ride," he said. "I was admiring it earlier."

The remark seemed oddly personal, as though he'd commented on the shape of her backside or the curve of her breasts or the scent of her hair.

And Melissa was immensely pleased.

"Thanks," she replied, her tone modest, her cheeks warm.

"One question, though," Steven went on, opening the

door of the ginormous blue truck parked next to the roadster. The dog went in first, then the little boy, who submitted fretfully to being fastened into a safety seat. Melissa waited for the question to come.

Steven didn't ask it until he'd shut the truck door again and turned to face her. "Where exactly do you live?"

Their toes were practically touching; Melissa breathed in the green-grass, sun-dried laundry smell of him, felt dizzy.

"I've never been very good at giving directions," she said, when she thought she could talk without sounding weird. "Why don't you follow me over right now? That way, when you come back later, you'll know the way."

"Okay," Steven said, with a little nod. His expression, though, had turned serious again. "I still think you've been painted into a corner here, Melissa, because you didn't want to hurt Matt's feelings about all of us having supper together, and while I certainly appreciate that, I'm not real comfortable with the idea of imposing on you, especially on short notice."

"It's only one meal," she pointed out.

If it was "only one meal," another part of her mind wanted to know, why was her heart beating so hard and so fast? Why was her breath shallow and why, pray tell, did she feel all warm and melty in places where she had no damn *business* feeling all warm and melty?

Steven was quiet, absorbing her answer.

It was disturbing for Melissa to realize that she even liked watching this man *think*.

"You're right," he said at last, with a sigh that was all the more wicked for its boyish innocence. "It's only supper. We'll be there at six."

"Good," Melissa said, wondering exactly when—and how—she'd lost her reason. Hadn't she been down this same road with Dan Guthrie a few years ago?

Dan, the sexy rancher, widowed father of two charming little boys.

Dan, the patient, fiery lover who'd turned her inside out in his bed on the nights when they managed to have the house to themselves.

Dan, who'd finally dumped her, in no uncertain terms, claiming she couldn't commit to a serious relationship, and had taken up with a waitress named Holly, from over in Indian Rock?

Dan and Holly were married now. Expecting a baby.

And the little boys Melissa had come to love like her own children called Holly *Mom*.

Inwardly, she took a step back from Steven Creed, and he seemed to know it, because a shadow fell across his eyes and, for just a millisecond, a muscle bunched in his jaw. He wanted to lodge a protest, she guessed, having sensed her sudden reticence, but he didn't know what *about*.

"Follow me," Melissa said, in the voice of a sleep-walker.

Steven sighed, like a man who thought better of the idea but couldn't think of an alternative, and nodded.

Melissa drove slowly from the parking lot of Creek-side Academy, out onto the main road, and straight into Stone Creek.

Every few moments, she checked her rearview, and the big blue truck was back there each time, Steven an indiscernible shadow at the wheel.

You just want to sleep with him, Melissa accused

herself silently. *And what does that say about your character?*

Melissa squared her shoulders and answered the accusation out loud, since there was no one else in the roadster to overhear. "It says that I'm a natural woman, with red blood flowing through my veins," she replied.

You'll start caring for Steven Creed. Worse, you'll start caring for Matt. It's a case of burn me once, shame on you, burn me twice, shame on me.

Have you forgotten how much it hurt, losing Dan and the boys? It was like losing your mom and dad all over again, wasn't it?

"Oh, shut up," Melissa said. "I'm serving the man *supper,* not a night of steamy sex." She sighed. She could really have used a night of steamy sex. "And the joke's on you. I *already* care for Matt."

You need a child of your own. Not a substitute.

"Didn't I ask you to shut up?" Melissa countered, almost forgetting to stop at a sign.

Sure enough, Tom Parker's cruiser slipped in between her car and Steven's truck, lights whirling. The siren gave an irritating little whine, for good measure.

As if she wouldn't have noticed him back there.

Swearing, Melissa kept driving the half block to her own house, and parked.

"Did you see that stop sign?" Tom asked cordially, climbing out of the squad car. His dog, Elvis, rode in the passenger seat. In Stone Creek, Elvis counted as backup.

"Yes," Melissa said tersely, "and I *stopped* for it."

"Just barely," Tom pointed out, glancing back at Steven's rig.

Melissa watched as the flashy blue truck, which

probably sucked up enough gas for four or five cars to run on, drew up alongside her roadster, and the front passenger-side window buzzed down.

"Is everything all right?" Steven leaned across to ask. His eyes were doing that mischievous little dance again, generating blue heat.

Tom waved at him, smiled cordially. "Everything's fine."

Steven studied Melissa for a long moment, and when she didn't refute Tom's statement, he seemed satisfied. "See you at six," he said.

And then he just drove away.

Just like that.

Not that that annoyed her or anything.

Melissa folded her arms. "What's this all about?" she demanded. "You know damn well you had no business pulling me over. *I stopped for that sign.*"

Tom was still gazing after Steven's truck. "I just wanted to say hello," he lied.

"What a load," Melissa replied. "The truth is, you're just as nosy as your aunt Ona. You saw Steven following me and you wanted to know what was going on."

"He said, 'See you at six,'" Tom went on, as if she hadn't spoken. "You two have a date or something?"

"Or something," Melissa said. "Not that it's any of your business." She flexed her fingers, then regripped the steering wheel, hard. "This is harassment," she pointed out.

Tom chuckled, shook his head. But there was something watchful in his eyes. "At least let me run a check on Creed's background before you get involved," he said. "A person can't be too careful these days."

"Oh, for Pete's sake," Melissa retorted, exasperated.

"A person *can* be too careful. Like you, for instance. When are you going to ask Tessa Quinn out for dinner and a movie, you big coward?"

Tom blinked. Straightened his spine. "When I get around to it," he said, in a mildly affronted tone.

"Have you run a background check on her yet?"

"Of course I haven't."

"A person can't be too careful," Melissa threw out. Then she sighed and changed the subject. "I was just coming from the Parade Committee meeting," she said pointedly. "You know, that little thing I'm doing because your aunt, Ms. Ona Frame, has to have her gallbladder out? You *owe* me, Sheriff Parker. And if you think I'm going to put up with being pulled over for no reason—"

Tom did a parody of righteous horror. Laid a hand to his chest. Back in the squad car, Elvis let out a yip, as though putting in his two cents' worth. Then Tom laughed, held up both hands, palms out. Elvis yipped again.

Melissa leaned to retrieve her purse and that stupid clipboard.

He laughed again. "He's got you pretty flustered, that Creed yahoo," he said, looking pleased at the realization. "I haven't seen you this worked up since you were dating Dan Guthrie—"

Too late, Tom seemed to realize he'd struck a raw nerve. He stopped, reddened, and flung his hands out from his sides. "I'm sorry."

"You should be," Melissa huffed, turning on one heel.

Tom followed her as far as her front gate. "It's not as if you're the only person who's ever loved and lost, Melissa

O'Ballivan," he blurted out, in a furious undertone. "Imagine how it feels to be crazy about a woman who looks right through you like you were transparent!"

"I can't *begin* to imagine that, for obvious reasons," Melissa replied, heading up the walk.

Elvis howled.

Tom stuck with Melissa until she'd mounted the first two porch steps and rounded to look down into his upturned face. "You deliberately misunderstood that," he accused, but he'd lost most of his steam by then.

Melissa sighed. "You were referring to Tessa Quinn, I presume?" she asked, though everybody in town and for miles around knew that Tom loved the woman with a passion of truly epic proportions. Everybody, with the probable exception of Tessa herself, that is.

Tessa was either clueless, playing it cool or just not interested in Tom Parker.

Tom thrust out a miserable breath. "You know damn well it's Tessa," he said.

Melissa cocked a thumb toward the squad car and said, "Get Elvis and come inside. I made a pitcher of iced tea before I went out."

But Tom shook his head. "I'm supposed to be on patrol," he said.

"Well, that's noble," Melissa replied, as the dog gave another long, plaintive howl, "but I'm not sure Elvis is onboard with the plan."

"I was just taking him over to the Groom-and-Bloom for his weekly bath," Tom said. He took very good care of Elvis; everybody knew that as well as they knew his feelings for Tessa. "He's just worried about missing his appointment, that's all. He's particular about his appearance, Elvis is."

Melissa smiled. Nodded. "Tom?"

He was turning away. "What?"

"Why don't you ask Tessa for a date?"

He looked all of fourteen as he considered that idea. His neck went a dull red, and his earlobes glowed like they were lit up from the inside. "She might say no."

"Here's a thought, Tom. She might say yes. Then what would you do?"

"Probably have a coronary on the spot." Tom sounded pretty serious, but there was a tentative smile playing around his lips. "Same as if she said no."

"So you're damned if you do and damned if you don't."

"That's about the size of it," Tom said.

"I dare you," Melissa said. When they were kids, that was the way to get Tom Parker to do just about anything. Of course, she hadn't tried it since playground days.

He flushed again, and his eyes narrowed. "What?"

"You heard me, Parker," Melissa said, jutting her chin out a little ways. "I double-dog *dare* you to ask Tessa Quinn out to dinner. Or to a movie. Or to a dance—there's one next weekend, at the Grange Hall. And if you don't ask her out, well, you're just plain—*chicken*."

Instantly, they were both nine years old again.

Tom stepped closer and glared up at her. "Oh, yeah?" he said.

"Yeah," Melissa replied stoutly.

"You're on," Tom told her.

"Good," Melissa answered, without smiling.

"What do I get if you lose?" Tom wanted to know.

Melissa thought quickly. "I'll buy you dinner."

"As long as you're not cooking," Tom specified, looking and sounding dead serious.

This was a bet Melissa *wanted* to lose. "I'll recruit Ashley," she said. "She can do those specially marinated spare ribs you like so much."

"Deal," Tom said, without cracking a smile. Even as a little kid, he'd been a sucker for a bet.

"Wait just a second," Melissa said. "What if *I* win? What happens then?"

"I'll take over as chairman of the Parade Committee," Tom told her, after some thought.

"Deal," Melissa agreed, putting out her free hand.

They shook on it, then Tom turned and stalked back to the gate, through it and down the sidewalk to his car. "Just remember one thing!" he called back to her.

"What?" Melissa retorted, about to turn around and open her front door.

"Two can play this game," Tom said.

Then he got into the cruiser, slammed his door and ground the engine to life with a twist of the key in the ignition, leaving Melissa to wonder what the hell he'd meant by *that*.

He made the siren give one eloquent moan as he drove on past her house and vanished around the corner.

"Damn," Melissa said, as the answer dawned on her.

Now she'd gone and done it.

Tom would lie awake nights until he came up with a dare for her. And it would be a doozy, knowing him.

But she didn't dwell on the problem too long, because she had things to do. Like go over to Ashley's, thereby braving the wild bunch, who might well be swinging from the chandeliers in their birthday suits, to steal a main course and a dessert from one of the freezers.

"NEXT TIME," Steven told the rearview reflection of a chagrined Matt, as they drove out of town, "it would be a *really* good idea to talk it over with me before you go inviting people to our place for supper."

Matt was no pouter, but his lower lip poked out a-ways, and he was blinking real fast, both of which were signs that he might cry.

It killed Steven when he cried.

"I was just trying to be a good neighbor," Matt explained, sounding as wounded as he looked. "Anyhow, I *like* Ms. O'Ballivan, don't you?"

"Yes," he said, tightening his fingers on the steering wheel, then relaxing them again. "I understand that your intentions were good," he went on quietly. "But sometimes, if that person happens to have other plans, or some other reason why they need to say no, it puts them on the spot. There's no graceful way for them to turn you down."

Matt listened in silence, sniffling a couple of times.

"Do you know what I'm saying, here?" Steven asked, keeping his voice gentle.

Matt nodded. "Yeah," he said. "I get it. I'm gifted, remember?"

Steven laughed. "There's no forgetting that," he said.

"Are you mad at me?"

An ache went through Steven, like a sharp pole jabbed down through the top of his heart to lodge at the bottom. "No," he said. "If I straighten you out about something, it doesn't mean I'm angry. It just means I want you to think things through a little better the next time."

Matt let out a long sigh, back there in the peanut gallery, one of his arms wrapped around Zeke, who was panting and, incredibly, managing to keep his canine head from blocking the rearview mirror.

"It's kind of weird, calling you Steven," Matt said, after a long time. He was looking out the window by then, but even with just a glance at the boy's reflection to go on, Steven could see the tension he was trying to hide.

"Who says so?" Steven asked carefully. Conversations like this one always made his stomach clench.

"I do," Matt told him. His voice was small.

The turn onto their road was just ahead; Steven flipped the signal lever and slowed to make a dusty left. "What would you like to call me?" he asked.

"Dad," Matt said simply.

Steven's eyes scalded, and his vision blurred.

"But that doesn't seem right, because I used to have another dad," Matt went on. "Do you think it would hurt my first daddy's feelings if I went around calling somebody else 'Dad'?"

"I think your dad would want you to be happy," Steven said. It was almost a croak, that statement, but, fortunately, Matt didn't seem to notice. They'd reached the top of the driveway, so Steven pulled up beside the old two-tone truck and shifted out of gear. Shut the motor off. And just sat there, not knowing what to say. Or do.

"If he was *Daddy*," Matt reasoned, "then I guess it would be all right if *you* were *Dad*."

Steven's throat constricted. He literally couldn't speak just then, so he shoved open the truck door and got out. Stood staring off toward the foothills and the mountains beyond for a few moments, until he'd recovered some measure of control.

When he turned around again, both Matt and Zeke had their faces pressed to the window, gumming it up big-time with their breaths.

He laughed and carefully opened the door, so Zeke wouldn't plunge right over Matt and his safety seat and take a header onto the ground.

"I think that's a great idea," Steven said.

"So I can call you *Dad?*" Matt asked.

"Yeah," Steven replied, ducking his head slightly while he undid the snaps and buckles. "You can call me *Dad.*"

"That's good," Matt said. A pause. "Dad?" He said the word softly, like he was trying it on for size.

"What?" Steven ground out, hoisting the little boy to the ground, and then the dog.

"How come your eyes are all red?"

Steven sniffled, ran a forearm across his face. "I guess it's the dust," he said. He pretended to assess the sky, sprawling blue from horizon to horizon. "A good rain would help."

"HELLO?" Melissa rapped lightly at her sister's kitchen door, though she'd already opened it and stuck her head inside. "Anybody home?"

There was no answer, but she could hear voices coming from the dining room.

Melissa hadn't seen a car parked outside, so she'd hoped the lively group had gone out, maybe to play miniature golf or take in a movie. She would have loved to raid the freezer and duck out again, unnoticed, but she was afraid one of the oldsters would wander in, be startled and collapse from a massive coronary.

So she moved to the middle of the floor and tried again. "Hello?"

This time, they heard her. "Melissa, is that you?" a woman's voice called cheerfully.

"Yes," she answered. Then she drew a deep breath, proceeded to the inside door and drew another deep breath before pushing it open.

The guests were gathered at one end of the formal dining table, playing cards. And they were all wearing clothes.

Melissa was so profoundly relieved that she gave a nervous, high-pitched giggle and put one hand to her heart.

How amused Ashley and Olivia and Brad would be if they could see her now. In her family, she did *not* have a reputation for shyness, and her sibs would have gotten a major kick out of her newfound fear of naked croquet players.

"Come and join us," Mr. Winthrop said, rising from his seat. "We're playing gin rummy, and I'm afraid we've all known each other so well, for so long, that there just aren't any new tricks."

I'll just bet there aren't, Melissa thought, but not with rancor. Initial embarrassment aside, she *liked* these people. They had spirit. Imagination. Wrinkles. Lots and lots of wrinkles.

"I can't stay," she said, and the regret in her tone was only partly feigned. She enjoyed gin rummy and, heck, everybody was *dressed,* weren't they? "I'm having company tonight, so I came by to borrow a few things."

She waggled her fingers at them, backing toward the swinging door. "Enjoy your game."

"Don't take the roast duck," one of the women sang out, shuffling the deck for another hand of cards. "Your sister promised that to us. It's Herbert's favorite, and he's turning ninety tomorrow."

"Hands off the duck," Melissa promised, palms up and facing the group at the table, and then she slipped out. She was smiling to herself as she headed for the large storage room, off the kitchen, where Ashley had two huge freezers, invariably well-stocked.

One was reserved for desserts, one for main courses.

She selected a container marked *Game Hens with Cranberries and Wild Rice, Serves 6,* Ashley's graceful handwriting looping across the label. Melissa hoped that Matt liked chicken, as most kids did, and would therefore accept a reasonable facsimile.

For dessert, she purloined a lovely blueberry cobbler.

Best with Vanilla Ice Cream, Ashley had written on the sticker. It was almost as if she'd known, somehow, that her twin would be breaking into her frozen-food supply soon and would need guidance.

Melissa set the food on the counter, went back to the inside door to poke her head in and say goodbye.

The card players were still clothed and so normal-looking that she could almost believe she'd *imagined* the notorious backyard croquet game. Maybe she really *was* going nuts.

"See you," Melissa said stupidly, her face strangely hot as she backed away from the door.

She turned, grabbed the food containers and boogied

out the back door, glad she'd parked her car in the alley, so she wouldn't have to walk around front, where she might have to stop and chat with one of her sister's neighbors. She wasn't feeling very sociable at the moment.

She made a quick stop at the supermarket for ice cream and a premade spinach salad, then hurried home.

When she got there, Byron was working, shirtless, in the front yard, pruning shears in hand, snipping errant branches off the maple tree and stemming its invasion of the sidewalk.

Nathan Carter, a local dropout with a history of misdemeanors to his credit and not much else, sat cross-legged in the as-yet-unmowed grass, watching him.

"I thought you couldn't come until tomorrow," Melissa said, addressing Byron but shooting a curious glance at Nathan as she spoke, then grappling with Ashley's plastic containers and the stuff she'd bought at the store. "Something about relining the Crocketts' koi pond?"

Nathan returned her look, smirking. She'd never liked the kid; a sort of latter-day James Dean type, he seemed to fancy himself a rebel without a cause.

He was also without a job, a house or a car, as far as she knew. He came and went, turning up every so often to bunk on his cousin Lulu's screened-in side porch and stir up whatever trouble he could.

Byron, sweating, paused and pulled an arm across his forehead. His eyes were wary, and oddly hopeful, as he watched Melissa and nodded once. "Got that done," he said. "Those fish are back in the pond, swimming around like they had good sense. I'll be back in the morning to finish up around here, but I thought I'd whack off some of these branches tonight."

Melissa looked from Byron to Nathan and back to Byron, tempted to take her temporary yard man aside and remind him that he ought to be careful who he hung around with, given that he was on parole.

"Byron, here," Nathan put in helpfully, "is a little short on cash."

"I could advance you a few dollars," Melissa said.

Nathan and Byron responded simultaneously.

"Awesome," Nathan drawled, his tone oily, like his mouse-brown hair and his filthy T-shirt and jeans.

"I wouldn't feel right taking money," said Byron, with a decisive shake of his head. "Not when I haven't finished the job."

Had this kid changed in jail, Melissa wondered, or had she misjudged him, way back when? There had never been any question of his guilt, that was true, but maybe Velda had been right.

Maybe she should have tried for mandatory treatment in a drug and alcohol facility instead of time behind bars…. No. She had considered every angle, consulted experts, lain awake nights. She'd done what she thought was right and there was no use second-guessing the decision now.

She turned her thoughts to her supper guests—Steven and Matt Creed. Nathan dropped off her radar, a nonentity.

And she immediately felt better.

The containers of frozen food, now beginning to thaw, stung like dry ice through the front of Melissa's top and she still wanted to tidy up the house a little, choose an outfit—nothing too come-hither—do something with her hair, and put on some makeup. A touch of mascara, some lip gloss, that was all.

Maybe a little perfume.

The message she wanted to send was, *Welcome to Stone Creek,* not, *Hey, big guy, what do you say we hire a sitter, slip out of here, and go find ourselves a place to get it on?*

She blushed, because the second version wasn't without a certain appeal, then realized she hadn't responded to Byron's last statement. "Okay, then," she told him, ignoring Nathan, tugging open the screen door with a quick motion of one hand and holding it open with her hip. "See you tomorrow."

Byron nodded and went back to snipping branches off the maple tree.

CHAPTER SEVEN

By 5:59 P.M., MELISSA WAS ready to serve supper—the game hens, warming in the seldom-used oven, filled her small, bright kitchen with their savory aroma. The cobbler, already thawed and heated through, sat cooling on the counter nearest the stove, covered by a clean dishtowel. The antique table, which too often served as a catchall for newspapers and junk mail, looked like something straight off the cover of *Country Living* magazine.

Melissa took a moment to admire the crisp white tablecloth, the green-tinted glass jar in the center, spilling over with perfect white peonies from the bushes on either side of the front steps. The plates, purchased on impulse in, of all places, an airport gift shop, were decorated with checks and flowers and polka dots.

She tilted her head to one side, considering the look. Fussy, yes. Feminine, definitely. Cheerful, to the max.

But was it *too* fussy, feminine and cheerful?

After all, this wasn't a reunion of her high school cheerleading squad; she was entertaining a little boy and a grown man.

And *what* a man. There should have been a law.

Melissa chewed briefly on one fingernail, fretting. With the exception of the flowers in the jar, none of this was at all like her—the fancy dishes had been gathering dust in the cupboard above the refrigerator for a couple of years, she hadn't cooked the food and she had exactly one tablecloth to her name—*this* one. It didn't even have any sentimental value, that tablecloth—it hadn't been passed down through generations of O'Ballivans, like the various linens Ashley and Olivia so prized. No, Melissa had bought it on clearance at a discount store, just in case she might need it someday—her share of the heirlooms were stored in a chest, out on the ranch. Did she have time to drive out there and grab some?

Deep breath, she instructed herself silently.

Just as she drew in air, a rap sounded at the front door. *They're here.*

No time to tone down—or tone *up*—the decorations now, obviously.

Melissa, feeling especially womanly in her summery dress, a multicolored Southwestern print with touches of turquoise and magenta, gold and black, went to greet her company.

Matt stood on the porch with his nose pressed into the screen door, his damp hair already beginning to rebel against a recent combing, springing up into a rooster tail at the back of his head and swirling into little cowlick eddies here and there.

Melissa's heart melted at the sight of him; a smile rose up within her and spilled across her face, warm on her mouth. Of course she was aware of Steven, standing behind the boy—how could she *not* have been aware?— but she didn't make eye contact right away.

No, she needed a few more deep breaths before she could risk that.

So she concentrated on Matt—unlocking and opening

the screen door, stepping back so he could spill into her house, all energy and eagerness and *boy*.

"You look very handsome," she told the child, resisting a motherly urge to smooth down the rooster tail with a light pass of her hand.

Matt's smile seemed to encompass her, like an actual embrace. "And *you* look *beautiful!*" he responded.

"Amen," Steven said huskily. That single word coursed right over Matt's head to lodge itself in Melissa like a velvet arrow.

Her throat caught, and her gaze betrayed her, going straight to him long before she was ready.

Steven wore jeans, a little newer than the ones he'd had on earlier, along with polished black boots and a white, collarless shirt of the sort men favored back in the Old West days. His hair was damp from a recent shower, like Matt's, but there were no cowlicks and no rooster tails, and he smelled like a field of newly sprouted clover after a soft rain.

A free-fall sensation seized Melissa, buffeted the breath from her lungs, as though she were skydiving without a parachute, or riding a runaway roller coaster.

The feeling was stunning. Terrifying, in fact.

And categorically *wonderful*.

"I hope you're both hungry," she heard herself say, and the normality of her tone amazed her, because on the inside, she was still being swept along, helter-skelter, like a swimmer caught in a fast current.

"We're *starved*," Matt answered, looking around the living room, as alert as a detective scanning for clues.

Steven smiled and cleared his throat slightly, raising one eyebrow when Matt turned to look up at him.

"Well, we *are*," the boy insisted, folding his small arms.

Steven grinned, unwittingly—or *wittingly*—sending a charge of electricity through Melissa. His eyes, so very blue and with a touch of lavender to them that reminded her of summer twilights and late-blooming lilacs, ranged idly over her, pausing here and there, lingering to light small fires under her skin. It seemed lazy-slow, that look, but she knew it couldn't have lasted more than a fraction of a moment.

"Then let's get you some supper," Melissa told Matt, extra glad he was there, and not just because she was already so fond of him. If she'd been alone with Steven Creed, considering her strange state of mind, she might have jumped the man's bones right there in the living room.

Okay, so maybe that was an exaggeration. But she was definitely attracted to him, and she couldn't shake the feeling that she was on dangerous ground.

Remembering her duties as a hostess, she led the way into the kitchen.

Matt started toward the table the moment they entered the room, but Steven caught the child lightly by one shoulder and stopped him.

"Where do we wash up?" Steven asked, looking at Melissa.

She pointed toward the hallway just to the left of the stove. "The bathroom is that way," she said.

The Creed men disappeared in the direction she'd indicated, then returned a couple of minutes later.

Melissa was just setting out the main course. Since

she didn't own a platter, she'd left the food in Ashley's freezer-to-oven casserole dish.

"Are those chickens?" Matt asked, eyeing the halved game hens dubiously.

Steven chuckled. "Yes," he said mildly. "They're chickens." And then he caught Melissa's eye, waiting for something.

After an awkward moment, Melissa pointed to one of the chairs. Steven pulled it back, let Matt scramble up onto the seat.

"Can I eat with my fingers?" Matt wanted to know.

Steven answered without taking his eyes off Melissa. "Thanks for asking," he said, in an easy drawl. "But no, Tex, you can't eat with your fingers."

It finally came home to Melissa that Steven wasn't going to sit down until she was seated. She moved toward the middle chair, oddly embarrassed, waited for Steven to pull it out for her and sat.

She noticed a sparkle in the man's eyes as he joined her and Matt.

"I don't think those are really chickens," Matt said, in a tone of good-natured skepticism, peering into the casserole dish in the center of the table.

Melissa began to wish she'd served something little-boy friendly, like pizza or hamburgers or hot dogs.

Steven, perhaps hoping to put her at ease, speared one of the game hens with the serving fork, dropped it onto his plate, and began cutting it into bite-size pieces. His movements were quick and deft, with a subtle elegance about them.

Don't think about his hands.

Melissa blinked, snapping out of yet another mini-daze.

Steven switched plates with Matt, who nibbled at a bite, then began to eat in earnest.

"Slow down," Steven said, helping himself when Melissa didn't move to dish up a portion of her own.

Matt nodded, chewing and swallowing. "You're a good cook," he told Melissa.

Melissa felt heat pulse under her cheeks, longing to fib and take all the credit—and completely unable to do so. She was terminally honest; it was her personal cross to bear.

"My sister Ashley is," she clarified. "I—well—sort of *borrowed* supper from her."

Steven's eyes danced with blue mischief, but he didn't offer a comment. He did seem to be enjoying Ashley's culinary expertise, though.

Everybody did.

"Oh," Matt said. Having taken the edge off his appetite, he paused, looking across the table at Steven. "Do you think Zeke is okay?" he asked.

Zeke? Then Melissa remembered the dog.

"Zeke," Steven said easily, "is just fine."

"I wanted to bring him with us," Matt confided to Melissa, who, by then, had begun to eat, however tentatively. "But Dad wouldn't let me. He said it wouldn't be polite to do that."

Melissa smiled, willing herself to relax. Steven Creed, with his broad shoulders and his quiet confidence and his mere *presence,* seemed to fill that small kitchen, breathing all the air, absorbing the light.

Absorbing *her.* The experience, though disquieting, had a certain zip to it, too.

"Zeke," Steven repeated, his eyes smiling as he looked at Matt, *"is just fine."*

"You could bring him next time," Melissa said.

Next time? Who said there was going to *be* a "next time"?

Matt cheered at the news.

"Bring it down a few decibels," Steven instructed.

Matt grinned. "I'm too loud sometimes," he said to Melissa, in a stage whisper.

She laughed and stopped just short of ruffling his hair. "That's okay," she whispered back.

After that, a companionable silence fell.

It wasn't until the meal was over, and they were contemplating dessert, that Matt got down to brass tacks.

"Are you married?" he asked Melissa bluntly. "Do you have any kids?"

Steven, so far unflappable, it seemed to Melissa, reddened slightly. Narrowed his eyes at Matt and started to speak.

Melissa cut him off before he could say a word. "No," she told Matt. "I'm not married, and I don't have any kids."

Matt's smile was glorious, like dawn breaking after a cold and moonless night. "Good!" he said. "Then you could marry my dad and be my mom. We'd help with the cooking, so you wouldn't have to keep borrowing supper from your sister, and even do the laundry."

"Matt," Steven said, fighting a smile.

Without thinking about it first—if she had, she would surely have stopped herself—Melissa rested a hand on Steven's forearm. Felt the muscles tighten and then ease again under her fingertips.

"It's okay," she said, very softly.

Matt looked from Steven to Melissa, and his small

shoulders stooped a little. "I guess I shouldn't have said that stuff about marrying Dad and me," he admitted.

"Ya think?" Steven asked.

Melissa smiled, anxious to reassure the child. "Know what?" she said, addressing Matt, finally removing her hand from Steven's arm.

"What?" Matt asked.

"If I'm ever lucky enough to have a little boy of my own, I hope he'll be just like you."

It came again, then. That beaming smile.

When this kid grew up, he was going to be a heart-breaker, no doubt about it.

"Really?" Matt asked.

Steven shifted in his chair, but said nothing.

"Really," Melissa confirmed. "Now, who wants ice cream and cobbler?"

MATT RESTED OVER STEVEN'S right shoulder, like a sack of potatoes. Once the kid hit the proverbial wall and gave himself over to sleep, that was it. His surroundings didn't matter—he was down for the count.

Melissa, looking better than any dessert ever could have, walked out to the truck alongside Steven, hugging herself against the chill of a high country night.

There was hardly anything to that sundress of hers, which was fine with Steven, except that he didn't want her catching pneumonia or anything.

"Thank you," he said gruffly, pausing on the sidewalk, turning toward her.

He wanted to kiss Melissa, but holding Matt the way he was, the logistics were just plain off.

Melissa smiled, reached past him to open the rear door of the rig.

Matt mumbled something as Steven set him in the car seat and began buckling him in but, true to form, he didn't wake up.

"He's terrific," she said softly.

"I agree," Steven told her, after Matt was secured. They stood facing each other now, on that darkened sidewalk. "Of course it *would* be a real plus if he'd stop proposing to women."

There was something flirty in Melissa's smile, but something vulnerable, too. "Does he do that a lot? Ask people to marry you, I mean?"

Steven chuckled, even though he felt inexplicably nervous, and shook his head. "No," he replied. "Actually, Matt is pretty discerning when it comes to women." A grin tugged at one corner of his mouth. "He doesn't suggest marriage and instant motherhood to just *anybody*, you know."

Melissa laughed at that; it was soft and musical, that sound, and it found a place inside Steven and stowed away there, perhaps for keeps. "He's sweet," she said.

Again—*still*—Steven wanted to kiss Melissa O'Ballivan. Full on the mouth, with tongue.

Since the direct approach might scare her away, he settled for leaning in and giving her a light peck on the forehead.

"Tonight was great," he said, resting his hands on her shoulders.

Given that the sundress left that part of her bare, the gesture might have been misguided. Melissa's skin felt warm and smooth under his palms, taut with vitality. Steven tightened his fingers, briefly and almost imperceptibly, then withdrew, letting his hands fall to his sides.

"Thanks," he said again, grinding out the word.

He saw the heat flash in her eyes, the knowing, a desire that might even match his own, and everything inside him soared.

It was inevitable, he realized. Written in the stars.

Right or wrong, for better or for worse, at some point, he and Melissa O'Ballivan *would* make love.

Whoa, you big dumb cowboy, said the voice of reason, causing Steven to sigh. *You just* met *the woman yesterday.*

Once, before Matt became a part of his day-to-day life, Steven would have countered the voice with a re-sounding *So what?* living, as he had, by the philosophy that he-who-hesitates-is-lost, especially when it came to beautiful women and the opportunity to bed them.

Melissa certainly qualified as beautiful, and that was the least of it. He sensed a vastness within her, a fasci-nating inner landscape he yearned to explore.

In time.

"Go inside," he told her, smiling down into her eyes, "you're shivering."

"Yes, I really should," she agreed, shivering harder.

But she didn't move and neither did he.

They just stood there, looking at each other.

Finally, Melissa rolled up onto the balls of her feet and touched her mouth to his, the contact light and brief, over almost before it began.

The kiss electrified Steven, left him confounded.

In the next moment, a wistful little smile playing on her lips, Melissa turned and hurried back through the gate, up the walk, across the porch, finally disappearing into the house.

Steven, wondering what the hell had just hit him, *still* didn't move.

Then he heard one of the truck windows open, with a whirring sound, turned to see Matt looking out at him, rubbing his eyes once with the heels of his palms and then grinning sleepily.

"Melissa *kissed* you," he said.

Steven chuckled and rounded the truck, climbed behind the wheel.

"She did," Matt insisted, as they pulled away from the curb. "I *saw* Melissa kiss you."

"Okay," Steven said, adjusting the mirrors. "She kissed me. It was no big deal, Tex. Just 'good-night.'"

"Melissa *likes* you."

"I like her, too."

"I bet she doesn't go around kissing *everybody* she likes," Matt went on.

"Go back to sleep," Steven responded, with a smile in his voice.

Matt giggled. He was wide-awake—so much for his usual tendency to sleep through anything. "Are you going to ask Melissa out for a date?"

Steven suppressed a broad grin. They were on the main street of Stone Creek now, headed in the direction of home.

Such as home was.

"You're five," he pointed out. "What would make you ask a question like that?"

Matt gave a huge sigh. "I know what dating is," he said, very patiently. "I watch TV. Guys on TV give lots of women roses and take them on dates, in limos. At the end of the season, the guy has to decide which one of them is a keeper and gets down on one knee and gives her a ring."

"And you watched all this stuff *when?*" Steven asked. In their household, television was strictly monitored, especially the "reality" kind.

"Mrs. Hooper has this big set of DVDs. We watched all of them."

Mrs. Hooper had been Matt's babysitter back in Denver. Steven had worked a lot of nights, tying up loose ends at his old law firm before making the move to Stone Creek.

"You didn't mention that at the time," Steven said dryly. Once they were past the city limits, he shifted gears and sped up a little.

"You never once asked me if Mrs. Hooper and I were watching smoochy dating shows on TV," Matt informed him.

"You'd make a great lawyer, you know that?"

"I don't want to be a lawyer," Matt said. "I want to be a cowboy." A pause. "I just need a *horse,* that's all. You can't be a cowboy without a horse. So, when are we going to build the new barn?"

Steven laughed and shoved his left hand through his hair, keeping his right on the steering wheel. "When I've had a chance to get some estimates and hire a contractor," he answered. "Until then, you'll just have to be patient."

Another sigh.

"What?" Steven asked.

"I was just wondering something."

"And that would be—?"

"Are you going to ask Melissa out on a date?"

Now it was Steven who sighed. "Guess what?" he

said. "That just happens to be none of your darned business, buddy."

"How am I *ever* supposed to get a mom if you won't go out with women?"

"I *do* go out with women, Matt."

"Okay," Matt conceded. "You went out sometimes when we lived in *Denver*. But this is *Stone Creek*."

"And we haven't even been here two full days," Steven said reasonably. "Give me a chance, will you?"

"So you'll do it?"

"So I'll do what?"

Matt sounded exasperated. "Ask. Melissa. Out. On. A. Date."

Steven laughed again, harder this time. They were bumping their way over a country road now. Their turn-off was just ahead and he switched on the signal, even though there was no one behind them. "Do you ever give up?"

"No," Matt replied, without hesitation. "Do you?"

Steven sighed. "No," he admitted.

"Because a Creed never gives up, right?"

Steven didn't answer.

"Right?" Matt persisted, through a yawn.

"Okay," Steven said. "Yes. That's right."

"And you're going to ask Melissa to go out with you, right?"

Steven stopped the rig near the tour bus, shut off the engine and turned in his seat to look back at Matt. "If I say yes, will you shut up about it?" he asked, not unkindly.

Inside the bus, Zeke began to bark.

"Yes," Matt said, and Steven thought his expression

might have been a little smug, though that could have been a trick of the light.

"Promise?"

"Promise," Matt confirmed. "But you have to promise, too."

Steven got out of the truck, went to open Matt's door and began unhitching the kid from his safety gear. "All right, I promise. But if she says no, that's it, understand?" He lifted Matt into his arms. "You don't get to pester me about it until the crack of doom."

Matt squeezed his neck. "Melissa *won't say no,* Dad," he said. "She *likes* you, remember? She *kissed* you."

Steven sighed. It sure felt good to be called "Dad," though.

Reaching the bus, he opened the door and stepped aside just before Zeke shot out of the interior like a hairy bullet.

"One other thing," Steven said.

Matt yawned again, watching fondly as Zeke ran in widening circles, barking his brains out. "What?" the boy asked, sounding only mildly interested.

Steven set him down, and they both waited for the dog to do his thing.

"When it comes to dating," Steven said, "three's a crowd, old buddy. You'll have to stay home with a babysitter."

Zeke raised a hind leg and christened the left rear tire of Steven's new truck.

"Okay," Matt agreed solemnly. "It's a deal."

When the dog was finished, Steven reached to switch on a light. Then the three of them went into the flashy tour bus with a silhouette of Brad O'Ballivan's head painted on the side.

Within a few minutes, Matt was washed up and in his pajamas, his breath smelling of mint from a vigorous tooth-brushing session at the bathroom sink. Steven tucked the boy in and pretended not to notice when Zeke immediately jumped up onto the mattress and settled himself in for the night.

Smiling slightly, Steven stepped out of Matt's room, remembering his own childhood. In Boston, he wasn't allowed to have a dog—his mother said the antique Persian rugs in Granddad's house were far too valuable to put at risk and besides, animals were generally noisy—but on the ranch outside Lonesome Bend, the plank floors were hardwood, worn smooth by a century of use, and the rugs were all washable. Nobody seemed to mind the occasional mess and the near-constant clamor of kids and dogs banging in and out of the doors.

There had been a succession of pets over the years; Brody and Conner each had their own mutt, and so did Steven. His had been a lop-eared Yellow Lab named Lucky, and when he arrived in the spring, right after school let out, that dog would be waiting at the ranch gate when they pulled in.

The reunions were always joyous.

The goodbyes, when the end of August came around, and it was time for Steven to return to Boston, were an ache he could still feel, even after all those years.

Of course, Brody and Conner had looked out for Lucky while he was gone, but it couldn't have been the same as when Steven was there. Brody had Fletch and Conner had Hannibal, and that made Lucky odd dog out, any way you looked at it.

Summer after summer, though, Lucky had been there

to offer a lively welcome when Steven came back, and the two of them had been inseparable, together 24/7.

His throat tight and his eyes hot, Steven tried to shake off the recollection of that dog, because he still missed him, no matter how much time had gone by. Lucky had been one of the truest friends he'd ever had, or expected to have.

Steven cleared his throat, then set about locating the drawings he'd been working on intermittently since he decided to buy fifty acres, a two-story house and a wreck of a barn outside Stone Creek, Arizona. Over the last several weeks, he'd redesigned the house a couple of times, and come up with what he considered a workable plan for the outbuildings, too.

Looking at the sketches, all of them scrawled on the now-scruffy yellow pages of a legal pad, Steven figured he was ready to hire an architect and start getting estimates from local contractors. Not that there were likely to be all that many in a community the size of Stone Creek.

He flipped through the pages, checking and rechecking. Somewhere along the line, he'd learned to multitask—a part of his mind was still back there on that sidewalk in town, face-to-face with Melissa O'Ballivan, who might as well have zapped him with a cattle prod as kiss him, even quickly and lightly, the way she had.

The effect had been about the same, as far as he could tell. On the other hand, he figured a *real* kiss probably would have struck him dead on the spot, like a bolt of lightning.

And then there was Matt, campaigning to marry him off ASAP, preferably to Melissa, but if that didn't fly, the kid was bound to zero in on another candidate without much delay.

Roses and limos and engagement rings offered on bended knee indeed, he thought, smiling.

A ringing noise jolted Steven out of his musings. He checked the caller ID panel on his cell phone—he didn't recognize the number—and answered with his name.

"This is Brody," replied his long-lost cousin. Brody's voice was so much like his twin brother's that Steven might have thought the call was from Conner, if it hadn't been for the opening announcement.

Relief and temper surged up in Steven, all tangled up. "Where the *hell* are you?" he demanded, in a ragged whisper. If it hadn't been for Matt, he probably would have *yelled* that question.

"It's good to talk to you again, too," Brody said, employing the exaggerated drawl he used when he didn't give a rat's ass whether he pissed off whoever he happened to be talking to. Which was all the time.

Steven let out a long breath, and he had to press it between his teeth, since his jaw was clamped down hard.

"You still there, Boston?" Brody asked.

The old nickname, once a taunt, enabled Steven to relax a little. And relaxing made it possible to work the hinges on his jawbones so he could open his mouth to answer.

"I'm here," he said. The second time he asked Brody where he was, he managed a civil tone.

Brody chuckled before he replied, "Now, cousin, if you followed the rodeo the way you used to, you'd know I've been out there on the circuit. In plain sight, you might say."

Steven's anger revved up again, like an engine locked in Neutral and pumped full of gas. "*Dammit*, Brody," he growled, braced on one elbow, with his fingers spread out wide through his hair. "I *did* follow the rodeo, online and sometimes in person, and I didn't hear your name or see your face even one time."

"I might have been in Canada for a while there," Brody allowed.

"Or doing time somewhere," Steven said, voicing his second worst fear. His first, of course, had been the distinct possibility that Brody was dead.

Brody laughed, and there was something broken in the sound. "I've been tossed into the hoosegow once or twice in my illustrious career," he replied. "But I've never served a stretch, Boston, and I don't mind admitting that I'm a little indignant over your lack of faith in the quality of my character."

Steven tried again. "Where are you, Brody?"

"Denver," Brody answered readily. "But I won't be here for long. Just passin' through, as they say."

"Have you been to the ranch?" Lonesome Bend wasn't that far from Denver; maybe Brody had paid a visit to the home folks. Mended fences with Conner, spent some time with Steven's dad and with Kim, both of whom loved both the twins like their own.

Even as the thought crossed his mind, he knew it was too much to hope for.

A Creed never gave up. Especially not on a grudge.

Brody gave another laugh, as raw as the last one. Maybe a little more so. "No," he said. "I'm not ready for that."

"It's been a lot of years," Steven said, straightening his spine, letting his hand drop to the tabletop. He glanced toward the hall, half expecting to see Matt standing there, watching him. "You planning on being 'ready' anytime soon?"

"Probably not."

"But you called me."

"Yeah," Brody agreed, with a sigh that said he didn't quite believe it himself. "I hooked up with a pretty girl in a cowboy bar last night, and it turned out that she used to work for you and Zack St. John, as a secretary or an assistant or something like that. Jessica, I think her name was."

Steven smiled sadly. Some things never changed. "You 'hooked up' with her, and you're not sure what her name was?"

"Hey," Brody said, "not everybody is detail-oriented the way you are, Boston. She was definitely a Jessica."

"Or maybe a Jennifer," Steven said. He'd never worked with anybody named Jessica, but there had been a Jennifer Adams at the law firm in Denver when he was there. She'd been a highly skilled paralegal.

"Maybe that was it," Brody admitted, with a chuckle. "Anyhow, she said you'd moved to Stone Creek, Arizona. When I heard that, I decided to get in touch, and damned if she didn't have your cell number handy."

"Whatever the reason was, Brody, I'm really glad to hear from you."

"There's a rodeo coming up," Brody went on, gliding right over any hint of sentiment, the way he always had. "There in Stone Creek, I mean."

"So I hear," Steven said mildly. "You mean to enter, Brody? Compared to what you're used to, it's small potatoes."

"It isn't so little," Brody said. "I've been there before.

Nice buckle and a good paycheck, if I draw the right bronc and the competition isn't too bad."

"It would be mighty good to see you again, cousin," Steven said, knowing full well that Conner would be in town then, too. It didn't seem right to keep that fact from Brody, but Steven didn't want to risk losing contact again, and he figured Brody was bound to hang up at the mention of his brother's name.

"I was hoping you'd say that," Brody answered.

CHAPTER EIGHT

MONDAY MORNING ROLLED AROUND way too soon, as it is inclined to do. Grumbling under her breath, Melissa practically *crawled* out of bed, went to the window and peered out between the slats of the wooden blinds.

Great.

The gray sky looked heavy-bellied with rain and, somewhere in the distance, thunder rolled, like a sound effect from the old Garth Brooks song.

The night before, feeling optimistic about the weather, she'd set out shorts and a tank top with a built-in sports bra, along with socks, running shoes and cotton underpants. Now, disheartened, Melissa opted for sweats, instead of the shorts and top, pulled her hair back and up in a ponytail, and went out into the front yard to stretch.

The fresh air, with its misty chill, did a lot to revive her, made her glad she'd overcome her first waking instinct of the day—to go straight back to sleep.

The lawn certainly looked a lot better, she thought, as she opened the gate in her picket fence and stepped out onto the sidewalk. Byron had spent the whole afternoon mowing and clipping and weeding, and the results were impressive.

Melissa breathed in the moist green scent of newly cut grass.

The branches of the maple tree no longer hung low over the sidewalk, and millions of tiny raindrops dotted the leaves, shimmering like bits of crystal, finely ground and then sprinkled on.

She started off at a slow trot, warming up. A light drizzle began before she got as far as the corner, and another clap of thunder sounded, way outside of town but ominous.

Melissa raised the hood of her sweatshirt and picked up her pace. She liked to vary her route and that day she circled the town's small, well-kept park three times before turning onto Main Street.

Most of the businesses were still closed, of course, since it was only about 7:30 a.m., but the Sunflower was open, along with the feed store and the auto repair shop.

Tessa Quinn stood outside her café, her long, dark brown hair tumbling down her back, pouring fresh water into the community dog dish. She smiled and waved as Melissa trotted past on the opposite side of the street.

Melissa waved back, pondering an idea that had been rattling around in the back of her brain for a while now: playing matchmaker by inviting both Tessa and Tom over for supper on the same night. Of course it would mean borrowing more food from Ashley's freezer stash—or even convincing her twin to whip up some culinary wonder befitting the occasion. Sure, it would be a risk—Tom and Tessa might wind up disliking not only each other, but *her* as well—but suppose luck was with them? Suppose it was the start of something big?

She smiled at the thought. Maybe, so she wouldn't feel like a third wheel, and *Tom* wouldn't feel outnumbered, she would ask Steven to come back, too. This time, of course, she wouldn't practically tackle the man on the sidewalk at the end of the evening and kiss his face.

Remembering, Melissa blushed. She'd had the remainder of Saturday night and all of Sunday to get over giving in to that one foolhardy impulse, but here she was, still obsessing about it. What *was* her problem? She decided to hold off on the matchmaking, at least until Ashley got back from Chicago and could serve as a sort of advisor.

Lord, she missed her sister.

Melissa jogged on, passing by the library, and the log post office, with its large green lawn, flag and flagpole, and the row of bright blue mailboxes facing the street. It was time to head for home, she decided, leaving Main for the oak-shaded residential street that lay parallel to it.

Every house was familiar; Melissa knew who lived there now and who had lived there before that, and before *that*. She knew the people and their histories and their hopes and the names of their pets, living and gone.

That was life in a small town for you.

Eventually, she reached Ashley's B&B, and was pleased to note a conspicuous absence of naked croquet players, at least in the front yard. Maybe it was the inclement weather, she thought, with a smile.

Or they could be around back, cavorting away.

Melissa was so distracted by those thoughts, and so used to running along that street in the early morning, that she wasn't paying attention, and nearly got run over as she crossed the dirt-and-gravel alley between the B&B and the Crockett sisters' place.

Brakes screeched, shrill as fingernails on some celestial blackboard, and tiny rocks peppered Melissa's skin. Even though the rain was still coming down, dust boiled up around her in a cloud. Trying to fling herself out of the path of doom, she leaped for the nearest patch of grass, stumbled and tore open the knees of her sweatpants when she fell just short of her aim.

Moments passed, taking their sweet time.

Everything seemed to vibrate around Melissa, like some void. Sounds dragged, as though someone had put a finger on an old vinyl record as it went around on the turntable.

And then Andrea was crouching in front of her, taking her firmly by the shoulders. "Are you all right?" the girl croaked out. "Oh, my God, Melissa, are you hurt?"

Melissa stood up, with some help from Andrea, trembling and coughing wet dust out of her lungs and shaking her head, all at once. It was then that she saw Byron standing nearby, looking worried, his hair sleep-rumpled. His clothes had that hastily put-on look.

Andrea followed Melissa's glance then focused on her face again and rushed on. "I'm sorry—I'm *so* sorry—"

"Maybe she ought to see a doctor," Byron said.

Again, Melissa shook her head. She'd gotten a scare, and she'd scraped her knees, but she wasn't seriously injured. At home, she'd shower and, if it turned out she'd broken any skin, she could apply antibacterial ointment and bandages.

None of which meant she was going to let the incident pass without comment, however. Yes, she should have watched where she was going, should have looked before sprinting across the alley. Yet that old car *had* been going way too fast.

"Who was driving?" she asked, looking from Byron to Andrea.

A flush of color moved up Byron's neck, and he shoved a hand through his hair.

"*I* was," Andrea said, a mite too quickly. "It's my car."

Melissa wasn't convinced that Andrea had been behind the wheel, but she'd made her point, and no laws had been broken, after all. She bent to pull the torn fabric of her sweatpants away from her knees, and the burning sensation made her wince.

Byron started to move, hesitated, and then took a resolute step toward her. "You might be hurt," he said.

A swift and wholly unexpected rage swelled within Melissa in that moment, stealing her breath away, no doubt triggered by the near miss she'd just had. Her mind flashed on the photos of Chavonne Rowan's small, broken body, taken at the medical examiner's office in Flagstaff. And those images were still vivid in her recollection; as if she'd seen them only moments before.

You might be hurt.

Hurt, indeed. The way Chavonne had been *hurt?*

"At least let us give you a ride home," Andrea pleaded, her expressive eyes brimming. "Please?"

Melissa paused, then nodded. Her house wasn't far away, but the rain was coming down harder now, and the flesh on her knees burned and she felt mildly sick to her stomach.

Byron didn't actually take her arm, though that had probably been his original intention. Instead, he just sort of herded her toward Andrea's car, opening the heavy door on the passenger side and waiting for her to get in. Andrea scrambled behind the wheel.

Melissa noticed that Andrea had to scoot the seat forward to reach the gas and brake pedals, but she didn't remark on it. She noticed a *lot* of things—being detail-oriented was part of her nature as well as her job—but even so, she tended to take most observations with a grain of salt. It was too easy to jump to conclusions.

Andrea's car was practically a relic, she reminded herself, and it was possible that the seat had to be adjusted every time she sat in it. Big John had owned an old rattletrap of a work truck like that once, back in the day. The seat had had a mind of its own and needed constant adjustment.

Andrea tightened her grip on the steering wheel and glanced at the rearview as Byron got into the back.

Melissa, understandably distracted, finally got it then. Byron had spent the night with Andrea, in her little apartment over the Crockett sisters' garage, and *whoever* had been driving had been in a hurry because neither of them wanted the elderly ladies to know about the rendezvous. Chances were, Velda wouldn't be thrilled that her son had pulled an all-nighter, either, especially so soon after getting out of jail.

It was no wonder the kids were rattled. They'd nearly flattened the county prosecutor under the front wheels.

"I'll be at work on time," Andrea told her boss a couple of minutes later, as she pulled the car to a stop at Melissa's front gate.

"Fine," Melissa said, shoving open her door to climb out. Since she was in good shape, it surprised her to discover that she was stiff all over, sore and achy.

Byron got out, too, and stood waiting on the sidewalk, the rain making his hair curl, watching her intently.

Melissa felt a sudden need to reassure him. Maybe it was that he looked so young, standing there, and so vulnerable, a regular Lost Boy.

"You did a great job with the yard," she said.

"Thanks," he said, and she realized he was waiting to walk her to her front door.

Melissa waved to Andrea and turned to go through the gate, only to find Byron one step ahead, holding it open for her. Her skeptical side—after all, she was a prosecuting attorney—warned her not to be too trusting. Being softhearted too often translated to being soft-*headed,* in her experience.

It might well be true that Byron was basically a good kid who'd made a serious mistake and paid the price for it. On the other hand, he could be putting on an act. The next drug fix, the next tragedy, might be right around the corner.

Rain slid off the roof over Melissa's porch, and she and Byron ducked through, like people passing beneath a waterfall.

Melissa wore her door key on a chain around her neck when she ran, and she pulled it out through the neck of her sweatshirt then, her hand still slightly unsteady. She'd gotten a powerful jolt of adrenaline a little while before, and it hadn't completely subsided.

Gently, Byron took the key from her hand, inserted it into the lock and opened the door for her, handed the key back when she turned on the threshold to meet his gaze.

"I'm sorry," he said hoarsely.

Melissa nodded. "Be more careful next time," she said.

He nodded. "You're sure you'll be okay?"

"I'm sure," Melissa replied, because she was. Growing up on a working ranch, she'd been thrown by horses and stepped on by cows. She'd fallen out of hay mows and off the backs of trucks and tractors, all with relatively little damage.

By comparison, this was nothing.

"Byron?" she ventured.

He still looked miserable. "Yeah."

"Choose your friends carefully. Nathan Carter is bad news, in case you've forgotten."

Byron absorbed that, his face pale and taut. "Right now," he answered, quietly and at some length, "I can't afford to be that picky. A guy needs friends, and right now, Andrea and Nathan are the only ones I have."

Sadness pinched the back of Melissa's throat. She said nothing more, but simply nodded in response to Byron's words.

Fifteen minutes later, having showered and gingerly dried herself off with little dabbing motions of her towel, she'd forgotten the brief conversation entirely. There were small cuts on both her knees, but they weren't deep, and the bleeding had stopped. The rest of her body felt bruised, though, as if she'd actually been struck by Andrea's car.

After bundling herself into a robe, she padded along the hallway to the kitchen, whipped up her protein smoothie, and gulped down a couple of over-the-counter pain pills with the first sip. In another few minutes, she told herself, watching dully as water sheeted down outside of the window over the sink, she'd be right as—well—rain.

Dressing took twice as long as usual, since every motion made some joint or muscle ache, but Melissa remained undaunted. She got herself into a pink-floral print skirt and a long white sweater, summer-light, and flicked on a few swipes of mascara and lip gloss.

Between the rain and her recent shower, her hair had frizzed out, and she was in no mood to spend half an hour taming it with a blow-dryer and a brush, so she clamped the stuff into a loose roll at the back of her head with an enormous plastic clip and called it good.

Tendrils drifted down around her cheeks and her neck—the look was softer than her usual tailored approach, more Ashley's style than her own, but it pleased her, nonetheless.

While she was inside, the rain had stopped, and the sun was out, bright as polished brass.

When Melissa limped into her office, just before nine, Andrea was already there, standing in the middle of the floor like a sentinel and grasping a plain glass vase containing a huge bouquet of purple and white irises, most likely appropriated from the Crockett sisters' garden, in both hands.

"These are for you," Andrea said anxiously.

Melissa smiled, took the flowers and started to go around the nervous young woman, toward her own office. "Thanks, Andrea," she said. "But you shouldn't have. It really wasn't necessary."

"You could have been badly hurt," Andrea burst out, "or even—"

Melissa paused, frowning. "I'm *all right*, Andrea."

Andrea's eyes clouded over with tears. "I know you

think—you think Byron was driving this morning, and that I'm covering for him, because of what happened before, to that girl, Chavonne. But *I* was behind the wheel, not Byron."

Melissa sighed, continued into her office and set the vase of flowers carefully on a corner of her desk.

They really were beautiful, dewy and vibrantly colored.

"What you do in your personal life is none of my business," she said, looking at the irises instead of Andrea. They'd both learned a lesson; now, it was time to move on.

"But—?" Andrea prompted, without inflection. Clearly, she wasn't ready to let the subject drop. Melissa, on the other hand, would have preferred to pretend that it hadn't happened.

"You've come a long way since your foster-home days, Andrea," Melissa replied, after drawing in and expelling a deep breath. "I hope you won't throw all that away by doing anything foolish."

Andrea blushed miserably. "Like going out with Byron Cahill?"

"I didn't say that," Melissa pointed out.

"You didn't have to," Andrea said. Still, there was no anger in her tone or her expression.

Melissa rested a hand on the young woman's forearm. "Okay, for what it's worth, here's my opinion. Byron has to be going through some major adjustments right now. He has a lot to deal with, and so do you. Maybe it would be better to let the dust settle a little before you get too—involved."

Andrea tensed slightly. "Because he was in prison."

"Partly, yes," Melissa answered. "And partly because both of you are young."

"Right," Andrea said, her tone turning crisp as she turned on one heel to leave Melissa's office. "I'll get your messages."

Bemused, and still aching all over from the tumble she'd taken into the gravel that morning, Melissa put her purse away, sat down in her chair and booted up her computer.

A tap at the framework of her open door alerted her to Tom's presence. Melissa smiled, and even *that* hurt a little.

Tom glanced in Andrea's direction and then came inside Melissa's office and closed the door.

"We've got trouble," he said. His tone was solemn.

Melissa looked up at him, her smile a thing of the past. "Sit down, Tom," she said.

But he shook his head. "I've had a complaint from Ashley and Jack's neighbors," he told her. "About the guests. Since it's sort of a—delicate matter, I wanted to run the report by you before I go over there."

Melissa closed her eyes for a moment. Dammit, that bunch of geriatric outlaws were running around naked again, and this time, someone had seen them.

She did *not* need this.

The B&B should have been Ashley's problem, not hers.

Tom cleared his throat, and his expression was diplomatic. His eyes twinkled, though, and he wasn't in any rush to state his business, it seemed to Melissa. "They're disturbing the peace," he said.

Melissa rolled her eyes. *"Disturbing the peace?"*

"Apparently, they're playing the stereo at top volume.

Practicing the tango on the back patio." Tom drew in a breath, his eyes still dancing with amusement. "The Crockett sisters are worried that the noise will scare their fish."

"Their *fish?*"

"You know. Those fancy goldfish they have."

"And this is *my* problem because—?"

"Well," Tom said, "because Ashley and Jack left you in charge of the B&B, for all intents and purposes. I thought you'd want to know what was going on."

"Good heavens," Melissa said.

Tom chuckled. "I'm fixing to go on over there and have a word with those good folks, of course," he went on. "I'm sure they don't mean any harm. You can come along or stay here—your choice."

Melissa groaned as the weight of twin responsibility settled on her shoulders. "I'd better go with you."

Tom nodded. "That would probably be a good idea," he allowed, his mouth twitching at one corner, "but maybe I should go in first, just in case."

"Just in case what?" Melissa asked, feeling testy. The over-the-counter pain pills she'd taken with her morning smoothie, before leaving home, were taking the edge off, but that was about it. "Last I heard, the tango wasn't dangerous. Not for spectators, at least."

Tom gave her a wry look as he opened the office door and waited for her to step through before following.

Andrea was just rising from her chair, the usual handful of pink phone messages clutched in one hand. She looked pale, and there were faint shadows under her eyes.

"Anything important?" Melissa asked, with a glance at the messages.

"I'm not sure," Andrea admitted. "There was a call from a woman complaining that one of her neighbors is buying too much toilet paper—way more than anybody needs, especially when they live alone."

Melissa frowned, puzzled.

But Tom gave a chuckle and a low whistle that brought the faithful Elvis click-click-clicking down the hallway from his master's office on canine toenails and said, "Sounds like the same old controversy Aunt Ona has to deal with every year when rodeo time rolls around."

"Mr. Creed called, too," Andrea added, while Melissa was still pondering Tom's cryptic remark. "I guess he didn't have your home number. Anyway, he said he and Matt really enjoyed supper last night and they'd like to reciprocate as soon as possible."

Melissa blushed slightly. "Okay," she said, avoiding Andrea's gaze. She could actually *feel* Tom's grin, though she didn't look at him, either.

"We'll be back in a while," Tom explained to Andrea.

Out of the corner of her eye, Melissa saw Andrea nod before turning and going back to her own desk.

Moments later, Tom, Melissa and Elvis were in the squad car.

Melissa flipped through the messages to make sure there was nothing urgent, then shoved them into her purse. All except for the toilet paper concern, of course.

The caller, not surprisingly, had been Bea Brady, one of the more vocal members of the Parade Committee. She'd spoken up during the meeting out at Creekside Academy, Melissa remembered.

"Some people," she said, with a long sigh, "have *way* too much free time."

Tom's mouth quirked at one corner. Elvis, meanwhile, sat in the middle of the backseat, behind the metal grill. "I suppose you realize," he said dryly, "that there are a few people around Stone Creek who'd say that about us. The big joke down at the barbershop is that I don't even need to load my service revolver—I can just carry a single bullet around in my shirt pocket, like Barney Fife."

A giggle escaped Melissa, in spite of everything, but when she spoke, she was utterly serious. "Sometimes I think I'm in the wrong line of work," she admitted, surprising herself as well as Tom.

Tom, already signaling to turn onto Ashley's street, cast a quizzical glance in her direction. "Really?" he asked. "You worked pretty hard to earn that law degree and pass the bar exam and then build a resume. What would you do if you weren't a lawyer?"

As the alley between the Crocketts' and the B&B came into focus, toward the end of the block, cell memory must have kicked in, because Melissa felt the impact of her fall all over again, as if it had just happened.

"Interesting question," she murmured in response. Before the breakup, she and Dan had agreed on a general plan: she would take a few years off from her career when she felt ready, help raise his two boys, have at least one baby, try out some of the domestic arts, like cooking and decorating, à la Ashley. "And I don't think I know the answer."

And that was probably the whole problem, she reflected. She not only didn't know what she would do if she didn't practice law, she didn't know who she would *be*.

She'd been so sure that she loved Dan, wanted to make a life with him, but when it came time to set a date and to actually *get married*, Melissa had panicked. Dan, who'd been patient for a long time, had been coldly furious, and then he'd delivered an ultimatum; she had forty-eight hours to make a decision, one way or the other: marry him, or call it quits.

Melissa hadn't needed forty-eight hours, or even forty-eight *seconds*.

She'd called it quits.

Of course, she'd expected Dan to come around in a day or two—a week at the longest—with flowers and sweet talk, the way he had every other time they'd ever disagreed about anything, large or small, but that time was different. There was no soft music, no steamy makeup sex, no anything. Within a week, in fact, Dan was dating a waitress, the woman he'd since married.

"Well," Tom said, drawing the cruiser to a stop in front of the B&B. "We're here."

"Yes," Melissa said, squinting her eyes and peering at the front of her sister and brother-in-law's gracious house. "Let's get this over with."

Tom chuckled, unfastened his seat belt and got out of the car. Reaching the sidewalk, he opened Melissa's door for her, then released Elvis from the back.

Even from where they stood, the sounds of merriment coming from behind the house were clearly audible. There was spritely guitar music, laughter, cheering and loud, enthusiastic applause.

"Damn," Melissa muttered, shaking her head, as Tom

opened the front gate and waited for her to walk through ahead of him.

"You can wait here if you want to," Tom offered, as Elvis trotted happily ahead, nose to the ground.

"It isn't as if I've never seen a naked man before, you know," she said.

Tom laughed. "Huh?"

Unwittingly, she'd just revealed her secret fear: that the B&B guests were naked again. "You know what I meant," Melissa replied, with a little snap to her tone.

Tom remained amused. "By the way," he went on, "what's the matter with you? You flinched every time I took a corner on the way over here, and I'd swear you're limping a little."

He'd taken the lead, following the walk that ran alongside the house and into the backyard with its high fences and sheltering trees, but he looked over his shoulder at her as he spoke.

Melissa raised and lowered her shoulders. Carefully. "I took a little spill when I was running this morning," she said. "It's no big deal."

Elvis, having reached the backyard, began to bark. The sound was the purest joy, and Melissa had to smile.

Tom stopped in his tracks as soon as he'd rounded the far corner of the house, and Melissa, bringing up the rear, almost collided with him.

"I'll be damned," he murmured.

She peeked around him.

And there was the Wild Bunch, the men dressed like matadors, except for their hats, the women in flamenco outfits and holding roses in their teeth, tangoing like mad across the wide stone patio.

The music, pouring from a boom box, was deafening.

Elvis stood near the edge of the patio, a delighted witness to the festivities, barking his brains out as he followed the action.

Spotting Melissa and Tom, John Winthrop hurried over to crank down the volume on the boom box. He was wearing one of those round hats trimmed with tiny pom-poms.

The other man in the group finished up the dance by dipping his partner.

Melissa, more impressed than she would have admitted to Tom Parker or anyone else, could only assume that osteoporosis wasn't an issue in this particular crowd.

Tom cleared his throat, then summoned Elvis to his side.

Melissa stepped up next to him, concentrating on one thing. Not laughing.

"Why, it's Melissa," said Mr. Winthrop, beaming, taking off his hat and bowing deeply. "How nice to see you again!"

"That's quite a costume," Melissa said.

"Rented," Mr. Winthrop replied. He drew in a deep, robust breath and let it out in a whoosh. "We got to talking about our trip to Spain—we went three years ago—and I guess we got a little carried away by all the memories."

"There's no costume-rental place in Stone Creek," Tom said, sounding suspicious.

"We called a shop in Flagstaff," Winthrop explained jovially. "They were kind enough to deliver."

"Oh," Tom replied, clearly at a loss.

"The neighbors are complaining about the music," Melissa told the gang. "It was too loud."

The women looked annoyed. The men were crestfallen. Melissa felt like the original wet blanket.

"Well, I guess there's no harm done," Tom allowed. "If you'll all just keep the noise down a little, everybody will be happy."

"Not everybody," said the woman in the in the red dress, trailing ruffles behind her and fiddling with the Spanish comb in her hair.

"We'll behave," Mr. Winthrop promised.

The woman in the red dress harrumphed, arms folded.

"Fair enough," Tom said agreeably.

By then, Melissa was wondering why she'd come along on this mission, since Tom didn't seem to need her help. If asked, she would have said it had seemed like a good idea at the time.

She smiled apologetically at the croquet/tango team. Winced when Tom took a light grip on her arm.

"That does it," he said to Melissa, as they walked away, Elvis ambling along behind them. "I'm taking you over to the clinic in Indian Rock."

Melissa sighed. "I'm just fine," she protested. "In fact, I was thinking I might like to try the tango—"

Tom flashed her a grin as he opened the door of the squad car for her and helped her to ease inside. "No way," he said.

"Why not?"

"Because," Tom said, with a wicked light in his eyes, "it takes two to tango, and I'll have no part of it, thank you very much."

Melissa groaned. "That was *such* a bad joke," she said.

But then she laughed.

Tom turned serious. "I still think you should see a doctor. I could run you over to the clinic in Indian Rock in no time—"

"I'm *fine,* Tom," she insisted. "And I'm not going anywhere but back to the office."

Tom didn't answer until he'd gotten behind the wheel again. "Not much going on there," he observed. "Andrea can probably hold down the fort. Why not stay home for the rest of the day, if you won't go to the doctor, and take it easy?" He indicated her purse with a nod of his head and another grin. "You could take care of all those phone messages. Reassure Bea Brady that you won't allow the toilet-paper contingent to get out of hand when it comes time to decorate the floats for the big parade. Tell Steven Creed you're hot for him and he's welcome to come by for supper anytime."

Melissa punched her old friend in the arm. *"I'm going back to work,"* she told her friend. "If I have to feel lousy, I might as well do it at the office as at home and, besides, my car is there."

"Never argue with a lawyer," Tom sighed, heading for the center of town.

"Maybe I *will* invite Steven over for supper again, though," she said, after musing a while. "Care to join us?"

Tom pulled the cruiser into the usual parking spot behind the courthouse and looked over at her. "I smell a setup," he said.

CHAPTER NINE

MELISSA GOT OUT OF THE SQUAD car, opened the back door for Elvis, who leaped nimbly to the ground, and semi-hobbled toward the side entrance to the brick courthouse. Tom's words echoed in her brain.

I smell a setup, he'd said, when she'd invited him to supper, moments before.

"You have a suspicious mind, Tom Parker," she accused.

"Part of the job," Tom admitted, holding open the heavy glass door for her.

It occurred to Melissa then, as it might have to Tom as well, that it was a shame their relationship had always been platonic. They'd have made a good couple, she guessed, but there was no spark on either side. Hanging out with Sheriff Parker was like being with her brother, Brad—easy, low-key and *safe*.

Keeping company with Steven, on the other hand, had the same charge as bungee jumping off a high bridge or riding a unicycle across the Grand Canyon on a tightrope.

"Taking risks is a part of your job, too," Melissa replied briskly, as they moved—man, woman and dog— along the corridor. "But when it comes to romance, you're nothing but a coward."

"So it *was* a setup," Tom said, with a note of triumph. "I knew it."

"I might have been thinking of asking Tessa Quinn to join us," Melissa answered, as they reached the outer door of her offices.

Melissa O'Ballivan, Prosecutor, read the faux-metal sign affixed to it.

She waited out a small rush of frustration. Once, she'd loved her work. Now, she was just marking time, it seemed, waiting for someone to break the law, so she could try them in court. Was that any way to live?

Tom frowned down at her, though there was a be-nevolent light in his eyes. "I'm looking forward to a platterful of Ashley's spare ribs," he said.

"You haven't won yet," Melissa pointed out. "In fact, the way you're dragging your feet—you've had plenty of time to ask Tessa out, it seems to me—you're looking more and more like the new chairman of the Parade Committee with every passing moment."

"I'll ask her," Tom said.

"Fine," Melissa retorted. "Let's see some action here. I'm not going to let you drag this bet out until we're all old and gray."

He huffed out a loud sigh. "Here's an idea," he said. "Why don't you just run *your* love life, O'Ballivan, and let me run mine?"

Melissa didn't have a reply ready, since neither of them actually had a love life, so she pushed open the office door and stepped inside, leaving Tom and Elvis in the corridor.

"As far as I'm concerned, the bet is off," Tom called after her.

"You wish," Melissa called back.

Andrea, though puffy-eyed, looked as though she'd rallied while Melissa was away. She smiled, pushed back her chair and hurried into the tiny break room, returning moments later with a steaming cup of coffee.

The fragrance was tantalizing.

"I made it myself," Andrea said, sweeping past her, into the inner office, and setting the cup down on Melissa's desk.

"I thought making coffee was against your principles," Melissa said lightly, extracting the stack of messages from her purse before putting the bag away in its usual cubbyhole.

"You're the one who said it wasn't in my job description," Andrea said.

Melissa smiled. "Nevertheless, Andrea," she replied, with a touch of irony that was probably lost on her assistant, "*thank you* for making the coffee. Did anyone call or stop by while I was out?"

For a fraction of a second, Andrea looked almost coy. "Mr. Creed was here," the girl responded. "About fifteen or twenty minutes ago."

Melissa's heart raced, though she was all-business on the outside.

Or so she hoped, anyway.

She sat down, reached for the cup, took a sip of coffee before saying anything at all. "Oh? Did he say what he wanted?"

Be casual.

"Lunch," Andrea said.

Lunch—an ordinary enough concept. When connected with Steven Creed, however, even the suggestion gave her that runaway roller-coaster feeling again.

Melissa merely nodded. She fanned the phone

messages out on the surface of her desk, just to give herself something to do.

"I could get Mr. Creed on the phone for you," Andrea offered, her tone eager, almost breathless.

Melissa didn't look up from the messages. "I'll do that myself, Andrea," she said. "But thank you."

"He's pretty hot," Andrea commented.

Melissa sighed. Agreeing that Steven was hot would have been like agreeing that the sky was blue.

Andrea hurried out of the office and closed the door behind her.

Melissa picked up the telephone handset, squinted at the written message with Steven's name on it and dialed.

While she waited, a miniature *Cirque de Soleil* sprang to life in the pit of her stomach, performing death-defying spins and leaps and dives.

This was ridiculous. Maybe Steven Creed was attractive—okay, he was *definitely* attractive—but he was a mortal man, not a Greek god, for heaven's sake.

Then again, that was the problem, wasn't it? He was *all* man—*too much* man—maybe even more man than she could handle.

As if.

"Steven Creed," he said suddenly, startling Melissa. She realized she hadn't actually expected him to answer the call—she'd planned on leaving a message. Counted, inexplicably, on that little buffer of time.

"H-Hello," she responded, all but croaking the word. *Get a grip,* she told herself silently. *You're a grown woman, dammit, not a teenager.*

"Melissa?"

"Yes." She cleared her throat. Squeezed her eyes shut

tight. "It's me. I'm sorry—I was planning to answer your call earlier, but then something came up and I had to leave the office and—"

"I just wanted to invite you to lunch," Steven said, with a smile in his voice, when she bogged down in the middle of her sentence. She'd have sworn he knew how rattled she was, and that only made her more so. "I'll understand, of course, if you're busy or something. It's pretty short notice."

Say you're busy, advised Melissa's inner chicken little. *He gave you an out.*

"I'm not busy," she said aloud.

"Great," Steven responded. "Meet you at the Sunflower Café at noon?"

Melissa checked her watch. It was quarter after eleven, so she had forty-five minutes to pull herself together. "Perfect," she said, sounding way more perky than she considered necessary.

Her "perky" quota was normally zero. Add Steven Creed to the equation, though, and she was about as sedate as a middle-school cheerleader at the first big game of the season.

"See you then," Steven said. "Bye."

"Bye," Melissa said, a few seconds after he'd hung up.

She took several sips of her rapidly cooling coffee, then squared her shoulders, raised her chin and started answering the messages Andrea had given her earlier.

A big believer in tackling the least appealing task first, she dialed Bea Brady's number. The older woman answered on the second ring, but not with a hello, or her name, the way most people would have done.

"It's about time you called me back, Melissa O'Ballivan!" she snapped, instead.

Melissa's temper surged, nearly breaking the surface of her professional composure, but she managed a pleasant tone when she replied. "I'm at work, Bea," she said. "Parade Committee business should probably be handled after hours."

"How do you know I'm calling about the parade?" Bea demanded, every bit as surly as before.

Melissa reread the message, hoping she'd transcribed Andrea's handwriting correctly. "It says here that you're concerned about someone purchasing toilet paper?"

"Adelaide Hillingsley bought a *truck load* of the stuff at one of those box stores in Flagstaff," Bea blurted. "She lives by herself. There's only one bathroom in her house. What would *one woman* be doing with so much tissue if she didn't plan on flouting the rules and using it to decorate the Chamber of Commerce float for the parade?"

Melissa closed her eyes, sat back in her chair and counted mentally until she was sure she wouldn't laugh. Adelaide *was* a force to be reckoned with; although she'd originally been hired as a receptionist, she'd been running the organization for years.

"Maybe you should ask Adelaide about that, Bea," Melissa said, when she dared to speak at all. "Since it's *committee business* and I'm at work—"

"Oh, don't give me that, Melissa O'Ballivan," Bea broke in. "Everybody knows you don't have anything to do most of the time anyway!"

Melissa counted again, but this time it was to keep from yelling.

"I beg your pardon?" she said, when she'd reached the double digits.

Bea backed off a little. "I didn't mean that the way it sounded," she conceded. She was a nice person, despite being a bit on the pushy side—as president of the local Garden Club, and an old-line Stone Creeker, she was used to being in charge, getting things done, that was all.

"I'm glad," Melissa said pleasantly, thinking the other woman's remark might not have stung so much if it wasn't so damn true.

"You'll speak to Adelaide? Remind her that the Parade Committee specifically voted *never* to use toilet paper in the construction of a float? It would be so tacky—"

"I'll talk to Adelaide," Melissa said, because she had other calls to make and she needed to move on to the next one. None of them were any more important or pressing than this one but, still. She *was* drawing a paycheck, and she was on county time.

"When? When will you talk to her?"

Melissa's cuts and bruises tuned up again, all at once, in a dull, throbbing chorus. "Tonight," she said. "Maybe tomorrow. But *soon,* Bea. I promise."

In those moments, Melissa went from wishing Tom would win their bet to wishing he'd *lose* and take over the Parade Committee.

Fat chance.

Bea was silent for a beat or two, but then she huffed out a sigh. "All right," she said. "But you mark my words, Melissa. Stone Creek will be the laughingstock of the whole state of Arizona if Adelaide has her way." She paused to sputter indignantly, then finished with

"*Toilet paper,* for heaven's sake. That woman is *obsessed* with toilet paper."

Melissa bit the inside of her lower lip as a means of corralling the obvious response —that Adelaide wasn't the *only* one with an obsession—before promising to attend to the matter at the first opportunity.

By the time she'd made the remaining calls, noon had rolled around and it was time to meet Steven for lunch over at the Sunflower Café. Because the small restaurant was close, and she thought the walk might be a remedy for some of her soreness, let alone her frustrations, she decided to leave her car at the office.

She and Steven arrived at the same time.

"I like the look," he said, taking in her skirt and sweater with a slow sweep of his eyes as they stood on the sidewalk in front of the café.

She let that pass. "Where's Matt?"

One side of his mouth kicked up in a grin. He looked better than good in his white shirt and well-fitting blue jeans. "At day camp," he replied, with a grin dancing in his eyes. "I spent the morning with an architect from Flagstaff. I'd like to have the house finished and the new barn up by fall."

Melissa looked down at the community dog dish, filled with clear water, and stopped just short of asking about Zeke.

Steven smiled again, opened the door for her, and held it wide. "Zeke's at home," he said, evidently reading her mind. "And he's fine."

It was disconcerting, the way this man could guess what she was thinking. What if he figured out that, even against her better judgment, just being around him made her want his body? She looked away quickly.

The café was crowded, as it usually was at that time of day, but Tessa seated them right away, at a corner table.

Melissa immediately reached for a menu, although her stomach was doing that nervous thing again.

"I had a great time last night, Melissa," Steven said. "So did Matt."

She looked at him over the top of her menu. Blinked once. It should have been easy to come up with an answer—so why wasn't it?

"I'm glad," she said, after a long time.

Steven didn't take the other menu, which was tucked between the napkin holder and the salt and pepper shakers. He just sat there, across the table, within touching distance, looking all warm-eyed and amused. "I'm glad you're glad," he teased, lowering his voice and leaning forward slightly.

She blushed then, because the way his eyes caressed her made her feel as naked as any of the croquet-playing oldsters she'd seen in Ashley's backyard the other day. They were in a very public place, she and Steven, but, even though they'd already drawn their share of glances, the Sunflower was so full of noisy good cheer that no one could have overheard their conversation—although a few people were sure to try.

"The club sandwich is very good here," she said helpfully, giving the menu a little wriggle. "So is the beef stew."

Steven smiled at her again.

Tingly waves of—*something* rippled under her skin.

"Okay," he said, his tone husky.

Melissa gave him a level look. "Lunch?" she reminded him.

"Supper, too, I hope," he said, without missing a beat. "Six o'clock? My place?"

Her heartbeat quickened. "Your place?" she repeated stupidly.

"I'm afraid Matt won't be there, though," Steven said, sounding mildly rueful. "Meg and Brad invited him to sleep over tonight. He and Mac are already great buddies."

Melissa swallowed. If Matt wasn't going to be home, of course they would be alone, she and Steven Creed.

Say no, warned her practical side. *You know what could happen, and you're not ready for that.*

"Isn't this a school night?" she asked.

Wow. She was a veritable genius when it came to small talk.

"Matt goes to day camp," Steven pointed out, after indulging in another of those slow, lethal grins. "Not Harvard."

"Oh," Melissa said.

"Are you coming, or not?"

She blushed again. Had he worded the question that way on purpose? "It's a little soon," she said.

"For what?" Steven asked, clearly enjoying her discomfort.

"You know damn well *for what,*" Melissa told him. She'd lost patience with herself by then. All this waffling was so unlike her—she was a direct person.

His blue eyes twinkled with mischief. And the promise of sweet, hot, languid things. "Do I?" he drawled. And then he reached out, took the menu from her hands, and set it aside. Closed his fingers around hers.

"Yes," Melissa whispered. "You do."

Just then, Tessa reappeared, pen and order pad in hand. "What'll it be?" she asked, smiling at both of them.

Steven ordered the club sandwich.

Melissa opted for beef stew, even though it was a warm day.

Still smiling, Tessa nodded and turned away.

"You were saying?" Steven grinned. He hadn't let go of Melissa's hand; indeed, he ran the pad of his thumb over her knuckles, very lightly.

Flames shot through her. "I forget."

"Liar."

"It's too soon," Melissa reiterated. There was something feverish in her tone.

"Are you trying to convince yourself, or me?"

"Steven, *stop it.*"

Tessa came back with their drinks then—both of them had ordered iced tea.

"You're okay, aren't you?" Tessa asked, giving Melissa much closer scrutiny than before. "Somebody at the counter just told me you were almost hit by a car this morning, while you were out for your run."

Small towns. Every incident, no matter how small, was grist for the mill.

"Just a little shaken up," Melissa said, aware of the change in Steven's face even though she wasn't looking directly at him just then. His grip tightened around her hand. "It was no big deal, Tessa. A miss is as good as a mile and all that."

"It could have been a *very* big deal," Tessa protested. "Did you see a doctor?"

"Tessa," Melissa said, with a smile and a shake of her head, "*I'm fine*. Really."

Tessa hesitated for another moment or so, then turned and walked away.

"You were almost run over by a car?" Steven asked. He was holding both her hands by then. And he no longer looked amused.

People were watching them.

Jumping to all kinds of conclusions.

She could *feel* it.

"I wasn't hurt," she insisted. It bothered her, how much she was enjoying his concern.

"What happened?" Steven asked.

"*Nothing*," Melissa answered. "That's why the word *almost* comes into play."

His fine jawline tightened briefly, relaxed again.

"Let's talk about something else besides accidents that didn't quite happen," she suggested, hoping to lighten the mood.

The grin was back, and it was as dangerous as ever. "Like what?"

"Well, not sex," Melissa said, and then regretted it.

He laughed. "I agree," he said. "It's better to just go ahead and *do* some things, rather than wasting time talking about them."

Melissa blinked. "Did you just say what I think you just said?" she demanded, whispering again. Leaning toward him.

"You were the one who brought up the subject of sex," Steven pointed out reasonably. "Not me."

He looked so damnably comfortable, sitting there, easy in his skin, with his glass of iced tea in front of him and his eyes that indescribable shade of blue-violet.

"Then I'm officially *un*bringing it up," Melissa said. "Forget I mentioned sex at all. It was totally inappropriate. A slip of the tongue—"

His grin flashed again.

She blushed even more. "I didn't mean—"

Mercifully, the food arrived then.

Since her stomach was still doing the circus thing, Melissa was surprised to realize that she was hungry. She picked up her spoon and focused on the delicious beef stew.

"What do you like to do, Melissa?" Steven asked, about midway through the meal. He'd made a pretty good dent in his club sandwich, and pushed away his plate to focus all his attention on her.

The feeling that gave her was exciting, in an unsettling sort of way. She was an attractive woman, and she knew it, but like many people, she felt invisible a lot of the time. "Do?" she echoed, confused. "I work. I read. And I jog."

"How do you feel about horses?"

"I grew up on a ranch," Melissa answered. "I rode a lot when I was younger. Not so much lately." And until she'd gotten over the effects of that morning's spill, she wouldn't be climbing into any saddles, thank you very much.

"I spent summers on the family ranch up in Colorado when I was a kid," he said. "Riding was about my favorite thing."

A picture flashed in Melissa's mind—she could imagine Steven as he must have looked growing up. That thatch of brownish-gold hair, those eyes, full of mischief. And probably a smattering of freckles, too.

"Just summers?" she asked. "Where did you live the rest of the time?"

"Boston." That was all. Just "Boston." And the way he said it was clipped, almost abrupt.

"I've been there a few times," Melissa said. "To Boston, I mean. It's a great city. I especially love the Common, and the swan boats."

Steven relaxed then, but Melissa saw that it took an effort, and that made her wonder what the rest of the Creeds were like, specifically his parents. She'd met the Montana branch of the family—Logan, Dylan and Tyler—when they visited their McKettrick cousins on the Triple M, over near Indian Rock. Those three hadn't had the easiest of childhoods, that was for sure, but they'd turned out to be fine men.

It had been Melissa's experience that some adversity made a person strong. She and Ashley, and certainly Brad and Olivia, were proof of that. Their mother, Delia, had abandoned them at a young age, and later on their dad, the classic man of few words but nonetheless the most solid presence in their lives, had been killed.

"Once my grandfather and my mother were both gone," Steven said, "that left my uncles running the show. Boston sort of lost its charm then."

It was a lot to absorb, and the café, however pleasant, surely wasn't the best place to discuss the things they were obviously destined to discuss.

Melissa figured things were getting too heavy. "Are we going to build our friendship around food, Steven Creed?" she asked. "We seem to be sharing quite a few meals these days."

Steven caught Tessa's eye, silently asking for the check.

Looking at Melissa again, he smiled. "I want to spend more time with you," he said forthrightly. "And out here in the countryside, that seems to include breaking bread together."

One of the waitresses brought the bill, since Tessa was busy with a fresh crop of customers, and Steven paid it on the spot, shook his head when the young girl asked if he wanted change.

Heads turned as they left the restaurant, as they had when Melissa and Steven came in, but Melissa was used to that. Stone Creek was, after all, barely more than a wide spot in the road, even a century and a half after the first settlers arrived.

"Thanks for lunch," she told Steven, when they were standing on the sidewalk again.

He looked around, probably for her car. "I could give you a ride back to work," he offered. "My truck is just around the corner."

Melissa smiled. "That's okay," she said. "The walk will be good for me."

Steven didn't look convinced of that, but he didn't argue, either.

"I'll be expecting you around six," he said.

She nodded, wondering precisely when she'd gone around the bend. She decided it must have happened when she got her first look at Steven Creed, because she'd certainly been sane before that.

The hike back to the office was a short one, but it didn't make Melissa feel better any more than the walk *over* had done. If she'd been anybody but her stubborn O'Ballivan self, she'd have taken Tom's earlier suggestion, gone home, gulped down something for the pain and climbed into bed.

When she arrived, Adelaide Hillingsley was in the outer office, chatting with Andrea.

"I came about the toilet paper rumor," the middle-aged woman announced forthrightly, as soon as she spotted Melissa. Pudgy, with thin, reddish hair and bright hazel eyes, Adelaide was a cheerful soul, and her family, like Bea's, went way back in Stone Creek's history.

Melissa managed not to roll her eyes, but just barely. Did *anyone* in this town understand that this was the prosecutor's office, not the official headquarters of the Parade Committee?

Resigned, she gestured toward the entrance to her private space.

"Shall I bring in some coffee?" Andrea piped up, all chipper efficiency.

Melissa gave her a look.

"That sounds nice," Adelaide said, sweeping grandly into the inner sanctum. "I'd like mine with a little cream and two sugars, please."

"None for me, thanks," Melissa said, putting a little point on the words. And then she shut the door with a firm push.

Adelaide, dressed in her customary cotton print blouse and elastic-waisted jeans, sat down without waiting for an invitation.

"Someone really should persuade Bea Brady to go straight out and shop for a *life*," she said. "My niece wore a toilet paper *wedding gown* when she got married, and she looked fantastic. The pictures were all over the internet for months afterwards."

Melissa sat down in her desk chair and tried to look serious. "I've gone over the bylaws for the Parade

Committee," she began, with dignity, "and there *is* a ban on using bathroom tissue to decorate floats."

Adelaide waved that off. "What about creativity? What about being resourceful, and the wise use of our funds—which, in case you don't know, are shrinking with every passing year?"

Melissa drew a deep, deep breath and let it out slowly. "Adelaide," she said, "creativity is certainly a good thing. Ditto resourcefulness and good fiscal management. But this is an issue that should be debated within the committee itself—not here, during working hours."

"You've always been such a—lawyer," Adelaide remarked, without rancor.

She looked around, smiling. "I don't see any crooks standing around, waiting to be hauled before a judge."

Melissa allowed herself a small and very diplomatic sigh. She'd been raised to respect her elders and, besides, Adelaide had been her and Ashley's Girl Scout leader when they were kids. She'd mothered them both, after a fashion, after Delia left. "I think that's beside the point, don't you?" she said mildly. "I grant you, this isn't Maricopa County, where the courts see a lot of action, but I'm still sworn to uphold the duties of this office, Adelaide, and I'm determined to do that."

Adelaide gave a responding sigh as Andrea ducked in with fresh coffee for the visitor and handed it over.

"If you wouldn't mind," the young woman said, "I'd like to leave early today. Since things are so quiet and all."

Melissa pressed her back teeth together, but kept smiling. Andrea's timing was priceless. "Go," she said.

Andrea blushed slightly. "It's just that there was a cancellation at the dentist's office today. If I go in for my cleaning now, I won't have to do it Saturday morning."

Melissa glared.

Andrea ducked out.

Adelaide, in no hurry to get back to her receptionist's job, apparently, took a loudly appreciative sip from her coffee cup. "Did anyone mention how grateful we are, Melissa—the members of the Parade Committee, I mean—that you were willing to step in and take over for poor Ona Frame?"

"Now you're just trying to butter me up," Melissa said, smiling again. Irritated though she was, she liked Adelaide Hillingsley, and that was that.

Adelaide cast an eloquent glance toward the place where Andrea had stood just a moment before. "It seems to be the most effective way to deal with you," she replied, looking pleased with herself. "This job has made all the difference in the world to that girl. Heaven only knows what might have happened to her if she hadn't had the good fortune to wind up in Stone Creek."

"Right about now," Melissa confided brightly, "I wouldn't mind throttling her."

Adelaide took another drink of coffee, raised her eyebrows slightly. After swallowing, she ventured thoughtfully, "I hear she's dating that Cahill boy. Seems to me folks ought to be more concerned about *that* than whether or not any of the parade floats are festooned with toilet paper."

Melissa leaned forward in her chair. "The tissue issue," she said, "will have to be settled by the committee. I want no part of it."

"But you're the chairperson," Adelaide said.

Thanks to Tom Parker, Melissa thought.

"I'm also the county prosecutor," she said.

"Then we'd better call a special meeting and settle the matter," Adelaide decided, in her take-charge way. "How does tonight sound? We might be able to get the community room at Creekside Academy, but I'm pretty sure the quilting club's already reserved it and, besides, your place is central."

Here it was, Melissa reflected. An emergency meeting of the Parade Committee. Just the excuse—however thin—she needed to get out of being alone with Steven Creed in the close and luxurious confines of Brad's former tour bus.

Except that she didn't *want* to get out of it, fool that she was.

"I'm afraid I have other plans," she said. "But feel free to call a meeting anyway. Naturally, I'll go along with whatever the rest of you decide, as long as there's a consensus."

"Does this have something to do with that Creed fellow?" Adelaide asked bluntly. There was a twinkle in her eyes. "First supper, then lunch. My, my. It would seem you're over Dan Guthrie at last, and none too soon, either."

"I've been 'over' Dan Guthrie for a long time," Melissa said evenly.

And it was true. She still missed his kids, though. Missed the life she'd *expected* to have.

How crazy was that?

Adelaide gave a girlish giggle, set her coffee cup down on Melissa's desk with a thump, and rose from her chair. "And it's none of my business," she chimed sunnily. "I could get you the instructions for my niece's toilet-paper wedding dress, if you want."

"Thanks," Melissa said. "But I won't be needing one of those real soon." She stood up, too, and walked Adelaide all the way to the corridor.

As soon as Adelaide had trundled off down the hall and outside, into the parking lot, Melissa turned and strode toward Tom's office.

He was sitting at his desk, with his feet up, studying the contents of a manila file folder.

"I resign!" Melissa announced summarily.

"From what?" Tom asked, dropping his feet to the floor and standing.

"From the damn Parade Committee!"

Elvis, sprawled on his side over by the water cooler, gave a concerned little whine.

Tom chuckled. "I never figured you for a quitter," he said, folding his arms.

Melissa knew he was playing her, but her cheeks went hot with indignation anyway. "Well, maybe you'd better just 'figure' *again,* bucko," she snapped.

"'Bucko'?" Tom repeated, grinning now.

"I must have been crazy to let you talk me into this," Melissa ranted on, pacing now. Hugging herself to keep from flinging her arms out wide in frustrated emphasis. "Why can't Bea Brady run the committee? Or Adelaide Hillingsley? They both *give a damn,* after all, which is more than anybody can say for me!"

"Whoa," Tom said. "Calm down, counselor. If Adelaide headed up the project, Bea would raise hell, and vice versa. And for the first time in fifty-odd years, there wouldn't be a parade to kick off Rodeo Days."

"Then *you* do it!" Melissa steamed. With one hand, she made a slashing motion in front of her throat. "I am *not* going to spend the next few weeks arbitrating disputes over toilet paper!"

To his credit, Tom was trying hard not to laugh. He made a clucking sound with his tongue and shook his head.

"Melissa, Melissa," he said. "Stone Creek *needs* you."

CHAPTER TEN

"'*STONE CREEK NEEDS YOU*,'" Melissa muttered to herself, still riled from the conversation with Tom Parker that afternoon, concerning the Parade Committee. It was five-thirty, and she'd already showered, replaced her unaccustomed skirt and sweater with an even *more* unaccustomed black-and-white polka-dot sundress, and spritzed on cologne. "What a load of manipulative crap. And I fell for it!"

In the end, much as she'd love to resign as chairperson, Tom had been right. She wasn't a quitter and that was that.

Melissa studied her image in the mirror on the inside of her closet door and went right on talking to herself. "You're not fooling anybody, Melissa O'Ballivan," she told the reflected woman glowering back at her. "The real reason you're all bent out of shape is that you're about to do something you damn well *know* you shouldn't!"

That something, of course, was spending an evening alone, in a private and relatively small space—with Steven Creed.

The man was a sin sundae, and she was so tempted to dig in.

If she had any sense at all, she chided herself silently,

she'd stay away from him until she stopped feeling quite so—well—*vulnerable*.

All right, it was true that she needed to get out of the house—and out of her own head. And it wasn't as if she didn't have options—Ashley, her favorite confidante, was still out of town, but Olivia would have listened without judging, and Meg, too. Her sister and sister-in-law were smart, savvy women, and if they gave any advice at all, it would be *good* advice.

On the other hand, they were both in committed, loving relationships with men they knew all about, not relative strangers like Steven Creed was to her. By now, they must surely have forgotten what it was like to be in her situation.

Bottom line, she wanted full-frontal contact with the delectable Mr. Creed, and that was that.

And so what if she did? Was that so wrong?

No, she reasoned, arguing the case in the courtroom of her mind, it *wasn't* wrong. Stupid, maybe, and probably shortsighted, but not wrong.

Having gotten exactly nowhere with this inner debate, Melissa slipped on a lightweight cardigan, not because she was cold, but because she had some bruises on her arms from biting the dust that morning, and she didn't want them on display. She found her purse, locked up the house and climbed into her car.

Melissa drove straight to Steven's demolition site of a place and parked behind the house, between two huge, overgrown lilac bushes. Stone Creek Ranch—and thus, Brad and Meg—were just down the road, and she didn't want either one of them to catch a glimpse of the car. A roadster sighting would lead to too many questions, ones she wasn't inclined to answer just yet.

While she was still thinking these thoughts, Steven emerged from the bus, cowboy-perfect in dark jeans and a spiffy white shirt, his hair a little too long and his boots showing just the right amount of wear.

He grinned in greeting.

The dog, Zeke, trotted over to her for a pat on the head.

"I thought you might back out at the last minute," Steven said, standing a few yards away, giving her space, his arms folded.

Melissa, who had been stewing over a variety of injustices ever since she'd left work, launched right in. "Just tell me this," she said, planting her sandaled feet and pressing her knuckles into her hips. "Why is it perfectly all right for a man to want sex and make no bones about it, say so right out, but a single *woman* has to come up with all kinds of reasons and excuses?" Not the most appropriate way to greet the man, she realized in retrospect, but the words had simply burst out of her.

Steven tilted his head to one side, and his grin was wicked, but he still kept his distance.

The scent of lilacs surrounded Melissa in a cloud, making her feel slightly drunk.

"I wouldn't say there were no bones about it," Steven drawled.

Embarrassment bloomed rose-pink in Melissa's cheeks. What was the *matter* with her? When had this—this *alternate personality,* perfumed and wearing a sundress—with a ruffled hem, no less—taken over her fine legal brain and caused her to forsake her tailored wardrobe?

In that moment, she couldn't think of a single sensible thing to say.

Painfully aware that she'd made a fool of herself—again—she actually considered jumping back into her car and zooming out of there. The problem was that just as quitting wasn't part of her constitutional makeup, neither was running away.

So she just stood there, feeling ridiculous.

Where were all her convictions about sex and the modern woman *now?*

Steven's grin softened, and he approached her slowly, the way he might have approached a frightened animal or a baby bird that had fallen from its nest.

When he was standing directly in front of her, he took her elbows into a gentle grip and looked down into her upturned and very flushed face.

"Hey," he said huskily. "You're calling the shots, Melissa. You can say 'now' or you can say 'never.' The whens and the ifs are entirely up to you. Meanwhile, why don't we just spend some time together and see how things go?"

Such a wave of relief passed over Melissa then that she was very glad Steven was holding on to her. If he hadn't been, she thought her knees might have given way.

"Thanks," she said, belatedly, breathing the word more than saying it.

He gave a low chuckle. Inclined his head toward the old dowager of a farmhouse; the paint was peeling away, and the flowerbeds were choked with weeds, but the blowsy old roses, splotches of crimson drooping under their own weight, gave it a singular appeal.

"Want a tour of the house?" he asked.

It was such an ordinary question. Such an innocent

one. Melissa, who had grown up in an old house and loved them for that reason and a few others, nodded.

Steven released her elbows, but immediately took her by the hand, and they walked toward the structure. The last dazzle before twilight turned the thick-glassed windows to pale purple.

They stopped just short of the back door, and Melissa looked up, shielding her eyes with her free hand.

"Don't you wish it could talk?" she asked wistfully.

Steven smiled. "I don't imagine all the folks who've lived here over the last several generations would consider that an entirely good thing," he said.

This man, Melissa thought.

One minute, he had her heart racing and her stomach doing flip-flops.

The next, he was soothing her, just by being who and what he was.

"I suppose not," she agreed. He stepped up onto the small, uncovered porch, and Melissa followed, trusting his lead. Suddenly, it was easy to talk to him. "This house has been here almost as long as ours, you know. The one old Sam O'Ballivan built, I mean."

"Sam O'Ballivan. The Arizona Ranger turned cattle baron."

Melissa nodded, mildly surprised.

"Brad told me a little about him," Steven said. "That's quite a story."

"The man from Stone Creek," Melissa replied, with another nod. "That was our Sam."

By then they'd entered the kitchen, and Melissa gravitated straight to the dusty, wood-burning cookstove in the far corner. "Wow," she said. "I'm surprised some antiques dealer didn't score this a long time ago. My sister Ashley would kill to have it at the B&B. She'd probably even *use* it."

Again, Steven smiled. "I take it Ashley's the domestic type," he said.

Melissa rolled her eyes. "You can say that again. That was her cooking we had last night at supper, remember. *My* culinary repertoire is limited to deli salads and stuff from the freezer aisle at the supermarket."

"Mine isn't much better, I'm afraid," he told her. Sunlight streamed in through a dusty window and cast an aura around him. "We're having meat loaf tonight, you and I, but it's takeout from the Sunflower Café. Matt will probably be blown away by supper over at Brad and Meg's place—a decent meal, for once."

Melissa left the stove, overwhelmed by a strange, swift tenderness unlike anything she'd ever felt before.

She swallowed. So much for his being easy to talk to.

"I think you take very good care of Matt," she said quietly.

"I try," Steven said, and she saw a flicker of sadness move in his eyes, quickly gone. "There's no denying that his mom and dad would have done a lot better job of raising him, though."

They were standing several feet apart, as they had before, out there in that bower of lilacs, but something electrical arced between them, undiminished by distance.

"What happened to them?" she asked. "Matt's parents, I mean."

For a moment, Melissa didn't think Steven was going to answer. When he did speak, he had to clear his throat first. "Jillie, Matt's mother, died of breast cancer close to two years ago," he said. "The grief got hold of Zack and it changed him. He was killed in a motorcycle wreck when Matt was four. I was named in both their wills as Matt's guardian."

"You must have been good friends, you and Jillie and Zack, if they trusted you to raise their child."

Pain moved in that handsome face, the features rugged and aristocratic, both at once. "We were good friends," he confirmed, after a long time.

She wanted very much to touch him then, not sexually, but to offer comfort, one human being to another. She was careful not to move. "You legally adopted Matt," she said. Judge Carpenter had told her that, the first day. The day everything changed for Melissa.

"I figured it made sense," Steven replied, "and Matt was all for it."

"It can't be easy, being a single parent."

"Oh, believe me," Steven said, smiling again, "it isn't. But, just the same, I'd be hard put to think of anything more rewarding." He held out his hand once more, and she crossed to him, took hold. "This place will be a lot different when the contractor and his crews get through with it," he added.

Melissa's throat tightened. "Don't let them change it *too much*," she said, without intending to say any such thing. It was none of *her* business what Steven Creed did to his house.

Steven cupped her cheeks in his hands then, and she knew by the touch of his palms that, professional man or not, he was no stranger to physical work. "I guess I probably shouldn't kiss you," he mused, his gaze focused on her mouth.

"I guess not," Melissa agreed, but weakly.

He kissed her—lightly at first, and then thoroughly.

She moaned and slipped her arms around his neck.

"It's too soon," she said breathlessly, when the kiss finally ended.

"I know," Steven rasped in reply.

After the longest moment of Melissa's life, he stepped back, away from her, let his hands fall to his sides. He was breathing hard, and a muscle bunched in his jawline, then smoothed out again.

They stood there, just looking at each other.

It was Steven who finally broke the silence, and what he said surprised her. A lot. "Tell me something about yourself, Melissa."

"Like what?"

Steven chuckled, standing there in a shifting mist of sun-speckled dust. Spread his hands. "What you love— what you hate—whether or not you believe in God. That sort of thing."

A smile tugged at the side of her mouth. She was relaxing a little—in spite of herself. "Oh, that," she said. She considered the question briefly. "Yes, I believe in God. I don't see how a person could help it, looking up at a sky full of stars, or in the early spring, when the grass comes up green, or watching a baby take those first few steps—"

So much for relaxing. Heat suffused Melissa's face. Why had she gone and blurted out a loaded word like *baby?* The man was going to think she was one of those women for whom all roads lead to marriage and children.

Steven was gracious enough to ignore her embarrassment, obvious as it was. "I agree," he said. "I'm convinced because of thunderstorms, the kind that seem to shake the ground itself. And because of the way little kids laugh, from way down deep in their middle, just because they're so full of joy they can't hold it in."

Melissa's eyes smarted, and her throat thickened, too. "Yeah," she managed to croak out, after what seemed like a long time.

Steven smiled, stretched out a hand to her.

Melissa hesitated only briefly, then took it. He led her out of the house, with its benign ghosts and soft, musty shadows, into the deep grass that was once a lawn.

With a sweep of his free arm, he indicated the surrounding countryside. "Now it's your turn, Melissa," he said, his gaze resting gently on her face. "Show me the Stone Creek Ranch you remember, the parts of it you loved the best."

The request quickened something inside Melissa. "Okay," she said.

They took his truck, since there wouldn't have been room for Zeke in the roadster and neither of them had the heart to leave the dog behind.

She directed him to the pioneer cemetery first, the place where generations of O'Ballivans were buried, along with her dad and Big John, her grandfather.

"Olivia and I used to come up here on horseback all the time," Melissa confided, with a slight smile. "We were hoping to see a ghost and absolutely terrified that we might get our wish."

Steven grinned. "You and Olivia? What about Ashley?"

"She didn't care much for riding horses," she answered. "And even less for ghosts."

He laughed.

She loved the sound of his laugh.

"So," Steven began presently, looking around that peaceful place, "did you ever get your wish? See a ghost?"

She knew her answer would surprise him. "Once or twice, I thought I did," she said softly, remembering. "But it happened in the ranch house, not here."

Steven arched an eyebrow, ever so slightly, and the breeze raised tendrils of his hair, as if offering a mischievous caress. And he waited for her to elaborate.

"A glimpse of a figure, out of the corner of my eye, that's all it was," she said. She'd been comforted, rather than frightened, by the experience.

After a few moments, during which the two of them tacitly agreed that it was time to move on, Steven whistled for Zeke, who'd gone exploring amid the tall grass, sheltered, like the graves, within the cluster of flourishing oak trees.

Their next stop was the high ridge, with its spectacular view of both Stone Creek Ranch and, in the near distance, the town as well. Melissa had hoped for a sighting of King's Ransom, the legendary wild stallion that sometimes put in an appearance, but that day, he kept himself and his band of mares and foals well hidden.

"There's still the house, of course," Melissa said, once she was settled in the passenger seat of Steven's flashy truck again, figuring the tour was complete, "but since it's occupied, that part will have to wait."

Steven smiled, looked back at Zeke to make sure he was settled, and started up the engine.

Something had definitely changed between herself and Steven, Melissa thought. There was still tension, of course, but the strange sense of urgency had passed. Being together seemed only natural now, and easy,

Things just sort of unfolded after that, with no hurry and no fretting and no drama.

"What will it be, Melissa?" he asked her, very quietly and after a long silence, when they were back at his place, inside the tour bus. "Is it now, or is it never?"

"How about now?" Melissa murmured, realizing, as her heartbeat quickened and her breath caught, that she was completely lost. If the scent of lilacs had made her drunk, this man's close proximity affected her like opium.

Of course she could have cited chapter and verse on why she shouldn't go to bed with Steven Creed—they'd only been acquainted for a couple of days, and that was just the start of it. He could be six kinds of bastard and a few besides, for all she knew.

But she also knew—*had* known from the moment they met, actually—that making love with him, for better or worse, for heaven or for heartbreak, was as inevitable as the turning of the seasons.

Melissa had only been inside her brother's fancy bus a few times—Brad had expressly forbidden any of his three younger sisters to consort with his band—but she knew where the main bedroom was. And knew they were headed straight for it.

Steven laid her down on the bed gently, his eyes at once troubled and hungry. "Are you sure about this?" he asked.

Melissa nodded, swallowed. "I'm sure," she said. *Like hell.*

He sat down on the edge of the bed, pulled off his

boots, tossed them aside. Otherwise, Steven was fully dressed, just as she was.

Turning his head to look down at her, he smiled very slightly. "You knew this would happen," he said. The statement might have been a mere guess, it might have been an accusation.

It might have been both.

"So did you," Melissa replied, scooting over, so he could stretch out beside her, which he did.

"Some things," he agreed, in that same gruff voice, "are written in the stars."

She smiled up at him. "You're a poet on top of all your other charms."

He laughed. "Woman," he said, easing the skirt of her sundress up over her knees and then higher still, to the middle of her thighs, "poetry is the *least* of my charms."

She felt so crazy-happy, and the emotion was all the sweeter because she knew it wouldn't last. The *real* Melissa was hardheaded and practical, and wherever she'd gone, she'd definitely be back. With a vengeance. "And you're *arrogant,* too."

But his face had changed. He sat up, frowning, touching her with just the tips of his fingers.

Melissa remembered the cuts and bruises she'd sustained that morning, though she couldn't actually *feel* a single one of them. No, all she felt was Steven's caress, and the desire for more contact and then still more.

"This happened today?" he asked. "When you were *almost* hit by a car?"

Melissa bit her lower lip. "Yes," she said. "But—"

He met her gaze, his expression grave. "You're hurt," he said. And just like that, he was up and off the bed, moving away from her. He disappeared into the bathroom and returned almost immediately with a drugstore first-aid kit.

Still adjusting to the shift in mood, Melissa nearly laughed, out of pure nervousness, and started to shinny upright.

Steven stopped her, though, with just a look.

"You keep a first-aid kit handy?" she asked.

Stupid question, since he obviously did. But there it was.

"I have a five-year-old son," he reminded her.

He set the white plastic box aside, on the table next to the bed, and that was when she noticed that he'd just happened to bring a small, easily recognizable packet along, too.

A condom. Anticipation returned, washing over Melissa in one great tsunami-like wave.

"Let's get you out of that dress," he said next.

And he simply whisked the whole thing right off over her head, without any sort of wasted motion.

Melissa had been undressed by a few men before, of course, but never in such a deft and matter-of-fact way. The yearning, strong before, pressed on her like a weight now, making it hard for her to breathe.

"That was—direct," she gasped, as a flush moved from her hairline to her toes. Goose bumps rose in its wake.

"I'm nothing if not direct," Steven said. Then he began applying some kind of medicine to her injuries, lightly and with skill.

"I've already used ointment," she struggled to say. Her body wanted to rise to him, to the touch of his hands, her back wanted to arch and her legs to part.

"Well, now you're getting more," Steven answered.

Oh, God, Melissa thought desperately, as his fingertips moved like a whispering breeze over the tingling flesh of her thighs and her knees, then her arms and shoulders.

He gave another of those raspy chuckles she was beginning to recognize as a hallmark of his personality. "Oh, lady, as roughed up as you are, you are *beyond* beautiful."

Apparently, they were past the first-aid stage.

Melissa suppressed a moan of pure need as she watched Steven stand up, unbutton his shirt partway, and then impatiently haul the garment off over his head.

His chest was broad, his muscle tone was good and a light dusting of hair, the color of brown sugar, caught the light.

"You're sure?" he asked again.

The longer she looked at him, the surer she was.

"Yes," she said. It was an ache, that simple word.

He didn't take off his jeans then, which was probably a mercy, Melissa figured, because she already wanted him so badly that she might have bolted right up off that bed and tackled him to the floor if she'd seen what was under them. Not that his erection didn't show, because it strained against that thin layer of denim.

The mattress dipped and he was beside her again, gathering her close, deftly unhooking her bra, so that skin met skin. Kissing her so deeply, so thoroughly, that she couldn't hold still any longer.

Her body flexed on the bed, already slick with need, and burning. Burning everywhere. She was on fire, and nothing had even happened yet.

She felt his thumb slide under the elastic on her

panties, and then those were gone, too, as easily as if they'd dissolved under the heat of his hand.

His hand. It was between her legs now, stroking her, teasing her, subtly parting her.

He kissed his way down her neck, stopped to nibble at her left breast, then her right. She was squirming, even whimpering a little, by the time he left the nipples, wet from his mouth and so hard that they nearly hurt.

He reached her belly, tasting her skin, his fingers still plying her.

Melissa's whole body buckled in reaction; if he kept this up, she'd have an orgasm *way* too soon. She didn't realize she'd voiced this concern aloud until Steven laughed and shifted, kneeling between her legs now.

"Go ahead and let yourself go if you need to," he drawled, leaning forward now, his hands gently possessive on her breasts. "There will be plenty more where that came from."

Another groan escaped her, fierce, almost primordial.

And then he lowered himself to her, parted her with his fingers, flicked at her with the tip of his tongue.

Melissa's hips surged upward, and she made a soblike sound, hoarse with lust.

He tempted. He teased. He feasted, and then withdrew, and then feasted again.

Melissa buried her fingers in his hair, frantic. Her body flew, but Steven stayed with her.

She began to quiver all over, and perspiration misted her skin, made wisps and tendrils of her hair stick to her neck and her cheeks and her forehead. Finally, she pleaded, in a scratchy rasp....

And the climax came, shattering, a thing of light and

heat and fire, blinding her, wringing guttural shouts from her throat, causing her heels to dig deep into the surface of the mattress.

Steven held her afterward, until the trembling had eased, until she could breathe, and then got up, a haze at the periphery of her vision, and got out of his jeans.

She hadn't seen his shaft—everything was blurry—but she *felt* it all right, because he was soon on top of her. The length of him, hard and hot, pressed against her abdomen and belly, a physical portent of what was about to happen.

Melissa moaned again, as all the melted-honey satisfaction of her recent climax instantly morphed into something greedy and feverish and utterly wild.

Steven shifted his weight slightly, careful not to crush her, and she knew he was putting on the condom. Even that move was graceful.

He kissed her again, then looked straight into her eyes and said, "Last chance to say no."

Melissa arched her back, inviting him inside her in that way as old as the human race, and now it was Steven who groaned. He was part of her in one swift, fiery stroke, sheathed to the hilt.

She reveled in the sensation of being conquered and, at the same time, conquering. By tacit agreement, they both lay still for a few long, delicious moments, simply savoring this most intimate of all connections.

As soon as he began to move, though, Melissa was lost.

She bucked under him, like a wild mare being broke to ride, and clawed at his shoulders and his back, and there was something so primitive, so freeing, in the joining that a terrible, consuming joy rose up inside her.

On and on it went, the delicious tension rising, rising—and then the peak. Melissa wept as she gave herself up to Steven Creed, completely, eagerly, without reservation or shame.

His whole body stiffened as, at last, he surrendered, his head thrown back, the muscles cording in his neck.

Then he collapsed beside her, one leg still sprawled across her thighs, and both of them lay gasping.

It was a long time—a very long time—before either of them spoke.

In the end, it was Steven who broke the silence.

Melissa's face was wet with tears, and he dried them with the side of one thumb, kissed the traces of them away.

"Did I hurt you?" he asked, and he sounded genuinely worried.

Melissa laughed softly. "*Hurt* me? Mister, if that was pain, bring on the next round."

His eyes, his wonderful blue eyes, remained solemn, and the chortling sound he made came out brief and a little raw. "Then why the tears?"

She crooned a sigh. She was soft everywhere, inside and out. And more deeply satisfied than she'd ever imagined it was possible to be. "Because it was so good," she said, tracing the line of his jaw with the tip of one index finger.

He ventured a smile then, shook his head. "Women," he said.

He got up, disappeared into the bathroom again, then came back.

Melissa looked at Steven, saw that he was hard again, and held out her arms to him.

THE MEAT LOAF WAS PRETTY GOOD, in Steven's opinion, and after several hours with Melissa O'Ballivan, definitely the hottest woman he'd ever encountered, in or out of bed, he was ravenously hungry.

He was managing to keep his misgivings at bay, but he knew they were slinking around like wolves on the fringes of the light from a campfire, waiting to pounce.

She sat across the table from him now, fresh from the shower they'd just shared, wearing his T-shirt and nothing else. He felt downright overdressed in his jeans and the shirt he'd been wearing earlier.

Melissa picked up her fork, but instead of taking a bite of food, she looked around. Smiled.

"What?" Steven asked, amused, but feeling a touch of something else, too. Something proprietary, though he wasn't ready to call it jealousy.

"It's ironic," she answered, with a saucy twist of her mouth and a twinkle in her beautiful eyes. "I've been inside this bus maybe three times in my life—Brad bought it for the guys in his band, while Ashley and I were still in high school, and Olivia had just started college. And none of us were allowed anywhere *near* it unless he was with us—he was that determined to protect our virtue."

Steven smiled. "Can't say I blame the man for that," he commented. "Looking out for three sisters—especially *kid* sisters—has to be a challenge."

Melissa took a few bites, looking pleasantly thoughtful. Then she asked, "Do you have sisters, Steven?"

He shook his head. "I'm an only child," he said.

"That sounds lonely."

"You know what they say. A person can be lonely in a crowd."

"That's true," Melissa admitted. "And I have to admit, there were times when I wouldn't have minded being an only child myself."

"Did you always want to be a lawyer?"

"No," she replied. "My first ambition was to reign as queen of Stone Creek Rodeo Days."

"Did you?"

"Sure did," Melissa answered. "When I was nineteen. Did *you* always want to be a lawyer?"

Steven paused a moment before shaking his head. "Nope," he said. "I planned on running a ranch, like my dad."

"What changed your mind?"

Steven was a little surprised to find himself discussing a matter he'd barely talked about with Zack, his best friend, or Brody and Conner, his cousins. "Ranching was in my blood," he said, "but so was the law, as it turned out. My grandfather founded one of the biggest firms east of the Mississippi. It was a family business."

"Was?" Melissa's tone was casual, but she was watching him closely.

"My uncles still run it. It wasn't the same after my mother and grandfather passed away."

"Wasn't there a place for you—afterward?" she asked.

Steven shook his head. "Not one I'd fit into," he said. "Zack—Matt's father—was a good friend of mine, from way back. He put in a good word for me where he worked, and I moved to Denver." He paused, looking back. It wasn't something he allowed himself to do very often; in his opinion, there wasn't much to gain by indulging in personal retrospectives. "Turned out I liked practicing criminal law a lot better than corporate. And I was good at it."

"But you didn't stay," Melissa said smoothly.

He grinned. "You must be pretty good in a court-room yourself," he observed. Though the remark had been prompted by her subtle way of going after sensitive information, Steven meant what he was saying. Melissa wasn't just beautiful, she was smart, and most likely successful at just about everything she did.

Take sex, for instance.

Melissa smiled, and that was almost Steven's un-doing. When the lady smiled, her eyes shone and her whole face lit up. "I do all right," she replied easily. Then she drew a deep breath, let it out, and squared her shoulders. "So," she went on. "What brings you to Stone Creek?"

"It's a great place to raise a kid," Steven said.

"So are lots of other places, like Denver. And Boston. And wherever else you've been in your travels."

Like Lonesome Bend, Colorado, he thought, with a touch of sadness.

He didn't see any need to tell Melissa about the ex-perience that had soured him on the place. So he merely raised and lowered one shoulder slightly in what was meant to serve as a shrug. "As you probably know, your sister-in-law and I are distantly related. Turns out the founders of the McKettrick and Creed clans were half brothers. Meg tracked me down online, and we started emailing back and forth. The more she told me about Stone Creek, the more it appealed to me. I paid a brief visit, met Meg and the rest of the McKettrick family, saw that this ranch was for sale and made an offer."

Melissa bit down on her lower lip, her eyes luminous with worried curiosity. "Today at lunch, you mentioned spending summers on a Colorado ranch while you were growing up. Is that near Denver?"

Steven nodded. "It's outside a town called Lonesome Bend. My dad and stepmother still live there, when they're not traveling around the country in their RV. My cousin Conner runs the operation now."

"Your cousin?" She arched one eyebrow. The woman didn't miss much. "If the ranch was your home, at least part of the time, why not make a life there?"

He sat back, folded his arms. Tessa Quinn's meat loaf was fantastic, but he was satisfied. When it came to food, anyway. "Conner and Brody's father was the firstborn son in his generation. He inherited the ranch when my grandparents were both gone, and even though my dad stepped in and took over after his older brother died, there was never any question of ownership. Legally, the ranch passed to my cousins when they turned twenty-one."

"And your dad was just out in the cold after that?"

Steven grinned. "Hardly. The executors paid Dad a good salary for taking care of the spread, not to mention raising Conner and Brody, and he had some money of his own to start with. He's a master saddle maker—there aren't many of those left—and he fills custom orders for a pretty elite list of customers."

Melissa smiled. "When he's not RVing with your stepmother?"

"It's a big RV," Steven answered. "Dad does a lot of work on the road."

Melissa, also through eating, rested her forearms on

the table and leaned forward a little way. "Does it bother you?" she asked.

"Does what bother me?"

"That your cousins each got a share of the ranch but you evidently didn't?

"No," Steven said. "That was the deal. I knew it from the beginning. And, anyway, Conner and Brody offered me a third of the outfit. I turned it down."

"Because?"

"Because I wanted to build a legacy of my own," Steven said.

She spread her hands. "And here you are," she said, with another of those wrenching smiles of hers.

"Here I am," he agreed.

"Have you ever been in love?"

Steven chuckled. "Yeah," he said. "At least, I thought so at the time."

"But you were mistaken?"

"I guess you could say that."

"What was she like?"

"Beautiful. Smart. Tough as nails."

They were quiet for a few moments, while Melissa mulled over what he'd said. For his part, Steven was content just to look at her, though he wouldn't have said no to more sex.

"How about you?" he asked, in good time. "Have you ever been in love?"

As soon as he'd asked that question, he regretted it, because the atmosphere changed. He saw Melissa draw further into herself; her smile wobbled and the happy light in her eyes dimmed a little.

"I guess it's only fair, your asking me that," she said.

"Since I asked *you* the same thing about two minutes ago."

His heart went out to her, and he wasn't sure it was going to find its way back where it belonged anytime soon.

He reached across the narrow table, took her hand, gave her fingers a light squeeze. "Another time," he said, watching her. Thinking he might just fall right into the blue of her eyes, tumbling head over heels forever, never hitting bottom.

"No," she said, shaking her head. "Fair is fair."

"If you don't feel like talking, Melissa, that's all right."

Melissa looked straight into his eyes, didn't move to pull her hand from his grasp, but it was a long time before she spoke. "His name was—*is*—Dan Guthrie. He wanted to get married, and he had these two great kids. I said yes. But every time we tried to go through with the plan and actually throw a wedding, I'd back off. Eventually, Dan got tired of that, and he—well—he's married to someone else now. They're going to have a baby."

Steven wanted to ask if she still loved this Guthrie yahoo, but he figured there had been enough soul-baring for one night.

Besides that, he wasn't sure he could stand hearing the answer.

CHAPTER ELEVEN

PINK AND GOLD CRACKS split the dawn sky as Melissa rose from Steven Creed's bed, being careful not to wake him, crept into the bathroom for a hasty shower and slipped back into the sundress she'd worn the night before.

Common sense said to get out while the getting was good—she definitely didn't want Brad or Meg to find her there at that hour, if they had to bring Matt home early for some reason, for instance—but she couldn't resist leaning down to plant a whisper-light kiss on Steven's forehead before leaving. And when she did, he took her by the shoulders and eased her down beside him.

Startled, she gave a little shriek as she landed. Then she laughed and scrambled right back up again, careful to stay out of his reach this time.

Steven yawned luxuriously and cupped his hands behind his head, watching her with a glint of mischief in his eyes and a grin resting on his mouth. "Leaving so soon?" he asked, in a teasing tone.

"'Soon'?" Melissa echoed, pretending indignation. "I got here at six o'clock last night, and now the *sun* is about to come up. I should have left *hours* ago."

"I'm glad you didn't."

She couldn't help smiling; she felt so good. "I'm glad, too," she admitted. "But I've got to go. All the neighbors will probably see me pulling in at first light as it is, and I'm due at the office in a couple of hours."

"Right," Steven said, sounding resigned. Outside in the narrow hallway, Zeke gave an anxious little whimper. "Dog needs to go outside," he added, sitting up and starting to throw back the comforter.

Knowing only too well what was *under* that comforter, Melissa turned on her heel and rushed out. "Come on, boy," she told the waiting canine. "I'll let you out."

As she retreated, Zeke hurrying along behind her, she heard Steven chuckle.

Moments later, he appeared in the doorway of the bus, barefoot and shirtless, with his jeans misbuttoned. Melissa had been waiting for Zeke to relieve himself so she could let him back into the bus before starting for town. Seeing Steven shook her resolve a little, though.

Did he have to look so damn good, even five minutes after he got out of bed? He hadn't shaved or showered or even combed his hair, and he still made her ache for more of the same.

"Call you later?" Steven asked, shoving a hand through his hair.

Melissa could still feel the silken texture of that hair between her fingers. "Okay," she said. "Thanks for—" Heat surged into her face. "Thanks for supper."

He grinned. "Thanks for coming," he said mildly.

Another blush followed the first one, winding up at Melissa's hairline, where she could feel it throbbing in time with her heartbeat. She was *damned* if she'd say, *You're welcome.* "Okay," she repeated, heading for her car as the dog frolicked toward his master.

Melissa jumped into her car, started the engine and

drove away. Fast. Her face didn't cool down until she was almost at the town limits.

After that, she thought about how conspicuous her car was. If she'd been driving a normal subcompact, or some kind of sedan, she might have a chance of going unnoticed. In a bright red replica of an MG Roadster— not so much.

Melissa straightened her spine. Breathed in the fresh morning air, and tried to think sensibly. She'd had a relationship with Dan, after all, and the whole town knew it. Why was she so worried that news of her night with Steven Creed would get around?

She bit her lower lip. It definitely wasn't about shame or embarrassment—that much she was sure of. So *what*, then?

It didn't take her long to figure it out. Her time with Steven was precious and, therefore, *private*. She needed a while to process all that had happened, to make some kind of sense of things.

Good luck with that, she thought.

She was especially careful to stay within the speed limit as she cruised through town, because all she needed right then was for an early-rising Tom Parker to pull her over and give her a ticket.

At home, she parked the car in her tiny detached garage instead of leaving it at the curb or in the driveway, feeling grateful that none of the neighbors seemed to be stirring yet. She made a dash for the back door, keys in hand, and ducked inside like some fugitive two steps ahead of the law.

This morning, she was determined, would be like any *other* morning.

She got into shorts and a sports bra and a tank top,

pulled on some socks and her running shoes, left again by way of the front door, pausing on the porch to lock up before slipping her ribbon strung key over her neck.

The cuts and bruises from yesterday's fall hadn't been magically healed, but they didn't hurt the way they did before, either, so she warmed up as usual and jogged through the gate and down the sidewalk, following her favorite route.

Running always straightened out any tangles in Melissa's brain, and this run was no exception.

Mentally, she reviewed the situation. Fact: she'd slept with Steven Creed. Fact: she'd enjoyed the experience, and she wasn't one bit sorry. Fact: she'd better watch out, if she didn't want her heart smashed to bits all over again.

She dried a stray tear with the back of one hand and picked up her pace.

She jogged along Main Street, not stopping in for a bottle of deliciously cold water as she passed the Sunflower Café after lapping the town park three times, then headed for home.

All was quiet at Ashley's but, hey, she thought, with a small smile, it was early. The ancient ones were probably still snoozing away in their various beds, but who knew what they'd be up to after a hearty breakfast.

Minutes later, cooling down in her side yard, Melissa heard the phone ringing inside, and the tone seemed oddly urgent. She unlocked the door and hurried inside,

"Hello?" she sputtered. Not her usual way of answering.

"Hello," Tom responded. "Any chance you can come in early today?"

A prickle danced up Melissa's spine and then back down again. "I guess. Why?"

Tom was quiet for a moment. "It's the Carter kid—Nathan," he finally went on. "One of my deputies ran him in last night for loitering—mainly so the boy would have someplace to sleep. This morning, Carter's claiming that Pete knocked him around, and he's got a shiner to prove it. Says he wants to press charges."

Melissa released a long sigh. Deputy Pete Ferguson, a solid citizen with a wife and four kids and a sterling reputation in the community. It was hard to imagine him abusing his authority in any way whatsoever.

"Great," she muttered.

"You're the prosecutor, O'Ballivan," Tom said, his tone light, but grim, too. "Ferguson is being accused of a felony. And he's beside himself over it. So you'd better get down here and decide whether or not the people have a case."

"I'll be there," Melissa confirmed. "Tell Pete to hold on."

She took a quick shower, got dressed and skipped the makeup, except for mascara and a swipe of lip gloss.

Melissa paused only briefly to check herself out in the full-length mirror before leaving the bedroom. Her tailored black slacks and peacock-blue silk blouse made her feel—and look—more like her old self. And that was important because, since last night, she hadn't been quite sure *who* the heck she was.

As soon as she set foot inside the municipal building, a sense of dread settled over her spirit. After pausing to steel herself for a moment, Melissa marched down the corridor to Tom's office, drew a deep breath outside his door, let it out again and went in.

Steven was standing by Tom's desk, all spiffed up for the day and yet still managing to look like a man who's just enjoyed a night of lively sex.

Which, of course, he was. Moreover, he was a lawyer, there to represent *someone*—Pete? Nathan Carter?

It was anybody's guess, at that point, but one thing was for sure. Steven would inevitably side against her.

Melissa felt dazed, as though she'd collided with an invisible brick wall, crazy as it seemed.

Steven looked as cool as could be, in no apparent hurry to do anything.

His mouth crooked up at one corner when his gaze connected with Melissa's, after a slow cruise from her feet to her face. He was trying to unsettle her, of course, and it was working.

Melissa felt strangely *exposed*, as though Steven had X-ray vision or her clothes had turned to cellophane.

"Morning," he drawled. His eyes and that faint grin said it all.

He'd played her body the way Charlie Daniels plays a fiddle, during the night, and he wasn't going to pretend it hadn't happened, much as she wanted to do exactly that.

Melissa hoped Tom hadn't picked up on the note of intimacy in Steven's tone. He'd razz her mercilessly if he knew what was going on.

"Good morning," she replied stiffly, as though she and Steven were mere acquaintances instead of very recent lovers. She glanced past him, as dismissively as she could, toward the cells, where Nathan stood behind bars, smirking at her.

Pete Ferguson, who had been fidgeting at his desk,

bolted to his feet. "It's a lie, Melissa," he blurted out. "You *know* I'd never rough up a prisoner—"

Carter simply pointed to his eye, which was nearly swollen shut, the flesh around it shot through with varying shades of purple and green as well as bruise-blue.

Nobody spoke for a few moments.

Then Steven cleared his throat and said, "In addition to the injury Mr. Carter suffered, there seems to be some question of Deputy Ferguson's reasons for detaining him in the first place."

Melissa felt as though she'd been kicked in the solar plexus. Hard. "You're representing Mr. Carter, then?"

Ferguson, tall and clean-cut, with a military haircut and pale blue eyes, looked sick. Tom just looked disgusted.

"It would be more accurate to say I'm advising him," Steven said. His tone was even, though a bedrock of resolve ran beneath it.

Melissa turned on Nathan Carter. He looked her over insolently, and the effect was quite different from when Steven had done almost the same thing. "What happened?" she asked.

"He was hanging around the park, and it looked like he didn't have any place to spend the night," Pete put in. "So I bought him a hamburger and let him sleep in the cell."

"You'll have your turn, Pete," Melissa said calmly. "Right now, I want to hear Mr. Carter's side of the story."

"I told the deputy I was fine with sleeping in the park," Nathan said. The smirk was gone now, replaced by a cagey narrowing of his eyes. "He said that was vagrancy and he had to take me in. When I argued with him, he put his fist in my face."

"That's not true!" Deputy Ferguson protested heatedly.

"Pete," Tom said, very quietly.

"But Carter already *had* that black eye when I approached him," Pete insisted. Color pulsed in his neck and his round, earnest face.

"I guess it's his word against mine," Nathan said, his tone dejected.

"Or not," Steven said mildly.

Melissa ignored him. "Were there any witnesses?" she asked, looking at Nathan.

Tom gave a derisive snort.

Melissa flashed him a look, which he returned in kind.

"Unless specific charges are being brought against Mr. Carter," Steven interjected, "I would suggest releasing him."

Melissa held her temper, while Tom made a production of jingling his keys, crossing to the cell and unlocking the door.

"You're free to go," he told the erstwhile prisoner.

"Whoop-de-do," Nathan mocked, waltzing through the opening and crossing the room to stand next to Steven. "How about locking up the deputy, there?" Again, he indicated his shiner. "I'm accusing him of police brutality."

Pete turned crimson.

Tom shut the cell door with a clang.

"Be quiet," Steven told Nathan, who remained in the sheriff's office.

Melissa turned to Pete. "What's your story?" she

asked him. He was an old friend, like Tom, but if he *had* struck Carter without adequate provocation, there would be repercussions.

Miserably, Pete recounted the events of the night before. He'd been on routine patrol, he said, and spotted somebody skulking around the bandstand in the town park. He'd gotten out of his car and walked over, with a flashlight, to investigate.

Carter had flipped him some attitude, but it was nothing serious. The boy had ridden in the front seat of the squad car, without cuffs, and they'd both had burgers and fries from the drive-through at McDonald's. Pete added that he'd thought about taking Nathan home with him, letting him sleep on the couch, instead of parking him in a cell, but he'd decided against that because of the wife and kids.

"Are you going to arrest him or not?" Nathan barked, when the tale ended.

"No," Melissa said. "Not without a credible witness to verify that Deputy Ferguson actually struck you."

"Then I want to sue the Stone Creek County Sheriff's Office," Nathan said. "I want to sue the whole damn *town!* My rights have been violated here!"

Melissa didn't look at Nathan Carter, but at Steven. "Have at it," she said.

"Just go," Steven told the younger man, holding Melissa's gaze with no problem at all. He produced a wallet from the inside pocket of his spiffy suit coat and handed Carter some money.

Nathan hesitated, then snatched the bills from Steven's hand and stormed out of the sheriff's office.

Over by the water cooler, Elvis yawned loudly, making his presence known for the first time, and then shook himself hard, so that his ears made a loud flapping sound.

That broke the silence that had descended after Nathan's outburst.

"Go on home," Tom said to Pete Ferguson.

"I'm not suspended, pending some kind of investigation?" Pete asked, turning to the sheriff.

Tom shook his head. "No," he said.

Pete left, giving Melissa a wounded glance as he passed her.

Tom, meanwhile, focused on Steven. "I guess your work here is done, counselor, for the moment, anyway,"

In other words, Melissa thought, *Get the hell out of my office.* She was inclined to agree.

Steven smiled, nodded politely and headed for the door.

Melissa would have waited until she was sure he was gone to duck out, but the fact was, she wasn't any more eager to deal with Tom than with Steven at the moment.

Steven was waiting in the hall. Melissa ignored him, walking on by. He stopped her by reaching out and taking a light but firm hold on her elbow.

Her temper flared. "I can't believe you would actually consider representing that scumbag!" she whispered, her fury at such a fever pitch that the words just formed themselves, seemingly independent of her brain, and came tumbling out of her mouth. "Pete Ferguson would step off the sidewalk and into the street before he'd *squash a bug* under his shoe, let alone manhandle anybody. And as for Carter—"

"Whoa," Steven said. "Everybody has a right to

counsel. Or were you out sick when they covered the fundamentals the first week of law school?"

Melissa jerked her elbow free, in no mood to be reasoned with. "Yes," she agreed tartly, "everybody *does* have the right to counsel. But before you take on any more clients, you might want to take the trouble to find out what kind of people they are!"

"It doesn't matter what kind of people they are," Steven replied moderately. "The law is the law."

She took a step back. "Pete Ferguson's father was the last sheriff," she said. "Before that, it was his grandfather, and before *that*, his *great*-grandfather. The Fergusons are some of the finest people in this community—"

Steven leaned in, so his nose was nearly touching hers. "*Beside the point,* counselor," he said. "If your friend, Deputy Ferguson, gave Nathan Carter a working over, I'll nail him for it."

For a long moment, they just glared at each other.

Then Steven turned and walked away.

Melissa didn't move until he'd disappeared through the outside doorway. It took her that long to calm down enough to set foot inside her office.

She was immediately met with a whole new Andrea. Gone were the jeans, the hair spikes, the too-tight T-shirts, the heavy eye shadow and the white lipstick. She was wearing a nice skirt, a white blouse and modest makeup.

Melissa couldn't help staring. "What happened to you?" she asked.

The girl straightened her spine and lifted her chin. The expression in her eyes was completely earnest, and she held Melissa's direct gaze without looking away. "I'm turning over a new leaf, that's all," she replied, with a little sniff. "Byron says it's important to look professional."

Melissa barely kept herself from smiling at that one. "Oh?"

Andrea nodded and then pushed back her chair and stood. "I even made coffee. It should be ready by now."

Melissa raised both her hands, palms out. "Sit down, Andrea," she said. "I was only teasing before. Making coffee really *isn't* in your job description."

"Can't a person do something nice for somebody?" Andrea asked. Her lower lip was wobbling now, and her eyes misted over.

"Sit down," Melissa repeated, but gently.

Andrea sagged into her chair.

"What's this all about? This big transformation, I mean?"

"I almost ran over you yesterday morning," Andrea burst out, and a tear slid down her cheek. "I—I guess I'm just trying to—well—*make up* for what could have happened to you, at least partly, if—if—"

Melissa felt a burning sensation behind her own eyes now. "You've apologized," she reminded her assistant. "You've promised to be more careful in the future. You don't need to do anything more, Andrea."

Andrea absorbed that in silence, looking straight ahead. Her hands rested on the surface of her desk, fingers tightly interlaced.

Melissa waited a few moments, then asked, "Were there any messages?"

"Mrs. Brady called," Andrea said, turning her head. "So did Mrs. Hillingsley. They agree on *one* thing, anyway, that the Parade Committee meeting didn't go very well."

Meeting? It was a beat before Melissa recalled the great toilet-paper debate, and how she'd suggested that the committee gather right away to settle it.

"Oh," she said.

"Half of them want to let Mrs. Hillingsley decorate the Chamber of Commerce float any way she pleases," Andrea went on, a smile creeping over her mouth as she spoke, no longer gazing off into the beyond, "and the other half say there'll be hell to pay if she embarrasses the whole town of Stone Creek by decking the thing with miles of toilet paper."

Melissa muttered under her breath. If troublemakers like Nathan Carter didn't give her a migraine, the Parade Committee would. "Did anyone else call?"

"Mr. Blake left a voice mail," Andrea said. "It was so long that I thought it'd be better if you just listened to it yourself, instead of me trying to write it all down. You know how he rambles on."

Oh, indeed she did.

"More space aliens landing in his cornfield and scaring his sheep?" Melissa asked.

Andrea nodded, then gave a little giggle. "Sorry," she said, after a moment, clearly insincere.

Melissa heaved out a sigh. "Okay," she said. "That's everything, then?"

"That's everything," Andrea said.

Melissa practically dove into her office.

Concentrating on her work proved to be a challenge for the rest of the morning—she kept thinking about Steven, and the things they'd done together the night before, juxtaposed against the cold, hard reality of their separate philosophies concerning the practice of law.

She was a prosecutor.

He was a defense attorney.

There were similarities between them, of course, but just then, the differences looked a whole lot bigger.

CHAPTER TWELVE

JUST BEFORE NOON, Melissa saved a computer document to the file labeled "to be reviewed" and noticed for the first time that she was hungry. That morning's after-jog smoothie had definitely worn off.

Too bad the residual effects of Steven Creed's *lovemaking* hadn't—or those of the confrontation outside of Tom's office after Nathan Carter's release from jail. The occasional faint aftershock *still* rocked her—at once delicious and annoying.

Melissa decided to remain in the office over her lunch hour, although the day was lovely and it would have been a lot more fun to munch away on a half sandwich and a fruit cup from the little market down on the corner.

So, silently telling herself to *get over it* all the while, she had strawberry yogurt from her stash in the break-room fridge instead.

And she waited.

When she couldn't sit still for another moment, she stood up and walked out of her private office, past Andrea and into the corridor.

Tom was sitting at his desk when she walked in, scribbling away at some form on a clipboard. Seeing her, he pushed the paperwork away and got to his feet. His desk chair creaked in the process.

She didn't speak right away, so he spread his hands wide and said, "What?"

"Do you have any idea what kind of problems you've opened yourself up to?" Melissa demanded. "Maybe it was all right to throw someone into jail just to get them off the street back in the day, but it isn't anymore!"

Tom's eyes twinkled, though he looked weary, too. "Tell it to Pete Ferguson," he said, slowly sinking back into his chair. "*He* made the arrest."

"*You* tell him," Melissa snapped in response. "You're his boss."

Tom arched an eyebrow. "Are you through?" he asked, with a grin he couldn't quite suppress, though he did make a visible attempt.

Melissa began to pace. "Carter *could* sue the county for false arrest," she reminded her friend. "And even if Steven Creed didn't take the case, some ambulance chaser from Flagstaff or Phoenix would be thrilled to do it!"

Tom nodded toward the chair facing his desk. "Sit down," he said. "You're making me nervous."

She plunked herself onto the seat, arms folded.

"Speaking of Creed," Tom said, when she didn't speak, "what's going on between you two?"

"Who says anything is 'going on'?" Melissa countered, perhaps too quickly.

"Oh, come on," Tom said. "The air was *flammable* in here this morning. Good thing nobody smokes in public buildings anymore, because the whole crowd of us might have gone up in a blast if anybody had flicked a lighter or struck a match."

Melissa folded her arms. "I'm not discussing Steven Creed with you," she said. She wanted to discuss Steven with *someone*—Ashley and Olivia were both likely candidates—but not Tom. Definitely not Tom, because he'd tease her to death if she admitted anything.

Tom chuckled. "All right," he said, spreading his hands in a gesture of affable acquiescence. "But don't think you're fooling anybody, because you're not."

Melissa took a step toward him. Let her arms fall to her sides. "Speaking of not fooling anyone," she said, "remember our bet? You were supposed to ask Tessa Quinn out for dinner or a movie—or have you forgotten?"

He reddened slightly, under the jaw.

Elvis made a rhythmic thumping sound against the floor as he scratched under his chin with one hind leg.

"You said the bet was off," Tom told her.

"No, I didn't," Melissa argued. "*You* did. And that's as good as losing, as far as I'm concerned." She leaned in, tucked her fingers under her armpits and flapped her elbows like wings. "Cluck-cluck-cluck."

"Look, it isn't that easy, okay? Tessa comes from a different *world* than I do. She's beautiful. She used to be on TV—God only knows who she's dated in the past and—"

"Cluck," Melissa said. "Cluck. Cluck—"

"Stop it," Tom ordered.

"Arrest me," Melissa challenged.

"That is tempting," came the raspy reply. Tom hooked his thumbs under his belt. "And if you think all this jabbering is throwing me off, you're wrong. I'm a trained investigator, remember. I know there *is* something going on between you and Steven Creed. In fact, I'd go so far as to say you weren't even home last night."

"What makes you say that?"

"I might have driven past your place once or twice."

Melissa raised one eyebrow. Tilted her head to one side. "Is that right? Well, let's assume, for one wild and crazy moment, that I *did* have something 'going on' with Steven. Why would that be any of your damn business?"

He smiled. "It wouldn't," he conceded. "But I'd be happy about it. The whole damn *county* would be happy, in fact."

Melissa's tone was dangerous, which was fine, since she wanted it that way. "Because—?"

"Because you don't have a life. Ever since you and Dan broke up, you've been—it seems like you're—"

"And I suppose *you* have a life?"

"I get by," Tom hedged.

"'Getting by' doesn't count. You're still a young man, Tom. You're nice-looking and honest and you have a steady job. *Lots* of women would be interested in you, and Tessa might just be one of them, for all you know. I can't *believe* that as brave a man as you are, you're afraid to risk one tiny rejection."

Tom didn't answer. He just stood there, looking like he was trying to think of a smart-ass comeback, but none was forthcoming.

"All right," Melissa said, "there's a dance at the Grange Hall Saturday night. Why don't you ask Tessa if she'd like to go?"

He let out a breath. "Tessa's always friendly when I stop by the café for coffee, or pick up something from the bakery side," he confessed, "so I get to thinking she might be up for dinner and a movie, anyway, but then at other times she seems pretty distracted, like a lot of things are worrying her. How do I know I'm not misreading the smiles and all that? After all, Tessa is nice to everybody, not just me."

Melissa felt a rush of sisterly tenderness and touched Tom's arm. "It's a *dance,* Tom. Ask her. Either she'll accept and you'll both have a great time, or she'll refuse, and you'll be able to stop wondering and move on."

He turned stubborn then. "I'll ask Tessa if *you'll* ask Creed," he said.

The depth of her reaction to the suggestion startled Melissa. Suddenly, she wanted to run back to her office and hide behind her work again.

Which was completely crazy, considering the things she and Steven had done in bed together just the night before.

Weren't parts of her still humming with sense memories?

Tom pounced on her hesitation and jumped in feet first. "*Now* who's chicken?" he asked.

Melissa forced herself to relax. Tried for a throw-away smile. "How do I know this isn't a trick?" she asked. "I invite Steven to the dance and then you conveniently fink out on asking Tessa. Where would that leave me?"

"Dancing with Steven Creed?" Tom teased, a grin in his eyes.

"You go first," Melissa said. "And I have to be there when you ask her."

Tom pretended to be horrified. "You don't trust me?"

"Not when it comes to this," she replied, lifting her chin. "You've been waffling for a year, telling me you're going to make a move and then backing off again."

"You expect to *be there* when I talk to Tessa?"

Melissa nodded. Glanced at her watch. "Nearly two o'clock. It would be entirely reasonable for us to go out on a coffee break right about now," she said. "We'll head over to the Sunflower, and when Tessa comes to the table to take our order, you just say something like, 'There's a dance this Saturday night and I was wondering if you'd like to go with me.'"

Tom considered long and hard. It was a measure of how much he really liked Tessa, maybe even *loved* her, that taking such a small risk scared him.

"All right," he finally said. He whistled for Elvis, who got to his feet and crossed the office. Holding the office door open for Melissa, Tom added, "After you, counselor."

"I'm proud of you," Melissa said.

She ducked into her office for her purse—Andrea still wasn't back—and ducked out again.

"There's a catch," Tom informed her, when they were both strapped into the squad car and Elvis had taken up his post in back, behind the folding grill.

Melissa's stomach fluttered slightly. "What kind of catch?"

"Fair is fair," Tom said. "If you get to hang around when I ask Tessa to go to the dance, then the reverse is true. I have to be there when you ask Creed."

Awkward, Melissa thought. Her most recent exchange with Steven hadn't exactly been a friendly one. And, anyway, there was a big difference in situations here—she'd *slept* with Steven Creed. Recently. There had clearly been no such intimacy between Tom and Tessa.

Still, how could she refuse without explaining? And

she certainly wasn't about to admit that she'd spent the night with the man, even though Tom had expressed his suspicions.

"You're on," she said finally. She'd think of a way out later.

Tom nodded and started up the cruiser, and they headed for the Sunflower Café and Bakery. Alice McCoy was out front on her three-wheeled cart, putting tickets on windshields, and she waved merrily to Tom, one crime fighter acknowledging another.

Tom smiled and waved back, but he looked a little pale around the jawline, and Melissa knew he was nervous.

She felt fairly sympathetic toward him, even—until they walked into the café that is. There was Steven, sitting on the same stool as the first time she'd laid eyes on him, sipping coffee and going over plans with Alex Royce, an architect from Indian Rock.

Steven turned immediately to face Melissa, and his eyes sparked when he looked at her. The corner of his mouth quirked up, too.

Tom was so pleased to see Melissa put on the spot like this that he must have forgotten his own mission, at least for a moment.

"We're on a coffee break," Melissa said, perhaps a touch too loudly.

Conversation ceased all over the small eatery, and everyone looked in their direction. A few people smiled to themselves before going back to their late lunches, early suppers or afternoon snacks.

Steven spoke to Alex, who nodded, and then rose from the counter stool to walk over to Melissa and Tom.

"Have you calmed down a little?" Steven asked,

unsmiling, gazing deep into Melissa's eyes. She felt as though she were being *undressed,* and her cheeks flamed.

She flushed, too tongue-tied to speak, while Tom grinned down at her, plainly enjoying her discomfort.

Steven's gaze held hers. "Evidently not," he said, apparently in answer to his own question.

Melissa glared at him. How was she supposed to ask this obnoxious man out on a *date,* for heaven's sake, and in front of half the town, too?

"I'm fine," she managed.

"That's good to hear," he said.

At the same moment, Tom gave Melissa a light poke with his elbow. "Go ahead," he said, in a stage whisper that probably carried clear past the jukebox and down the short hallway to the restrooms. "Ask him to the dance."

Melissa tallied up her chances of getting away with murder and decided they weren't good. Too many witnesses, for one thing.

So she had to let Tom live. For the moment.

Steven's grin was even more crooked than before. He might have thrown her a lifeline of some sort, said *something,* but not a word came out of that highly kissable mouth. He simply stood there and waited.

Melissa cleared her throat, painfully aware that everybody in the place had an ear cocked that way. "There's a dance at the Grange on Saturday night," she said, because there was no way out. "And I was wondering if you'd like to go." She paused. "With me, I mean."

"Is it Sadie Hawkins' Day?" some redneck joked, from one of the booths.

"Say what?" someone else called.

Steven leaned in, not touching her, though his breath made her lips tingle. "Yes," he said. "I'll go to the dance with you, Melissa O'Ballivan, but only if you agree to pick me up in the roadster."

The tension subsided slightly.

"What's going on?" a customer yelled to a friend on the other side of the café.

"Melissa asked that Creed fella to the Grange Dance!" the friend boomed.

"It's about time she had a date," commented someone else.

"Good," Melissa said. Then she turned on Tom and glowered up at him. At the edge of her vision, she saw Tessa coming out of the kitchen, looking lovely in her jeans, sleeveless white top and blue cobbler's apron smudged with flour. "Now it's *your* turn."

Steven, after one lingering look of sheer appreciation, excused himself quietly and went back to the counter, where Alex waited with the plans.

The clientele was still being unusually quiet.

"Have a seat," Tessa said, her glance moving questioningly between Melissa and Tom. "Ella will be right with you." Ella was the other waitress.

Melissa flashed Tessa a bright smile. "We were hoping you could wait on us personally," she told her friend. "Would you mind?"

"Not at all," Tessa replied, dusting the flour smudge off her front with a few slaps of one hand. "On my way."

As soon as Melissa and Tom had seated themselves at a table in front of the window, Tessa was there, order pad in hand, pencil at the ready.

"Coffee for both of us, please," Melissa said.

Tom sat directly across from her, brooding. He wouldn't look at either Melissa or Tessa.

Melissa kicked him under the table.

Tom started, as though he'd been off in some other world and had just come in for a crash landing.

He looked up at Tessa, his hands so tightly interlocked that his knuckles showed white, and blurted out, "I guess you wouldn't want to go out with me or anything."

Melissa sighed.

Tessa's cheeks turned pink. "I—I mean—"

And nobody in that café, except for Steven and his architect that is, made any pretense of minding their own business.

"See?" Tom said to Melissa.

"Are you talking about—a date?" Tessa faltered.

"Probably wants you to go to the Grange Dance with him on Saturday night," said that same helpful redneck who had spoken up before.

"Oh," Tessa said.

Tom ears turned bright pink.

Tessa spoke again. "Tom Parker," she said, "look at me."

Surprised, Tom did as he was told.

Tessa leaned down, so that her nose was almost touching his, and said, "Now, say whatever it is you want to say. I want to hear it from you."

A sunburst of a smile broke over Tom's face, a mix of hope and cautious joy. "Will you go out with me? To the dance on Saturday night?"

Tessa straightened. Her face revealed nothing whatsoever.

Tom didn't move.

Melissa didn't breathe. If she'd thought for one

moment that Tessa would turn Tom down, she wouldn't have opened her big mouth in the first place.

"Yes," Tessa said, at long last. "I think I *will* go to the dance with you."

The whole place erupted in cheers and whistles then, and Tom went even redder than before.

Melissa let out her breath and sneaked a sidelong look at Steven. By then, even he was caught up in watching the saga unfold, just like everybody else in the café.

"That's good, then," Tom said. Now that he'd made his pitch, he seemed to be at a loss for titillating conversation. "That's real good."

Tessa smiled, her own color a little high, and turned to go behind the counter for the coffee order.

"Thanks for kicking me," Tom said to Melissa. "I think you broke my shin."

"She's going to the dance with you!" Melissa whispered, thrilled that her good friend hadn't been shot down, especially with the whole town looking on. It would have been her fault, at least in part, if that had happened.

"And you're going to the dance with Creed," Tom replied very quietly, grinning. "Not that I thought for one second that he'd turn you down."

Melissa looked toward Steven, just to make sure he was still out of range and, seeing that her Saturday night date was busy shaking hands and exchanging parting words with Alex, turned back to Tom. Raised both her eyebrows. "What made you so sure?" she asked, under her breath.

Tom bent toward her. His eyes sparkled. "Because you're already involved with him," he said slowly, and with a note of cocky triumph. "*That's* why."

"Says who?"

"Says you. Do you think I can't read simple body language, after all these years as a cop? Hell, Melissa, you might as well have hired a skywriter—the pulses in your throat and wrists are pounding so hard, they're visible." He paused, spread his hands in that way he had. "Case closed."

"Oh, shut up," Melissa said, just as Steven started toward their table.

She loved the way he walked, the way he moved, easy in his skin.

She loved the way he did a few *other* things, too, but that was beside the point.

He was trouble—the way they'd butted heads in Tom's office that morning should have been proof enough for anybody, including her.

So what was she doing?

"I'll be looking forward to Saturday," Steven said, when he reached them.

"Me, too," Melissa said, without intending to say anything of the kind. She definitely needed some space, a chance to figure things out, at least a little bit, but she also wanted to get up from that booth and follow him home.

Steven checked his watch. "Time to pick Matt up at school," he said.

Melissa's heart slowed and warmed at the thought of the little boy. "Tell him hi for me," she said.

"I will," Steven told her. Then he nodded to Tom and walked out into the midafternoon sunshine.

Melissa must have stared at the empty space where Steven had just been standing for a beat too long, because when she met Tom's eyes again, he was grinning like a fool.

She made a face at him.

Tessa brought the coffee. Along with two slices of fresh peach pie and forks rolled up in napkins. She blushed when she set Tom's down in front of him.

"Thanks," he said, turning shy all over again.

Tessa turned and hurried away.

Melissa unwrapped her fork. She'd had a carton of designer yogurt for lunch and it wasn't enough. Suddenly, she was starving.

GIVE HER SOME ROOM, warned a voice in Steven's mind, as he walked around to the side parking lot and unlocked his truck with the key fob.

He wanted to turn on his boot heel and go right back inside the café, grab Melissa by the hand and take her home with him. Smooth over the awkward stuff. Hear her laugh. Watch the late afternoon sunlight glinting off her hair. And, yes, he wanted to make love to her again.

Steven sucked in a breath and got into the truck, started it up. *Slow down, cowboy,* he thought.

She was a complex woman, that was for sure. In bed, she'd been a tigress. Ditto that morning, when she'd showed up at the jail. And yet asking him to a country dance had made her turn pink from her collarbone to her hair.

Easing out of the lot and onto the street, Steven shook his head, marveling at the things that were going on inside him just then. Not that he could identify any of them—the fact was, he'd never felt quite this way before.

Never wanted to know everything there was to know about a woman, and more besides.

He reached Creekside Academy within a couple of minutes, and Elaine Carpenter brought Matt out, holding his hand as they came down the front walk.

Matt, a big piece of drawing paper in his free hand, glanced in Steven's direction then turned his attention back to Elaine.

Steven shut off the truck and went to meet them at the curb.

"I made a picture!" Matt crowed, as Steven leaned down to scoop the boy up.

Elaine smiled. "As first days go," she said to Steven, "this one rated an A-plus."

"Thanks," Steven said to her.

"Don't you wanna see the picture?" Matt all but shouted.

With a chuckle, Elaine turned and headed back into the school.

"Sure," Steven told Matt, "but let's get into the truck first."

He carried the boy to the rig and buckled him into his safety seat. Matt waved the piece of paper in Steven's face the whole time.

"All right, already," Steven said, laughing. He took the paper and looked at it.

Three stick figures—man, woman, little boy. A stick dog and a stick horse stood with them, in front of some kind of building leaning hard to the right.

Something fluttered in Steven's heart. It wasn't sorrow, exactly, but it wasn't happiness, either. If he'd had to put an adjective to the emotion, he would have said *bittersweet*.

"That's you," Matt said, stabbing an index finger into the chest of the stick man, but soon moving on to the woman. "And that's Melissa." He, of course, was the child, and the dog was Zeke. The horse was evidently there as a reminder.

"That's—great," Steven said, after a moment or two. He kept thinking he'd get used to things the boy said, but so far that hadn't happened. A glimpse inside Matt's mind always choked him up and, sometimes, like now, it made him afraid. He searched for the right words, a way to warn the little guy not to get his hopes up as far as Melissa was concerned without shooting down all that bright-eyed faith.

Nothing came to him.

"Next time I see Melissa, I'm going to give her this picture as a present," Matt said, as Steven set him on his feet.

Steven's throat ached, and he couldn't quite look at the boy. "Matt—"

"I know, I know," the five-year-old broke in sunnily, "you and Melissa aren't married yet, and I shouldn't get carried away and make all kinds of plans—"

Steven could picture himself married to Melissa— though he hadn't really tried before now—but there was no telling what *her* take on the matter might be.

Sure, they'd had a great time in bed together, but he hadn't forgotten the hurt he'd seen in Melissa's eyes, during the interlude between bouts of lovemaking, when they'd sat at his table eating take-out meat loaf. The last guy she cared about had done a serious number on her, and she wasn't over it.

On top of that, she had a career, a house, a *life,* quite independent from his own. What would someone like

Melissa O'Ballivan really have to gain by tying herself down at this point?

Sex? She didn't need marriage for that, any more than he did.

"Dad?" Matt jolted him out of the thought tangle by tugging at the fabric of his shirt.

Steven blinked, looked down at his son. "What?"

Matt was pointing in the general direction of the ranch house. "Whose truck is that?"

Seeing that old beater was like taking a punch in the gut. The black Dodge, dented and scraped and still sporting Wile E. Coyote mud flaps, even after all these years, belonged to none other than Brody Creed.

"Stay here," Steven told Matt, putting out a hand briefly to emphasize the point before striding off toward his cousin's truck.

The kid might as well have been born a Creed as get adopted into the family, because he never listened. Steven got all the way to Brody's truck, which sat in the high grass with its windows rolled down, before he realized that Matt was right behind him.

"Didn't I tell you to stay put?" Steven asked the boy.

Matt folded his arms and looked up at him, that stubborn glint in his eyes. "You might need some help," he pointed out manfully.

Steven sighed and shoved a hand through his hair in frustration. Then he stepped up onto the running board on the driver's side and looked in.

Brody lay across the seats, his hat over his eyes and his knees drawn up.

Steven jerked the door open, causing it to give way under Brody's booted feet, and he scrambled upright, ready to fight, as always. He shoved the hat back, so he could see, and an instant grin spread across his face.

"Dammit, Boston," he said, "you scared the hell out of me."

Steven was glad to see Brody—no question about it—but there was some anger there, too. The man disappeared for years at a time, with nothing but a ratty Christmas card, always arriving in mid-January, to indicate that he was still alive.

"You look just like Uncle Conner," Matt marveled, his piping voice a much-needed reminder that there was a child present and that meant no more swearing and no landing a fist in the middle of Brody's face. "But you're *not,* are you?"

Brody got out of the truck, resituated his hat, which, like everything else he owned, had seen better days. "Nope," he said, putting out a hand to Matt. "I'm his brother. Name's Brody. And who might you be?"

"Matt Creed," Matt responded, gazing wide-eyed up at Brody.

They shook hands solemnly.

"The rodeo," Steven said, "is still three weeks away."

Brody swung his ice-blue gaze to Steven. It was unnerving how much he looked like Conner, though it shouldn't have been. They were identical twins, after all. "Don't you worry, Boston," he said, in a slow drawl, tucking in his shirt. "I'm not here to stay—just passin' through."

"How come he calls you 'Boston,' Dad?" Matt wanted to know.

"I'll explain later," Steven said, ruffling the boy's hair and handing him the key ring. "You'd better go let Zeke out of the bus. He's probably crossing his hind legs by now."

Matt glanced once more at Brody, eyes full of curious interest, then dashed off toward the bus.

Once he and Steven were alone, Brody folded his arms. "Quite a spread you have here," he said.

It might have been a jibe, considering the state of the house and barn, but Steven didn't know for sure, so he let the comment pass with a quiet, "Thanks."

"Look," Brody said, rubbing his chin, which was bristly with dark gold stubble, "if you want me to hit the trail, just say so."

Steven laid a hand on the front fender of the truck, and he smiled as youthful memories rose in his head, brightly colored and glowing around the edges. "You're welcome here, Brody," he replied, "and you damn well know it."

Brody grinned again. "When did you get married?" he asked, with a gesture toward Matt, now bounding out of the bus behind the sheepdog-bullet that was Zeke.

"I didn't," Steven replied.

Brody arched one eyebrow, and his eyes danced. "I see."

"No," Steven told him, slapping him on the back to head him in the direction of the bus, "you *don't* see. And where the hell have you been all this time?"

CHAPTER THIRTEEN

MELISSA, JITTERY WITH SILLY, schoolgirl thoughts of what she would wear to the dance on Saturday night, decided as she left the office to steel herself and stop by the B&B to look in on the guests. Ashley would be back from Chicago soon, and Melissa wanted to be able to say she'd tended to business.

She smiled as she maneuvered the roadster out of the parking lot behind city hall. The breeze was fresh and the afternoon sunshine was glorious, and Melissa was glad she'd left the top down on the roadster that morning, even though the wind was playing havoc with her hair.

When she reached Ashley's place, there was a familiar SUV parked in front of the garage door, and Melissa's spirits rose even further at the sight of it. Ashley and Jack and little Katie were back from Chicago, at last.

Melissa parked hastily at the curb, maybe a shade too close to the fire hydrant, and barely remembered to grab her purse before dashing across the sidewalk, through the front gate and up the porch steps.

Ashley opened the screen door, grinning from ear to ear, two-year-old Katie balancing on one hip.

They were so different, Melissa and Ashley, that strangers were always surprised to learn that they were twins. Melissa's hair was dark brown, and she preferred to dress for success, while Ashley, a delicate blonde, generally wore pastels, gauzy skirts and ruffled things.

Their eyes, though, marked them as sisters, because they were precisely the same shape and the same shade of blue.

They hugged, Ashley's embrace one-armed because she was still holding Katie, and Melissa's eyes burned with happy tears.

"You were gone *way* too long," Melissa accused, when they were inside the entryway.

Katie, blond like her mother but with her dad's dark eyes, strained toward Melissa, who gladly took her and planted a noisy kiss on one pudgy—and slightly sticky—little cheek.

"And that goes for you, too, Missy," Melissa told her niece.

"We missed you, too," Ashley said. She was barefoot, wearing white shorts and a matching top that showed off her light tan, and her hair was tumbling down from its Gibson-girl do in a way that was almost a signature. "Follow me to the kitchen," she said, and turned.

Melissa followed, carrying Katie and looking around for Mr. Winthrop and the rest of them as they passed through the long, cool hallway between the big living room and the equally spacious dining room.

Ashley's kitchen was the heart of the house, a welcoming place, cheerful and bright, always shining-clean and usually smelling of something delicious—as it did now.

Melissa sniffed. "Brownies?"

"Double Chocolate *Death* Brownies," Ashley replied, twinkling as she turned, took her daughter from Melissa, and gently plunked the child down in her playpen. "And you're going to have at least two, because you've lost weight since we've been gone."

Ashley tended to mother Melissa. Also Brad and Olivia, when they allowed it. She was a born homemaker and a good businesswoman in the bargain.

"You, on the other hand," Melissa responded, tilting her head to one side as she looked her sister over, "are getting a tummy."

Ashley patted her abdomen. "Of course I am," she said happily. "I'm pregnant, remember?"

"Yes," Melissa answered, letting her nose lead her to the counter, where the batch of brownies was cooling, "but I don't have that excuse."

"You're too skinny," Ashley said, filling the electric teakettle at the sink.

"I am not," Melissa replied, good-natured bickering being pretty much their pattern. "And don't think I'm going to gain weight to keep you company for the next six months, either."

"We're twins," Ashley reasoned, hiding one of her sunshine-bright smiles. "The least you could do is pack on some sympathy pounds."

"In your dreams," Melissa said, but it was all she could do not to make quick work of that plate of brownies.

Ashley laughed, and inclined her head toward the table. "Sit down," she said. "And tell me what's been going on in Stone Creek over the last couple of weeks."

"Where do I start?" Melissa said, only partly in jest. She scanned their immediate surroundings. "Are your guests around?"

"They're in the backyard," Ashley answered, with a twinkle. "Practicing the tango."

Melissa shook her head. "I don't hear any music."

"They make their *own* music," Ashley said.

"You can say that again," Melissa retorted, recalling the nude croquet match. She wasn't sure she'd ever be able to put the shock of it behind her.

Ashley sighed. It was a happy, contented sound that made Melissa feel both love and envy, all in the same moment. "I like them," she said. "I wish they were staying longer. So does Jack."

"Where is Jack, anyway?" Melissa asked, looking around. Ashley's husband was one of those men who seem to fill a house with their presence, almost making the walls bulge.

Like Steven Creed.

"He went out to Brad and Meg's to fetch Mrs. Wiggins," Ashley said. "You know—our cat? The one you didn't want to keep at your house because she makes you sneeze?"

Instead of sitting down, Melissa went to the back door and looked out through the screen. Mabel, clad in plaid Bermuda shorts and a red T-shirt instead of the Flamenco dress she'd worn last time, held a rose in her teeth as she and Herbert tangoed their way across the patio.

"Amazing," she muttered. "I need to find out if those people take vitamins and if so, what kind."

Ashley laughed, moving to stand beside her. "They *are* pretty incredible," she agreed mildly. Then she nudged lightly with her elbow. "I hear *your* wild side has been coming out lately."

Melissa narrowed her eyes at her sister, who walked

away to attend to the now-whistling teakettle. "Who told you that?" she demanded, though quietly.

Katie had curled up on the soft bottom of the playpen, and she was sleeping like an angel, with one thumb in her mouth.

Ashley poured hot water into the china teapot that had belonged to their grandmother on the O'Ballivan side, after scooping in some loose tea leaves. "I never betray my sources," she said primly.

Melissa chuckled. "Tom Parker," she said, making a not-so-wild guess. "He's been emailing updates all along."

"Texting," Ashley corrected.

"I swear he's a worse gossip than his aunt Ona," Melissa fretted. "What did he tell you?"

"That he thinks you're sleeping with somebody named Steven Creed," Ashley said, without missing a beat.

With anyone else, Melissa might have fibbed, and with a lot of protestation, too. But lying to her sister was just plain useless; they knew each other too well. "He has his nerve," she said, hedging. That didn't usually work, either, but sometimes she could pull it off.

Maybe Ashley was jet-lagged.

No such luck. "Is it true?" she asked.

Melissa double-checked to make sure Katie was sleeping and the white-haired guests were still tangoing to the music only they could hear before she answered, "Not in the *ongoing* sense, however Tom might have made it sound."

Again, Ashley giggled. She would have looked like a Victorian lady, standing there in front of the cupboard, waiting for the tea to steep, if it hadn't been for the shorts and top. "The 'ongoing sense'? What the heck does *that* mean, sister mine?"

Melissa sank back into her chair at the table again. She felt weirdly agitated and, at the same time, crazy-happy. "It means it happened *once*," she said, in a whisper. "Last night. We've known each other for all of five days. He's a lawyer and his name is Steven Creed. Do you have any other questions?"

"Only about a million," Ashley said.

Outside, voices rose on the warm summer air, and a plaintive meow rang out. Jack was back, with Mrs. Wiggins.

"Guess they'll have to wait for a while," Melissa said.

"Guess so," Ashley agreed, pouring tea.

Jack opened the screen door and came inside, the family cat a fluff of white inside its plastic carrier, and Ashley put one index finger to her lips and pointed toward the sleeping toddler with the other.

The man's face fairly glowed with love for his wife and daughter, it seemed to Melissa. He nodded, kissed Ashley smartly on the mouth and carefully released Mrs. Wiggins from the carrier.

With all that, he still managed a brotherly wink for Melissa. He mouthed the word *hi*.

Ashley, an animal lover, stooped to pet the cat.

Mrs. Wiggins, no doubt indignant over her people's long absence, twitched her tail, gave one petulant meow and vanished through the dining room door.

Melissa sneezed.

"Oh, for Pete's sake," Ashley said. "You're *not* allergic."

Melissa sneezed again.

Jack, a dark-haired, outdoorsy type, agile and fit, cocked a thumb over one shoulder, evidently indicating the backyard. "Mamie Crockett just waylaid me in the driveway," he told Ashley in a be-quiet-the-baby's-sleeping voice. "She said our guests have been raising three kinds of hell ever since they got here."

"Mamie," Ashley said, "is a sweet old thing, but she's also a curmudgeon."

"It's true," Melissa said.

Jack grinned admiringly and shook his head. "I sure hope *I'm* still getting into that much trouble when I hit my nineties," he said. "If somebody calls the cops because the tango music is too loud, I'll count that as a real accomplishment."

"Not to mention just *making* it to that age," Ashley added, slapping Jack's hand when he reached for the brownies and grabbed three of them in one swoop.

"I wonder if they skydive," Jack teased. "And ride mechanical bulls."

"I wouldn't be a bit surprised," Melissa replied.

Just then, Katie awakened, hauled herself upright by gripping the rails of her playpen, and let out a wail. "Potty!" she yelled.

"Your turn," Ashley told Jack, helping herself to a brownie before carrying the plate to the table and setting it down in the middle.

Jack swept the toddler up and kissed her on the cheek. "Too late," he said, after patting Katie's diaper-cushioned bottom.

With that, he and Katie disappeared through the dining room doorway, headed upstairs.

It was hard to believe that Jack McKenzie, able diaper-changer, had so recently headed up a top-notch security company, personally rescuing men, women and children from South American jungles and other politically volatile environments. Although he still owned the firm, and occasionally met with clients and with his key employees, always somewhere far from his wife and child, he seemed content to live in Stone Creek. Riding the range with Brad and Tanner, Olivia's husband, seemed to be all the adventure he needed these days.

"Now we can talk about the new man in your life," Ashley said to Melissa.

"He's *not* 'the man in my life,'" Melissa insisted. "I barely know Steven."

Ashley, sitting across the table from her now and nibbling at one of the brownies, raised an eyebrow. "You know him well enough to *sleep* with him," she said.

"Be quiet," Melissa whispered, as the screen door creaked open and the first of the guests entered into the kitchen.

"I smell brownies!" Herbert whooped.

THEY'D WALKED THE PROPERTY, checked out the ramshackle old house and the ruins of the barn, now partially removed by the work crew that had been there earlier, but Brody still hadn't answered Steven's question. Still hadn't said where he'd been since he and Conner got into a fistfight in a parking lot in Lonesome Bend one night, two weeks after graduating from college, and parted ways.

Brody hadn't even gone home to pack up any of his belongings, as far as anybody knew. His old dog, always riding shotgun, was with him, and the two of them just lit out without so much as a "Go to hell" to the rest of the family.

Now, watching as Matt and the dog played tag in the softening afternoon light, Brody hooked his thumbs in the belt loops of his threadbare jeans and smiled to himself. "You gonna tell me how you happened to come by a kid, Boston?" he asked, his voice low-pitched and gruff with some private emotion.

Steven explained about Zack's and Jillie's deaths, and how he'd adopted Matt when they were both gone.

"That's doing things the hard way," Brody commented, and Steven couldn't be sure whether he was referring to Zack and Jillie, for dying, or Steven himself, for stepping up to raise a child.

But sympathy flickered in Brody's eyes as he watched the boy and the dog playing their games. He was one tough cowboy, and that was as true a thing as any statement ever had been, but deep down, he was a sucker for kids and critters. Always had been.

He slanted a glance at Steven, slapped him hard on the back. "I figured you'd be married by now," he said.

Steven laughed. "Why?"

Brody gestured toward Matt. "Because you're the marrying kind," he said. "Unlike me."

"'The marrying kind'?" Steven repeated. "Excuse me?"

"Face it," Brody said, and another grin splashed across his face. "You were born to be a husband and a father."

"Unlike you?" Steven prodded lightly.

"Unlike me," Brody affirmed. "No good woman

would have me, and while I might sleep with a bad one, I'd never put a wedding ring on her finger."

Steven couldn't stand the wondering any longer. "Brody," he said, his tone firm now, his gaze direct. "Where have you been?"

"It's like that old Johnny Cash song," Brody said. "I've been everywhere, man."

"Not good enough," Steven challenged. "Do you have any idea how much Dad and Kim worry about you?"

Something changed in Brody's face; he looked older than his thirty years, and sadder than a man that young ought to be. "I thought about going home a million times," he said gruffly. "But my pride always got in the way, and I couldn't seem to find a way around it."

Steven thought of Zack and Jillie as he watched their child, and of how unlikely it seemed, even now, that they could be gone. "You gonna wait until somebody dies, Brody? Trust me, if that happens, you'll be a long time regretting it."

Brody's look was sharp as he turned his head toward Steven. "Is one of them sick—Davis or Kim, I mean?"

Steven shook his head. Was Brody implying, by deliberately omitting a third name, that it would be just fine with him if *Conner* were sick? "No," he said. "And neither is your brother. But you ought to know as well as I do how fast things can change."

Before Brody could reply, Matt rushed them, head back and arms out like airplane wings, as good as flying. Zeke ran, barking, behind him.

"I'm *starved!*" Matt declared loudly.

Brody reached out and ruffled the boy's hair. "Me,

too," he said. He looked at Steven again. "What's for supper, Boston?"

"Leftover meat loaf and canned ravioli," Steven said, leading the way toward the door of the bus.

"How come you call my dad 'Boston'?" Matt piped.

"'Cause that's where he's from," Brody said. "*Steven*'s too formal for me—can hardly bring myself to say it—and he won't answer to *Steve*. So I call him Boston."

They were inside now.

Matt picked up Zeke's empty bowl, ready to hike back to the little room where the water heater and the washer and dryer were, that being where the kibble was kept. So far, he'd kept his promise to look after the dog.

"I'm from Denver," Matt said to Brody, "that's where I was born. But nobody calls me that."

Brody pretended to size up the little boy, take his measure the way he might do with a grown man.

It made Matt throw back his shoulders in pride and puff out his chest a-ways.

"I don't reckon *Denver* suits you all that well," Brody said, after some time had gone by. "Nope. If I was going to give you a nickname, I'd pick the *Colorado Kid*."

Matt's face lit up. "Like *Billy* the Kid?"

"Yeah," Brody said, grinning. He'd never met the man, woman or child he couldn't charm straight into next week.

"Feed the dog," Steven told Matt.

Matt nodded and started down the hallway, followed by said dog.

"Do me a favor," Steven said to Brody, keeping his voice down.

Brody's grin faded. "What?"

"Don't set Matt up for a fall, okay?"

Brody took offense, which was more like him. "What the hell do you mean by that?" he rasped, glaring at Steven.

"You said it yourself. You're just passing through. So go easy on the avuncular charm, because I don't want Matt to get too attached to somebody he might never see again."

Brody didn't get the opportunity to respond, because Matt and Zeke reappeared. Matt set the bowl down in its accustomed place and the dog began to crunch loudly on his supper.

Steven, who could do with some supper himself, washed his hands and then went to the full-size refrigerator and took out the leftover meat loaf. There was a lot, because Melissa hadn't eaten much and, as for him, he'd wanted second helpings of something else entirely.

"This is quite a rig," Brody said, looking around.

"It belongs to Brad O'Ballivan," Matt said. "And he's *famous.*"

"I figured that," Brody replied, "from the big head painted on the side, along with his name airbrushed in letters three feet tall."

Steven put the meat loaf in the microwave and took a family-size can of ravioli, the old standby, out of the cupboard. He was annoyed, and he was worried, but he couldn't help the grin that tugged at one corner of his mouth.

"It's just like a house," Matt said, raising his voice to be heard over the dog chomping on kibbles. "There's even a washer and dryer. And I've got my own room, with bunk beds."

Brody gave a low whistle of appreciative exclamation. "Is there a shower? Because I've been on the road for a while, and I could sure use a good sluicing off and a close shave."

Steven opened the ravioli can and dumped the contents into a saucepan. Turned on the gas underneath.

"Yep," Matt said. "There's a shower. Did you know Brad O'Ballivan is famous?"

Brody grinned. "Yeah," he said. "I like his music. Looks like you and him must be pretty good buddies."

"He's a *grown-up,*" Matt responded, as though that precluded friendship. "His son, Mac, is my friend, though. I slept over last night, at Mac's, I mean. We rode on his pony before *and* after supper."

It was the first Steven had heard about the pony ride; Matt hadn't mentioned it that morning, on the way to day camp. He smiled at the thought.

"I see," Brody said.

The timer on the microwave dinged. Steven let the meat loaf sit while the ravioli heated up and he put three plates and some silverware on the table. Surveying it, he realized he'd forgotten to buy milk again. Good thing there was melted cheddar on top of the meat loaf.

Brody went off to wash up for supper, and Steven hoisted Matt up so he could soap his hands and rinse them off in the kitchen sink.

"I like Brody," he whispered to Steven, as though imparting a confidence.

"Me, too," Steven answered.

Brody came back, and they all sat down to supper.

Brody told stories about his life on the rodeo circuit,

both in the States and north of the Canadian border, all of them noticeably devoid of personal information. His cousin might have been an alien from another planet, posing as Brody Creed, for all the connection Steven felt. Once, they'd been as close as brothers, the two of them.

Except for Brody's looks—even in need of a shave and a haircut and decent clothes, he was still a dead-ringer for Conner—he was practically a stranger.

It bruised something in Steven, even thinking that.

Brody. A stranger.

How was that possible?

After supper, Matt reluctantly agreed to take his shower and get into his PJs.

Brody cleared the table, and when everything was in the sink, he paused to pick Matt's drawing of the stick family up from the desktop, pondering it solemnly.

"Everybody wants the same thing," he murmured, holding the sheet of paper as though it were somehow sacred. "A family."

Steven's throat tightened. "Yeah," he managed, when he could get the word out. He went to check on Matt next, because his eyes were burning, and while the boy probably wouldn't notice, he couldn't risk letting Brody see.

When he came back, after toweling Matt off and digging out the pajamas he'd forgotten to bring into the bathroom with him, the door was standing open and Brody was gone.

Had he left again, already, without even a good-bye?

Considering the possibility, Steven felt his heart skip

a beat or two before common sense overtook him. The dog was outside, and Brody was with him.

He went to the doorway.

Brody was hauling a suitcase from under the tarp in the back of his truck. That piece of luggage looked like it was bought at a thrift store, beaten with a tire chain and then dragged down five miles of rough road behind a tractor.

But, then, so did Brody. Life had used him hard, that much was clear.

He might want to talk about it eventually, or he might never say a word. Cussed-stubborn as he was and, conversely, unpredictable, it might go either way.

Brody brought in the suitcase, along with a couple of tattered blankets, the kind they sell cheap in the markets of Tijuana and Nogales, and set everything down on or near the couch.

Steven didn't say anything. He just went to the door and whistled for Zeke, who was chasing some kind of flying bug around the yard. It was a comforting sight, somehow, a dog playing in the twilight, with the old house standing watch in the near distance.

"I'm done with my shower!" Matt announced turning up at the end of the hall. "And I brushed my teeth, too!"

"Good deal," Steven said.

"I don't need a story tonight," Matt added manfully. "You probably want to talk to Brody and everything."

Steven smiled. "There's always time for a story," he said. Ever since Matt had come to live with him, scared and small and confused, clinging to his blanket and his toy skunk, they'd read out of a book every night. Even when Steven wasn't home, he'd made sure the babysitter kept up the ritual.

"I'd just like to look at my picture for a while," Matt said. He sounded mighty philosophical, for a short guy.

My picture. The photo of Zack and Jillie, skydiving on their honeymoon, Steven thought. He was about to say it was right where they'd left it, on Matt's bedside table.

But the boy scampered across the living-room–kitchen and claimed the drawing he'd made at day camp.

That's you, and that's Melissa, and that's me.

Steven's eyes started burning again. "If you change your mind about the story," he said, his voice hoarse, "just let me know."

Matt nodded, then gave a wide grin. "'Night, Dad. 'Night, Brody."

Steven just nodded.

"Good night, Colorado," Brody said seriously.

Matt beamed at that. Summoned the dog. "Come on, Zeke," he said. "It's time for bed."

Zeke, who had been sniffing at his empty kibble bowl, obediently trotted over to Matt, and the two of them vanished down the hallway and into the second bedroom.

"All right if I take a shower?" Brody asked Steven when they were alone again.

"Of course it's all right," Steven said, maybe a touch more abruptly than he should have. "You need anything?"

Brody grinned. "You mean, like a toothbrush, Boston? Hell, I haven't sunk *that* low."

"You're not going to tell me about the time you've been away, are you?" Steven asked, already knowing the answer.

"Not yet," Brody said, with sadness in his eyes, briefly resting a hand on Steven's shoulder. "You asked me for a favor earlier. Now, I'm asking you for one. Let me get around to talking in my own way and my own time. I'm still sorting through things myself."

Steven nodded in agreement.

Brody left the room without another word, and a few seconds later, Steven heard the shower running.

FOR THE NEXT FOUR DAYS, Melissa's life ran smoothly.

She worked. She gained two pounds after having supper with Ashley and Jack and the one-time flashers on several nights. The tenants, meanwhile, remained on their best behavior, probably because, one, there was a child in the house and two, Jack clearly wasn't the sort to put up with any nonsense.

After work, she happily weeded her little patch of garden. She mediated more disagreements, thankfully minor, between the members of the Parade Committee, and ran into Steven fairly often—in the post office, in the grocery store, once at the Sunflower Café, when she stopped for a bottle of water during her run, and another time at the dry cleaner's next door to his new office. He introduced her to his visiting cousin, Brody.

These encounters, mundane as they were, both unnerved and excited Melissa, but she'd said it herself: Things had been moving pretty fast between her and Steven. She was grateful for a breather—and equally grateful that she saw him almost every day.

On top of all this, the weather was flat-out perfect. Warm, but not hot. Sunny, but not glaring.

Happily, there were no confrontations with Velda and no calls from Eustace Blake, lodging his interminable complaints about space visitors.

Nathan Carter had apparently left town again, because Melissa hadn't seen him around, which was a weight off Deputy Ferguson's mind, and hers, too.

Her cuts and bruises healed, and the last of the soreness faded away, although she could still feel ecstatic little catches of physical pleasure sometimes, when she allowed herself to remember how it was, making love with Steven Creed.

Rummaging through Ashley's closet one evening, she even found a killer dress to wear to the dance on Saturday night—an aqua-blue sundress with thinnest-of-thin vertical silver stripes shimmering through the silky fabric.

Life was downright idyllic, all things considered. Which was precisely why she should have been prepared, she would think later.

On Saturday morning, she met with the members of the Parade Committee, as agreed, for the walk-through—a sort of rehearsal, but without the costumes and the floats.

Bea Brady and Adelaide Hillingsley were still on the outs over the toilet-paper question, but the ice was broken when Tessa Quinn and a few assistants showed up at the meeting place in the park with coffee and a big bag of fresh doughnuts, her contribution to the community effort.

Melissa, suitably clad in blue jeans, sneakers and a T-shirt, her hair pulled up into a Saturday ponytail, her face bare of makeup, shepherded everybody into line—Tom had temporarily closed Main Street by placing a sawhorse at each end—and appropriate gaps were left for the high-school band and drill team, the sheriff's posse, and the annual offering from over in Indian Rock.

Stone Creek and Indian Rock tended to be a little competitive, as far as their town floats were concerned, but that only served to up the quality of the event.

Oscar Vernon, who owned a used-car dealership and salvage yard outside the city limits always put the Stone Creek float on the road, and he was invariably secretive as far as colors and subject matter were concerned. He was keeping his mouth shut this year, too—wouldn't give so much as a hint of what he planned—but since he'd done the place proud every year since 1978, nobody really pushed him for answers.

Everyone was poised to begin when Steven and Matt sprinted across the grassy expanse of the park to join in.

Melissa's heart did a thing her granddad Big John would probably have called a twenty-three-skidoo, whatever that was, and she wished she'd bothered with lip gloss and mascara and maybe even a little perfume.

"We're here to help," Matt informed all and sundry, in a piping voice. "What are volunteers supposed to do, anyhow?"

Steven chuckled and ruffled the boy's hair, but he'd locked gazes with Melissa as soon as he came to a stop, and he wasn't letting go.

"Well," Melissa fumbled, reminding herself that Steven had graciously offered to help out on the Parade Committee, managed to shift her eyes to Matt's upturned face, "you could walk where the sheriff's posse will be riding on the big day. That'll give us a better sense of—spacing. Between the floats, I mean."

Steven smiled, well aware, obviously, that she was disconcerted and enjoying the fact. Someone pointed out where the posse went, and Matt ran to the area, earnest and eager.

Before joining him, Steven moved closer to Melissa and gave her a heated once-over, very private.

Her nipples pressed hard against the fabric of her bra, and things warmed and softened inside her.

She blushed.

Steven grinned down at her. "You haven't forgotten about our date, have you?" he asked.

Melissa bit her lower lip and rummaged up a smile, for the sake of curious onlookers—of which there were many—rather than Steven. "I haven't forgotten," she said. Then she looked past his shoulder, pretending to search for someone. "Where's that drop-dead gorgeous cousin of yours?" she asked, just to take some of the smugness out of the man's grin.

It didn't work. Steven Creed looked every bit as cocky as before; maybe even more so. "Brody left yesterday," he said. "He had to be up in Oregon for a rodeo by tonight."

"Oh," Melissa said.

Steven turned, mainly because Matt was calling for him to do his part holding the gap for the sheriff's posse, but he looked back at her over one shoulder and his smile was so intimate that she felt as naked as any member of the infamous croquet team over at Ashley's B&B.

CHAPTER FOURTEEN

"Now, DON'T GO WEARING a three-piece suit on your hot date, Boston," Brody warned, via cell phone, at around four-thirty Saturday afternoon. He'd called, as ordered when he left, to let Steven know he'd gotten to Oregon with no mishaps along the way. "You're going to a dance with a pretty lady, not arguing a case before the Supreme Court."

Steven laughed, standing there in his bedroom in Brad O'Ballivan's tour bus and grimly assessing the limited wardrobe he'd brought along from Denver. Most of his clothes, like the furniture and the lion's share of his and Matt's personal belongings, were in storage until the farmhouse was ready to live in. "Point taken," he said. "What *do* guys wear to a country dance these days, anyway?"

"Well, *that's* a dumb-ass question if I've ever heard you ask one—which I have, of course," Brody responded, his tone jocular. The way he talked, nobody would guess that he'd turned his back on the whole family almost a decade before and cut off all communications except for a once-a-year greeting card. "Wear jeans. Pretty new, if you have them, along with a halfway decent Western shirt and good boots, polished to a shine. You can dispense with the hat—you look like a dude when you wear a hat. Oh, and iron the jeans and the shirt, too."

Steven pretended to be aggrieved. He and Matt had both missed Brody since he hit the road. "Are you through?"

Brody chuckled. "OK," he conceded, "you looked all right in a *real* hat, back when you were rodeoing and punching cattle, but don't try to get away with anything fancy, because it won't work."

"Got it," Steven said. Then he asked if Brody had signed up for his events yet, and when he thought he might be rolling back through Stone Creek.

During Brody's visit, they hadn't discussed the past much. Only a few words about Davis and Kim had passed between them, and they hadn't talked about Conner at all. Steven felt a prickle of guilt, wondered if he shouldn't tell Brody that his brother was planning on coming to Stone Creek's rodeo, and then clue Conner in, too. But since he knew neither one of them would show up if they so much as suspected the other would be there, too, he kept that knowledge to himself.

It was a little like being the only person in the world who knew that, at a certain hour, on a particular day, a colossal meteor would strike the planet.

Steven had considered warning his dad and Kim, in case they decided to change their travel plans and swing by in their RV for that visit Kim had mentioned. They'd be more than ready to spend some time with Matt, whom they missed sorely, and they had to be curious about the new place. He was still undecided on that score, because he knew Kim, the eternal optimist, might not be able to resist telling Conner. She would naturally think the twins' long overdue reconciliation was a sure thing.

Steven knew it was anything but. In fact, it might be a

replay of that long ago summer night, when Conner and Brody had lit into each other with fists flying and blood in their eyes. Some risks were worth taking, though—there was always the chance that Kim was right.

"Tell the Colorado Kid I'll be seeing him again soon," Brody finished. He'd already established a bond with Matt, but would he hold up his end of the bargain?

No telling.

Steven swallowed hard. "I'll do that," he said, and rang off.

Matt was spending the night over at Brad and Meg's again, with Mac, because of the dance, and Zeke had gone with him.

That left Steven feeling a lot more alone than he cared to.

He dropped his cell into his shirt pocket, ran a hand through his hair and sighed. Not surprisingly, he had Melissa on his mind. He wondered if he ought to go for more sex, or keep on giving her the space he sensed she needed. In the end, he decided he'd have to play it by ear.

He got out his best pair of jeans, the only ones that were still clean as a matter of fact, and chose a shirt with snaps instead of buttons and a Western cut to the yoke. He poked around the bus until he found an iron and a fold-down ironing board, and he managed not to scorch the duds while he pressed the wrinkles out and the creases in. Then he showered and dressed and polished his good boots with spit and a wad of paper towels, since he hadn't bought a tin of the waxy stuff he normally used to shine up his shit-kickers.

Even with all that done, it was only 5:30 p.m., and he wasn't supposed to pick Melissa up at her place until

7:15. Too restless to stay home, without even a dog for company, he grabbed his keys, fired up the new truck and headed for town. Once there, he'd find some way to kill time, and he wanted to track down a nice bouquet for his date.

He shook his head and chuckled as he began the short drive down to the road. When had he ever been this excited about spending an evening with a woman? Hell, not since high school—if then.

And since he wasn't all that crazy about dancing in the first place, there were some serious implications here.

She's a prosecutor, he reminded himself. *Just like Cindy.* And, just like Cindy, Melissa had worked hard to carve out a career for herself. She'd loved Dan Guthrie, loved his kids, too, but she hadn't been willing to give any ground at all to save the relationship.

Briefly depressed, Steven shook off those thoughts and moved on to new ones. Work on the house and the new barn would begin on Monday—he had the contractor's word on it, and the guy had a solid reputation for honesty and hard work. Matt was settling in just fine at school, and Stone Creek was already proving to be a good place to call home.

In an unpredictable world like this one, that was enough.

Reaching the edge of town, Steven glanced down at the gas gauge and decided to fill up. That would use up the better part of fifteen minutes, he calculated.

He pulled in at the combination convenience store–gas station, where there were exactly two pumps, one of which dispensed diesel. He shut off the truck, got out and read the handwritten sign taped to the paper-towel dispenser.

"Machine broke. Pay inside."

Steven started for the door, passing a rusted-out Bonneville with cardboard in place of the glass that should have covered the rear window. Besides his truck, it was the only rig around.

Business must be slow this time of day, he decided.

A plump woman stood behind the counter, in front of the register, and her nametag said "Martine."

Steven glanced to one side, spotted the probable owner of the Bonneville over by the cooler, evidently shopping for beer. The guy was young—maybe under the legal drinking age—and nobody he recognized, but that didn't mean much. After all, Steven was new in Stone Creek; there were still a lot of people he didn't know, small as the place was.

He said hello to Martine, who smiled at him as she returned the greeting, and ran his debit card through the machine to make advance payment for whatever a full tank of gas wound up costing.

"Well," Martine responded, "welcome to Stone Creek. It's nice to see somebody moving into this town instead of out. Seems like there was a mass exodus after the mill closed down."

"Thanks for the welcome," he said. He knew she'd read his name off the credit card, but he offered it up just the same, since that was the polite thing to do.

"You got a wife, Mr. Creed?" she asked.

Steven wasn't exactly pressed for time, so he lingered longer than he might have done otherwise. "No, ma'am," he said. "It's just me and my son, Matt."

Martine tilted her head to one side and studied him,

a mischievous light dancing in her clear-as-creek-water eyes. It crossed Steven's mind that she might know all about his rendezvous with Melissa, that being typical of a small town like Stone Creek.

"We can always use another eligible bachelor," she said finally. "Not that you'll be on the market long, a good-lookin' cowboy like you."

The remark made Steven feel uncharacteristically shy. "Thanks," he said, for the second time, feeling his earlobes burn a little. Now, he fled.

"I've got a daughter!" Martine called after him. "Her name is Jessica Lynn and she's going to be a full-fledged dental assistant in another six weeks!"

Steven pretended not to hear the pitch, but he couldn't help chuckling as he took the nozzle off the fuel pump and stuck it into the tank's opening.

He'd been so busy trying to figure out Melissa O'Ballivan, it hadn't even occurred to him that he might be the subject of some matchmaking. How many other mamas, besides Jessica Lynn's, were eyeing him through the matrimonial crosshairs, right at that very moment?

Since the tank was nearly empty, it took a while to fill it. Steven washed the windshield, checked the tire pressure and wiped a few bugs off the grillwork.

When the gas pump shut down, he went back inside to sign the credit slip and get his receipt.

Martine had acquired some more customers by then, and she was too busy at the register, ringing up jugs of milk, lottery tickets and cigarettes to try to sell him on Jessica Lynn again.

Thinking ahead to that evening's dance at the Grange Hall, which would probably be attended by just about everybody in Stone Creek and maybe Indian Rock, too, he couldn't help wondering just what he might be letting himself in for.

He grinned to himself as he drove away.

Maybe he'd attract enough attention to make Melissa a little jealous.

Wouldn't *that* be something?

MELISSA STOOD IN FRONT of the mirror on her closet door, scowling at herself. Now that zero hour was approaching, she didn't like the aqua dress half as much as she had before.

She sucked in her stomach. "There they are," she said, pointing at her reflected backside. "The two pounds I gained eating *your* food."

Ashley, sitting on the bed and holding Katie on her lap, smiled and shook her head. "Please. You could gain ten *more* pounds and still fit into every pair of jeans you own."

"As if I'm going to let *that* happen," Melissa said, with a little sniff.

Ashley laughed softly. Her eyes shone with contentment and good humor. Once upon a time, she'd been pretty tense herself, but since Jack's arrival in her life, and then Katie's, she'd mellowed considerably.

Which was sometimes annoying.

"Are you planning on spending the night with him?" Ashley asked.

Melissa turned and made a big deal of cupping her hands loosely over Katie's little pink ears. "What a thing to say in front of a *child,*" she said.

Ashley rolled her twinkly blue eyes. "Katie is *two,*"

she reminded her sister. "And anyway, you're just trying to stall."

Melissa uncovered Katie's ears, sighed. "I don't know," she said.

More twinkling. Happiness looked wonderful on Ashley, just as it did on Olivia and Meg. "You don't know if you're stalling?" she teased.

"I don't know if I'm going to—" Melissa glanced down at Katie, who was holding Ashley's long, golden braid in both hands and gazing at it in wonder, and lowered her voice, "sleep with him."

"What's the holdup?" Ashley asked.

Melissa plunked her hands on her hips and mimicked, "'What's the holdup?' Easy for *you* to ask, Ashley O'Ballivan McKenzie, when you have the whole rest of your *life* laid out like a path between two rose gardens!"

"Stalling," Ashley repeated, singing the word.

Katie giggled and sang her own version.

Melissa stumbled over her answer. "It's just—well— we hadn't known each other very long when—"

"Maybe," Ashley reasoned, "it's a matter of knowing each other *well* enough, instead of *long* enough."

Melissa arched an eyebrow, her hands still resting on her hips. Which felt slightly wider under her knuckles, though that was probably an illusion brought on by concern over consumption of her sister's incomparable lasagna. "Whose side are you on, anyway?" she asked.

"There are *sides?*" Ashley countered, raising her own eyebrows. "Who knew?"

Melissa let out a big breath and sat down beside her sister on the bed. "I'm trying to be sensible, here," she said.

"Love isn't sensible," Ashley informed her.

"Who said anything about love?" Melissa countered. "This is a case of lust. If I were in *love* with Steven Creed, don't you think I would have noticed?"

"Not necessarily," Ashley chimed. "For such a smart woman, you can be pretty obtuse when it comes to men."

"Obtuse?" She took a slow, deliberate breath, in a bid for patience. "Just because you're married now, Ash, you're suddenly an expert on men?"

"I'm an expert on *one particular man,*" Ashley responded, a little smugly. "That's all I need to be."

Melissa studied her twin in silence for a long moment. Then her shoulders slumped slightly. "Don't you ever get scared?" she asked, very softly.

Ashley took her hand, squeezed lightly. A slight furrow appeared in her forehead. "Scared?"

"Caring so much," Melissa murmured. "It's, well— it's *dangerous.*"

Ashley's entire countenance softened, along with her face. "Oh, honey," she said. "Is this about the breakup with Dan? That's why you think it's dangerous to care too much? I know you were hurt, but honestly, what are the odds of something like that happening twice in one person's lifetime?"

Melissa sighed again. "Have you checked the divorce statistics lately?" she asked. Her stab at humor fell flat.

"Statistics are statistics," Ashley said. "And people are people. Every couple is different, Mel. It's all about finding someone who wants the same things out of life and has similar values, and then both partners trying like hell to make it work. There aren't any guarantees, obviously—not for any of us."

"So you never get scared. Never worry that something could happen to Jack or, God forbid, Katie or the baby?"

"Of course I worry sometimes," Ashley replied. "I'm only human, and I have some of the same abandonment issues as you do, because of Mom leaving and Dad dying so young. But I try never to dwell on all the things that could go wrong. Melissa, so many things go *right*, every single day, for everybody, but nobody notices that."

Melissa leaned closer and let the side of her head rest against the side of Ashley's. "You're amazing," she said.

"Yes," Ashley replied, with comical primness, "I am, rather, aren't I?"

They were quiet for a while, content just to be side by side.

Then, perhaps because she'd missed Ashley so much while she was away visiting Jack's family, Melissa asked a question she might have kept back, saved for another time.

"Ash, did you ever feel as though your own life didn't fit you anymore?"

Ashley squeezed Melissa's shoulders. "Before Jack, I did," she replied quietly. "I had everything I'd ever thought I wanted—you and Olivia and Brad, this house, my own business, all of it. But I finally had to face facts after Jack turned up again. Something was definitely missing, and that something was a man to love and be loved by." She paused, sighed happily, and kissed the top of Katie's head. "A man I could make babies with. Share dreams with. Even argue with."

Melissa sighed, too, but it wasn't out of contentment. She felt confused, as though she'd reached some kind of crossroads and didn't know which way to turn. "We're so different," she reflected, "despite being twins. You've always been old-fashioned, baking pies and wearing aprons with ruffles on them, seemingly glad to stay right here in Stone Creek until the end of your days, while I always wanted to take on the world, prove I could hold my own against the best of them."

Ashley smiled, but her eyes were serious, and full of tender concern. "Maybe we're not so different as you'd like to believe," she said. One corner of her mouth quirked mischievously, which meant there was a zinger coming, for sure. "You'll probably never be a decent cook," she went on, "but I think you'd really *like* to have a home and a husband and some kids."

"I *have* a home," Melissa said, thinking of her tidy, mortgage-free cottage.

"You have a *house*," Ashley corrected her gently. "That isn't the same thing at all."

"Ashley O'Ballivan McKenzie," Melissa challenged good-naturedly, "are you saying a woman can't live happily ever after without a man in her bed and a gold band on her finger?"

"Of course not. Lots of women thrive on being single. Men, too. But that's them and this is you, Mel. Olivia and Meg and I have been worrying about you for a long time—since you and Dan called it quits, especially. You put on a good show, sister mine, but we—your nearest and dearest—are not so easily deceived."

"All right, so I get lonely sometimes," Melissa retorted. "Who doesn't?"

"*I* don't," Ashley said. "And I don't think Olivia and

Meg do, either." She paused again, looking thoughtful. "In my opinion, you've gotten so used to being lonely that you think it's normal to feel that way."

Melissa huffed out a sigh, ready for the conversation to be over. Ashley's comments struck a little too close to the bone. "What would you suggest I do?" she asked, going against her own decision to change the subject. "Shall I just cut some poor, unsuspecting guy out of the herd, throw him down on the ground and hog-tie him?" She pretended to ponder the plan. "He'd have to be a pretty slow runner, of course."

Ashley gave a soft hoot of laughter at that. The woman twinkled all over, like a tree bedecked with fairy lights. Was it even *legal* to be that happy?

"Do you know what your problem is, Melissa?" Ashley challenged, with a note of smugness in her tone.

"A twin sister with a penchant for minding my business instead of her own?" Melissa teased.

Ashley stopped smiling then, and the fairy lights dimmed a little. "Your whole life is geared to wins and losses. No gray areas for you—and you *really* don't like to lose. When your relationship with Dan went under, you saw it as a personal defeat. After that, you were scared to try again."

"Nonsense," Melissa said, but her tone was decidedly hesitant.

"I was always the old-fashioned type," Ashley maintained gently. "And you were always competitive. Because you weren't the one to put an end to the whole thing, instead of Dan, you counted it as a rejection."

Melissa's throat tightened, and she swallowed, but

it didn't help. She didn't have the words to contradict Ashley, or the conviction, either.

On some level, the breakup with Dan *had* left her with the idea that love worked for other people, but not for her.

Still holding Katie, Ashley stood, bent to kiss the top of Melissa's head. "Just have a good time tonight," she advised.

And then she and Katie left the room.

ONCE HE WAS THROUGH at the gas station–convenience store, Steven drove around town for a while, marveling at his own sense of blithe aimlessness, and finally realized he was hungry. He headed for the only drive-through burger place in town, ordered a cheeseburger and a cola, and ate in the driver's seat, being careful not to spill anything on his clean shirt or his best jeans. He'd pressed them both, and he wanted to stay spiffy as long as he could.

Even when the burger was history, there was lots of time to go before he could reasonably knock on Melissa's front door.

He found a flower shop, after some searching, but it was closed. From there, he proceeded to the supermarket. He'd seen roses and various houseplants in the produce sections of grocery stores lots of times. He'd have preferred something a little fancier, a big bouquet with exotic blossoms and ribbon tied around the vase, but for tonight anyhow, he'd have to make do.

Inside the store, Steven chose between daisies, rosebuds just opening up, and what was probably some kind of lily. He considered buying several bunches and putting them together, but he wasn't sure which colors went with which. So he settled for a dozen yellow roses, stuck them, stems dripping, into their vase-shaped plastic bag, and headed for the checkout counter.

All the lines were long. Folks with shopping carts filled to overflowing, toddlers wailing with boredom or fatigue or some combination of the two. A few last-minute Louies—like himself—who'd stopped in for flowers.

Steven waited patiently. After all, a line was a line and he had plenty of time, anyway. He was caught off guard when another cart in front of his rammed into his from the side, lightly but still with a startling crash of metal.

Tessa Quinn, from over at the Sunflower Café, was standing there, grinning at him. "Oops," she said. "Sorry. I wasn't watching where I was going."

"Hey," he greeted her, with an easy smile.

She took in the yellow roses. "Nice flowers."

Steven sighed. "Yeah," he said.

Tessa blew out a good-natured breath. "Not another man of few words," she lamented cheerfully. "We've already got a surplus of those in this town."

He chuckled. "Looking forward to the dance tonight?" he asked, having decided to make more of a social effort. Up on the ranch, outside Lonesome Bend, Kim was forever claiming that she'd trade the whole bunch of quiet Creed men for someone who spoke in complete sentences.

Tessa's smile dazzled. "Oh, yes," she said. "I thought Tom Parker would *never* ask me out."

The line moved, and Steven held back to let Tessa go ahead of him. "And I thought Melissa would never ask *me*," he joked. No matter how things turned out between

them, he figured he'd never get tired of the memory
of that woman swallowing her formidable pride, right
there in the Sunflower Café, in front of half the town,
to invite him to a dance.

Tessa laughed. "That *was* a surprise," she said. "Tom
must have tricked her into it." The expression on that
well-known face was priceless as she realized how the
remark must have sounded to Steven. She even blushed.
"It's just that—well—the two of them have been buddies
since they were little kids. After Dan Guthrie broke Melissa's heart into about a million pieces, people thought
she and Tom might finally get together—" She fell silent
again, looking miserable.

"But they didn't," Steven said, trying to help the poor
woman off the hook.

Tessa shook her head. "No," she confirmed. "They
didn't."

He might have asked her to tell him a little more
about Melissa's broken heart if the time and place and
circumstances had been different, but the clerk was waiting none too patiently to ring up Tessa's purchases and
the line behind them stretched clear back to the freezer
aisle.

When Tessa had finished with her transaction, she
grabbed her grocery bags and almost *ran* out of the
store.

Thoughtfully, Steven paid for the flowers and headed
for his truck.

Once there, he got in, snapped his seat belt into
place and then just sat for a while, staring through the
windshield.

So Melissa had some emotional baggage, he thought.
Didn't everybody, himself included?

Cindy had done a number on him, back in the day. So had a few other women, though to lesser degrees. And as much as he loved Kim, he'd spent a lot of time wishing, as a kid, that his stepmother had never entered the equation in the first place. Why, he'd wondered privately, couldn't his mom and dad have gotten married, and raised him together, like normal people, instead of shunting him back and forth between two very different worlds until he was old enough to make his own choices?

Finally, Steven had been forced to accept the pertinent facts. Life was messy. It was unpredictable. And 99.9 percent of the time, it didn't make any damn sense at all.

For all that, it was still good.

It was a gift.

The trouble arose, he reasoned, when he tried to swim upstream, against the flow.

He sighed.

It was a warm summer night. He was going to a country dance with a beautiful woman.

He decided to let that be enough, for the time being.

MELISSA FELT A LITTLE QUIVER of excitement in the pit of her stomach when she opened her front door to find Steven Creed standing on the porch, a bouquet of yellow roses clasped in one hand.

For a moment, she was a teenager again.

Wishing Ashley had stayed to meet Steven, instead of taking Katie home, she stepped back to let him in.

His gaze drifted over her in an appreciative way that

didn't rankle, as it would have with some men. "You look fantastic," he said.

Melissa smiled. *You don't look so bad yourself, cowboy,* she thought, letting her eyes speak for her.

Steven shifted, looking somewhat uneasy. "I'm probably a little early," he said.

Still smiling, she took the flowers. "I'll just pop these into a vase and we'll go," she told him, leading the way into the kitchen.

There, she filled a vase with water and clipped an inch or so from the end of each of the rose stems, so they'd last longer.

"They're from the supermarket," Steven said, from somewhere behind her. He wasn't touching her, but he was close enough that she could sense the hardness and the heat of him.

Or was that her imagination?

"The florist's shop was closed," he added.

She turned, holding the vase full of yellow roses, and said sincerely, "All roses are beautiful. Thank you, Steven."

A spark of something—possibly relief—lit his blue eyes. "You're welcome," he said, and his voice sounded hoarse. He crooked an elbow at her. "Shall we?"

Melissa laughed. "Let's."

Outside, he hoisted her into the passenger seat of his pickup, his hands strong on the sides of her waist, stirring up all sorts of deliciously uncomfortable sense memories.

They kept the conversation light during the drive—Steven said his barn would be going up fast, because the contractor had talked him into a prefab, and the concrete foundation was scheduled to be poured on Monday. The house would take a little longer, he told her, but it would be livable in a couple of weeks.

"I guess that tour bus is starting to feel a little cramped," Melissa said, and instantly regretted the remark.

Talk about sense memories.

Out of the corner of her eye, she saw the slightest grin flicker across Steven's mouth. "Actually," he said, "it's pretty comfortable."

Melissa was relieved to see the Grange Hall up ahead. The building was historic, dating back to Sam O'Ballivan's lifetime, and the never-painted walls were weathered by a century of hard rains, deep snows and long, ground-cracking dry spells. Thanks to Brad's generosity, the place was much sounder than it looked, the roof solid, the dance floor level, the small stage equipped for live music and the productions of the local amateur theater group.

Tonight, cars and pickup trucks jammed the gravel parking lot, and there was a buzz of anticipation in the air. The twang of electric guitars spilled into the sultry evening, a nearly tangible vibrato, and the whole scene reminded Melissa, in a bittersweet flash, of a time long past—back when she and Ashley and Brad and Olivia were kids, their mom not yet gone and their dad still young and vital.

How Delia had loved a community dance—looked forward to it all week long. Wore her freshly shampooed hair up in rollers all day Saturday, and often squeezed the cost of a dime-store lipstick out of the grocery budget because, as she put it, a new shade always made her feel prettier. Delia had favored dresses with full skirts, the better for twirling, and she'd primp in front of the mirror on top of her bureau, as if she was practicing her smile for the upcoming occasion.

Or maybe she wasn't practicing for the dance at all, but for the men she'd meet after she got on the bus one day and left Stone Creek—and her family—behind for good.

Melissa sighed. Delia was gone now; she'd died of hard living and the effects of long-term alcohol use a couple of years ago. By then, the woman had been a stranger for so long that the loss felt impersonal; Melissa had done the bulk of her grieving as a small child.

Back then, Melissa's dad, a quiet man, thoughtful and maybe a little shy, had watched Delia's antics with smiling admiration glowing in his eyes, as if he'd never seen a more beautiful picture than the one his wife made, spinning to make the hem of her dress fly out around her shapely legs.

Whole families had attended the dances in those days—not just the mothers and the fathers, but babies and kids of all ages, and old folks, too. Melissa recalled running wildly around the Grange Hall, inside and out, with her brother and sisters and a flock of other local children, until they all finally ran down.

As the evening wore on, the younger kids would collapse from sheer delighted exhaustion, one by one, and, lie down to rest on a makeshift bed, usually consisting of horse blankets or suit coats, to be carried out to the family rig around midnight, when the festivities ended.

For a moment, Melissa was back there—she could smell her dad's aftershave and the fresh-air scent of the jacket he wore for dress-up, feel the warmth and strength of his shoulder, where her head rested. He'd carried her in one arm and Ashley in the other, and remembering brought a lump to Melissa's throat and a sting to the back of her eyes.

Steven paid the modest price of admission—the money collected went partly to the band and partly to the local historical society—and she knew he'd picked up on her mood by the way his eyes narrowed slightly when he looked at her.

He moved nearer to her and, since the noise was intense, leaned close to her ear to ask, "You look a little peaked. Are you okay?"

She nodded, swallowed. She felt a little deflated, though, the way she always did when she remembered the demise of her parents' marriage and the vast emptiness left behind when it was over. "I'm fine," she told him, but it was herself she wanted to convince.

It was a long time ago, she thought. *Let it go.*

Melissa was good at shaking things off—and it helped when she spotted Olivia and Tanner waltzing on the other side of the hall, lost in each other's eyes, seemingly oblivious to the fast song the band was thrumming out and the dancers spinning and gyrating around them.

Her sister and brother-in-law were happy together, as were Ashley and Jack and Brad and Meg. There was no antilove curse looming over the O'Ballivan family.

When the band struck up a slow tune, Steven drew Melissa into his arms and claimed a space for them on the crowded dance floor.

Melissa drew in the delicious, fresh-air-and-green-grass scent of his skin and hair. Reveled in the hard heat of him, though the sensation wasn't about sexual attraction—though God knew there was plenty of that—

but instead came from a sense of being protected and even cherished.

Steven's breath was like a balmy breeze against her ear. "I'm issuing a blanket apology, in advance," he told her, with a note of laughter in his voice. "I've never been much of a dancer, and if I step on your feet, please assume it's unintentional."

She smiled, tilted her head back to look up at him. She could see the underside of his chin, the strong line of his jaw, but only part of his face. By then, the memories of her youthful parents had been carefully folded and tucked away in the softest places in her heart.

"You're doing just fine," she said.

He drew back just far enough to look her full in the face. She saw tenderness in those periwinkle eyes of his, and something that glowed like light. "Thanks," he replied.

And they danced.

Dan Guthrie passed, with Holly in his arms, and Melissa waited for the pang she usually got when she saw them together, but it didn't come.

When the song ended, the crowd parted, women laughing and fanning their flushed faces with their hands, men looking relieved to get a break from dancing.

Dan and Holly, hands clasped, came right through the path that had opened for them and straight to where Melissa and Steven were standing.

"Hello, Melissa," Dan said, his tone solemn, his eyes fond as they rested on her for that first moment. His gaze almost immediately shifted to Steven, and he put out a hand, the way men do when they introduce themselves to a stranger, and added, "Dan Guthrie."

Steven accepted the handshake. "Steven Creed," he replied. "Good to meet you."

Holly, a pretty thing, skinny except for the prominent baby bump pushing out the front of her cotton sundress, wore her blond hair pulled up into a ponytail that night. It bobbed near the top of her head. She couldn't seem to stop smiling.

Dan slipped an arm around Holly's waist and said, "This is my wife, Holly."

Steven smiled and said hello.

It was all so ordinary, Melissa thought. So comfortable.

She and Dan might have been old friends, perhaps one-time classmates, instead of former lovers.

"How are Michael and Ray?" Melissa asked, as Steven took her hand.

Dan grinned proudly at the mention of his young sons. "They're growing like weeds," he said. "I swear, a bunkhouse full of hardworking cowpunchers couldn't put away more food at a sitting than those two."

Melissa laughed, felt a whisper of tenderness deep in her heart, not for Dan, but for what they'd once had together, and for his children. She opened her mouth to make some comment she wouldn't remember two seconds later, but a burst of happy laughter from near the entrance stopped her.

Tom and Tessa had arrived, Tom looking handsome in civilian clothes—jeans and a nice Western shirt—Tessa exquisite in a sundress with a blue print and ruffles.

Seeing Melissa, Tom grinned and pointed an index finger at her before pulling Tessa through the throng of Stone Creekers to approach the group.

Dan and Tom shook hands, and the music started up

again, compelling Dan and Holly to drift off into the swirl of sweaty noise and motion.

Melissa and Tessa chatted briefly, but since conversation was almost impossible, they soon gave up.

She sighed, looking up at Steven, as the other pair moved away. "They make a great couple," she said.

Steven responded with a nod and then they, too, were dancing again.

After an hour or so, they stepped outside to get some fresh air and admire a sky full of stars. As the strains of a romantic ballad spilled from inside, Steven took Melissa into his arms and they waltzed in the shadows of the old building.

His smile was tender as he looked down at her. "I warned you about my dancing, didn't I?" he drawled.

She laughed, enjoying the sheer masculinity he exuded, the controlled strength, the hard muscles of his arms and chest, the clean, woodsy scent of his cologne.

"You're doing just fine," she told him.

And they continued to dance, even between songs.

For Melissa, it was a time out of time. They'd stopped, and she'd just tilted her head back for the kiss she knew was coming, when someone drove into the lot at top speed, tires flinging gravel in all directions.

"What the hell—?" Steven muttered, still holding Melissa's shoulders in his hands, but distracted now.

She peered through the darkness, saw Martine, who worked over at the Stop & Shop, jump out of her beat-up sedan.

"Help!" Martine yelled. "Somebody, *help!*"

The music drowned out her voice, but Steven and

Melissa heard her plaintive cry, and they rushed toward her.

"Martine—" Melissa sputtered "—what on earth?"

"There's been a robbery!" Martine choked out. "A man wearing a ski mask—he took all the money in the till and made me open the safe—he had a gun—"

"Breathe," Melissa ordered, taking Martine's hands.

"I'll get the sheriff," Steven said from somewhere at the fringes of Melissa's awareness, and she nodded without looking at him.

"Are you hurt?" Melissa asked, and Martine shook her head, still half-hysterical.

"No—I did what he said—there was nobody else in the store, thank God—"

Melissa steered Martine, who was trembling violently by then, back to her car. Seated her on the passenger side.

Tom arrived quickly, with Tessa and Steven and several other people following. Melissa moved aside, and Tom crouched next to Martine's car, looking up into her pale face.

"Tell me what happened," he said gently.

Martine repeated what she'd told Melissa. A man had come into the store, waving a gun and wearing a ski mask. She'd been so scared—certain he meant to kill her, he was so jittery—and she'd done what she was told. Given him all the money she had access to, including the contents of her own wallet.

Tom asked if she'd recognized the man.

Martine shook her head, bit down hard on her lower lip.

"What?" Tom prompted, very quietly. "Tell me, Martine."

"I was practically out of my head with fear, but—but something made me look out the window—I guess I wanted to make sure he wasn't coming back—and I saw him get into a car and drive off." She paused again, looking miserably uncertain. "I can't swear to it, Tom, but it sure looked like that old heap of Velda Cahill's."

Melissa felt a tightening in the pit of her stomach.

Dear God. *Byron?*

Tom straightened, turned to Tessa. "I'm sorry," he said, his voice gruff.

Tessa nodded, reached out to touch his arm. "I can get home on my own," she said. "You be careful."

Call it a premonition, call it common sense. Whatever the feeling was, it washed over Melissa like ice-cold water.

For now, maybe forever, the fun was over.

STEVEN AND MELISSA took Tessa home, pulling into the alley behind the Sunflower Café, where an outside stairway led to the apartment upstairs.

Leaving Melissa in the truck, Steven saw Tessa to her door, waited while she worked the lock, leaned inside to switch on the living room lights. A visible shudder moved through her as she paused on the threshold.

"It's creepy," she said. "Knowing a criminal might be running loose in Stone Creek, I mean."

"We could wait," Steven offered. "Until your brother and his wife get here, at least."

"I'll be all right," Tessa replied quietly. "Olivia and

Tanner won't be long—they just wanted to go by their place and make sure the kids were okay."

Tessa might have been a lot of things, but "all right" wasn't among them. She looked scared to death.

"We wouldn't mind hanging around for a while," Steven reiterated.

Tears glimmered in Tessa's eyes. She sniffled and shook her head once, as though to fling away her fears. "This guy threatened Martine with a *gun*. What if— what if something happens to Tom—?"

"He strikes me as the type who can take care of himself," Steven said truthfully. "And, besides, he has deputies to back him up."

"If anything happened—" Tessa fretted, more to herself than to Steven.

Steven didn't answer. He wasn't about to throw out a flippant "Don't worry, everything will be all right"; experience had taught him that that wasn't necessarily so. Nor did he feel right about leaving quite yet.

"I've never told Tom that I love him," Tessa said, looking directly into his eyes. "What if I don't get a chance to tell him?"

Steven touched her arm. "What if you do?" he countered gently.

Just then, another truck appeared in the alley below, sitting headlights-to-headlights with his own rig.

"Looks like Tanner and Olivia are here," Tessa said, with obvious relief.

Melissa had gotten out of Steven's rig to speak to them. The two women were embracing, while Tanner took the stairs two at a time.

Steven nodded to him and stepped back, and Quinn pulled Tessa in for a quick, brotherly hug.

"I'm all right," Tessa insisted. Then she made introductions, and the two men shook hands.

"Thanks for looking out for my sister," Tanner said.

Steven merely nodded, then headed down the steps. At the bottom, he met Olivia, Melissa's sister, for the first time.

Not a word passed between him and Melissa until they'd both gotten back into his truck and he'd backed out of the alley and onto a side street, coming to a stop at the only traffic light in Stone Creek.

A right turn, and they would be headed for her place. A left, for his.

Steven was torn. He didn't want to leave Melissa alone, but suggesting that she spend the night with him didn't seem right, either.

"Where to?" he finally asked.

"The courthouse," Melissa said, not looking at him.

She didn't offer any further explanation, but Steven knew all too well why she wanted to go there. She meant to wait, either in her office or in Tom's, until there was some kind of news.

"Okay," Steven agreed, and when the light finally changed, he turned neither left nor right, but drove straight through the intersection, headed for the parking lot behind the courthouse.

The whole building was blazing with light, and Tom's cruiser, along with two others, sat at angles from the main entrance, as though quickly abandoned. One of the motors was still making a ticking sound, in fact.

A group of onlookers stood watching.

"Showtime," Melissa said, under her breath, without even a semblance of humor.

Steven kept pace with her, nodding to various locals as he passed them.

They reached the large glass doors, and he opened one of them, then waited while Melissa crossed the threshold.

"You don't have to stay," she told him, when they were inside the corridor.

Noise spilled from Tom's office at the other end of the hallway—a woman was alternately sobbing and shriek-ing, and a dog, probably Elvis, was barking.

Steven made no response.

Melissa gave a small sigh of apparent resignation, and they walked toward the sheriff's office.

VELDA CAHILL REELED, wild-eyed, when Melissa stepped through the doorway, but the woman was look-ing past her, to Steven.

"You've got to help my boy!" she cried. Word that he was a defense attorney must have gotten around.

Melissa stiffened slightly, but that was the only outward indication she gave that she knew what was going to happen. In some strange way, she'd known it all along.

Byron Cahill hadn't lasted long on the outside. Most likely, she'd be filing charges of armed robbery against him by morning, if not before then.

Steven spoke quietly to Velda; Melissa didn't attempt to listen in. She exchanged glances with Tom Parker and then swung her gaze toward the old-fashioned cells at the back of the office.

Byron sat on the cot in one of them, his head down,

his hands hanging between his knees, fingers loosely intertwined. Elvis peered in at him, through the bars, reminding Melissa momentarily of one of the scenes in the Pirates of the Caribbean ride at Disneyland.

"What happened?" Melissa asked, speaking to Tom but still watching Byron. She had a sinking feeling in her middle, and she knew the trouble went beyond the sure and certain knowledge that she and Steven would be on opposite sides of the coming fight.

They were emotionally involved so, technically, anyway, she and Steven could not legally oppose each other in a courtroom.

She could handle the prosecution, or Steven could defend Byron Cahill, but not both. One of them would have to withdraw.

And it wasn't going to be her.

CHAPTER FIFTEEN

STANDING BESIDE MELISSA as she gazed at Byron Cahill through the bars of the cell, Tom explained what had happened after he'd spoken to Martine in the Grange Hall parking lot. He'd started for the Stop & Shop, intending to begin his investigation where the crime had taken place, and had nearly been hit by the Cahill car as it shot out of an alley.

Tom had stuck his portable light on the roof of his personal vehicle and set it flashing, wishing he had a siren, too.

The driver hadn't slowed; in fact, if Byron hadn't swerved to miss a cat running across the road in front of him, and pitched his mother's car into the ditch in the process, the chase would still be on.

"I didn't do anything wrong," Byron said, lifting his eyes at last, looking out at them with an expression so hopeless that Melissa felt that drowning sensation again, like a swimmer going under.

"You didn't stop when I pulled in behind you and turned on the light," Tom reminded him calmly.

"I was scared," Byron answered. "I knew you wouldn't believe me!"

"Know why I don't believe you, Byron?" Tom inquired, his tone smooth. Even. "Because on top of trying to outrun me, you happened to be carrying a ski mask and a backpack full of $5, $10 and $20 bills in the trunk of your car."

Melissa folded her arms. She didn't want it to be true; if only for Andrea's sake and for Velda's, she'd hoped Byron would keep his nose clean. Make a new start.

But the evidence was stacked against him.

"If you didn't rob the Stop & Shop," she ventured, watching Byron's faced closely, "who did?"

Elvis made a slight whimpering sound, full of sympathy.

Byron looked away. "I don't know," he said.

Years of taking depositions and reading juries had taught Melissa to spot a lie, and Byron Cahill was definitely not telling the truth now.

"Do we have a case?" Tom asked Melissa.

It was a rhetorical question, of course.

"I'm afraid so," Melissa answered wearily. "I'll file formal charges in the morning. In the meantime, since Mr. Cahill did his best to evade you when you tried to pull him over, it would be best to keep him here."

Byron was on his feet, knuckles white where he gripped the bars with both hands, looking past Melissa and Tom. "Can they do that?" he demanded. "Can they hold me when no charges have been filed?"

Steven joined the group in front of the cell. Melissa slanted a sideways glance at his face, through her lashes, but said nothing.

"Depends," Steven answered.

"I can always file charges tonight," Melissa told Byron crisply, "if that's what you want."

Steven sighed.

Byron spun away.

"That went well," Tom observed, leaning down to pat Elvis on the head.

When Melissa turned around, she was surprised to see that Velda had left.

"I asked Mrs. Cahill to wait in my truck," Steven said. "I'm taking her home."

"That's very nice of you," Melissa said, without inflection.

"You might as well go on home," Tom interjected. "Both of you. There won't be much going on here for the rest of the night."

Cautiously, Steven touched Melissa's elbow. "I'll drop you off at your place," he said.

"No, thanks," Melissa replied lightly, but with an edge. "I'll call someone."

A look passed between Steven and Tom. Tom walked away, whistled for Elvis, who remained in front of the cell, keeping watch over the prisoner.

"I'd like a word with you, in private," Steven told Melissa.

Melissa gave one abrupt nod and followed Steven out into the corridor.

She surprised herself by being the first one to speak. "You know damn well you can't ethically defend Cahill," she said, glaring up at him. "Not while I'm the prosecutor."

"And you do intend to prosecute?"

"Of course I do," Melissa answered impatiently. "It's my job."

"Has it occurred to you that the kid might be innocent, just as he claims?"

"He'll have a public defender," Melissa pointed out.

"No," Steven argued, his tone and his eyes stone cold. "He won't."

"You can't defend him, because—because of—"

"Us?"

"Yes," Melissa said, fighting a humiliating urge to break down and cry.

"You're right, counselor," he said, maintaining the chill. "You and I can't oppose each other in court. But I know some other lawyers who'll be willing to take the case pro bono."

She blinked. "Why are you pushing this?" she asked.

"Because I think Cahill is innocent," Steven answered.

"He was caught with the mask and the money! How *could* he be?"

"Ask the dog," Steven said.

And with that, he turned and walked away, leaving Melissa standing alone in the corridor outside the sheriff's office.

Ask the dog, Steven had said. What the *hell* did that mean?

She opened Tom's door quietly and slipped back into the office.

Elvis was still sitting in front of Byron's cell. The prisoner was sprawled facedown on his cot. And Tom was seated at his desk, entering data into his computer.

Melissa approached, sank into a chair nearby. Glanced at Elvis.

"What's up with your dog?" she asked, after a long time.

Tom sighed. "I'm not sure," he said, so quietly that Byron wouldn't have heard. "I've never seen Elvis behave like that before." He paused. "I don't mind admitting that it bothers me a little, though."

"Why?" Melissa asked, wishing she were at home, in her own bed, that the night hadn't happened.

That *Steven Creed* hadn't happened.

"Well," Tom said, at some length, "Elvis has always been a pretty fair judge of character."

IT WAS HIS NIGHT for walking women to their front doors, evidently.

Steven squired Velda Cahill along the dirt path leading to her rusted-out single-wide. A plastic gnome stood guard on a little porch jerry-rigged from mismatched scraps of lumber.

The trailer door swung open, and Melissa's assistant, Andrea, stood framed in the light from inside. Even with her face in shadow, Steven could see that she'd been crying.

"Where's Byron?" she demanded.

"He's in jail," Velda said. She'd been frantic earlier in the evening, but now she seemed beaten down.

Andrea gave a little wail of despair.

"You'll help him, won't you?" Velda almost whispered, turning to look up at Steven. "You'll make sure my boy doesn't go back to prison for something he didn't do?"

"I'll do what I can," Steven answered, just as a young man replaced Andrea in the doorway, easing her to one side.

Steven had never seen the guy before.

"Nathan Carter," he said, stepping aside long enough to sort of steer Velda into the trailer, then putting out a hand.

"Steven Creed," Steven answered.

"Somebody's got to look after these women," Nathan said, although no one had asked what he was doing there. He sounded regretful as he spoke, but his eyes told another story. On some level, he almost seemed to be enjoying the excitement.

Steven hesitated a moment, reluctant to leave and, at the same time, eager to be gone. He finally nodded to Carter and turned to descend the three rickety steps to the path.

It was late, so, as he and Meg had agreed earlier, he didn't stop at Stone Creek Ranch to pick Matt up. By now, the boy would be sound asleep.

Back at the tour bus, Steven let Zeke out into the yard, waited while the dog made good use of the front yard and followed him inside.

Zeke stood looking up at Steven, wagging his tail. For a dog, he sure was expressive.

And so was Sheriff Parker's four-legged deputy, Elvis.

"Things don't look real good for Byron Cahill," Steven told Zeke, leaning to pick up the mutt's nearly empty water dish to refill it at the sink. He set the bowl down on the floor and watched as the animal lapped up a drink. He remembered the expression on Melissa's face, there in the corridor outside the jail. "Come to think of it," he added, falling just short of a smile, "they're not looking all that good for me, either."

IT WAS TOM WHO DROVE MELISSA home that night.

She was thoughtful during the ride.

He and Elvis walked her to the front door, waited until she was safely inside and left again. She knew

Tom planned on spending the night on the couch in his office, rather than leaving the prisoner unattended until morning.

Melissa locked up, then wandered into her bedroom and stood in front of the full-length mirror, shaking her head at the bedraggled figure staring back at her.

The aqua dress, which had made her feel so pretty and so feminine earlier in the evening, seemed to mock her now.

Her hair drooped, her mascara made faint shadows under her eyes and she'd long since chewed off her lipstick.

With a sigh, she grabbed her robe and headed for the small master bath just off her bedroom. There, she stripped, stepped under a hot shower and scrubbed until her skin squeaked.

After that, she dried off, put on the robe and headed for the kitchen. What she needed, she decided, was a nice cup of herbal tea.

Or a shot of whiskey.

She decided on the tea, and was sitting at the table near the windows, sipping from a mug, when someone pounded on the back door.

"Melissa!" yelled a familiar female voice. "I know you're in there—let me in!"

Andrea.

Melissa went to the door, turned the dead bolt and then the knob. She didn't ask what Andrea was doing there, at that hour of the night no less, because she already knew.

The young woman was obviously upset; she'd been crying, hard, and her eyes were so red they looked raw.

"Sit down," Melissa said gently.

Andrea collapsed into a chair at the table and, after locking the door again, Melissa prepared a second cup of tea and set it down in front of her midnight visitor.

For a moment, Andrea looked as though she might send the mug and her tea flying with one angry swipe of her arm. Fortunately, she seemed to think better of the idea in the next instant and carefully lifted the cup to her mouth, her hands shaking.

"Were you with Byron tonight, when he held up the Stop & Shop?" Melissa asked.

Andrea flung a beleaguered look in her direction, but she retained her composure.

"I was with Byron tonight," she said. "But he didn't rob the Stop & Shop."

Melissa merely waited, her own tea cooling, forgotten, on the table.

The set of Andrea's jaw was obstinate, but only for a moment or two. Fresh tears brimmed along her lower lashes, and one trickled, zigzag, down her cheek. She wiped it away with the back of one hand, but only after the fact.

"I'm telling you, Byron didn't do anything wrong," the girl insisted.

"You know," Melissa said carefully, when Andrea lapsed into another silence, "I keep hearing that. From you. From Velda. But Byron was heading out of town at top speed when Tom caught up with him, and later, the money from the robbery was found in the trunk of his car, along with a ski mask like the one Martine described when she reported what happened."

"We were in bed," Andrea said, in a broken whisper. "Byron and me."

"Where?" Melissa asked. She still suspected her

assistant of making up an alibi for her boyfriend, but she was willing to listen.

"His place," Andrea said, meeting Melissa's eyes only with an effort.

"Velda must have loved that," Melissa commented.

Andrea bristled. "She was at work," she said. "Byron and I had the place to ourselves. Velda called from the cocktail lounge around nine-thirty and said she didn't feel very well and she needed to come home, and would Byron pick her up. That's when he found out the car was gone."

"Gone? You mean, stolen?"

"Byron knew who'd taken it. It was that loser, Nathan. He's been hanging around the Cahills' place lately—he and Byron ran around together when they were younger—said he needed someplace to stay. I guess Byron felt sorry for him or something." Andrea tossed her head slightly; a good sign. She was turning back into her old, spirited self. "That Nathan, he's a sneak. He tried to borrow money from me a couple of times—I turned him down. And he bragged that he had a case against Deputy Ferguson because of that black eye, and the county would have to give him some kind of settlement to keep the story out of the news—" She stopped, took a shaky breath, and then rushed on. "Deputy Ferguson didn't give Nathan that shiner. Velda did."

The tale was just crazy enough to be true. "Velda?" Melissa asked, intrigued and more than a little uneasy. "Why?"

"She said she caught him going through her purse," Andrea said. "Byron and I weren't around at the time. She told us later that she slugged Nathan because he gave her some back talk, and then she kicked him out."

Another sigh. "Of course, he came back, and Velda decided the cops were out to get him and so she'd let him stay at the trailer a while longer."

"Were you planning on mentioning this to me at some point?" Melissa asked archly. "The accusation Nathan Carter made could have ruined Deputy Ferguson's career—or even his life."

"We didn't know he'd accused anybody of anything until he started bragging about it," Andrea said, sounding miffed. "I wouldn't have let Deputy Ferguson be blamed, and neither would Byron. He's a good person, Melissa."

"I really want to believe that," Melissa said slowly.

"But you don't?" Andrea challenged, and the tears were back again.

Melissa didn't answer.

"Don't you see?" Andrea pressed, looking and sounding desperate now. "*Nathan Carter* robbed that store, not Byron!"

It wasn't beyond credibility, but there was one obvious problem. Nathan hadn't been trying to get away from Stone Creek with the money taken at gunpoint from the Stop & Shop—*Byron* had been the one at the wheel when Tom caught up to him. And Byron probably wouldn't have stopped at all if he hadn't run off the road.

"Then why wasn't he driving Velda's car, Andrea?" Melissa asked, after taking a few moments to collect her own composure. "If Nathan went into that store, wearing a ski mask, and stole that money, why was Byron the one who tried to get away?"

"I don't know," Andrea said.

"You don't know," Melissa repeated, absorbing that.

"After Byron realized his mom's car was missing, he told me to go back to my apartment and stay there. He said there was going to be trouble, he could feel it, and he didn't want me to be involved."

"And you went home? Just like that?" Melissa was skeptical. The Andrea she knew wasn't fond of taking orders.

"Yes," Andrea replied. "Byron was really upset, and I was scared. Not of Byron, but of whatever had scared *him* so much."

"So you've been home, in your apartment, since Byron sent you away?"

Andrea bit her lower lip, then shook her head. "No," she answered, after a few beats. "The Crockett sisters heard about the robbery over their police scanner, and they couldn't wait to tell me that Sheriff Parker and all his deputies were out hunting for Byron. I panicked and went over to Velda's, and Nathan was there. He told me Byron was in big trouble, that he'd pulled a heist with a deadly weapon and Velda had gone to the jail to try and do something to help—"

A chill trickled down Melissa's spine. "And after that?"

"Steven Creed brought Velda home. She's a basket case. Nathan's making like he's all caring and everything—he made her a hot toddy and everything."

"And you decided to come and talk to me." It was a statement, not a question. Melissa's mind was racing, but she knew she appeared calm on the outside. She'd had a lot of practice at that.

Andrea nodded hard, glanced nervously in the

direction of the door. "I knew Byron thought Nathan had taken the car, and when I heard about the robbery and headed over to Velda's, and Nathan was there, I knew what had *really* happened. I sneaked out while he was making a fuss over Velda, making her a drink and everything, and then I was scared to go home, because Nathan knows where I live."

Melissa rose from her chair, crossed to the wall phone, and picked up the handset.

Tom Parker answered on the first ring. "Stone Creek County Sheriff's office," he said. "This is Tom."

Melissa launched right in, telling Tom everything Andrea had told her.

He didn't interrupt, but simply listened.

"I'll check it out," he said, when she'd finished. "Keep Andrea there with you, and make sure all the doors and windows are locked up tight."

"Tom," Melissa said, after catching her breath. "Be careful, okay?"

"Always," he promised, with a smile in his voice. "I'll leave Elvis here to guard the prisoner."

Melissa didn't comment. "Call me," she said.

"Lock up tight," Tom responded.

And then he hung up.

Melissa checked the front door and all the windows. She brewed more tea, and she and Andrea moved to the living room, where there were draperies over the windows.

Melissa was definitely creeped out, and she knew Andrea was, too, although neither of them said much. Andrea seemed exhausted, and little wonder, after the night she'd put in.

Eventually, Andrea fell asleep on the couch.

Melissa covered her with an afghan Ashley had crocheted for her years ago, as a Christmas gift, and sat down in her easy chair again, huddled inside her bathrobe.

The clock on the mantel ticked ponderously. Every passing second seemed like a full minute to Melissa, every minute an hour.

At some point, she nodded off.

ANDREA AWAKENED HER with a cry of alarm. "My car is gone!"

Melissa straightened, blinking, surprised to find herself in a chair instead of her bed.

Andrea was standing by the window, holding back one of the drapes. Cold light spilled over her puffy face, and her cheeks were streaked with mascara and last night's tears.

"Wh-what?" Melissa said, bumbling to her feet. Yawning.

"My car!" Andrea wailed. "I parked it right out there, at the curb, last night. And now it's *gone!*"

"Are you sure?" It *was* a stupid question, but, despite years of getting up at the crack of dawn to go out and run, in actuality, Melissa wasn't a morning person.

"Of course I'm sure!" Andrea replied. "It was there, and now it's gone!"

Melissa sighed. Time to put in another call to Tom.

She picked up the cordless handset in the living room and punched in his office number.

"Stone Creek County Sheriff's office," he answered.

"Andrea's car has been stolen," Melissa blurted.

Tom was quiet for so long that Melissa spoke up again.

"Tom? What's going on?"

He gave a raspy sigh. "I'll tell you when you get here," he said. "In the meantime, put Andrea on. I'm going to need as much information about her car as she can give me."

"But—"

"When you get here, Melissa," Tom repeated, sternly patient. "Oh, and fair warning. You're bound to run into Steven Creed. He's on his way here right now, to oversee Byron Cahill's release."

"You're letting him go?" Another stupid question. She needed coffee. Pronto.

"Yep," Tom said.

Melissa turned to find Andrea standing wide-eyed at her elbow. "The sheriff wants to ask you some questions about your car," she said to the girl.

"They're letting Byron go?" Andrea asked softly.

Melissa nodded. "Sounds like it," she said.

While Andrea was trying to remember her license-plate number and other pertinent details, Melissa hurried off to her room.

She dressed quickly, donning a black pantsuit, pulling her hair back and fastening it in place with a barrette. She applied minimal makeup and rejoined Andrea in the living room.

The girl was still standing there, looking dumbfounded with joy. Sure, her car was gone, possibly for good, but Byron was getting out of jail.

For Andrea, it was all good.

They both hopped into Melissa's roadster, keeping the top up because it was a misty morning, and headed for the courthouse.

As fate would have it, the first person Melissa

encountered was Steven Creed. He was dressed for lawyering, as Big John would have said, in a tailored suit and shoes polished to such a sheen that they almost made her blink.

Andrea dashed past him, anxious to see Byron.

Steven's expression was just short of smug, but something in his eyes made Melissa wary.

"What?" she finally whispered, standing there in the corridor, looking at him.

He straightened his tasteful tie—pale blue silk with very thin gray stripes running diagonally—and even though his mouth didn't shape itself into a smile, he looked amused.

"So this is your evil twin," he said, taking in her mean-business pantsuit, slapdash makeup job and prim, no-nonsense hairstyle. One of his eyebrows rose slightly. "I must admit, I like the other Melissa better, the one with no hard edges."

Evil twin? Hard edges?

"Get out of my way," Melissa said.

Steven didn't move except to shove his hands into the pockets of his perfectly tailored trousers and cock his head to one side. "Temper, temper," he scolded, with syrupy insolence. "Your edges are showing."

She tried to go around him, but he blocked her way.

"Before you go in there, there's something I need to tell you."

Again, Melissa felt that quiet alarm. She drew a deep breath, let it out slowly, and silently instructed herself to calm the heck down. It was downright unprofessional, letting this man rattle her the way he did.

And even worse that he knew exactly what he was doing.

"All right," she said, finally. "What is it?"

His face tightened almost imperceptibly, and he actually averted his gaze for a moment. "Velda Cahill was assaulted last night."

"What?"

Steven relaxed a little, took a light hold on Melissa's shoulders. "She'll be fine in a few days," he assured her. A muscle bunched in his cheek, and she saw a combination of anger and regret flare up in his eyes, gone as quickly as it appeared. "Carter knocked her around some last night, when he realized Andrea had slipped out of the trailer behind his back. He stole Velda's watch and the contents of her tip jar and took off."

Melissa felt cold all over. "Poor Velda," she said. "That woman cannot catch a break."

"She's an inpatient at the clinic over in Indian Rock. I thought I should let you know ahead of time because Byron hasn't been told yet. He's bound to be shaken up, not to mention furious, and I figure he'll want to go after Nathan Carter himself. If he does that, obviously, he'll be back in jail for sure."

Melissa nodded slowly. "Do you have a plan?"

"If it weren't for Matt, I'd have Byron stay at my place until he settles down or Carter is in custody, whichever comes first. There are too many unknown factors in the equation, of course, and I'm not about to risk Matt's being hurt. Tom and I talked it over, and he's willing to take the boy in, since it's just him and Elvis. God knows whether Byron will agree or not."

Melissa pondered the idea. Given Byron's history

with the sheriff, it didn't seem likely, but stranger things had happened.

"Thanks," she said stiffly, and this time when she moved to enter Tom's office, Steven didn't get in her way.

BYRON WAS OUT OF THE CELL and back in his civilian clothes, plunked sullenly in a chair next to Tom's desk. Andrea stood behind that chair, her hands resting on Byron's taut shoulders.

Following Melissa into the large, open room, Steven shifted his focus from her shapely posterior to the tasks at hand.

His gaze snagged with Tom's.

"You must be out of your mind," Byron blurted, glaring at the sheriff.

Elvis slunk over, placed his muzzle on the young man's blue-jeaned thigh and made a soft sound full of sorrowful affection.

Byron automatically stroked the dog's head, but he went right on trying to bore a hole through Tom Parker with his eyes.

Tom, perched casually on a corner of his big desk, looked unflappable. Initially, Steven had pegged the man for a rube, but he'd since revised his opinion. "I reckon three-quarters of the people I know would agree, since I just invited you to bunk on my screened-in sunporch for a while."

"Why would I want to do that?" Byron snapped. Andrea's fingers tightened noticeably, and he shrugged her off.

Tom glanced in Steven's direction, and Steven nodded in response. Cleared his throat.

"Byron," he said, "your mother has been hurt—"

Byron leaped to his feet and whirled around so fast that his chair toppled over and both Elvis and Andrea had to jump out of the way. "What happened to my mom?" Byron demanded. "How bad is—?"

Steven held up both hands, palms out. "She'll be *fine,* Byron. They're keeping her at the clinic a day or two, mostly for observation, but she's going to be all right."

Byron reddened, and clenched both fists at his sides. "*He* did it, didn't he? That son-of-a-bitch Nathan Carter *hurt my mother!*"

Melissa went to stand beside a trembling, wide-eyed Andrea, putting an arm around the girl's shoulders, giving her an encouraging squeeze. Essentially, holding her up.

Tom spoke next, quietly and with authority. "That's what she told Deputy Ferguson when he took her to the clinic last night," he said, watching Byron. Like Steven, he was poised to land on the kid if his temper got any further out of hand. "Velda has some cracked ribs, two black eyes and a split lip. And if there's one thing your mother *doesn't* need right now, it's for you to get yourself into trouble all over again."

Byron calmed himself a little, but not quite enough for Steven and Tom to let down their guard. He swore under his breath and thrust a hand through his rumpled hair, and his eyes filled with angry tears.

"You must have known it was Nathan who robbed the Stop & Shop," Steven said reasonably, watching Byron. "Why didn't you tell me, or Tom?"

Byron seemed to deflate, like a balloon two days after the party. He groped his way back into his chair.

Glanced up at Andrea with an expression of such profound concern that Steven himself was moved by it. "I would have, when the time was right," he finally replied, "but I was in here and Carter was out there where he could do anything he wanted, and I was afraid for the people I care about."

"Are you ready to tell me where you were headed last night, when you wrecked your mother's car and Sheriff Parker hauled you in?" Maybe Tom had gotten an answer to that question in the interim, but Steven was still in the dark.

Byron's shoulders sagged, and he spent a few moments petting Elvis before he made his reply. "I just panicked, that's all," he confessed. "I didn't know where I was going. I just wanted to get away and hide out someplace, so I wouldn't have to go back to prison."

Tom's response surprised everybody. "I can see why you'd freak out," he said. He paused, gave a sigh, but his gaze was steady on the younger man's face. "There's an APB out on Carter," he went on, "and we'll get him. But it's my job—mine and the department's—to bring him in, not yours. You try to take matters into your own hands and you *will* go to jail, for violating your parole at the very least."

Byron swallowed, nodded again.

Andrea moved away from Melissa and approached Byron's chair. Laid a hand on his shoulder, like before. "You ought to stay with Sheriff Parker," she said, very softly. "It's good of him to offer, Byron. He's trying to help you."

A smile crooked the corner of Tom's mouth. "Elvis is all for taking in a roommate," he said.

Byron didn't move for a long time. Then he put his hand on top of Andrea's, gently squeezed her fingers.

"Okay," he said.

And one matter, at least, was settled.

Now, Steven thought ruefully, *to settle everything else that's gone wrong lately.*

As though reading his mind, Melissa looked at him and narrowed her eyes, in a like-hell sort of way. She told Andrea to take the day off, asked Tom to keep her posted on the statewide hunt for Nathan Carter, and breezed past Steven like he wasn't even there.

The door snapped shut behind her.

Steven immediately followed. He knew he was probably making bad matters worse, but he damn well couldn't help himself.

He caught up to her at the door of her office.

"Melissa," he ground out. "Wait—"

"Go away," she said. "I don't want to deal with you right now."

He steered her inside the room where Andrea normally worked, and closed the door. "Well, that's just *tough,* counselor, because you *are* going to deal with me."

She glared up at him, folded her arms. Her words flew like well-aimed bullets, staccato and dead on target. "It was all a mistake. You and me, I mean. I should have known better. Case closed."

"Melissa," Steven heard himself say, "that's crazy."

She was on a roll. "You do criminal defense. I'm a prosecutor. We don't think the same way."

"Of course we don't think the same way," Steven countered easily. "Why would two intelligent, independent adults even want that?"

"Do the math," Melissa persisted. "We might as well be from different planets."

"Mars and Venus?" Steven teased.

"Very funny," she replied. But she didn't look or sound all that amused.

Steven tried again. "What I meant was—"

"I don't *care* what you meant, Steven."

"I can see that," he answered calmly. "So, what happened, Melissa? Was your mother scared by a member of the Dream Team when she was pregnant with you?"

"Ha-ha," Melissa said.

"Can't we just agree to disagree?"

"Yes," she said, after swallowing visibly. "We can agree to disagree. How about forever?"

Steven whistled, long and low. "Hello? Don't you think you're overreacting just a little here?"

"All we have to do is pretend nothing happened—"

"No," Steven interrupted flatly. "We aren't going to do that."

"Why not?"

Damn, she was stubborn. Too bad he found that quality so attractive in a woman. Or, at least, in *this* woman.

"Because it *did* happen."

"Now you're just nitpicking," she protested.

Steven rolled his eyes. "We went to bed together," he said slowly and with emphasis.

"Keep your voice down!" Melissa retorted, glancing toward the door.

He flung out his hands. "I give up."

"Good," Melissa said. "It's about time."

He leaned in, so their noses were almost touching. *"For now,"* he clarified. Then he left her standing there, and strode out into the corridor, headed back to Tom's office.

He had business to attend to—and he'd better put Melissa O'Ballivan out of his head.

CHAPTER SIXTEEN

"This is an intervention," Olivia announced solemnly, a week and a half after Melissa's last conversation with Steven Creed.

Melissa looked around Olivia and Tanner's living room, sweeping Meg and Ashley up in an indignant glance.

"You tricked me," she said, in an accusing tone. Olivia had suggested that all four of them meet at her place that Thursday evening, after Melissa got off work, to discuss the parade, which was scheduled for the following night. Ostensibly, her devoted sisters and sister-in-law were supposed to assist her with last-minute logistics.

What a sucker she was.

"We had to do something," Ashley said earnestly, near tears. "You've gone around the bend."

"You're definitely not yourself," Meg added, plainly concerned. She took in Melissa's outfit. "Since when do you go to work in sweats and sneakers?"

"Without makeup," Olivia pointed out.

"And look at your *hair*," Ashley all but wailed.

"Plus you haven't been running," Olivia contributed. This whole confrontational thing had probably been her idea—she'd always been the bossy big-sister type.

"Maybe I'm a little depressed," Melissa admitted,

feeling defensive. "It'll pass as soon as they catch Nathan Carter and this damn parade is over."

"Even after you and Dan parted ways, you didn't let yourself go like this," Ashley pressed, waving off Melissa's words as she spoke. "We're worried about you."

"You're falling apart," Olivia said.

"I think this *mood* you're in has something to do with Steven Creed," Meg insisted. "You've been different ever since he hit town."

Olivia and Ashley nodded in unison.

"No, it does *not* have to do with—him," Melissa lied. The truth was, she couldn't seem to get the man out of her mind, even for her own good.

"Level with us," Olivia urged, her eyes softening. "We want to help you."

"I need help with the parade," Melissa said. "Not my personal life."

Olivia, Ashley and Meg all looked at each other, exchanging unspoken messages.

Melissa stood up.

"Sit down," Olivia said firmly.

Melissa sat. "This is silly," she said.

"Are you in love with this Steven Creed person?" Ashley wanted to know.

"No," Melissa said, hoping she sounded convincing. By then, she was so confused, she didn't know *what* she felt. Was wanting somebody—not just physically, but emotionally and mentally and even *spiritually*, for pity's sake—the same as *loving* him? "It was just a case of temporary lust." She waved one hand dismissively, much as Ashley had done earlier. They were, after all, twins. "Anyway, it's over."

"What happened?" Meg asked.

"That," Melissa said, "is none of your business—any of you—but I'll answer anyway. Yes, there was an attraction. But Steven and I are both lawyers. Worse yet, we have very different viewpoints, since he's Defense, and I'm Prosecution. While that may not seem like a big deal to *most people,* it constitutes irrevocable differences in our private philosophies. When it comes to our philosophies of life, we're polar opposites."

Ashley shook her head, marveling. "What a lot of gobbledegook," she said.

"I'd call it BS," Olivia interjected.

"Now you know why I didn't want to talk about this," Melissa said loftily. She stood up again, and this time she meant it. She was leaving. "I knew none of you would understand. And why should you? All three of you have children, and happy marriages—"

"Melissa—" Ashley said.

Melissa picked up her purse, ferreted inside it for her car keys and headed for the Quinns' front door. There, she paused and turned to assess—very coolly— the three other women who had summoned her on false pretenses. "The parade starts at six tomorrow night," she said. "We're gathering at four, in the parking lot behind the high school. If any of you actually want to *help,* be there."

Nobody said anything.

Naturally.

Slinging the strap of her purse over one shoulder, Melissa left with a flourish.

IT HAD BEEN OVER A WEEK since he'd seen Melissa, except at a distance, and Steven did his damnedest to carry on as if nothing had changed.

Every morning, he fed Matt and the dog breakfast, made do with stale, reheated coffee himself. At night, he slept heavily, mired in mixed-up dreams he couldn't remember two seconds after he opened his eyes, and he sure as hell didn't feel rested—more like a wino, hung over after a three-day binge.

Quite a trick, since he hadn't had anything to drink since before Brody left.

Leaving the tour bus that Friday morning, locking it behind him, Steven was mildly pleased to see that the renovation crew had already arrived to put in another day's work. The barn, a nifty-looking prebuilt structure, already had walls and a roof and, by Monday, the stalls would be in, as well. He stopped to confer briefly with the foreman, who told him they were putting up drywall in the bedrooms that day, and they'd start installing the kitchen and bathroom fixtures tomorrow.

"If you don't watch it," Steven said, only half kidding, "you're going to give the contracting business a good name."

The foreman smiled at the comment, puny as it was, and informed Steven that the company was family-owned, had been in business for four generations and there had been at least one member of the clan on one crew or another from the first.

The watchword, Steven thought, was *continuity*. It was a way of life with most of the Creeds—the Mc-Kettricks and the O'Ballivans, too. And it was what Steven wanted for Matt, for himself, and for any descendants inclined to live out their lives on a ranch.

He hadn't reckoned on Melissa when he'd decided to put down roots in Stone Creek, but life was full of things nobody had reckoned on, wasn't it? A man had to do the best he could with whatever hand he was dealt, press on, take the good with the bad.

Some family histories just happened. Others were deliberately created.

Steven intended to build a dandy one, and to do that, he'd need a wife. Eventually.

Things would turn out just fine, he assured himself, while he was buckling Matt into his safety seat in the truck, as long as he stayed away from lady lawyers— Cindy aside, he'd never been able to get along with them, outside the office or the courtroom, even when they played on his team.

Insanity, the saying went, was doing the same thing over and over again and expecting to get different results.

Melissa was beautiful and funny and smart, everything he admired in a woman, but when push came to shove, she had the prosecutorial mind-set: The accused was guilty until proven innocent, not the other way around. And Steven, to the roots of his being, was *all about* the other way around.

Matt brought him out of his reflections with a jolt, his tone worried. "You look really sad."

"Maybe I am a little," Steven said, once he'd helped Zeke onto the seat, next to his pint-size master.

"Because you're not going out on dates with Melissa anymore?"

"Partly," Steven replied. He never lied to the boy, but he wasn't inclined to burden a five-year-old with adult problems, either. He just wished Matt hadn't developed a shining set of high hopes as far as the Stone Creek County prosecutor was concerned.

In Matt's mind, Steven was sure, Melissa was on the

fast track to becoming his new mommy. His drawing of the stick-people family was still taped to the refrigerator door, and he wouldn't hear of taking it down, except to pore over it and add a detail here and there, with a pencil or a stub of crayon.

"I guess it's grown-up stuff?" Matt asked, with a certain resignation.

Steven grinned, though he felt hollow inside. "Grown-up stuff," he confirmed. "Nothing you need to worry about."

"Okay," Matt agreed, but he didn't seem convinced.

Steven shut the door, walked around the truck and hauled himself up behind the wheel. He was only thirty-five, but he felt about eighty that morning.

The dreams he couldn't remember still weighed on him.

He shoved a hand through his hair and started the engine.

Matt was quiet during the drive into town; Steven could almost hear the gears grinding in that little head.

When they pulled up at Creekside Academy, Matt didn't seem happy to be there, as he usually did.

Kids, Steven reassured himself, as Matt dawdled along the sidewalk, delaying entering the building for as long as he could, are resilient.

Must be nice, he thought, trying to remember what it felt like, being good at bouncing back.

He watched until Matt was safely inside the building, then turned and got into the truck again. Zeke, still in back, craned his neck and laved the side of Steven's face once with his sandpaper tongue.

Steven chuckled, checked all the mirrors and backed out of the parking space.

The Stop & Shop was back to business as usual, had been since the morning after the robbery.

Talk about resilience.

On impulse, he turned into the lot and parked.

Martine was back at work, as he'd hoped—she'd taken some time off after the robbery, and Steven hadn't wanted to bother her at home.

After adjusting the windows and telling Zeke he'd be right back, he walked into the store.

Martine was there, looking a little pale around the gills, but otherwise she seemed pretty cheerful.

A plain young woman standing at the counter paid for her purchases—a half gallon of milk and two lottery tickets—and nodded to Steven as she passed him on her way out of the store.

Steven nodded back, waited until he and Martine were alone, then reintroduced himself. They'd already met, of course, but she'd been through a trauma and he figured she might not remember.

"Hello, again," Martine responded, with a wan smile, proving him wrong. He recalled last time's reference to her unmarried daughter. "What can I do for you, Mr. Creed?"

"Steven," he corrected, approaching the counter. "I'd like to ask you a couple of questions about the other night, if you wouldn't mind."

Martine looked reluctant, almost pained, but she nodded. "You and half the cops in the state of Arizona," she sighed. Evidently not one to be idle, she wiped ineffectually at the glass countertop with a cloth as she spoke. "It started out as a normal night. Things were quiet, so I went back to the storage room to call my boyfriend on my cell. We've been having some trouble lately, him and me. Anyhow, when we were finished talking, I was too antsy to finish my break, so I headed for the front of the store. And the guy with the ski mask was standing there, right about where you are now, with a gun in one hand—" she paused to point, blanching as the experience replayed itself in her mind.

"And you recognized Byron, even with the ski mask covering his entire head?"

"I recognized Velda's car," Martine stressed. "I was too scared to identify anybody, notice eye color or height or anything like that. I just wanted to give the robber whatever he wanted so he'd get out of here—without shooting me."

Steven nodded. "Any customers in the store right before your break?" Steven asked moderately.

But Martine shook her head. "As I said, it was quiet. Everybody in town was over at the dance." She paused, gave a husky, rueful chuckle. "Everybody except George and me, anyhow."

George, Steven assumed, was the boyfriend, the one she'd been on the outs with on the night in question. He didn't pursue the subject. "No strangers came in? Say, early in your shift?"

Another shake of the head. "Last strangers I recall seeing were an older couple traveling in an RV, and that was at least a couple of days before—before it happened."

Steven didn't respond directly. Since he hadn't gotten around to having cards printed yet, he helped himself to a stenographer's notebook resting on the countertop, along with the accompanying pen, and wrote down his cell and office numbers. "I'd appreciate a call if you remember anything else," he said. He started to turn away, but Martine stopped him with a remark meant to sound offhand, most likely, but falling a ways short.

"I hear you're serving as Byron Cahill's lawyer."

"Not exactly," Steven said, after an inaudible sigh. "As you know, Byron is no longer a suspect. I'm just trying to help out in whatever way I can."

"It was good of Tom to take the boy in for a while," Martine said. "Byron and Velda haven't had it easy, that's for sure. Do you think they'll catch Nathan Carter anytime soon?" She stopped for a breath, shuddered slightly. "It gives me the heebie-jeebies, knowing he's still out there. What if he comes back and tries again, since he didn't get to keep the money last time?"

"I don't think he will," Steven said in parting.

It wasn't much, but at the moment, it was all he had to offer.

Feeling as if he'd made no progress at all—what else was new?—Steven left the Stop & Shop and drove to his office, passing the Sunflower Café on the way. The place was doing a brisk business, as usual, the parking lot packed with cars, motorcycles and pickup trucks.

Steven cruised on past the courthouse next, casually stealing a glance in that direction, as he did every time he came into town for any reason. Melissa's roadster was parked in its usual place, with the top up and a reflective shield across the inside of the windshield.

He considered stopping by to say hello—*hello?*—but soon discarded the idea.

What was there to say? Melissa had made up her mind about him, and about what he did for a living. She was an intelligent woman, a practicing attorney; at least in principle, she definitely understood that under the American judicial system, faulty though it was, everyone—guilty or innocent—has the right to counsel.

It seemed more probable that she was merely using that difference of opinion as an excuse to avoid anything remotely resembling a lifetime commitment. She'd admitted to caring a lot for Dan Guthrie, once upon a time, and Steven had seen what could only be called regret in her eyes when she spoke of Dan's children, the two boys she'd expected to raise as her own.

She was clearly fond of Matt—a point in her favor, of course. Unless she'd been attracted to Steven *because* of the child, and only because of him.

He parked alongside his building, got out of the truck and almost forgot Zeke in the backseat. A cheerful yip reminded him that he wasn't alone, so he retraced his steps, hooked a leash to Zeke's collar, and lifted the dog out of the truck, setting him on the ground. Waiting.

Zeke sniffed the gravel for a while, checked out various thatches of weeds at the edges of the lot, then lifted a hind leg in front of the weathered log marking the boundary of the property on the Main Street side. Steven was still stumbling around in his own thoughts, too distracted, by his own reckoning, to be good for anything much—that day, at least.

He rubbed the back of his neck with one hand, remembering the wild time he and Melissa had shared in his bed. Male egotism aside, he knew she hadn't been faking her responses—he'd felt the subtle flexing of her body as she'd reached one orgasm and then another, felt the moisture of exertion on her silky skin and thrilled to her uninhibited cries of pleasure.

Steven shifted uncomfortably. Tried to turn his thoughts in another direction.

Zeke finished up and they headed for the side door.

Inside, Steven unsnapped the leash and left the dog to wander around the inner and outer offices until he'd found just the right place to curl up for a morning snooze. This involved some circling, some pawing at the carpet, and a couple of big sighs, but Zeke finally settled himself in a patch of sunlight in front of the window to the street, dropped off to sleep and began to snore.

Steven checked his messages.

Zip from Melissa, of course.

Two from Velda Cahill; she'd been calling regularly since her release from the clinic in Indian Rock a few days back, wanting to know what was being done to find Nathan Carter and making a lot of noise about how Byron ought to come back home ASAP.

Byron, on the other hand, seemed happy enough bunking with Tom Parker and Elvis—the kid did his share of the yard and household chores to earn his keep, according to the sheriff, and although not much was said, they all got along just fine. In his spare time, Byron helped out over at the animal shelter, and there was talk about his getting hired steady, bringing home a paycheck, however modest.

So far, so good.

Except that Carter was still at large, of course.

Settled at his desk, Steven booted up his computer, checked his email for the first time that day.

Conner was on his way, he learned, and Davis and Kim were coming along, too, bringing their RV. Everybody was up for a visit and a good old-fashioned rodeo, according to Conner's brief message.

Steven sighed. Brody was headed for Stone Creek, too, planning on competing in the bronc-riding events, both bareback and saddle.

His twin cousins were about to meet up, after all this time, though neither one of them knew it.

Once again, Steven wondered if he'd made the right decision by keeping the impending collision of Creed tempers under his hat, so to speak.

It was the hope—however frail it might be—that Brody and Conner would finally work things out and get on with being brothers that prevented Steven from issuing a storm warning. Those two were both stubborn to the bone, and if either found out that the other one was going to be in Stone Creek for the rodeo, *neither* of them would show up.

Therefore, Steven thought, as he tapped out a response to Conner's email, revealing nothing, the chips would have to fall where they may.

MELISSA WENT FOR A RUN on Friday morning—something she hadn't done for a few days—and took special care with her hair, makeup and clothes when she got back home.

It *wasn't* because of that stupid "intervention" Olivia, Ashley and Meg had sprung on her the evening before, though. No, sirree. She would be leaving her office early to put the finishing touches on the parade that would kick off Stone Creek Rodeo Days that night, and after that, the whole thing would be *over*.

Looking good was her way of celebrating, that was all.

The morning went by quickly, for once.

She skipped lunch, feeling too nervous to eat, and,

conversely, loaded up on coffee. At three forty-five, leaving her assistant to hold down the fort for what little remained of the workday, Melissa headed out.

Ferociously hungry all of a sudden, and telling herself that relaxing her dietary standards a little didn't mean she was on a greased track to hell, she downed a burger from the drive-through place and then, after steeling herself, drove over to the high school, where the Parade Committee had gathered, together with the parade participants and their various floats.

Horses were arriving in trailers, all of them on loan from Stone Creek Ranch, since the sheriff's posse didn't actually ride much, except for occasions like this one. They definitely didn't saddle up and chase outlaws into the hills, as Sam O'Ballivan and his pals had back in those thrilling days of yesteryear.

Brad and several of his ranch hands were supervising, while members of the posse—all of them honorary deputies—argued over who'd put on the most weight since last year's parade.

Although some of the floats hadn't lumbered in yet, there were nearly a dozen crepe paper–bedecked monstrosities in evidence. The standout float was the Chamber of Commerce's contribution—a massive replica of a nearby ski slope, made almost entirely of toilet paper. It even had trees, the branches weighted down with white tissue "snow," and spangles of glitter made the whole shebang sparkle in the sun.

Adelaide Hillingsley and Bea Brady, both wearing their best polyester pants suits and sporting fresh perms, were already nose to nose.

"You're just mad because our float is better than yours!" Adelaide challenged.

Bea looked as though she might be getting ready to throw a punch, so Melissa maneuvered herself between the two women.

"Ladies," she said, "let's remember that we're all friends here."

"Not anymore," Bea scowled.

Adelaide gestured toward the toilet-paper extravaganza. "It's beautiful and you know it!"

The thing really *did* look good.

Over the course of the holiday weekend, folks would drop slips of paper, their vote for the best float in that year's parade, into a mammoth plastic raffle drum set up in the middle of the fairgrounds. On Sunday afternoon, the votes would be tallied and Bill Norman, who always emceed the rodeo, would announce the winner.

A trophy would be presented.

And Melissa had figured out this much, anyway: Both Bea and Adelaide wanted the honor.

Melissa cast an imploring glance in her brother's direction, but Brad didn't look her way, though even from a distance she could see a little grin resting lightly on that famous mouth. Unless she missed her guess, he was pretending that he hadn't noticed what was going on.

"It's too late to do anything about the float now," Melissa said to Bea, in what she hoped was a sympathetic tone. "Let's have a look at yours, shall we?"

Bea looked apoplectic, but she led Melissa away from the offending mobile ski slope to show off the Garden Club's entry, a giant bouquet of colorful papier-mâché flowers of all types and sizes, the whole display perched precariously on top of somebody's farm tractor.

"It's lovely," Melissa said, and she meant it. Enormous amounts of thought, effort and plain old hard work had gone into the construction of that float, and the others, too.

Bea was still upset. "Rules are rules," she exclaimed. "Adelaide Hillingsley thinks they apply to everyone but her!"

By then, cars were pulling up, spilling out uniformed members of the Stone Creek High School marching band.

Melissa thought quickly. "We have to set a good example in front of the children," she said. "So let's keep things as dignified as we can."

Bea huffed at that, but her temper seemed to subside a little.

Melissa patted her back, cast another admiring look over the Garden Club float. "You've outdone yourselves, you and the Garden Club," she said. "As always."

The band kids began to toot on horns and beat on drums right about then. Mercifully, conversation was impossible.

Melissa fled, taking care to avoid Adelaide Hillingsley and her float as assiduously as she meant to avoid Bea.

Just get through this, she told herself. *One crisis at a time.*

She sought Brad out next, found him still over by the horse trailers, making sure the animals were unloaded properly.

"Thanks for all the help," Melissa said, putting a sharp point on the words in case her brother failed to notice the irony in her tone *and* in her expression.

Brad grinned at her. "There was a problem?" he asked innocently. "I guess I missed it."

Melissa punched him in the arm, but it was a

halfhearted move. If there had been a *real* problem, she knew, her big brother would have been the first one to jump in and help.

"I see the intervention worked," he said, when she didn't say anything.

She gave a derisive little snort. "That wasn't an intervention," she said. "It was just plain *meddling*."

"You know Meg and Ashley and Liv love you," Brad told her. His eyes were still twinkling. He went through the motions of looking at the watch he wasn't wearing. "They ought to be here anytime now," he added. "Meg said you needed their help with the parade."

"If I don't keep Bea and Adelaide apart until this is over," Melissa replied ruefully, "I may need help from the *National Guard*."

Brad laughed, laid a hand on her shoulder, but his eyes had turned serious. "You all right, shortstop?" he asked her.

The childhood nickname, familiar as it was, made Melissa's throat tighten a little. "Not you, too," she managed to say.

"When Meg worries, I worry," Brad replied gently. "It's part of my job description as a husband-father-brother."

"I'm fine," Melissa insisted.

"Not so much," Brad said.

Ashley showed up then, dressed in jeans and a short-sleeved yellow blouse, her fair hair falling in a long braid down the center of her back. Joining her brother and sister, she smiled. "I *told you* I would be here to give you a hand with the parade," she said brightly, rubbing her palms together in anticipation and ignoring Melissa's somewhat impatient glance. "What needs doing?"

Before Melissa could answer, Olivia and Meg arrived, Meg standing on tiptoe to kiss Brad on the cheek. He slid an arm around his wife and held her against his side for a moment.

"This had better not be another intervention," Melissa warned. She was still a little insulted by the whole concept, frankly.

Olivia was, as usual, completely undaunted. She'd once treated a wild stallion for injuries, up in the hills, and it took more than an irritated younger sister to throw her off her game.

"The last one must have worked," she said, after looking Melissa over. "Your hair has been combed and you're wearing makeup."

Melissa made a face, but then she had to laugh.

"You're impossible," she said, addressing Olivia, Meg *and* Ashley, all together.

"Looks like the ice cream shop's float is in trouble," Ashley said, shading her eyes as she watched the giant cone, made of cardboard and crepe paper, teeter wildly to one side.

Meg pushed up the long sleeves of her fitted blue T-shirt. "Let's go see what we can do to help before that thing falls over and spooks one of these horses or something," she said to Ashley and Olivia. There were at least a dozen of the animals nearby, waiting to carry the sheriff's posse on a triumphant sweep along the relatively short length of Main Street.

"Good idea," Melissa said. And they were off.

The horses, as it happened, were doing just fine— Brad and his wranglers had brought them to town and unloaded them early for the express purpose of giving them time to get used to being off the range and in a fairly unfamiliar environment.

"They mean well," Brad told Melissa, watching the three women march over to take charge of the giant ice cream cone and the overwhelmed junior management type trying to contain the thing.

"I know," Melissa said, with a little sigh. Then, as a farewell, she added, "Later."

"Later," Brad confirmed.

It was surprising, Melissa discovered over the next couple of hours, how many things could go wrong with one small-town parade.

The convertible that was supposed to carry the mayor of Stone Creek, that year's grand marshal, threw a rod.

The tractor supporting the Chamber of Commerce's infamous toilet-paper float stalled out, and the teenage rodeo queen had to borrow a horse from Brad, because her own turned up lame.

And those were the *easy* things.

Nonetheless, Melissa found herself enjoying the distraction. At least, being so busy, she wasn't brooding over her life in general and Steven Creed in particular.

By five minutes to six, all the participants had taken their proper place in line. The high-school marching band was in formation, tuning up their instruments for the umpteenth time. The sheriff's posse, led by Tom Parker, of course, were all safely mounted on patient horses—the kind Meg and Brad generally reserved for inexperienced dudes.

The oversize ice cream cone had been stabilized.

Another convertible had been found to replace the one that had broken down earlier, so the mayor was riding high and all set to wave to the crowds on the sidewalks, and the rodeo queen was sporting a dazzling smile and plenty of sequins.

Ona Frame, well along the road to recovery after her gallbladder surgery, looked on from a place of honor.

It was all good.

"Melissa!"

She turned at the sound of her name and saw Matt Creed about half a block farther along Main Street, perched on Steven's shoulders. They were clearly part of a group, Steven and Matt; a good-looking couple in their fifties, dressed Western, stood close by.

The man had to be Steven's father, Melissa thought, distracted in spite of her better intentions. Same build, same hair color, same innate sense of quiet confidence. The sight of them all made her throat catch, for some reason, and caused the backs of her eyes to tingle slightly. She smiled and waved to the little boy, pretending not to notice the man, and turned to give the signal that would start the parade rolling.

Folks along the way cheered, their faces alight with pleasure in this simplest of all small-town-America celebrations. Many of them were people Melissa knew, lifelong residents of Stone Creek and Indian Rock and the surrounding areas, but others were strangers, passing through. The annual rodeo, with its customary trimmings, always drew plenty of fans, along with competitors from all over the country.

Melissa felt as though she'd been swept up in something, and was being carried along, watching that parade pass. She was, in those moments, ridiculously proud of her hometown, and the stalwart people who inhabited it.

She was even a little proud of *herself,* for sticking with it, for seeing the task through to its fruition.

Not that she ever intended to get roped into heading the Parade Committee again, as long as she lived, because she most certainly didn't. Next year, someone else would have to oversee the project, keep Bea Brady and Adelaide Hillingsley from coming to blows, and make sure no one wound up pinned beneath an enormous cardboard ice cream cone.

She looked over toward the fairgrounds—the rodeo would start at noon the following day and run well into the night, and the festivities would be repeated on Sunday, the Fourth, with a finale of spectacular fireworks. Meanwhile, the Ferris wheel loomed neon-pink against the darkening sky. As the parade noise subsided, the tinny music from the carousel and all the other rides and games would settle over the town like a blanket.

Once the last float had wobbled down Main Street, people would head over to the carnival, kids in tow, to fill up on roasted corn, served on sticks, barbecued meat and chicken, cotton candy and plenty of other nutritional disasters as well.

Some of Melissa's first memories were of that carnival and the big rodeo, before the family had splintered apart. The old sequence played out in her mind, yet again. Delia had left them, getting onto a bus one day and never coming back. Not long after that, their dad was killed. Then Big John died, too.

A strange mix of sadness and gratitude overtook Melissa, right there on Main Street, with friends and strangers all around her. She'd lost a lot in her life, but she still had Brad and Olivia and Ashley, their spouses, and all her nieces and nephews.

She was part of a close and ever-growing family, and that was more than a lot of people could say. So why wasn't it *enough?*

STEVEN KEPT TRACK OF MELISSA as best he could, given how crowded the sidewalks were. He'd lose sight of her, then get onto the balls of his feet and crane his neck to find her again, all the while trying to look like he wasn't looking.

Kim was beside him; she and Davis had rolled in that afternoon, their new RV almost as fancy as Brad O'Ballivan's tour bus. Brody was still missing in action, and Conner, apparently, had been temporarily detained up in Lonesome Bend. He'd be there by morning.

For now, it was just the four of them.

"Where's Melissa?" Kim asked, nudging Steven lightly in the side when there was a lull between the high-school marching band and the sheriff's posse on horseback. "Point her out to me."

Steven was a little taken aback—as far as he could recall, he hadn't mentioned Melissa to his folks—and while he was still trying to come up with a response, Matt leaped into the conversational breach.

"That's her!" he fairly shouted, shifting excitedly atop Steven's shoulders to point. "That really pretty lady with the twisty curls in her hair!"

Matt's voice carried far and wide, and Melissa, looking country-delicious in her well-cut jeans and peach-colored off-the-shoulder blouse with lots of little ruffles, reappeared from the throng and turned her head in their direction.

"Melissa!" Matt called out, overjoyed, it seemed, to see her. By then, he was waving so wildly that Steven had to tighten his grip on the kid to keep him from tumbling to the sidewalk. "Melissa! Over here!"

Steven watched her scrounge up a smile, and then crank up the wattage for Matt's sake.

"Nice parade!" Matt complimented her, when she entered their small family circle. "You did a *great job,* Melissa!"

"Thanks, cowboy," she said, with tenderness in her voice as well as her eyes, as she reached up to tug at Matt's "rodeo" hat. It was one of several presents Kim and Davis had brought along.

"I'm Kim Creed," Steven's stepmother said warmly, putting a hand out to Melissa. "And this is my husband, Davis."

Davis's eyes twinkled as he shook hands with Melissa. "Well, now," he said, giving a tug at the brim of his own hat, a larger version of the one Matt was wearing, but otherwise a near duplicate. "It's nice to meet you in person, though I will admit that I feel like I already knew you."

Melissa blinked at that, and her cheeks turned almost the same enticing shade of peach as her blouse as she darted a confused glance at Steven, looking as though she might be wondering if he was the type to kiss and tell.

So to speak.

"Matt's been talking about you pretty much nonstop," Kim explained, smiling at Melissa.

"I showed them the picture I drew," Matt piped up. "You're in it. It's you and me and Dad and Zeke and my pony, looking like a family."

Inwardly, Steven groaned. Outwardly, he managed to keep his cool.

If Melissa had any reaction at all to the boy's remark, it didn't show.

"Not that I *have* a pony," Matt added, when no one else spoke up right away. "Even though Dad *promised* we'd both have horses as soon as the barn was finished."

Davis chuckled at that. "Give your dad a chance, boy," he said easily, looking up at Matt. "It was just yesterday that the shavings were put down in the stalls and the water supply was hooked up."

Steven was grateful to his father for saying something, because his own tongue still felt like a twist of rusted barbed wire. Though he couldn't stop staring, he hoped Melissa would be too distracted by Matt and Davis and Kim to notice.

I love you, Melissa O'Ballivan, said something inside him.

Steven was, oddly, as shaken by that silent voice as Melissa and the others would have been, if he'd said it out loud. Thank God, he hadn't. Had he?

She looked up at him, her expression curious. Somehow unsettled.

Then she recovered, smiled a brilliant smile that skirted over him but took in Davis, Kim and especially Matt.

"I'd better be going," she said. "Once the parade wraps up, I'll be expected to offer my congratulations to one and all."

With that, she walked away.

Steven didn't make a sound. He couldn't see where Matt was looking, but it wasn't hard to guess.

Davis and Kim, of course, were watching Melissa

hurrying alongside the last straggling remnants of the Independence Day parade.

"I want Dad to marry Melissa," Matt said, with so much enthusiasm that more people than just his grandparents heard the statement and turned to grin as they registered it. "But I'm not getting anywhere with it."

Steven reddened, starting with his neck and ending somewhere above his hairline.

Kim smiled, and reached up for Matt with both arms. "The parade's almost over," she said, as the boy went to her, readily. "Let's head over to the fairgrounds and get a jump on the line for the Ferris wheel."

Matt nodded eagerly.

"And you," Kim said to Steven, holding the child comfortably in those strong, ranch-woman's arms of hers, "can probably find something constructive to do while your dad and I spend a little time with our grandson."

Davis chuckled again, and slapped Steven on the back.

And then all three of them walked away and left him standing there, looking like a damn fool who hadn't figured out that the parade had already passed him by.

CHAPTER SEVENTEEN

STEVEN FELT LIKE A STALKER, but he trailed Melissa to the supermarket parking lot at the other end of town, where the parade was already breaking apart into colorful segments, like some snake undergoing a mysterious rite of renewal.

There was a lot of hugging and hand-shaking, and then more hugging. The kids from the marching band stripped right there in the open, shedding uniform coats and creased pants to reveal the shorts and T-shirts underneath. Then they tossed the discards, including their hats with the spiffy gold insignia above the brim, into the backseats of various minivans and SUVs. They were off to the carnival, traveling in noisy packs, thinning the crowd as they went.

Steven tried to stay out of sight, but, as luck would have it, Brad O'Ballivan, there with a few ranch hands and several large horse trailers, spotted him and called out. Which made Melissa turn her head toward him and then away again. Quickly.

Feeling like an idiot, Steven managed a grin he hoped looked easy and unconcerned, and walked over to where Brad was standing.

"Need some help loading these horses?" he asked.

"Sure," Brad replied. His gaze, while not unfriendly, seemed a little more intent than usual.

Steven busied himself with work he could do without thinking, removing saddles, replacing bridles with halters, leading weary critters up hoof-scarred ramps and into trailers that smelled pleasantly of hay and horse, securing them there, so they could make the trip home in safety.

All the time, he thought about Melissa, though he didn't dare look in her direction. Stupid, he decided, since she was the whole reason he'd followed the parade to this parking lot in the first place. But there it was.

By the time the last of the animals were loaded and the doors on the trailers shut and bolted, she'd vanished. Brad approached and said thanks, and the two men shook hands.

"Looking for Melissa?" Brad asked, after a few moments of awkward silence.

"Was it that obvious?" Steven countered, discouraged.

Brad grinned. "Oh, yeah," he said. "It was that obvious." Then he sobered again. "This is the part where I ask you if your intentions are honorable, as far as my sister is concerned."

"And if they are?"

"I'll be real pleased," Brad answered affably. Then he leaned in slightly and commenced to using John Wayne's voice in place of his own. "On the other hand, Pilgrim, if it turns out that you're just looking for a good time, I'll have to personally feed you your own ears, one at a time. And after that, I'll hurt you."

Steven laughed. He reckoned if he'd had a sister, he'd have felt much the same way. "Fair enough," he said.

"Melissa caught a ride back to the other end of town, where she left her car before the parade," Brad went on, back to being himself again, though his imitation of the Duke had been more than passable. "She's worn out—plans on going straight home, as I understand it, and heating canned soup for supper."

After a short hesitation, Steven nodded, said thanks, and turned to walk back to the center of town. He'd left his own rig parked beside his office, and he hurried toward it now, cutting between buildings instead of taking a more direct route, which would have led him past the courthouse. He still felt the pull of habit, even though he knew she hadn't gone back to work.

He didn't know what he'd say to Melissa once he caught up to her, but as he reached his truck, got inside and started up the engine, he felt a peculiar sense of urgency, as if there was no time to waste.

That, of course, was crazy. Brad had told him what Melissa meant to do—collect her car from the parking lot behind the high school and then go home. She probably *was* exhausted, after all the rigmarole of making sure the Fourth of July parade came off with no notable hitches, and the wiser course would almost certainly be to leave her alone.

Steven couldn't do that, for whatever reason. Something compelled him to find her and say—what? What, exactly, was there to say?

Damned if he knew, but he had to see her, without Matt and his parents around. When he looked into her eyes, the words would come to him—or not.

He pulled out onto Main Street, now dappled with horse manure the clowns with brooms had missed, multicolored bits of confetti and the remains of the wrapped pieces of hard candy the mayor had tossed from his perch in the convertible, and was gratified to see Melissa one intersection over, at the wheel of her roadster.

She'd put the top down, since the weather was good, and even from that distance, Steven could see the last spangles of daylight catching in her hair.

There wasn't another vehicle in sight, in either direction, and the effect was eerie, almost postapocalyptic. He'd missed the green light, since he wasn't paying attention, and watched with some surprise as Melissa turned right, instead of left, which would have taken her in the direction of home.

She cruised past Steven, and he pulled out behind her.

Sure, she'd see him, but he was tired of skulking around like some character in a bad spy movie. He'd defended a stalker or two in his time, but he'd never expected to be one. He did have a little more insight into the nature of obsession than most people, which he wryly supposed was a plus.

When she signaled her intention to turn in at the Stop & Shop, Steven got that spooky feeling again, as if he ought to stay close by, keep her in sight.

Melissa stopped at the gas pump, got out of the roadster to swipe her credit card and fill up.

Steven drove right past her, to a parking space in front of the store, which looked deserted, like the rest of town, feeling ridiculously self-conscious again.

She looked up, smiled vaguely and went back to fiddling with the nozzle on the pump hose. Her brow creased into a frown as she clicked away at the starter lever, getting no response.

Steven sighed, turned, and forced himself to walk casually toward her.

"Hi," he said.

"Hello," she responded. She didn't sound unfriendly, just distracted, as though she knew they were acquainted, but she couldn't quite place him.

Oh, yeah, he imagined her saying, as realization hit, tapping her forehead with the heel of one palm, *that guy I went to bed with.*

"Where's Matt?" she asked. There was a certain distance in her tone, and they might as well have been facing each other from opposite sides of an electric fence—with razor wire strung along the top.

"He's over at the carnival, with my parents," Steven answered, in a perfectly normal tone of voice, which was amazing because on the inside, he felt as though he'd swallowed a hive full of bees, all taking flight, all buzzing.

"Oh," Melissa said, averting her eyes.

Something had to give. Break through the barrier, get them talking like adults instead of feuding teenagers. "Melissa—"

"What?"

"I—we need to talk."

One of her perfect eyebrows rose slightly. "About—?"

"About us, dammit," Steven said.

Her voice was sugar-sweet. "And what 'us' would that be?"

Exasperated, Steven gestured toward the gas pump. "Maybe you've noticed that that thing isn't working," he told her.

She sighed, sounding put-upon. "I guess I'll have to go inside to pay," she answered. "Get Martine to flip the switch."

With that, she walked away, moving toward the glass doors of the entrance at an impressive clip.

Steven followed, double-stepping to catch up. "I can't stop thinking about you," he was surprised—and mortified—to hear himself say.

Melissa favored him with a winning smile, waited while he held one of the doors for her, and whispered, "Try a little harder, then."

She was inside in the next moment, Steven right behind her.

"There has to be a way around this lawyer thing," he whispered back, nearly colliding with Melissa when she stopped abruptly.

The store was silent, and yet the air seemed to vibrate.

Martine was indeed behind the counter, and Nathan Carter was right beside her, with the barrel of a pistol pressed up hard under her fleshy chin. Her eyes were round with fear and they flitted between Steven and Melissa, begging for help.

Steven acted instinctively; caught Melissa by one arm and fairly threw her behind him.

"Put the gun down," he told Nathan, his voice calm.

Melissa was back, and she tried to edge around him, but, with one arm, he eased her behind him again.

Carter merely cocked the pistol, a flashy move, like he'd watched a lot of old Westerns on TV or something, and then practiced endlessly.

Oddly, it struck Steven then, and certainly not for the first time, that if criminals put the same effort into honest work as they did taking illegal shortcuts, they wouldn't need to turn to crime.

Martine made a small, whimperlike sound. "The armored car service came today," she said weakly, her eyes awash in tears now, "picked up most of the cash we had on hand. All I have is a couple hundred dollars, so I can make change."

"Shut up," Carter rasped, poking Martine harder with the gun.

"Easy," Steven said, in a tone he usually reserved for spooked horses and unfriendly dogs. "You don't want the kind of trouble you'll be in if Martine gets hurt. Believe me, you don't."

Carter was sweating, and his pupils seemed to be spiraling in the centers of his eyes. He was high, or drunk, maybe both. Very bad news. Drugs, alcohol and stupidity didn't make a good combination.

"She's lying about the money," the thief growled. "She won't tell me where the money is!"

"I just have what's right here in the till," Martine insisted, in a frantic squeak. "We've been selling a lot of gas and beer and soda and stuff, with all these people in town for the parade and the rodeo, and the boss wanted most of the money in the bank—"

"I *told* you to shut up," Carter said. Then, quicker than Steven would have thought anybody could move, especially when they were stoned, he turned the pistol in his hand and used the butt of it to whack Martine hard in the side of the head.

The sound was like a baseball bat striking a watermelon.

Melissa screamed, more in objection than fright.

And Steven pitched himself over the counter at Carter, who, in that split second, was fumbling with the weapon.

A shot ripped through the air, shattered the glass in the front window.

The alarm began to shriek.

Steven landed on Carter and they both went down, in a tangle, not far from where Martine lay, perfectly still and bleeding.

The quarters were close behind that counter. Carter still had the gun—Steven could feel it pressed sideways between him and his adversary, knew the other man was groping for the trigger, and if he managed to get a finger around it—

Sirens sounded in the distance—too *far* in the distance.

The struggle for control of the gun seemed neverending, although it couldn't have lasted more than a few seconds. When the pistol went off, Steven froze, waiting for the bullet to tear through him.

But it was Carter who'd been hit.

He looked up at Steven, smirked and then closed his eyes.

Steven raised himself slowly, got as far as his knees, then took the gun from the dead man's fingers—there was blood everywhere by then, some of it Carter's, some of it Martine's.

Melissa scrambled, half crawling, around the base of the counter, her eyes huge, her face chalk-white. Her gaze found Steven, clung to him for a fraction of a moment, skittered over Nathan Carter and fixed itself on Martine, who was beginning to stir. Moaning a little.

"Are you hit?" Melissa asked. And when she didn't get an answer in the next second, she repeated, *"Steven, are you hit?"*

"No," he said. The bloody pistol made a thunking sound as he reached up and set it on the counter.

She wriggled past him, and Carter, to reach Martine. "Hold on," she murmured to the other woman. "Please, hold on. Help is coming. Do you hear the sirens? You're all right now, you're safe—"

The sirens were louder.

Closer.

Steven hauled himself to his feet, dazed.

Flashing lights swiped at the windows, a slap of red, a slap of blue.

He blinked.

Melissa was still on the floor, trying to comfort Martine.

Tom Parker burst in, gun drawn, still wearing his fancy parade uniform. "What the hell—?" he said.

"You can holster that thing," Steven told him, in a remarkably calm voice. "The shooting is over."

Tom hesitated as two deputies piled in behind him, their own service revolvers out and ready.

Tom raised a hand, evidently a signal that any immediate danger was past, and ordered, "Tell the EMTs it's okay to come in, and make sure—make *damn sure*—nobody else sets foot in here. I don't want this scene messed up."

The deputies obeyed.

Things had been happening at warp speed right along, but now time seemed to move even faster.

The EMTs appeared.

Steven took Melissa's hand, and pulled her out from behind the counter, held her close while the medics worked to stabilize Martine.

"I'm all right," Martine said, over and over again.

Steven tightened his arms around Melissa when she began to cry.

Martine was carried out on a stretcher, and loaded into a waiting ambulance.

Tom rounded the end of the counter to look down at Nathan Carter, who was so obviously dead that the paramedics hadn't bothered with him.

"What happened?" Tom asked, in the thunderous silence.

Outside, the world was still a noisy place, a thrumming void, threaded through with panicked shouts and carnival music and the screech of tires on asphalt as the ambulance sped away. Instead, that store was like the bottom of a lake. Or an ocean.

Melissa buried her face in Steven's shirt, avoiding the blood for the most part, and trembled against his chest.

Slowly, Steven recounted what had happened.

The State Police arrived, along with their crime scene techs. The store was secured, and Tom told Melissa and Steven to go on home, because there was nothing more to be done here.

"You can't let Matt see you with blood all over your clothes," Melissa said, when they were outside in the warm night.

The statement reassured Steven that she was all right. She was coming back to herself. Back to him.

"I know," he said, weary to the core of his soul.

Bystanders shouted questions to them, questions Melissa fielded with an upraised palm and, "Tom will make an announcement when that's appropriate. In the meantime, I hope you'll all cooperate and let the authorities complete their investigation with no interruptions."

"Is Martine gonna make it?" someone called out.

"Yes," Melissa said, her arm around Steven, just as his was around her.

He wasn't sure who was supporting whom.

The roadster was still parked at the pumps, its paint job shining under the outside lights.

Steven steered Melissa in the direction of his truck—whatever happened, he wasn't ready to let her go—and they were almost to the driver's-side door when a man in a hat stepped out of the shadows.

"Boston? Does all that blood belong to you or somebody else?"

Brody. Steven felt a rush of emotions, but at the moment, relief was the only one he recognized.

"I'm all right," he said.

Brody swept off his beat-up old hat, nodded politely to Melissa. "How about you, ma'am?"

She simply nodded, leaning into Steven a little.

"Dad and Kim are over at the fairgrounds, with Matt," Steven said to his cousin. "Find them and bring them out to the ranch, will you?" He paused, looked down at his clothes. Tom hadn't said so, but the police would probably want them as evidence, and he'd be questioned, without a doubt. This was likely to be a long night.

Brody nodded. "I'll do it," he said. He took Melissa's arm and escorted her to the other side of the truck, helped her into the passenger seat.

He could be a gentleman, when he chose.

Steven was behind the wheel by the time Brody returned to look in at him through the open window.

"Maybe you'd like a little time to get out of those duds," Brody observed gravely. "If Kim and the little guy see you looking like you lost a gunfight, they'll freak for sure."

Steven nodded. "Give us an hour," he said.

He shifted into gear, backed the truck out, shifted again.

"Do you want me to drop you off at your place?" he asked Melissa, as an afterthought.

Steven was more than relieved when she shook her head no.

They drove to the ranch in relative silence; both of them were probably in shock. When she saw that there were lights burning in the old house, and Brad's tour bus was gone, replaced by Davis and Kim's RV, she sat up a little straighter.

"You've moved into your house?"

"It's more like we're camping out," Steven answered, smiling. It felt good—and strange—to smile, as if he'd forgotten how to do it and then suddenly remembered. "But it's shaping up. Matt's in his room and I'm in mine. The kitchen works, and so do the shower and the bathtub."

She looked down at her clothes, when Steven stopped the truck and shoved open the door, causing the interior lights to come on.

"I'm a mess," she said.

"You can borrow something of Kim's," Steven replied, getting out.

Before he could go around and open the door for her, Melissa had alighted on her own.

They met behind the truck.

"You're—you're really okay, Steven?" she asked.

He started to touch her, drew back his hand at the last

moment. "You might say I've seen the light," he said, after giving a nod.

She moved to his side, slipped an arm around him, and they started toward the house.

Inside, Zeke was barking his head off, waiting to greet them.

Eager to greet *anybody*.

They entered the house, and Steven acknowledged the dog, then crossed the kitchen and plucked a couple of garbage bags from the box under the new stainless steel sink. He offered one to Melissa, pointed her in the right direction. "You take the first shower," he said. "There's a robe on the hook on the back of the bathroom door."

"What about you?" she asked, her voice quiet, worried. "Matt would be beside himself if he saw you—"

"Brody will make sure he doesn't," Steven said. His cousin was about the least dependable person he knew, but when it mattered, Brody always came through.

"Still," Melissa argued.

Steven put a hand on the small of her back and steered her to the bathroom door.

"Go," he said from behind her and close to her ear. "I'll go out to the RV and swipe something for you to wear. Put your clothes in the garbage bag—there's a good chance the forensics people will want them."

She nodded, without turning around to look at him, then pushed open the door and disappeared into the bathroom.

He waited until he heard the shower running, then retraced his steps to his bedroom. He stripped and stuffed his clothes into the second bag, and pulled on a pair of sweatpants he'd been meaning to throw away. After one last hurrah, their time would come.

Steven got out a shirt, socks and sneakers. He heard the shower stop, and imagined Melissa stepping naked out of the stall, drying off quickly, reaching for his robe and shrugging into it, cinching the belt up tight. The thought made him smile.

It also made him want to hold her. Skin to skin, yes. But the desire was more about knowing that Melissa was safe than it was about sex.

They met in the hallway.

"I'll make coffee," she said.

"Good idea," Steven replied.

Fifteen minutes later, when he joined her, she was sitting at the kitchen table the movers had brought from his condo in Denver—it looked too modern for a ranch house and too small for that kitchen—but Melissa looked just fine.

She turned her head and he knew by the look in her eyes that her brain was in top gear.

Amazing, considering what she'd been through earlier in the evening.

"Hold on," he said, sounding gruff. "I'll be back in a minute." He took the keys to his parents' RV from the hook beside the back door and headed outside, taking Zeke with him. While the dog sniffed around and lifted his leg against an old wagon wheel half buried in the dirt, Steven unlocked the fancy RV and went in.

There were a couple of suitcases on the bed in the master space, both open, but Davis and Kim hadn't unpacked yet.

Steven helped himself to a likely looking pair of jeans and a T-shirt with "Lonesome Bend Pioneer Days" imprinted on the front, but he didn't touch the bras and panties. He didn't know for sure, but he figured it was a fairly good bet that women didn't like wearing each other's underwear any better than men did.

No, Melissa would just have to go without. The thought made him smile again. And that was remarkable, considering.

He returned to the house, Zeke frolicking happily at his heels, and offered the jeans and T-shirt to Melissa.

Still sitting at the table, she accepted the neat little pile of clothes without comment, got up from her chair and went back to the bathroom to put them on.

She returned in time to drink the fresh coffee Steven had just poured into her mug. She reached for the cup and breathed the aroma in gratefully.

Kim was taller than Melissa, so the jeans and T-shirt looked a little big on her, but she didn't seem to care.

"What happens now?" she asked, after dropping back into her chair.

Zeke walked over and laid his muzzle in her lap, as if to offer comfort.

"Tom calls us in for questioning," Steven said, though he was sure she'd only asked rhetorically. "Maybe tonight, probably tomorrow." He turned a chair around, sat astraddle of it, with his arms resting across the back. "We're witnesses, counselor."

And I killed a human being, Steven thought.

A brief flash sparked in her eyes. "I *know* that," she said. "I was talking about—I meant—what happens between us?"

A grin tugged at the side of his mouth. "Not too long ago, a lady told me, with some emphasis, that there *is* no us."

Melissa sat up straighter, one hand curled around her cup, the other stroking Zeke's head. "That was before she—I—came face-to-face with my priorities. That happens, when you think you might die."

Steven nodded. His heartbeat quickened, but she had no way of knowing that, of course. A good thing, to his way of thinking.

"What are *your* priorities, Steven?" she asked.

He took his time replying, even though the answers lived in the very cells of his body, little holograms, each one containing the whole. "Matt. His health and happiness and freedom, my own, my family's, and everybody else's. Knowing, when I'm about to fall asleep at night, that I did what I thought was right that day, even if things didn't turn out the way I hoped they would." He allowed himself a measured pause. "What about you? What are your priorities, Melissa?"

"The people I love matter most," she said, after taking a few sips of coffee. Her gaze was fixed on the far side of forever. "The law matters, because without some kind of social order, we're all in trouble." She looked down at Zeke. Smiled tenderly. "Animals mean more to me than I ever realized—they're so devoted and so loyal."

"Thinking of getting a pet?" Steven asked, when another silence fell.

She smiled, shook her head. "Not right away," she said. "But I think I'd like to work for Olivia's foundation, once my term as prosecutor is up. Livie and I used to talk about it a lot, how I could serve as a kind of animal advocate."

Steven took that in, along with a few sips of coffee. Tried not to look too pleased by what she'd just revealed. He would have bet his best saddle that this woman would remain the Stone Creek County prosecutor until her hair was tinted blue.

"That's—interesting," he said.

Zeke lifted his head off Melissa's lap and started barking again.

They heard the sound of an engine, the slamming of a door.

Brody poked his head into the kitchen a few seconds later. "Is the coast clear?" he asked.

"It's clear," Steven said.

Brody's smile broke over his face like a summer sunrise, full of light. "Good," he replied. "I'll go get Kim and Davis and the boy."

As quickly as that, he was gone again, and Zeke went with him.

Zeke had long since appointed himself the official welcoming committee.

Melissa bit her lower lip. "I know I should ask you to take me home, but—"

Steven closed his hand over hers. "But?"

"But I don't really want to be alone, and my family would make such a fuss over all the things that *could* have happened—I don't think I can face that, tonight, anyway."

"Stay with me," Steven suggested, husky-voiced. "I'll hold you. Nothing more than that, I promise."

Tears filled her eyes as she searched his for any sign of deception.

"Okay," she said, just as Matt burst into the house, with Kim and Davis and Brody and Zeke close behind.

MELISSA NOTICED THE PICTURE taped to the refrigerator door only after Steven had given Matt and the others a watered-down version of that night's events. Kim and Davis and Brody all listened intently.

He left several pertinent details out of his account—the fear they'd all felt when Martine was struck down with the butt of Carter's pistol, the struggle for that weapon, the shot that ended the robber's life—but he still managed to convey a lot.

Yes, someone tried to rob the Stop & Shop. Yes, Melissa and I were scared. Both of us. No, I wasn't a hero.

"Yes, he was," Melissa disagreed, pulling her gaze away from the drawing of the stick-family Matt had mentioned earlier, in town, when the parade was about to end.

Kim smiled and tugged Matt onto her lap. "Why don't you get your pajamas and your toothbrush and come spend the night in the RV with your grandpa and me?"

The boy's eyes widened. He looked tired, but the things Steven had said had apparently calmed his fears.

"You'll be okay, Dad?" he asked.

"I'll be fine," Steven promised.

Matt turned to look up at Kim. "Can Zeke come, too?"

Davis answered for her. "Sure, he can," he said, his gaze moving to Brody, who was leaning against the counter, with his arms folded, watching them all. "There's plenty of room out there," he added.

Brody grinned, gave a little salute as an answer.

He was good-looking, Melissa thought, strangely detached.

"Will you still be here in the morning?" Matt asked,

coming to stand next to Melissa's chair and looking up at her with what she read as a combination of concern and hope.

It was a tricky question. Melissa looked to Steven for help, but he said nothing.

Suddenly, Matt dashed over to the refrigerator and fetched the drawing, bringing it proudly back to the table to show Melissa. Tape still clung to its now ragged edges.

Steven cleared his throat. "Maybe you ought to go and get your pajamas and your toothbrush, as your grandmother asked you," he said to his son.

The glow in Matt's little face barely flickered. He nodded in response to Steven's words, but he was focused on Melissa and on the drawing.

"See?" he said. "It's the one I told you about, at the parade. There's me, and there's my dad, and there's Zeke. And there's you."

Melissa's throat ached. Her crayon image wore her hair up, and she had on what looked like a suit and carried either a very large purse or a briefcase.

"And this?" she said, indicating an equine-shaped creature.

"That's my horse. I'm getting one any day now. Grandpa Davis says if Dad doesn't get me a pony, *he* will."

"Is that right?" Steven asked his father, in a low drawl.

"Let's all get us some shut-eye," Davis said, with bluster, exaggerating the yokel-speak a little. "There's a rodeo tomorrow, and I don't know about the rest of you, but I plan to be there in time to get a good seat in the bleachers, and that means I need my sleep."

Reminded of the rodeo, Matt forgot about the drawing and dashed for his room, returning pronto with the things he would need for the impromptu sleepover.

Melissa felt a little guilty, knowing she was the reason Brody and Matt were sleeping in the RV instead of the house. Given what had happened, Matt might *need* to be close to his father tonight, if only for the reassurance that Steven was safe.

That *he* was safe.

Brody and Davis went outside, engaged in some quiet conversation of their own. Steven and Matt had gone back to Matt's room to get a clean pair of pajamas to replace the ones the little guy had chosen first.

"Steven seemed to think you wouldn't mind if I borrowed some of your clothing," Melissa said to Kim, when it was just the two of them, even more embarrassed than before.

Kim patted her hand and smiled. "Don't you worry," she said. Her gaze moved to the drawing, still in Melissa's hands.

Matt's voice echoed in Melissa's head. *There's you... there's you...*

"Are you sure you're all right, Melissa?" Kim asked.

Melissa tried hard to smile. Shook her head. "I don't think so," she confessed. "It was so awful, especially when the gun went off a second time and I thought Steven had been—I thought he was dead or badly hurt—"

Kim rested a hand on Melissa's shoulder; her touch was light, but firm enough to be comforting, too. Out of the blue, Melissa thought of her mother, who had never really been there for any of her four children, and couldn't be there for her now, and a stab of regret and resentment hit her so hard that she nearly bent double.

"Maybe you should see a doctor," Kim suggested.

"No," Melissa said. "I'll be fine in the morning."

Just then, Steven returned with Matt, who was now outfitted in a pair of cotton PJs covered with tiny covered wagons, cacti and tepees.

"I'm the Colorado Kid!" he exulted, raising both hands as if the pajamas represented proof of his preferred identity.

"You're a nut," Steven said, with affection, ruffling the boy's hair with one hand.

Kim stood, after giving Melissa one more concerned look, and made a big production of yawning and stretching.

"We'd better turn in soon, Colorado," she told her grandson. "It's getting late."

"Good night," Steven said to his stepmother and his son.

Melissa sat at the table, and Steven stood where he was for long moments after everyone else, including the dog, had left the house.

Melissa, who had spread the stick-family drawing out on the table in front of her, looked down at it. Her eyes were burning, and her throat felt thick.

Steven finally crossed to her, took her hand, raised her to her feet. Then he cupped her face in his hands and tilted her head back so he could look straight into her eyes.

"All I want to do is hold you," he said. "But if you'd rather spend the night in Matt's room, that's fine, too."

"I want to hold *you*," Melissa replied.

He smiled. "Then we're on the same page," he told her.

His room, like Matt's, was on the main floor.

The bed was huge, and oddly modern-looking, given the rustic nature of the ranch house, and brass lamps shed pale gold light onto thick pillows. The linens were Egyptian cotton, unless Melissa missed her guess, with a very high thread count.

Was she channeling Ashley?

No, Melissa nodded. She was nervous, that was all. And it was silly to be nervous *now*, when she was perfectly safe.

As calmly as if they slept in the same bed every night, Steven left Melissa to her hesitation and disappeared into the adjoining bathroom. By the time he returned, she'd appropriated a T-shirt from a chest of drawers and pulled it on. She'd left Kim's clothes folded and resting on the seat of a chair.

Her eyes widened when she saw Steven—he was totally naked. *Gloriously* naked.

Melissa reddened as all sorts of things quickened inside her.

"I sleep like this," he explained.

"Oh," she said.

He got into bed on his side and, after a few more moments of silent debate, Melissa joined him. They lay far apart, staring up at the ceiling.

Then Steven stretched to flip the switch on his lamp, and both lights went out, leaving the room dark, except for a skim of moonlight that made the bedding glow white.

"Still okay?" Steven asked, after a long, long time.

"Still okay," Melissa confirmed. "You?"

"Better than okay," he said. And he drew her into his arms, held her close against the hard warmth of his body. "What would you say if I told you I think there's a very strong possibility that I love you?"

A terrible joy spread through Melissa before she had a chance to raise her usual defenses. Long moments had passed when she was finally able to answer. "I'd say," she replied, snuggling close to him and soaring inside, "that you're probably just shaken up by everything that happened tonight."

"Suppose it's more?" Steven suggested, propping his chin on the top of her head. "What then?"

Melissa started to cry. "I'd say it was a good thing," she told him.

A chuckle moved up through his chest, and his arms tightened around her. She couldn't remember when she'd last felt so safe.

"Which means?" Steven prompted.

Melissa sighed, sniffled. "Which means," she answered, "that I'm 99 percent sure I feel the same way about you."

"But you wish you didn't."

"Don't you?"

Steven considered before countering, "Not much use in that now, is there?"

"It is what it is," Melissa responded.

"Think you could maybe work up a little more enthusiasm?" Steven teased, turning now, so his lips hovered just over hers.

She smiled, slipping her arms around his neck. "Yes," she said. "But I'll need some encouragement."

CHAPTER EIGHTEEN

STEVEN DID NOT MAKE LOVE to Melissa during the night; he'd promised to hold her, and he kept his word. But when dawn broke, and the first pinkish light of a new day tickled her awake, everything in Melissa seemed to catch fire.

It was a slow, smoldering burn, all the hotter for that.

Last night, she'd been in shock and vulnerable.

Some men would have taken advantage of her—but not Steven Creed.

She slipped out of bed, scurried into the bathroom and returned with an empty bladder and, thanks to a bottle of mouthwash she'd found in the medicine cabinet over the sink, fresh breath.

She stood looking down at Steven, willing him to open his eyes.

"I know you're awake," she finally said.

A grin crooked the corner of his mouth and, just as he raised his eyelids, Melissa peeled off the T-shirt and tossed it aside.

Steven muttered an exclamation.

"Did you mean it?" Melissa asked, enjoying her brief moment of power. Once Steven got her under him, she knew full well, the balance would shift; he would be in command.

Mostly.

"Did I mean what?" Steven hedged. He scooted upright, sat with his bare back against the headboard, the pillow fluffed behind him.

"When you said you thought there was a good possibility you might be in love with me," Melissa said. "Did you mean that?"

He grinned, and his whole face changed, seemed to light up, like the world beyond the bedroom windows. "Actually," he said, reaching out with lightning speed, clasping her hand, and pulling her down onto his lap, "I understated the matter considerably."

She blinked, still breathless from being yanked, however gently, off her feet. "You mean—?"

"I'm sure of it now," Steven said, his gaze holding hers, direct and unflinching. "I love you, Melissa. I have from the first—it just took me a while to admit it to myself, that's all."

"Are you just saying that because you want sex?" Melissa challenged. She was sitting on his lap and therefore had proof positive that he wanted sex.

He leaned forward, kissed her. The faker, he'd just been pretending to be asleep. He smelled tantalizingly of toothpaste and soap, and his hair was faintly damp. He'd been up well before Melissa.

"I can't deny that I do want sex," he said with a smiling acknowledgment of his arousal. "However, the fact remains, counselor, that I do. Love you, I mean."

Melissa wanted it to be true, was so afraid it wasn't. "How can you be so sure?"

He grinned again, stroked her hair with one strong, calloused hand. "I'm sure," he said, as the same hand moved down, skimming the bare flesh of her shoulder, setting it to tingling, and then curved around her breast. With the side of his thumb, Steven chafed her nipple. It tightened deliciously, ready for his mouth, and Melissa groaned.

Steven turned her, so that she was straddling him, and tasted her with just the tip of his tongue.

Fresh heat surged through her.

He suckled at her breast, gently at first, and then with a growing hunger.

Melissa whispered something senseless, let her head fall back, offering herself to him.

The night before, he'd shown restraint. This morning, he was all over her, attending to her breasts at leisure, rolling her onto her back, burying his head between her legs after kissing the length of her inner thighs.

He nibbled. Teased.

Melissa cried out and plunged her fingers into his hair, unsure whether she wanted to push him away or pull him closer still. The pleasure was excruciating, almost beyond her ability to bear.

"What about—?" Her question came out as a stran-gled croak.

"Let—go—" Steven assured her, between flicks of his tongue. "We're—alone—

Melissa moaned, pleading incoherently. She needed the tension to end, and to *never* end.

Steven took his time, taking her to the verge, then withdrawing. Finally, though, he gave her what she wanted.

Or she took it.

The orgasm seemed to unspool, like gossamer thread, wild and glittering loops of incomprehensible satisfaction.

Melissa held nothing back, and by the time she'd stopped responding, her body flexing and easing and flexing again, in the throes of helpless release, Steven, too, had lost control.

He must have had a condom ready, because he'd put it on and entered her, deeply, in almost the same motion.

Melissa, having just descended from the heights, didn't expect to be aroused again, especially so quickly, but with that first thrust, she was flung back into the same ecstatic desperation as before.

Only more so.

They climaxed simultaneously, Melissa's body arching under Steven's. Steven driving deep inside her and thrusting his head back as he uttered a low, guttural shout of relief.

The recovery took a long time, but hearing Zeke barking outside set them both scrambling. Melissa got the first shower, as she had the night before, and it was a good thing, because when she got to the kitchen, Matt and Davis and Kim and Brody were all there. And so was Tom Parker.

Melissa blushed, tugging at the waistband of her loose, borrowed jeans.

Seated at the table, a cup of fresh coffee steaming in front of him, Tom favored Melissa with a saucy grin that said, "So," long and drawn out, as clearly as if he'd spoken the word aloud.

"Fancy meeting you here," he drawled, his eyes dancing with amusement.

"Just imagine," Melissa said, but she kept her tone moderate, because Matt was there, and Steven's folks, and his cousin Brody. And all of them were watching her.

"Did you sleep over?" Matt asked Melissa, with frank innocence, his voice carrying all over that big kitchen.

The adults hid their amusement with coughs or by turning away. Except for Tom, of course. He was enjoying Melissa's discomfort *way* too much.

"Yes," Melissa told the child, because she knew Steven's policy toward his son didn't include lying. "I did."

Matt, still wearing his Southwestern pajamas, ran over and threw his arms around her. "Will you stay for breakfast? Please?"

"Blueberry pancakes," Kim said, patting the reusable shopping bag in her arms. You had to like a woman who brought her own ingredients *and* was willing to cook. "You're welcome to join us, Sheriff," she added, for Tom's benefit.

He agreed readily. Tom might have been quiet, but he wasn't shy. Except as far as Tessa Quinn was concerned, that is.

"We'll be having bacon and eggs, too," Davis Creed said.

"*You* won't," Kim replied, leveling a look at her husband. "I want to keep you around for a while, if you don't mind."

Something crackled between those two, Melissa would have sworn. They loved each other, without a shadow of a doubt. Loved each other deeply, passionately—and permanently.

It *was* possible, then, for a marriage to last through

good times and bad, not just over a few years, but over the ups and downs of *decades.*

Theoretically, Melissa had known that, of course. But emotionally, because of her parents' experience, and her own, she hadn't quite dared to believe it.

Melissa helped Kim by setting the table, enjoying the talk, the laughter, the wonderful smells of breakfast cooking.

The meal was noisy and delicious, a family affair, for sure.

Steven seemed on edge, though; his gaze kept straying toward the windows, or the back door, and when a horn honked out on the country road that ran past his property, he actually started slightly.

"What's the matter with you, Boston?" Brody asked, from behind a stack of pancakes that rivaled the Leaning Tower of Pisa.

Melissa watched with interest, out of the corner of her eye, as Steven's neck reddened, the color climbing into his face. He stabbed at his food with his fork, but he wasn't actually eating.

"Nothing," he said, and his glance held a warning for Brody: *don't push this.*

Surely Steven wasn't worried about Tom's presence, Melissa reasoned. It was true, of course, that both of them would have to answer a million questions, and testify in court, too, eventually, but the case itself was pretty straightforward.

With his training and experience in criminal law, Steven had to know he wouldn't be blamed for Nathan Carter's death—so what was bothering him? She studied him closely.

Tom's cell phone buzzed before anyone could speak

again, though Brody certainly looked as though he'd meant to do just that. Defiance flashed in his blue eyes, and his mouth was pressed into a hard line.

Brody Creed, Melissa concluded, didn't like being told what to do. Big surprise there.

"Tom Parker," the sheriff said, into the mouthpiece of his phone. "Yes? That's good. That's *really* good. Sure, I can stop by the office in a little while, but I have to pick Elvis up at home first. He loves the rodeo."

Melissa smiled, though her stomach was tight with sudden tension. *What,* she wondered, *was "really good"?*

"Thanks," Tom said, ending the exchange by shutting the phone and dropping it back into his shirt pocket.

Everyone was watching him, and *nobody* was even pretending to eat.

"That was a doctor at the hospital in Flagstaff," the sheriff explained, taking up his fork again. "Martine will be fine. They're releasing her today."

Melissa choked up again. Now that she didn't have to hold thoughts of what had happened to the other woman at bay to keep from panicking, relief rushed in, bringing tears to her eyes.

"Thank God," she said.

"It's not that you're not welcome, Sheriff," Steven said, when some of the emotional energy zipping around the table had subsided, "but you must have had a reason for driving clear out here on a Saturday morning."

Tom glanced at Matt, who was busy trying to sneak a piece of bacon to Zeke, and therefore distracted from the conversation between the grown-ups. "I'll need the clothes you were wearing," he said, looking directly at Steven now. "As well as Melissa's. The—er—interviews

can wait until Monday, when the rodeo is over and the
dust has settled a little."

The hard line of Steven's shoulders seemed to soften
slightly. "Okay," he said. And he glanced toward the
window again.

Who was he looking for?

Melissa didn't get the opportunity to ask until the
meal was over and the dishes had been put away and everybody was ready to head into town, including Tom.

And by then, she'd forgotten she'd had a question in
the first place.

STEVEN WAITED in Melissa's living room while she disappeared to exchange Kim's clothes for an outfit of her
own. She returned looking five kinds of wonderful in
black jeans that fit her only slightly more loosely than a
second skin, and a blouse just like the peach one she'd
had on the day before, except that it was turquoise. And
not soaked in blood.

To complete the look, she'd pulled on a pair of su-
perfancy boots, also turquoise, and decorated with
shining silver conchos and a few rhinestones for good
measure.

"Wow," Steven said. She wouldn't be mucking out
any stalls in those boots, that was for sure.

"The last time I wore these," Melissa replied, "I was
Queen of Stone Creek Rodeo Days."

Steven cleared his throat. "They've held up well," he
said, sliding his gaze upward from the boots, past all the
hidden places where he'd touched and kissed her in bed
that morning, until he reached her face. "And so have
you."

She laughed. "Nice save," she said.

Steven shifted. "We can do this, can't we?" he asked.

Melissa crossed to him, slipped her arms around his waist, stood on tiptoe to kiss the cleft in his chin. "Do what?" she countered softly, her eyes twinkly and warm.

For a moment, he felt as though he might tumble right into those eyes, and fall end over end, forever.

"Make it work," Steven said. "You. Me. Us."

"We can make it work," Melissa confirmed gently, splaying her hands over his shoulder blades now. "All we have to do is keep trying, Steven. If we give things time, and we don't give up, we'll be fine."

He smiled, bent his head to nibble at her lips. "Spoken like someone who comes from sturdy pioneer stock," he teased.

"Just like you do," she breathed, against his mouth.

"We could be a little late for the rodeo," he suggested.

"What rodeo?" Melissa asked.

At that, Steven scooped her up in his arms and carried her to bed.

MELISSA COULDN'T STOP SMILING, which was crazy, since she'd nearly been killed the night before, in the Stop & Shop. Steven's lovemaking, in his bed and later in hers, had left her feeling as though every step she took was part of a dance.

Was it a risk, letting herself love a man so completely?

Of course it was. But, just as Steven said, she was descended from pioneers, people like Sam and Maddie O'Ballivan, and generations as strong as they were. They hadn't been afraid to open their hearts to that special person, and Melissa wasn't, either.

Nor were Brad and Meg. Or Olivia and Tanner. Or Ashley and Jack.

All of whom, as it happened, were sitting in the same part of the bleachers as Davis and Kim and Matt when Steven and Melissa arrived, holding hands. Matt, in fact, was playing chase with Mac, in the aisle between rows of seats, waiting out the lull between events.

Olivia, Ashley and Meg were immediately on their booted feet, rushing Melissa, each of them hugging her in turn, all of them crying and saying over and over again how glad they were that she was safe.

The men, Melissa noticed, despite the onslaught of sisterly love, just shook their heads.

When the emcee announced the bareback bronc-riding event, they all returned to their seats. Brody was competing in this round.

Or was he? Melissa blinked at the man coming up the aisle, his hat in one hand, a grin spreading across his handsome face. He looked exactly like Brody.

But he wasn't.

Melissa felt Steven stiffen beside her.

The stands were packed, and a roar went up as the emcee announced the first rider. "We have an out-of-towner with us today, folks," the familiar voice boomed out, over the loudspeakers. "Let's hear a real Stone Creek welcome for #32, Brody Creed, out of Lonesome Bend, Colorado!"

The roar intensified.

Melissa missed the whole eight seconds of Brody's ride, because she couldn't tear her eyes away from the man in the aisle.

Not a vestige of his grin remained, and his hands were clenched into fists at his sides.

"Uh-oh," Davis said, low. Then, by some tacit agreement, he and Steven both got to their feet.

"Who *is* that?" Melissa asked Matt, who had stationed himself in her lap.

"That's Conner," Matt said. "Him and Brody are twins, just like you and your sister. Only they're the kind that look alike."

Conner, his face hard with anger, looked at Davis and Steven and turned to head back down the aisle.

Melissa looked to Kim, and saw that the other woman was worried.

Davis and Steven followed Conner, and soon, all three of them were out of sight.

"What's going on?" Melissa asked Steven's stepmother.

"World War III, probably," Kim answered, but there was a flicker of something in her eyes, despite her serious expression. On some level, she was *pleased* by this development.

"Are we just going to sit here?" Melissa asked, fretful.

"Yes," Kim replied firmly. "For Matt's sake, if no one else's."

"Where did Dad and Grandpa go?" Matt asked.

"They're getting hot dogs," Kim said, without missing a beat.

Melissa looked at her in surprise.

But Kim just smiled and turned her attention back to the rodeo, where Brody's score was just being posted on the big board above the announcer's booth.

The numbers were impressive; he'd be hard to beat.

But a whole bunch of other cowboys were ready, willing and able to give it a try.

CONNER WAS ABOUT to climb back into his dusty black truck and speed away when Steven and Davis caught up to him.

Davis reached out and spun his nephew around, thrust him hard against the side of the rig. "Didn't you get the memo, Conner?" he asked, through his teeth. "A Creed doesn't run. From anything."

"Tell that to my twin brother!" Conner spat furiously, his eyes shooting azure-blue flames.

"Why don't *you* tell him?" Steven asked, folding his arms. His boot heels were planted hard in the gravel of the fairgrounds, and he'd widened his stance slightly, too, just in case Conner threw a punch.

Stranger things had happened.

"I'm not telling him anything," Conner said, the words raspy and raw, like they'd scraped their way past his throat. He glared at Steven. "But I've got something to say to *you,* that's for damn sure. You set this up. You *knew,* cousin. And I don't know if I can forgive you for that."

"Grow up," Davis told Conner. A few stragglers, late for the rodeo, glanced in their direction, but nobody looked like they were fool enough to interfere in what was obviously a matter between close kin. "Whatever happened between you and Brody, it's time to get past it and move on. Dammit, we're *family.*"

Conner ran the back of his hand across his mouth. He was still pissed off, but out of good sense, respect for his elders, or both, he didn't speak his mind to Davis.

Then again, he didn't *have* to. It was written all over

him. He was mad from the top of his hat to the soles of his battered boots, and he wouldn't be over it anytime soon. If ever.

He turned to open his truck door, and this time Davis didn't make a move to stop him. Neither did Steven.

It took them all by surprise when, before Conner could start up that truck of his and drive away in the proverbial cloud of dust, Brody appeared, thrusting his way between Steven and Davis and lunging at Conner.

The whole scene reminded Steven of two bucks in rutting season, circling, preparing to lock antlers.

It was unclear whether Brody pulled open the truck door, or Conner pushed from the other side, but the next thing anybody knew, the brothers were rolling around on the ground, throwing punches, grunting and obviously bent on killing each other.

Steven sighed and started toward them, but Davis caught hold of his arm. The old man might have been in his fifties, but he was still strong.

"Let them settle it," Davis said.

Conner and Brody were so equally matched that Steven figured the fight would run into the middle of next week. Instead, they both wound up exhausted and rolled onto their backs in the dirt, breathing hard and cursing like a pair of old salts with seawater in their veins.

Davis grinned.

One of Tom Parker's deputies rushed over, red-faced. "We don't allow fighting inside the city limits," he blustered. An older man, significantly overweight, the deputy probably should have retired years before.

Brody hoisted himself upright and, beside him, Conner did the same.

"This isn't settled," Brody gasped out.

"You're damn right it isn't," Conner retorted, just as short of breath.

Brody got to his feet. "I've gotta go," he said.

"You scared I'll kick your ass?" Conner asked, rising, too.

"No," Brody bit out, "but I paid good money to compete in this rodeo, and I've got another event to ride in."

"I'll be waiting," Conner told him.

"You'd be one chickenshit son-of-a-bitch bastard if you weren't," Brody retorted. He bent to retrieve his hat from the ground and whacked it against one thigh, making the dust fly.

Conner made a move toward Brody, but Davis put out his hand again, making contact with the younger man's chest this time.

"Go make your ride," Davis told Brody, though he was smiling warmly at the deputy the whole time. "Everything's fine now, officer. We won't trouble you again."

Brody strode off toward the arena.

Conner swore and picked up his own fallen hat, punched the inside of the crown back into shape with so much force that Steven half expected his cousin's fist to break through. He rolled his broad shoulders and then glared at Steven before plunking his hat back on his head.

"You don't know what you've started," Conner bit out. There was sadness in his eyes now, along with the lingering anger. "If you did, Steven, you'd have left Brody and me alone."

Steven ached inside. As kids, the three of them had

been close. Their summers were almost magical back then, straight out of *Huckleberry Finn.*

When had that changed? What had gone so wrong between Brody and Conner that they couldn't even look at each other without tying in with fists flying?

"I guess I was hoping you'd gotten over whatever it was that came between you," Steven said quietly.

"Or *whoever*," Davis put in.

Steven turned to look at his father, suddenly wondering if Davis had known what the trouble was all along.

"She's long gone," Davis went on, still watching Conner. "Isn't it time you and Brody put that whole business behind you and moved on?"

A woman, Steven thought. He should have guessed that much but, back when the split happened, and Brody and Conner went their separate ways, he'd been too wrapped up in his own problems to really put his mind to it.

He'd been reeling then, from his granddad's death, following so quickly after his mother had passed away unexpectedly. He'd been embroiled in a battle with his maternal uncles over his inheritance. Busy making a name for himself in the Denver firm where Zack worked.

In those days, he'd believed that Brody and Conner would simply work out their differences. After all, identical twins or not, they'd always had *plenty* of differences.

Instead, a decade had gone by, with both of them holding their grudges, unwilling to give so much as an inch.

The waste made Steven grind his back teeth. All

those Thanksgivings and Christmases, when Brody's chair at the big dining room table was empty. All those weddings and births and deaths. All those years when they could have been, *should* have been, a family.

When tragedy struck Jillie down, and then Zack, Davis and Kim and Conner had been there for Steven. But he'd missed Brody sorely during those days, just the same.

Now, he felt a strong and sudden—or maybe not so sudden—urge to throttle Conner, right then and there, then find Brody and do the same thing to him. To keep himself from doing just that, Steven turned on one boot heel and headed back to where Matt and Melissa were.

His cousins could do whatever they damn well pleased—they always had—but Steven was through wasting time. He was through waiting and hoping, and being scared of getting things wrong. He knew what he wanted, and he meant to get it.

Soon.

MELISSA TOOK STEVEN'S HAND when he sat down beside her in the bleachers, his face still flushed with temper. "Where's Conner?" she asked, whispering because even though Matt had moved up a few rows to sit with his buddy, Mac, she didn't want to take the smallest chance of his overhearing.

"I don't know," Steven said coldly, "and I don't care."

"I don't believe that," Melissa said.

His shoulders, tense before, loosened a little as she reached up to rub Steven's back with her palm. He gave her a sideways glance and grinned, albeit wanly.

"I love you," he said softly.

She smiled. "Well, that's convenient, cowboy, because I love you right back."

"I wish we could leave—right now."

Her eyes sparkled. "And miss the rodeo? Sacrilege! Besides, my sisters and Meg would know *exactly* what we were up to."

"I'm thinking they know already," Steven pointed out.

"Let me stay in denial as long as I can," Melissa said.

Steven laughed, and she laid her head against his shoulder for a moment, and he forgot, at least for the time being, what it meant to be unhappy, or lonesome, or scared.

All he felt then was a quiet joy, the kind that weathers every kind of sorrow, the kind that lasts.

Forever.

"Will you marry me?" he asked quietly, his hand tightening around hers.

She smiled sweetly. "Eventually," she answered.

And Steven kissed her, right there in the stands at the Stone Creek Rodeo, in front of God and everybody.

Let 'em look, he thought.

EPILOGUE

One year later...

MELISSA AWOKE TO STEVEN'S KISS, and his hand moving gently over her pregnancy-distended belly. The birth was still two months away, and she could feel their twin sons moving within her, wondered if they were already at odds, like Conner and Brody.

After the rodeo, Steven's hardheaded cousins had gone their separate ways—again.

Conner returned to the ranch up at Lonesome Bend, as did Davis and Kim.

Nobody knew for sure where Brody had gone. He'd been conspicuously absent from the wedding, held in Ashley and Jack's spacious front room at the B&B, barely three months after Steven and Melissa had first met. Even though it had been a wonderful, happy day, Melissa knew Steven missed having Brody there.

Now, Steven's hand was moving lower on her belly.

Melissa caught hold of it and stopped his progress, which would inevitably lead to serious delay. Also, alas, serious *pleasure*. They didn't make love in the usual manner these days, since she was well along with the twins, but Steven had his ways. Oh, yes, he definitely had his ways.

"There's a wedding today, remember?" she said. "And it *starts* at noon."

Tom Parker and Tessa Quinn were finally tying the knot, in the First Congregational Church, and the whole town was thrilled. Like her sisters and Meg, Melissa was involved in the preparations.

They still had crepe-paper streamers to hang in the reception hall, and folding chairs to set up, and programs to fold for the special service preceding the wedding itself. There was simply no time to waste.

Steven caressed her.

Melissa moaned. "Steven Creed," she murmured.

"What, Melissa Creed?" he asked.

"You know damn well I can't resist you when you do that—"

He chuckled, the sound throaty and innately masculine, and kissed her neck. And he intensified his efforts.

"Think of it this way," he murmured, against her flesh, already kissing his way down her body. "You'll be glowing with—happiness—"

Melissa groaned. *"Steven—"*

He kissed her belly, one hand playing gently with her breast, the other parting her, preparing her for pleasure.

"Do you want me to stop?" he asked.

Melissa's back arched slightly as he worked her with easy circles of his fingertips. "I'll—be—*late*—" she protested, forestalling the inevitable. When it came to sex, her husband always got his way, and she always wound up glad he had. Still.

"Melissa?"

"What?"

"Do you want me to stop?"

Melissa swallowed and finally gave in. "No," she gasped. "Damn you, *no*."

Steven chuckled at that, and went on about his business, and five long minutes later, Melissa was in the throes of a glorious orgasm, the first of several.

ELVIS WAS SPORTING a little kerchief, made to resemble a tuxedo front, and his coat gleamed with a recent grooming. Byron Cahill, the dog's fast friend, crouched beside him, stroking his ears, offering encouragement. Matt was nearby, too—during the ride to town, he'd beamed up at Melissa and said, "Now Tessa and Tom will be a family, like us!"

And her heart had melted into a warm pool of love for the earnest little boy, the one she already loved as completely as if she'd borne him herself.

Now, Melissa smiled. Only in Stone Creek, Arizona, would a dog serve as best man at a formal wedding.

"I hope you made sure he's—comfortable," Melissa said to Byron, who was now a fixture at the animal shelter and also training as a veterinary assistant, under Olivia's guidance. She saw him practically every day, now that she was working for her sister's foundation.

Byron flashed a grin at Melissa as he stood. "We were just outside, weren't we, Elvis?" he said.

Andrea came to his side, and he slipped an arm around her, squeezed. Since Melissa had finished out her term as county prosecutor and declined to run for a second one, the office was held by a seasoned attorney from over in Indian Rock, and Andrea worked for him now.

Tom appeared, wearing a real tux, fiddling with his

string tie. He was clearly nervous, and glanced down at Elvis, who seemed eager to take their places in front of the altar and wait for the wedding march to begin.

"Relax," Melissa counseled, fixing her friend's tie for him and then kissing his cheek. "The fuss will be over soon, and you'll get to spend the rest of your life loving Tessa."

The sheriff's face lit up at the reminder. "Thanks," he said.

Melissa turned him bodily in the right direction and gave him a little push. Tessa, resplendent in her wedding dress, was already on her mark in the church's entryway, on the arm of her brother, Olivia's husband, Tanner, who would give the bride away.

"Go," Melissa ordered.

Tom looked back at her, then down at Elvis. He grinned.

"Showtime," he said.

* * * * *